FAMINE

Lavabrook Publishing

Published in the United States by Lavabrook Publishing, LLC.

Cover by Regina Wamba
www.maeidesign.com

For Jude,

I love you endlessly.

When He broke the third seal, I heard the third living creature saying, "Come." I looked, and behold, a black horse; and he who sat on it had a pair of scales in his hand.

—*Revelation 6:5 NASB*

Yond Cassius has a lean and hungry look; He thinks too much: such men are dangerous.

—William Shakespeare, *Julius Caesar*

Chapter 1

Year 24 of the Horsemen
Laguna, Brazil

I always knew I would see Famine again. Call it intuition, but I knew that fucker would come back.

The coastal breeze blows against my skirt and ruffles my dark hair. Nearby, a woman gives me a dirty look.

I stand with what's left of my town, our bodies lining the road. I don't know why the rest of Laguna is still here; they don't have the same excuse that I do.

I glance at Elvita. The aging madam's face is resolute. If she's frightened, she doesn't show it. She *should* be frightened, but I don't tell her that.

I follow her gaze to the empty road that curves out of sight around one of the hills Laguna is nestled against.

It's ominously silent.

Most of the seaside town where I spent the last five years is abandoned. Our neighbors have locked up their homes, packed up whatever valuable possessions they own, and retreated. Even most of the bordello's inhabitants have slipped out when no one was looking. I don't know if they'll come back. I don't know if anything will go back to the way it once was.

I'm not entirely sure how I feel about that.

An older woman bumps my shoulder as she passes by.

"Slut," she says under her breath.

I turn, catching her icy gaze.

"Last night your son called me something a little different," I say, giving her a wink.

The woman gasps, looking thoroughly scandalized, but bustles on.

"Stop picking fights," Elvita chastises me.

"What?" I say, giving her an innocent look. "I'm defending my honor."

She huffs out a laugh, but her eyes are back on the road, the weathered skin around them pinched.

Alongside me, people hold jugs of wine, sacks of coffee beans, buckets of freshly caught fish, baskets of flower petals to shower the ground with, purses filled with jewelry, stacks of the finest fabrics—and everything in between. All of it tribute fit for a ruler.

I'm not sure the horseman is going to give a shit.

In fact, I'm pretty sure sticking around was a supremely bad idea, and this is coming from the queen of bad ideas.

At least I have my own excuse. Elvita and the rest of these people have none.

The minutes turn to hours, all of us silent and somber.

Maybe he's not coming after all. Laguna is a slip of a town, hardly worth a horseman's notice.

Anitápolis was hardly worth his notice either, but that didn't stop him from wiping it clear away.

A murmur rises through the line of people, interrupting my thoughts. My pulse quickens.

He's here.

Even if the crowd hadn't reacted, I'd sense the change in the air itself.

At the thought of Famine, I feel a cocktail of emotions. Curiosity, old pain—anticipation most of all.

And then I see him, the Reaper.

He sits astride his coal black horse, his bronze armor shining so bright that it nearly obscures the huge scythe strapped to his back. He comes to a stop in the middle of the battered highway that bridges the two sides of my city.

Even this far away, my breath catches, and my eyes actually sting. I can't say what I'm feeling, only that my professional façade is slipping away at the sight of Famine.

He's more otherworldly than I remembered. Even after revisiting the memory of him over and over again, the sight of him in the flesh is startling.

Next to me, Elvita sucks in a shocked breath.

The Reaper—so named for the scythe he carries—and his horse are still as statues. He's too far away for me to make out those piercing green eyes of his or his curling hair. But I can tell he's taking us all in. I can't imagine he's much impressed.

After several long minutes, Famine nudges his steed into action, and his horse begins to trot down the bridge. People toss flowers into the road, littering the path with brightly colored blooms.

Ever so slowly he gets closer and closer to me.

My heart is thundering.

And then he's passing me by, looking like a god. His hair is the color of melted caramel, his sun-kissed skin only a shade or two lighter. There's the sharp, chiseled line of his jaw, the high brow and cheekbones, and the haughty curve of his lips. Most striking of all are those moss green eyes of his. Devilish eyes.

His shoulders are broad, and that bronze armor, embossed with spiraling floral designs, fits snugly against his powerful, sculpted physique.

Up close, his beauty is a shock to my system.

Far, far more otherworldly than I remembered.

Despite Famine's handsome features and my own breathless excitement, the first true tendrils of fear take root.

Should've left with the others, reunion be damned.

Famine doesn't see me as he passes; his gaze never wavers from the street ahead of him. I feel a wave of relief, followed, quizzically, by a hint of disappointment.

I stare after him and his horse as the rest of my town cheers, acting like this isn't the end of our world when it so obviously *is*.

I stare until he's far out of sight.

Elvita grabs my arm. "Time to go, Ana."

Chapter 2

Long before Famine and his black steed ever set foot in Laguna, we knew he was coming. It would've been impossible not to.

In the weeks prior to his arrival, dozens—then hundreds, then thousands—of people made their way up the highway and through our city. The women I worked with at The Painted Angel joked about walking bow-legged for weeks after the influx of new clients. At the time.

But then some of these newcomers began to talk. They mentioned fruit withering on the vine and strange plants that could crush full grown men, and the very air itself seeming to change.

"Fucking crazy-ass bastards," Izabel, one of my closest friends, had muttered after hearing the rumors.

But I knew better.

And then Famine had sent an envoy ahead of himself to make demands of our town. The horseman wanted casks of rum. Jugs of oil. Garments and gold and food and a grand house to stay in.

I shouldn't even know this much. I probably wouldn't

either, had Antonio Oliveira, the town's mayor, not been a regular customer of mine.

Elvita and I walk in silence. I'm not sure what's running through her head, but the closer we get to the mayor's house—the home Famine will be staying in during his visit—the more unease settles low into my belly.

I should be packing up and fleeing, just like I made my friends at the bordello vow to do.

Elvita finally breaks the silence. She clears her throat. "I hadn't expected him to be so ..."

"Fuckable?" I finish for her.

"I was going to say *well-fed*," she says drily, "but *fuckable* works too."

I raise my eyebrows at her. "You were hoping to throw me at some emaciated bag of bones?" I say. "I'm offended."

She snorts, daintily. Everything she does is dainty and feminine, all of it meant to lure men in, even though these days, she rarely beds clients herself. That, she saves for the rest of her girls.

Like me.

"You screwed Joao," she says, "and he was the closest thing to a skeleton I've ever seen."

An unbidden memory of the old man comes to mind. He *was* little more than a bag of bones, and his plumbing was next to useless.

"Yeah, but he sent me flowers every day for a week and told me I looked like a goddess," I say. Most customers couldn't give a shit about my feelings. "I'd screw him until Kingdom Come for that alone."

She swats me, stifling a grin.

"Oh, don't act like you wouldn't gobble up every cent that man was willing to throw at you," I say.

"God rest his soul, I would."

At the mention of God, I sober up. I crack my knuckles nervously.

It's going to be alright. Famine doesn't hate you. This might work. This will work.

The rest of the walk is spent mostly in silence. We wind through the streets of Laguna, passing sagging homes and faded storefronts, the plaster chipped in most places.

Other residents are walking the same way we are, many of them carrying offerings.

I didn't realize so many people knew where the horseman was staying ...

Assuming, of course, that they're headed his way. That's where we're going. And here I'd hoped that simply showing up at the Reaper's doorstep would be enough to grab his attention.

Eventually, the worn, weathered homes and broken cement streets of Laguna end. There's empty space, and then in the distance, a hill rises, and on it rests the mayor's house, overlooking the glittering water.

We approach the old Oliveira mansion, with its red tile roof and blown glass windows. For as long as I can remember, the mayor and his family have lived here, amassing a fortune on the ships that move goods up and down the coast.

Up close, the home's opulence is even more striking—there's a cobblestone drive and a manicured yard and ...

There's already a line of people congregating near the door.

Motherfucker.

There goes my edge.

Just as we head up the front drive, the home's double doors bang open. Two men drag Antonio out, his face bloody. He shouts obscenities over his shoulder as he struggles against the men.

I stop walking altogether, my lips parting in shock.

The men holding Antonio cart him around the building. Not even a minute later, Antonio's wife and two daughters are hauled out after him. His wife wails, and it's like nothing I've heard. Their children are sobbing and crying out for their mother.

No one does anything. Not the people in line, not even me and Elvita. I don't think anyone knows what to do. That would require understanding what's going on, and that's anyone's fucking guess at this point.

I meet Elvita's startled gaze.

I'm not sure the madam's plan is going to work after all. My eyes return to where I last saw Antonio and his family.

But if her plan doesn't work ...

I'm afraid what failure will look like.

Reluctantly Elvita and I step up to the back of the waiting line of visitors. A few of them have broken away from the line and are hustling off the property.

I stare after them, thinking they're the most sensible ones out of the lot of us. But even as they flee back the way they came, more people are heading towards us from the city.

We might still have time to pack up and leave. I could forget about having my moment with Famine. Maybe it's not too late for me and Elvita ...

The sentiment only deepens when I hear several screams come from the back of the property. The hairs on my arms stand on end.

I turn to Elvita, opening my mouth.

She stares straight ahead. "It'll be fine," she says resolutely.

Years of listening to this woman have me shutting my mouth, even as a hard knot of dread grows within me.

The men who dragged the Oliveira family away a moment ago now return empty-handed, the Oliveiras nowhere in sight. Most of these men re-enter the house, but two of them move to stand in front of the doors, their faces grim. My eyes scour their dark clothing and the exposed skin I can see. There are wet patches that I swear are blood splatter ...

A knock comes from the inside of the door. One of the guards opens it, stepping aside.

One of the people in line ahead of us is ushered inside. Then the door closes once more.

Over the next twenty minutes, the people ahead of us in line enter the house one by one. None of them leave out the front doors—if they leave at all.

What is going on in there? The damnable, curious part of me wants to know. The rational, spooked side of me wants to get the hell out of here. I still haven't seen Antonio or the rest of his family, and I'm legitimately worried—not just for them, but for the rest of us as well.

Elvita must have realized I was a flight risk because she took my hand ten minutes ago, and she's held it tight ever since.

Eventually, we're the next in line.

My pulse races as I wait. I dart a glance at one of the guard's forearms. What looked like a line of moles from far away now looks alarmingly like blood.

Oh God—

A knock comes from inside the house, and a moment later the door opens. Both guards step aside, allowing Elvita and me to enter.

I ... just can't get my feet to move.

My boss gives my hand a tug. "Let's go inside, Ana." She says it sweetly enough, but her eyes are sharp and her eyebrows are arched just so. I've received enough orders from her to know this is yet another one.

I wet my lips, then force myself to step over the threshold.

This is the reunion you've spent years imagining, I reassure myself.

It'll be okay.

Chapter 3

I've never been inside the mayor's house, which is a weird thought, considering he's been inside *me* many, many times.

My eyes sweep over everything, taking in delicate porcelain vases full of withered blooms to the cut glass chandelier. There's a huge painting of Antonio and his family hanging in the living room. It was clearly commissioned a few years ago because his children are younger versions of themselves.

Sitting right beneath that painting, his scythe draped across his lap, is the horseman.

My breath catches. Once again I'm overtaken by the sight of him, with his wavy hair and glittering green eyes. He looks cut from stone, distant and untouchable.

I try to resolve this hardened thing with the very first memory I have of him.

His neck is a mess of blood and sinew. His face and head are covered in mud and blood, his hair matted to his cheeks—

"And what have we here?" His voice is like honeyed-wine, and it snaps me back to the present.

I stare and stare and stare. My whip-sharp tongue fails me now.

When neither Elvita nor I speaks, Famine's gaze rakes over me. He pauses a little when he gets to my eyes, but there's no recognition there.

There's no recognition there.

All that guilt and shame I pent up for years and *Famine doesn't even recognize me.*

I hide the crushing disappointment I feel. Not once in the last five years that I worked for Elvita had I mentioned that I'd met the Reaper before. I only agreed to this stupid plan of hers because I had unfinished business with the horseman.

Unfortunately, that business hinged on the horseman remembering me.

Elvita steps forward. "I brought you a gift," the madam says smoothly.

The horseman looks between the two of us, his expression bored. "And where is it? Your hands are empty."

Elvita looks over at me, willing me to speak. Normally, I have a decent amount of confidence, and what I lack in confidence, I make up for in posturing. But right now, all I want to do is sink into the ground.

Do you remember me?

I nearly ask it. The two of us are like an unfinished conversation hanging in the air.

"I'm the gift," I say instead, falling back to Plan B.

"*You?*" He raises his eyebrows, his mouth curving into a mocking smile. His gaze flicks over me again. "What could I *possibly* want with you?"

"Maybe I could warm that cold, cold heart of yours." There's my cutting mouth.

Now the Reaper looks halfway intrigued. He lifts his scythe and stands.

Famine steps up to me, his boots clicking against the ground. "What even *are* you under all that paint?" he says, coming in close. "A cow? A pig?"

I feel my cheeks heat. It's been a long time since I've felt the burn of humiliation. I'm suddenly aware of how many other people are in the room—not just Famine and Elvita, but half a dozen guards—all of them witnessing this.

The horseman sneers at me. "You thought I'd want your body? Is that it?" His voice is cruel.

Yes. That's exactly it.

"You pathetic creature," Famine continues, scrutinizing me. "Have you heard nothing of me? I don't want your putrid flesh." His eyes flash as they move between me and Elvita. "You two were better off when you hadn't caught my attention."

I feel the energy in the room shift then, and I remember the way the mayor's family was dragged away not an hour ago. And now that I'm thinking about it, I realize with alarm that though offerings line the nearby wall, the people who brought them are notably absent.

We have drifted into dangerous waters.

Next to me, Elvita looks undeterred. "Have you ever bedded a mortal?" she asks, ever the saleswoman.

Famine's gaze moves to her, and he cracks a sly smile, like he's enjoying himself for the first time today. His eyes, however, are as cold as I've ever seen them. Sex and flesh seem like the very *last* thing on his mind.

"And what if I haven't? Do you really think a few pumps into this bag of flesh would change anything?"

I raise my eyebrows. I'm used to vulgar, degrading comments; I'm not used to ... I'm not even sure what sort of insult that was.

Bag of flesh? Bitch *please.* I know I look good.

"You clearly haven't been inside one of *my* women," Elvita continues, clinging to this idiotic plan.

"*Your* women?" Famine's attention returns to me.

Squaring my jaw, I meet his gaze.

Does he recognize me? Does he know?

His unsettling green eyes take me in, and they're so

shrewd. There's no spark of familiarity. If he remembers me, he doesn't show it.

"How terrible it must feel," Famine says, "to be owned and used like property."

I open my mouth to tell him he's wrong, to tell him to fuck off, to tell him that if only I could be alone with him for a moment, I might just jog his memory. Maybe then I can finish that old business between us. When it comes to him, my hope and my hate are old.

For a second, the horseman hesitates. I think he almost feels it. But then his expression sharpens.

Famine's eyes move over our heads. He whistles, gesturing to a few nearby men.

"Get rid of them with the others."

This was a mistake.

That much is clear when Famine's men roughly grab me and Elvita, dragging us away.

"Get your hands off of me!" my madam commands.

The men ignore her.

I fight against their grip as well. I only have eyes for the horseman, who resettles himself on the plush chair we found him on, his scythe laid once more across his lap.

"Don't you remember me?" The words finally rip free.

But Famine's no longer paying attention to us—the ridiculed whore and her desperate madam. His eyes have drifted to the front door, where the next supplicant will be entering.

"I saved you!" I shout at him as I'm dragged away. The men that hold me and Elvita haul us towards a door that leads out to the back of the mayor's estate.

Famine doesn't so much as look at me. I assumed that once I said something on this subject, he would stop and listen. I hadn't anticipated that he both wouldn't recognize me *and* wouldn't hear me out.

Old hurt and indignation bubbles to the surface. If it weren't for me, neither of us would be here right now.

"No one else would help you!" I call out to him. I trip a little as one of his guards tows me outside. "No one but me. You were hurt and—" The door slams shut.

I—I missed my chance.

I'm still staring at the door when I hear Elvita's sharp inhale. Then—

"Jesus fucking Christ." Her voice is shrill, the pitch of it too high.

I tear my gaze away from the door, turning to where—

Holy mother of God.

Ahead of us is a huge pit, the steep earthen walls of it smooth. Antonio had mentioned once, months and months ago, that he was going to install a pool for his daughters. I remember the conversation only because a pool sounded like a nightmare to upkeep.

Rich people and their toys.

Now ... now I'm staring at the beginnings of that pool. Only, there are splatters of blood on the stone pavement around it, and inside the earthen pit—

At first my eyes don't want to make sense of what I'm seeing. The strangely bent limbs, the blood-soaked bodies, the glassy eyes. Over a dozen people lay in that pit.

Dear God. No, please, no.

My nausea rises, and I begin struggling in earnest.

I hadn't survived this long to have it all end like this.

Elvita is cursing as she fights like a wildcat against her captors.

One of the guards holding Elvita now releases her, and for an instant I think she actually managed to partially free herself. But then the man withdraws a dagger from his hip holster.

"Please," she begins to cry. "I will do anyth—"

He runs her through, stabbing her over and over again

before she can even finish begging for her life. I scream as her blood sprays, and I jerk against the men who hold me, feeling like a fish on a hook.

They kill her. Right in front of me they do it. I scream and scream as she bleeds out.

That's when the first knife enters my body—while I'm still watching my friend die. For a moment, my cries cut off, the action taking me by surprise. But then it's my body the men are stabbing over and over again.

I can't catch my breath around the pain. My legs fold as warm liquid trickles down my body.

Fuck, it hurts. Worse than anything I've ever felt. I want to scream, but the sharp agony of it closes up my windpipe.

I go limp in the men's arms. They grab me by the legs, hoisting me off the ground. The world tilts, and I finally manage to release a low, tortured moan as my body sways back and forth, back and forth.

"*One ... two ... three.*"

The men release me, and for a single second, I'm weightless.

And then I hit the bottom of the pit.

I think I pass out from the pain, but I can't be sure. I'm slipping down a hole of agony and delirium. I'm too weak to focus on much of anything else, otherwise I might have noticed the particular hue of the sky above me or the shape of the dead around me. I might have even tried to focus on the arc of my sad, brief life or that I might finally be reunited with my family.

But the pain crowds my thoughts, and all I really notice over it is how cold I am and how hard it is to breathe.

My mind drifts and my eyes close.

This is the end.

I feel death creeping into my bones. This is where people rally and fight for their lives.

I don't.

I give in.

Chapter 4

I have this recurring dream of Famine walking through a field of sugarcane. His hand reaches idly out, his fingertips brushing the stalks. Beneath his touch the plants curl and blacken, the decay spreading out around him until the entire field has withered away.

It's eerily silent. I can't even hear the wind whistling through those dying stalks, though they sway in some phantom breeze.

I'm back there now, standing like a sentinel as the Reaper moves through the field, killing that crop. There's another, darker figure that looms somewhere behind me, but I don't pay him any attention.

As I watch, Famine moves farther from me, and as he does so, the silence seems to close in on me, until it's a deafening ring in my ears.

From behind me, a strong hand grips my shoulder, squeezing tightly.

Lips press against my ear.

"*Live*," the voice breathes.

That's what wakes me.

My eyes flutter open. I squint against the heavy, oppressive shine of the sun, the pungent smell of decay thick in my nostrils.

Hazy with pain and weakness, I draw in one shaky breath, then another.

I shift a little. At the movement, sharp, blinding pain rips across my torso.

Fucking *ow*.

I go still, waiting for the pain to abate. It does ... somewhat, dulling to a steady throb. I take a shallow breath, inhaling bits of dirt as I do so.

I cough, and Satan's balls, it feels like I've crossed through the gates of hell. The pain reignites.

Hurts so damn bad.

Dirt shifts over my body, skittering off me as I push myself up. My arm brushes something soft, something that isn't dirt. Then it's my leg that touches that same object.

My teeth grind against the pain as I force myself to sit up. I cry out at the action, my body hurting in a dozen different places.

Don't throw up. Don't throw up.

When the pain and nausea pass, I look around me. Vaguely, it registers that I'm sitting in that unfinished pool, and that someone has thrown mounds and mounds of dirt back into the craterous pit. But that's not what's truly snagging my attention.

Little more than a meter away, I see a face peering up through the soil like some newly sprouted plant, its mouth slightly agape, dirt lightly sprinkled across its open eyes, which stare blankly into the distance.

A sound slips out of me as my gaze darts over the rest of my surroundings. To my left I see a leg and part of someone's torso sticking out from the dirt, to my right I see a shoulder and the arm of yet another body.

My hand braces itself against something lumpy and vaguely

hard. I glance down only to realize this whole time I've been pushing against the face of the mayor's wife, two of my fingers are brushing against her teeth.

My scream comes out as a choked cry.

Dear God.

I snatch my hand away, causing a dozen flies to take flight before resettling.

The woman's daughters are laying nearby. All of them then haphazardly covered with dirt.

Buried in a shallow grave. Left to die.

And me along with them.

Elvita.

My eyes dart around, searching frantically for the woman who took me in five years ago.

I don't see her, but the longer I stare about, the more I realize that the pit is *moving*. There are others who survived the rampage, others like me who have been buried *alive*.

And now that I'm actually paying attention, I can hear their soft, dying groans. Those of us still living might not be for long. My mind rallies against that thought.

I want to live.

I *will* live.

And then I will get my revenge.

I can't say how many minutes it takes to force myself to my feet. The whole time I'm sure that one of Famine's men is going to come out here and check on us to make sure the dead stay dead. That all my effort will come to a swift, sharp end. But no one comes.

I dust the dirt off my body. It's everywhere—in my hair, down my shirt, coating my clothes, between my toes and inside my mouth. I'm too cowardly to look at the wounds on my chest, but I bet if I did, I'd see dirt in them as well.

Pushing myself up, my gaze sweeps over the pit. The sides of it are too steep to simply walk out of, but thankfully one part of the pool is shallower than the other, and in this shallow area someone thought to create steps leading out.

But in order to get over to those steps, I have to walk over the partially buried bodies.

Pinching my eyes shut, I draw in a deep breath, release it, then start to move.

Instantly, the pain sharpens, stealing my breath and making my movement almost unbearably agonizing.

I take one shaky step, then two, then three.

Just a little farther.

My foot slips on a bloody arm, and I fall. I hit the ground.

Blinding pain—

I think I pass out because I'm suddenly blinking my eyes open even though I don't remember closing them.

Once again I'm lying on a dirt-covered corpse, my cheek nestled against something wet and sticky. The pain, the horror—all of it has my nausea rising. I barely have time to turn my head to the side before I retch.

My entire body is shaking, both from exertion, and from my terrible reality.

I let myself lay there for a moment, my face crumpling as I begin to sob. I don't think I can do it. I want to live, but this is all *too much.*

Those awful flies land on me and that is what causes me to snap.

I will not be food for some fucking flies. I won't.

I force down the last of my nausea and, gritting my teeth against the pain, force myself up once more.

Again, I begin walking towards those steps. And this time, I don't fall. I make it up the steps and out of that deadly pool.

A relieved cry slips out once my feet touch solid ground. But it only lasts a few seconds. I can still hear the faint moans of the still living.

I glance back at the pool looking for anyone still alive.

Maybe Elvita survived. It's possible.

I stare out at the sea of partially covered bodies. I don't see the madam, but I do see the mayor, though he's almost unrecognizable, his face drenched in blood. He's one of the ones still clinging to life.

I wrap a hand around my stomach to stave off as much of the pain as I can, and then I begin to stumble over the edge of the pool nearest him.

He was an inconsiderate lover and a terrible tipper, but he didn't deserve to die like this—and his wife and children certainly didn't as well.

When I get close, I crouch next to the edge of the pool and reach down. I don't know how I'm going to get an injured adult male out of this pit, but I can't *not* help him.

He shakes his head, seeming to choke on air. Only now do I notice the tear tracks that snake down his cheeks.

"Take my hand," I insist, pleading with him.

He doesn't.

His dark eyes find mine. "Kill ... me ..." His voice is barely a whisper.

I give him a distraught look. "What?"

"Please ..." he wheezes.

I rear back, horrified. My wild eyes look everywhere but him, and that's when I see the back of Elvita's blood-drenched body.

A sound slips from my lips. For a moment, the mayor's plea is forgotten. I rise to my feet, then stumble over to the edge of the pool nearest her, my vision darkening from the pain. I don't bother to muffle my cries, even though a small part of me worries that it will draw the attention of Famine's men.

I fall to my knees and frantically reach for her. She's close enough for me to touch, but the moment my fingers brush her, I know she's gone. Her skin feels nothing like living flesh.

A sob slips from my lips.

Elvita is gone.

Truth be told, I have—I mean, I *had*—a complicated relationship with this woman, one that was equal parts resentment and gratitude. I know she used me—exploited me even—but she was also a friend and confidante, and she protected me from the worst of our world. This plan of hers—to throw one of her girls at the horseman—wasn't supposed to end like this.

Over the last five years, my old anger towards Famine stayed with me like a scab, and now it's as though he picked it open.

He took everything from me *twice*.

It's time he pays.

Once I've gathered myself, I stand, moving away from the pool and the flies that circle it.

All this time I've been too distracted to notice that neither Famine nor any of his men have approached this backyard. And for that matter, the pit is filled in. Their business here must be done.

I stumble towards the front of the house, grinding my teeth at the impossible pain.

I shouldn't be alive, and how badly I'm regretting that fact right now, when my body feels flayed wide open.

I round to the front of the house. The front door hangs open. The place looks abandoned.

How long was I lying inside that pit?

I stagger home, taking in shallow, ragged breaths. I have to pause numerous times to catch my breath when my vision clouds or the pain and exhaustion become too unbearable. I gasp out hushed cries.

As I walk, I skirt around large plants that have broken through the asphalt road. Perhaps if I'd been less focused on making it through each step I would have noticed how quiet my surroundings had become. Quiet and empty. I would've noticed the putrid smell stinging my nose and the road's altered appearance.

I'm more than halfway home when I finally notice the drone of buzzing flies, a sound that's accompanied me for most of the walk. Even then, I don't process the noise until I lean against one of those trees growing in the middle of the street—a tree, now that I think about it, that wasn't there the last time I used this road ...

The buzzing is nearly deafening, and that's when I finally realize something's not right.

I glance above me, towards the sound, and I swallow a scream. Dangling from the boughs of an enormous paraná pine tree is a twisted body, the feet bare and discolored. As I watch, the corpse gently sways in the breeze. A swarm of flies circles what I think used to be an old man, flying and landing and flying and landing round and round the corpse.

As my eyes move over the canopy of leaves, I notice another body, this one a young woman. Her limbs are tangled up in the branches, her eyes bulging.

I've seen this before—Lord help me but I have.

I've seen trees like this one grow spontaneously from the ground, and I can easily imagine how it plucked men and women off the street and squeezed the life out of them like an anaconda squeezes prey.

Not that it makes it any easier to process.

I lean over once again and heave. But there's nothing left in my stomach to expel.

I think of how all us townspeople lined the road, waiting for the Reaper, our arms full of gifts meant to placate him. Then I remember his face when he ordered my death. All because I caught his attention.

This is how our fear and generosity are treated.

A flash of anger eclipses my pain and horror for a moment.

None of us deserved this. Well, *maybe* one or two of my shittier clients deserved this, but not everyone else.

I push away from the tree and continue on. Now I really

notice the trees and brambly shrubs that have broken through the cracked streets of Laguna. In each one, bodies are held captive, their forms contorted.

No one besides me walks down the street. All the people are gone and the flies have moved in—them and the semi-feral dogs who tug at some of the more accessible bodies.

I eye the plants around me like at any moment they might scoop me up and crush me. So far, they haven't, and I'm really fucking hoping my luck holds out.

By the time I get to The Painted Angel, nestled between a tavern and a gambling hall, I'm still alive. Alive and alone. I haven't seen another living soul.

I pass under the wooden sign depicting a naked angel whose wings barely cover her tits and pussy, and I slip inside the only home I've known for half a decade. The door slams shut behind me, the sound echoing throughout the space.

I come to a standstill inside the main parlor.

Normally at this time of day, the girls are lounging about on the jewel-toned couches that fill the space. Sometimes there's a midday caller, but usually this is the time when—if we're not sleeping off the night's work—we're sprawled across these couches, coffee or tea in hand, playing *Truco* or gossiping or singing or doing each other's hair—or a million other things.

Today, the bordello is as still as the grave. And for good reason. Three giant, thorny bushes grow in the middle of the room, and caught in their clutches are—

Luciana, Bianca, and Cláudia.

All of them had decided to stay behind, unwilling to leave this life they'd built for themselves. But now they're gone anyway, and all their hopes and dreams are gone with them.

My throat is working. I'm trying desperately to not fall apart. I just hope to God that the women who fled before the horseman's arrival are still alive and safe.

I shuffle past the bodies of my former housemates.

"Hello?" I call out, but I already know no one is left. Famine doesn't leave anyone alive.

I drag myself towards the kitchen. All I want to do is sleep, but my lips are cracked and my throat is scratchy from dehydration. Rummaging around, I find a few pieces of fruit that are past their prime, some stale bread, and a hard rind of cheese. That's all that remains of the normally well-stocked kitchen. The icebox hangs open, its shelves bare, and the pantry, with its links of hanging sausages and bags of grain, has been cleaned out.

I grab a partially empty pitcher of water that sits on the countertop, and bring it directly to my lips, draining it dry. I tear into the bread, only pausing to take large bites from the cheese and the shriveled fruit.

I feel nauseous again, like maybe my stomach isn't really fit to hold food. That thought nearly has me retching up my meal.

God, I really hope this isn't going to be some long, lingering death that takes a fucking month.

I almost lay back down on one of those couches, my body is that ready to give out. But I can't bear the sight of any more dead, so I stumble up the stairs and to my room, and thankfully, I see no more unnatural plants.

I fall into bed, dirt and blood getting all over my sheets. Elvita isn't alive to yell at me, and frankly, if there still *is* anyone left to yell at me, I gladly welcome it.

Because I'm pretty sure that I'm well and truly alone.

Chapter 5

I don't die. Not that day or the next or the one after that.

I don't know why, out of all the many people in Laguna—people who had good, enviable lives—it's my miserable one that gets spared.

Those first several days are a fever-filled blur. I am certain I dragged myself outside to the well to refill the pitcher at some point, and I managed to hoist myself out of bed to go to the bathroom, but the memories are fuzzy. I only remember eating once or twice.

It has to be roughly a week before my fever subsides. My head finally clears and my stomach is cramping with hunger, despite the awful, rotting smell that fills the room.

Ugh. I want to die.

Pretty sure death *would* be easier than bearing this horrible pain, but for whatever cursed reason, I'm forced to live through it.

A memory tugs at the back of my mind, of a hand on my shoulder and something whispered into my ear—

But then the memory is gone, and it's not coming back.

I push myself up to a sitting position.

For the first time in nearly a week, I see my surroundings clearly. There's the trunk at the foot of my bed with some of my more interesting toys and costumes, there's the closet that's crammed with soft, skimpy outfits that tease and reveal all the most tantalizing parts of flesh. On the windowsill are my collection of plants, most now wilted. And then there's the vanity, lined with glass bottles of perfume and makeup. It's as though my room didn't get the memo.

The world has ended. Get with the program.

Pushing off the bed, I force my achy muscles to move, wincing at the agonizing pull of my wounds. Even now, the pain is terrible, but I can bear it enough to focus on other things.

Like the fact that at least two other rooms I walk by are filled with Famine's frightening plants, more of my fellow housemates lying limp in their clutches, their bodies badly decayed.

Fear and the overpowering smell drive me outside. I take in several lungfuls of air then, gathering together my courage, I wander into the tavern next door, looking for food.

There are more plants, more dead people, more horror. I keep my eyes down and mostly hold my breath as I make my way to the kitchen.

I have to work around another twisting tree as I search for food, ignoring the dead cook. Decomposing bodies, I'm quickly discovering, are nightmarish things.

I'll never be able to wash away the sight of them.

Most of the tavern food has gone bad, but I quickly grab what little remains, and then I leave.

That night, I sob as I wash my wounds.

Partly the tears come from the pain. Several of the cuts are deep and they're still infected. But another part of it comes from the fact that I cannot escape the rotting city that surrounds me. There's death in the streets and inside every building, and I feel like the horror of it is going to break my mind—if it's not already somehow broken.

And then I cry for the women I worked alongside—for Elvita who sheltered me, and Bianca and Cláudia and Luciana who, if they were here, would've helped me tend to my injuries, just as the women did every time a client crossed the line.

And then I cry for the other girls, dead in their rooms or strung up in the trees somewhere else in this city.

I cry until my head pounds from the effort. When it feels like I have no more tears left in me, I draw in a long, ragged breath, then another.

Each breath feels like a small victory. I shouldn't be alive, I really shouldn't. And with every breath I take, my resolve hardens.

I'm going after him.

Even if it means certain death, I'm doing it.

That evil fucker made one huge mistake coming here: he didn't make sure I was dead.

And now he's going to pay for it.

Chapter 6

I spend the next couple days breaking into homes and businesses and grabbing what supplies I can.

To properly go after the horseman I need some form of transportation. My shaky legs carry me down the streets of Laguna. I grimace at the sight of birds screeching at one another as they fight over the remains of some poor soul.

For the love of God, Ana, look away.

I take a steadying breath, trying to force down my nausea.

The first time I saw what Famine could do to an entire town, I hadn't stuck around long enough to see the bodies decompose. Now, my injuries have given me no choice.

As it is, my breath is ragged, and I sway unsteadily.

I make it to the post office, where they have horses and carriages and—

They're all gone. All the horses.

Inside the post office's stables, the horse stalls hang open, each one empty. The only explanation for how they came to be that way are the spindly plants that snake up the front posts of each stall, their vines still curled around the latches.

Famine released the horses?

I stare for a little longer before I leave the stables. It's probably for the best that the animals are gone. I'm in no position to feed and water and shelter a creature—especially one that spooks easily.

The post office also has rows and rows of bikes on their property, several which are already hitched to carts. I snag one of these, and roll it back to the bordello. From there it's simply a matter of dumping all my supplies into the cart. Food, water, blankets, a first aid kit, a tent. *Shit, Ana, who knew a hussy like you had a campy side?*

I stack a hefty amount of weaponry into that cart too. I don't know who I'll come across, but considering how my last encounter with an outsider went, I'm feeling pretty fucking stabby at the moment.

By the time I'm done, the cart is nearly overflowing with supplies. I feel a small spark of excitement.

I'm leaving Laguna. Permanently. I never thought I'd actually escape this city.

But before I do so, I make a final stop back inside my room. I stand just inside the threshold for several seconds, taking the place in. These four walls have been mine for years, and I have all sorts of memories in here—most of them unnerving, some degrading, but then I have plenty of happy memories here too. It's a funny, uncomfortable thing, remembering it all. I'd practically sold my soul to The Painted Angel. I thought this was all I'd ever be.

Slowly, I begin to meander around the room. My eyes pass over a series of paintings hanging on my walls of nude women lying in various, suggestive positions. Elvita called them tastefully sensual when she had them put up. Leaning against one wall is a gilded mirror. Across the room is the window with my mostly dead plants and near that is a single shelf that holds a blown glass vase, a book of erotic poetry and a basket full of seashells.

My gaze drops to the chest at the foot of my bed before

moving to my closet and the filmy clothing hanging inside. Lastly my gaze stops at my vanity, with the glass vials of perfume and my bag of makeup. I move over to the low table, my fingers skimming over the wood. There's a small wooden jewelry box next to a jar of lotion and my oil lamp.

All of it is so impersonal. The closest I get to any meaningful belongings is in a box pushed to the back of my closet, but even that holds nothing much of value. Just a small, carved horse I bought with my first paycheck, a stack of letters several different admirers wrote to me, a bracelet Izabel once braided for me and a couple other knickknacks.

None of it is particularly sentimental, and I find that I don't want to take any part of this past of mine with me. Not the makeup, not the clothing, not any of the mementos. These things are reminders of who I have been forced to be. But I don't intend to stay that woman. Not any longer.

On a whim I blow the room a kiss and walk out of there, shedding the past like a second skin.

I leave the city and get out just far enough to leave the stench of death behind. Then I stop and pitch the tent, and I stay put for well over a week, letting my wounds heal. I keep my weapons close—highwaymen are infamous for committing all sorts of crimes against travelers—but my fear is unnecessary in the end. I don't see or hear a soul.

Once my wounds are healed enough, I begin traveling. And traveling and traveling. The days blur together, one bleeding into the next until the days become weeks. My progress is slow, both because of my injuries, and because I have to stop to scavenge for food—which is a pretty way of saying that I have to enter more cities full of the rotting dead, and I have to break into more homes and steal food from those who no longer need it.

There's also the issue of following in Famine's wake. There's no one to ask for directions, so I have to use my intuition when tracking the horseman. To be honest, it's not too difficult. The man kills off crops wherever he goes, so it's a simple matter of following the dead fields and orchards.

And everywhere I go, there are bodies. In trees, next to fields, strewn across the road, outside of homes and outposts, and everywhere in between—all of them caught up in those awful plants. The sound of flies buzzing has become almost constant. I was foolish to think that leaving Laguna would somehow insulate me from the sight of so much death. That's all that's left of these towns and cities.

But even though the journey is full of horrors, there's beauty too. I see kilometer after kilometer of the Serra do Mar, the mountain range that stretches like a reclining woman along the coast. I hear the call of birds and insects that I never heard so crisply while living in the city. And sometimes, when the night is clear, I forgo the tent altogether and sleep under the stars, staring up at those distant lights.

So it's not all bad.

Not to mention that living through the end of the world means no more sex work for me, and *that* means I don't have to give a shit what my face or body looks like. Which is nice. Also, I don't have to have a horny, heavy body bearing down on me. That's nice too.

Fuck it, even after everything, I'm still an optimist.

The entire time I ride, I only end up seeing one other soul. I happen across him while passing through the coastal town of Barra Velha. I don't know who he is or why he was spared, but my best guess is that he was a fisherman out at sea when Famine struck his town. It makes me wonder if during that first feverish week after the horseman's attack some other local fishermen docked back in Laguna, coming ashore only to find a city full of death. The thought has the hairs along my arms standing on end.

I don't approach the weeping man—though I do wave at him when he glances up at me, his eyes going wide. A month ago I might've stopped to talk to him and make sure he was okay, but a month ago I had a little more heart and a little less vengeance.

The trail I follow turns inland, and the bodies I pass seem ... fresher. That's when I know I've just about caught up to Famine. By then, it's been roughly a month since I was stabbed. I can't imagine I'm even a flicker of a thought in the horseman's mind.

Just considering that has my anger rising anew. He might've forgotten me—twice now—but I have to live with the horrors he's inflicted. Movement still pulls at my wounds, and then there's all the pain that isn't physical. I couldn't forget that if I tried.

I finally catch up to the horseman in Curitiba, and I know it only because I can hear the moans carried on the wind.

I stop my bike, gazing at the city's skyline. I've seen skyscrapers before, but I've never seen so many, all of them clustered so close together.

Humans made those.

Sometimes people talk about what it was like before the horsemen came, their voices full of wistfulness. The past sounds like a dream, one that, most of the time, I can't believe. But then there are moments like this one, when I stare at the incredible evidence that once man's abilities rivaled God's.

It's only as I get closer that I notice how decayed they are. Many of them look like molting snakes, half of their surfaces fallen away. Vined plants seem to have taken root in the bones of these skyscrapers, making them appear even more ancient than they must be.

The horsemen only arrived a quarter of a century ago, and yet this city looks a thousand years old.

A moan tears my gaze from the buildings.

Not three meters from me a young woman is caught up in the twisting branches of one of the horseman's plants, this one producing clusters of bright berries. There's a thick vine wrapped around her neck, but it's not tight enough to suffocate her—yet anyway.

Dismounting off my bike, I grab one of the knives I packed. Approaching the plant, I begin to rip away at the branches. In response, the branches encircling the woman tighten, causing her to choke. Her eyes bulge a little—either from fear or suffocation. Frantically I begin hacking away, trying to get to her. All at once the plant squeezes the woman impossibly tight. I hear some awful, snapping noises. The woman's eyelids flutter and the light leaves her eyes.

"*No.*" I choke out.

I drop the knife and back up, staring at the plant. My stomach churns at the disturbing sight. It's all I've seen for weeks and weeks.

The shock of all this death has worn off, and beneath the horror only one thing remains.

Rage.

I am full of it. So full it's hard to breathe.

I get back on my bike and begin to ride again, moving through the dying streets of Curitiba. Street vendors have had their wares upended by these savage plants, and in some areas where there was heavier foot traffic, whole forests have sprung up in the streets, making roads inaccessible. Just like in most of the other cities I've visited, the plants here seem to have swallowed these people up within minutes.

What's the point of a Reaper blighting the land if he's going to kill people before anyone can starve to death?

He wants to watch them die. The thought whispers through my mind. I can see the cruelty on his face still. He wants to watch the earth squeeze the very life out of us.

I ride around the city, hunting for the horseman. There's a very real chance that Famine is still here in Curitiba. The thought thrills me, though finding him in such a large place is going to prove challenging.

I'm almost to the center of the city, where the structures appear especially dilapidated, when I hear another choked cry, this one coming from inside a building that showcases woven baskets, pottery, ceramic figurines, and some traditional Brazilian clothing.

Bringing my bike to a stop, I lean it against the building and head inside.

Inside, the store is dim, but it's not dark enough for me to miss the four separate trees that rise from the floor, their canopies pressed against the ceiling. Caught in each one of them are dark forms. One of these forms shifts, letting out another pained sob.

My eyes snag on the figure. Slowly, I approach.

"I can't cut you out," I say by way of greeting. "The last person I tried to help was killed by that ..." I can't bring myself to say *tree*, "*thing*."

In response, I think I hear soft sobs. The sound twists my gut.

"Can you speak?" I ask.

"He killed my children and their children too," the man rasps out. "He didn't even have to touch them to end their lives." He begins sobbing again.

"I'm looking for him," I say. "Is he still in the city?"

The man doesn't answer, just continues to cry.

I step in closer. Way up in that tree, I can just barely make out the man's eyes.

I pause, assessing him, before I lift my shirt, showing him my own grisly wounds. I can't say how many times I've stripped for men, or how many eyes have taken in my naked flesh. This, however, is one of the few times I've showed my skin for something other than money or pleasure.

After several seconds, the man goes quiet.

"He tried to kill me too," I say, letting the stranger take in the various scars from my knife wounds. "I intend to return the favor. So, do you know where he is?" I say.

"God has spared you, girl," he wheezes out. "Leave this place and live your life."

I want to laugh at that. I took that option once; it landed me in a whorehouse. I'm not taking it again.

"God spared me *nothing*," I respond. "Now, do you know where he is?"

The man is quiet for a long time, but finally he says, "Seven kilometers east of here, there's the neighborhood of Jardim Social. I've heard that he's staying somewhere in there."

Seven kilometers. I could get there within an hour or two—assuming I can find the place.

"Thank you," I say.

I hesitate then, feeling like I owe the man something.

"Leave me," he wheezes. "I belong here, with my family."

The thought sends a shiver through me.

"Thank you," I say again, then turn to leave.

"It's suicide," he calls out to my back.

I don't turn around. "It's revenge."

Chapter 7

I follow the old man's directions the best I can and head east. If there was once fear in me, there is no longer. It takes me a long time to find the house Famine is staying in, though eventually I find it. It doesn't in any way stand out from the houses around it. In fact, I might've ridden right past it if it weren't for the mean-looking men that loiter around the property.

One of them sees me, taking several ominous steps forward before he retreats into the house. Someone has clearly gone to tattle on me. Which means ...

Famine is in that house.

My heart begins to beat like mad.

Famine is in that house and in a few moments, he will know there's still someone alive in this blighted city.

Before the rest of the men standing guard can do anything else, I ride away, only stopping three blocks later when I come across an abandoned house, a relic of a different era.

Grabbing several of the weapons from my cart, I wait for one of Famine's men to come hunt me down—or worse, for one of those unnatural plants to spring up from the ground and crush me to death. I'm all but ready for it, but nothing happens. The minutes tick by, and the sun makes its way across the horizon.

The Reaper is here, in this city, mere blocks away. My adrenaline is spiking at the thought, and a part of me wants to charge over to that mansion, kick down its doors and push my way in. Instead, I force myself to wait, coming up with a plan of sorts while the sky darkens.

I wait until it's pitch black outside before I leave. I've strapped two blades to my hips and another across my chest, the leather straps feeling strange against my body. Two months ago, this would've been excessive for most law-abiding citizens. Now it might not be enough protection against Famine and his men.

I creep back towards the house he's staying in, my heart beginning to pound. I know enough about the horseman to understand that nothing humans have done has killed him. That doesn't slow my step.

Ahead of me, I catch sight of the mansion. I couldn't miss it. It's the only house anywhere in the city that's lit up. Oil lamps glow, and yet again a handful of men linger outside. Some are standing, a couple of them sit and smoke cigarettes and cigars on the front lawn. One of them is pacing, gesturing wildly as he does so; he's saying something, but I'm too far away to hear.

I move to the block that runs behind the house, sticking to the shadows. No one's posted back here, among these dark, empty homes. It's not surprising; Famine probably isn't expecting any sort of attack now that he's killed off most of the city's population.

Once I figure out which home backs up against Famine's, I cut across the home's yard, making my way to the back of the property. Everything is chillingly quiet.

I climb over the stone fence that separates the two properties, then drop down inside the mansion's yard, my feet landing in soft dirt.

My heart begins to pound in earnest, my breath coming in shallow pants. This is the point of no return. Up until now I could've taken that old man's advice and fled with my life. I could've existed. It would've been lonely and it would've looked nothing like the life I knew, but I would've survived, which is better than what I can say for most people.

I take a step forward, then another and another, ignoring the scared, rational part of my brain. This part of the property is dark; there are lamp posts back here, but they don't burn.

I realize why a moment later when I hear the groan of some dying soul. I squint into the darkness. After several seconds, I make out a pile of bodies.

Jesus.

I swallow a scream, my own memories swarming in. For a minute I simply stand there, riding out the old pain and fear, which doesn't seem so old at the moment. Then, when I've managed to wrestle my emotions back into place, I take a deep breath and continue on, skirting around the bodies.

My hand touches the hilt of my weapons. I've never stabbed a person before. I've scratched, slapped, and punched a few people in my time—and I've kicked men in the balls more times than I care to admit—but that's about it.

Tonight ... tonight will truly be my first time using a dagger. I try not to think about that too hard; I don't want to lose my nerve.

I head over to a back door and, reaching out, I try the handle. It gives beneath my touch.

Unlocked.

Because who would *dare* break into Famine's house after he decimated the city?

I swear I can hear my own heartbeat as I push the door open. I glance around at the cold living room beyond me. A few candles flicker, the wax dripping down their stems. The dim light illuminates a couch, a set of side chairs, an enormous vase, and an oiled wooden bust of a woman. No one's in here.

Silently, I step into the room.

Where are all the guards? I saw nearly a dozen of them outside, but in here they're nowhere to be seen.

After a moment, I hear a soft tapping sound. The sound drags my gaze to the right, where I take in a dimly lit dining room. My chest stills when I see Famine's silhouette sitting in one of the chairs, his back to me.

His armor is gone, but his telltale scythe rests on the table in front of him, just beyond the open book that's resting where a plate should be. The Reaper, however, doesn't seem to be reading. Based on the angle of his head, he's staring out the windows across from him, his fingers drumming absently on the table.

The Reaper sits so still that if it weren't for those fingers, I would've assumed he was just another pricey decoration put on display in this house.

For a moment, I wonder if this is some sort of trap. There aren't any guards posted in here, and there probably should be. And Famine is right there, alone and seemingly unaware of my presence.

I wait in the shadows for a long time, staring at his broad back and his caramel colored hair. Long enough for the teeth of any trap to close on me. The seconds pass and nothing happens.

Eventually, I begin to creep closer, cutting through the living room, my steps silent.

I reach for one of the knives sheathed at my side, drawing it out as quietly as I can.

Kill him and leave unnoticed. That's the plan. I know it's no permanent solution. After all, *he cannot die.*

That's one of the first things I learned about Famine long ago. There is no ending him.

It doesn't really matter at this point. Killing him—no

40

matter how temporary—is the only solution any of us humans have left. So I push my misgivings aside. I've come too far to stop now.

As I round the couch in the living room, I nearly trip on a body.

I have to bite down on my lip to stifle my yelp.

Dear God.

Just when I thought there were no more surprises.

The man at my feet has been gutted from navel to collarbone. He stares blankly off in the distance, laying in a pool of his own blood.

Bile rises up my throat, and I have to choke it back down. The whole time, I'm sure that Famine is going to hear me.

And yet he doesn't, so far as I can tell. He just continues to drum his fingers on the table and gaze out the windows.

Skirting around the corpse, I make my way to the dining room on silent feet. My heart, which was beating madly just minutes ago, has now slowed. I feel eerily calm. Gone is my fear, my nerves, and that terrible anger that's churned inside me for weeks.

This is what it must feel like to live without a conscience.

I step up to the back of Famine's chair, and in one smooth movement, my dagger makes it to his neck.

I hear the horseman's sharp, surprised inhalation.

Threading my fingers into that pretty hair of his, I jerk his head back, my blade pressed tightly against his skin.

"You made an example of the wrong girl," I whisper into his ear.

Beneath my touch, the horseman feels rigid.

"You are either very brave or very foolish to cross me," he says, his jade green eyes staring straight ahead.

"You *bastard*," I say, tightening my grip on his hair. "Look at me."

He does, his gaze moving to my face, his neck brushing against my blade as he turns his head. The Reaper wears a smirk as he meets my eyes, though he's in no position to find this funny.

"Do you remember me?" I ask.

"Forgive me, human," he says, "but you all look so *very* similar."

It's supposed to be an insult, but I'm beyond insults. So far beyond them.

After a moment, however, a spark of recognition sharpens his features and his brows lift. "You were the girl whose flesh was offered to me—weren't you?" he says. "My, what a difference face paint makes."

Another insult.

My grip on his hair tightens, and I press the dagger a little deeper into his neck. He doesn't react, but I swear he's agitated—very, very agitated.

His gaze scans over my body. "And you're still breathing," he notes. "Did one of my men succumb to your pitiful wiles and spare you?"

My blade bites into his skin now, drawing out a line of blood. After years of enduring men's demands of me, it is *awfully* nice to push my will onto someone else, and I cannot think of a more deserving creature to endure it.

The Reaper takes in my expression. After a moment, he laughs.

"I'm sorry, am I supposed to be scared?" He sounds so calm that I almost believe him. But his arms are tense, his muscles taut. And then there's the memory of the last time we met. For all the suffering he inflicts, I don't think he has much taste for it when it comes to himself.

"You still don't truly remember me," I say. "Think further back."

"What is the *point* of this exercise?" Famine says, exasperated. "I don't make it a habit of remembering humans."

I loosen my hold on his hair just a fraction. "I *saved* you once, back when no one else would."

"Did you now?" Famine says, amused. But unlike his expression, his eyes glint with anger. I sense that he's biding his time, waiting for me to screw up before he pounces.

"It's a mistake I've regretted every day since," I admit, my throat tightening.

"Is that right?" he says, and now I swear he *is* entertained. "And tell me, brave human, how did you save me?"

"You don't remember?" I say, actually somewhat shocked. How could he ever forget? "It was raining when I found you. You were covered in blood and your body was missing ... pieces."

Slowly, Famine's shitty little smile melts away.

Finally, the reaction I was looking for.

My grip on his hair tightens again. "Remember me now, motherfucker?"

Chapter 8

Five years ago
Anitápolis, Brazil

I don't believe the rumors. Not until I see him.

For the last couple years, there had been whispers in my town of the immortal man who raised the seas and split the earth. The horseman who came to our land and tried to cross us humans. Rumor was that he was caught and, as punishment, locked up somewhere in the vast Serra do Mar. Somewhere near our town.

I hadn't given the rumor much thought until now.

Through the torrential downpour, my eyes snag on a lump laying off to the side of the dirt road.

Don't look too hard.

I know I shouldn't. I know that once my mind pieces together what I'm seeing I'm not going to like it. But it's impossible to look away. My shoes squish against the mud as I close in on the thing. Eventually I realize I'm staring at a muddy, bloody torso. One that's been mutilated nearly past the point of recognition.

My breath comes fast, and I nearly drop my basket of jabuticabas, the dark fruit rolling perilously around.

Who could've done this to another human?

Get home—now.

Whoever attacked this person, they could still be out here, and this poor soul who's been left for dead, there's no sense helping them now. They're clearly dead.

As I walk past the body, I can't help it—I slow, my curiosity getting the better of me. That's when I notice something odd. The skin that rings what must be the person's neck and chest ... it *glows*.

Is it a necklace? What piece of jewelry *glows*? I stare at the bare torso, noting absently that it's a man.

Stop staring and go home. Whoever he is, he's dead, I'm soaked to the bone, and if I arrive home late again, Aunt Maria will have my hide.

Not to mention that a killer might be hiding in the forest that presses up against the road. He might be watching me at this very moment.

With that spooked thought, I push myself to my feet and reach for my basket, the rain still pelting down on me. Just as I start to walk away, I hear a ragged, broken sound at my back.

I spin around, and now the jabuticabas do spill out of my basket.

My gaze scans the trees around the road, certain the killer is going to spring out at any moment.

That's when I hear the sound again, only this time, it clearly comes from the bloody carcass in front of me.

Holy *shit*.

Could the man still be ... *alive?*

The thought is beyond terrifying. He's been shredded to pieces.

I swallow, taking a step towards the body, dread pooling in my stomach.

Just check to make sure he's dead ...

Still, I hesitate before I touch him. He's missing an entire arm; it's just *gone*. His other arm ends at his elbow, the frayed edges of it a pulpy mess.

My gaze moves down to his chest, which is crisscrossed with lash marks all the way down to his groin. His legs haven't been amputated, but like his torso, they seem to be flayed open in several spots. Rivulets of watery blood snake away from the naked man, mixing with the rainwater.

The sight of so much pain makes me want to weep.

What happened to you?

The man is so still. *Too* still. Whatever sound I heard earlier, I must've been mistaken.

There's no way a human could survive these wounds.

My skin is still prickling, instincts telling me to run before whoever did this attacks me too.

Before I get up, I place a hand on the man's chest, right over his heart—just to be sure he's well and truly gone.

Beneath my palm, he's utterly still. There's no intake of breath, no thump of his heart.

Dead.

I start to withdraw my hand when my attention snags on the soft green light glowing only centimeters away from my fingertips. I squint as I take it in—

What in the hell?

My hand moves of its own accord, my fingers trailing over the glowing markings. This is no piece of jewelry. The markings are a *part* of the man's skin.

My eyes flick to the stranger's face, which is hidden by his matted hair. My pulse begins to quicken.

Could this actually be ... ?

But that would mean that the rumors were true. Those ridiculous, frightening rumors.

Surely that can't be right. Any being strong enough to shake the earth and kill crops couldn't possibly be contained by

46

humans.

But now I can hear my pulse pounding between my ears and I'm still staring at that face, hidden behind a curtain of wet hair.

On a whim, I reach out and push the dripping locks away from the man's face, tucking them behind his ear.

At my touch, his eyes snap open, his irises a brilliant green color.

I scream, falling back on my butt.

God and all the saints! What in the actual *fuck?*

"Help," he whispers to me, and then his eyes fall shut again.

I'm shivering, staring at the horseman's unconscious form.

He's alive. The horseman. The creature sent from God to kill everyone. He's *alive* and he's missing appendages, and now he wants my help.

I hug my arms together. What am I supposed to do?

Tell the town. People need to know the horseman has come.

Would anyone even believe me? An hour ago *I* wouldn't have believed me.

So what if they believe you're a fool? Tell them and let them make up their own minds.

I get to my feet and begin to walk away, my steps hurried.

But then ... then I stop. I cast an unsure glance over my shoulder.

That man—supernatural or not—is too hurt to harm anyone. And judging by his wounds, he's not the great monster the stories made him out to be.

Someone did that to him. Someone who was surely a human.

I stare at his crumpled form for a little longer.

Help. He'd used his only breath to ask for my help.

The thought makes my chest tighten.

If this truly is the horseman ... I really should just walk away.

Still, I linger there, in the middle of the road, my eyes fixed on him.

I think about my aunt, who hardly gives two shits about me. If I were lying in a ditch, I'm not sure she'd save me.

I know what it's like to not be wanted.

And if I were the one hurt and begging for help, I'd want someone to care. Even a stranger.

I swallow.

Fuck, I'm going to do this.

Rain pelts my skin as I grab the horseman under the armpits, my gaze moving up and down the muddy road. There's no one on this backcountry trail. No one but me and the horseman But someone *will* come, it's just a matter of time.

One painstaking step at a time, I drag the horseman off the road and towards an abandoned house that I used to play inside when I was a kid. Even missing appendages, he weighs more than a freaking cow—and a *fat* cow at that.

The whole time, my heart pounds. Whoever did this to him really could still be out there.

And they're probably looking for him.

Once I'm inside the building, my legs buckle, and I fall, the horseman collapsing on top of me.

For several seconds I lay beneath his bloody body, struggling to breathe. Of course this is how I would meet my end—suffocating to death under the weight of this gargantuan man. Only I would get myself into this stupid situation.

Can't believe I'm actually trying to save a fucking *horseman* of the apocalypse.

Grunting, I push the man off of me, letting his body roll to the side.

I glance at the horseman's twisted form, frowning.

Maybe *save* is the wrong word. The man seems pretty dead. And yet still I'm here, hanging out with his body when I should be getting home.

This is why my Aunt Maria doesn't like me. I can hear her even now. *You're more trouble than you're worth.*

At the thought of her, I remember the basket of fruit I left back on the road. If I'm not only late getting home but I somehow also manage to lose both the fruit and her basket, she's *definitely* going to disown my curious ass.

I drag myself back outside into the pouring rain and fetch the stupid basket, half hoping that the horseman is somehow gone when I return to the abandoned building.

But of course he's not. He still lays in the bloody, dripping heap where I left him.

It's not too late to walk away—or to tell someone about him.

Of course, I'm not going to.

Too sentimental, my cousins call me.

I set the basket aside and crouch near the horseman. My muscles still tremble from my earlier exertion, but I force myself to lay the horseman out, trying to situate him in as comfortable a position as possible. The whole time I grimace at the cold feel of his body.

He *has* to be dead.

But the last time I thought that, he wasn't, and that's enough to keep me inside this damn house.

So I sit across the room from him as the rain pelts against the leaky roof, ignoring my rising anxiety that I'm not home and will most definitely get a beating for it. I close my eyes and lean my head back against a nearby wall.

I think I might've nodded off because when I blink open my eyes it's nearly dark outside.

On the other side of the room, I hear a terrifying, keening sound. My eyes cut to the source, and there's the horseman, his weird glowing tattoos giving the house an eerie green glow. In the fading light, I can see the whites of his eyes. He looks confused and frightened.

He *is* alive after all.

I haven't exactly thought through what I'm doing when I get up and move over to him, kneeling at his side. He's staring at the remnants of his arms, which I *swear* look as though they've regrown ...

I place a soothing hand on his bare chest. At my touch, the horseman flinches, as though he expects a hit to come. My throat tightens at that. I know the feeling all too well.

"You're safe," I whisper.

The horseman's gaze snaps to me. His face is still swollen and bruised but I think—I think beneath all those injuries he has a beautiful face.

Why are you thinking about his face?

He tries to move his arm—I think to push me away—but there's not enough arm *to* move.

"I'm not going to hurt you," I vow, my voice resolute. I hadn't fully committed to helping this man before, but now, seeing him hurting and frightened, I won't leave him.

"Are you thirsty?" I ask.

He studies me, those green eyes almost as piercing as the markings on his chest. He doesn't respond.

He must be thirsty. He hasn't drank anything all day. I unhook the canteen I carry at my side and move it to his lips.

The horseman gives me one hell of a distrustful look.

I raise an eyebrow. Does he think I poisoned the water? As *if* I'd go to that much trouble.

Just to prove to him that the water is fine, I bring the canteen to my lips and take a swallow. I lower it from my mouth and bring it to his.

He gives his head a shake.

"You must be thirsty," I insist.

"I'm fine," he whispers, his voice low and hoarse.

"Suit yourself," I say, setting my canteen aside.

"Why?" he grits out.

Why are you helping me? he means.

"It's what any decent person would do."

He lets out a disbelieving huff, like there's no such thing as a decent person.

The two of us sit in silence. I want to ask him all sorts of questions now that he's awake, but I bite them back. He's in pretty rough condition.

Just as the thought crosses my mind, he makes a low noise, his chest rising and falling faster and faster.

"What's wrong?" I whisper. I don't know why I'm whispering.

I hear his teeth gnash together and the high pitched sound of a bottled up scream.

Oh. Duh, Ana. The man is in major pain.

Without much forethought, I reach out and run my fingers through his hair. My father used to do this to soothe me when I was sick.

Another pained sound slips out of his mouth, and I withdraw my hand, thinking that maybe this isn't so calming after all. But then the horseman leans his head towards my hand, seeking out my touch.

Feeling brave, I scoot closer, until his head is nearly in my lap. Then I resume running my fingers through his hair. The action seems to soothe the horseman. As I watch, his eyes flutter closed and his breathing evens out.

"What happened to you?" I murmur.

He doesn't answer, and I don't expect him to.

What are you doing, Ana? Of all the mistakes I've made, this may be my worst one yet.

Problem is, I don't regret it, even though I should.

I most definitely should.

I wake up in the middle of the night to distant shouting. I push myself up, blinking around me. Last I remember I was running my fingers through the horseman's hair. But then I'd gotten tired and laid down ...

I rub my eyes and stifle a yawn. It's still dark out and—

"... *got away! ... motherfucker ... away!*"

That wakes me up quickly.

The horseman is still lying next to me. The green glow from his markings illuminates his face; his eyes are open. He's already aware of them.

I glance out the window, straining to hear what's going on.

"... *all the men ... dead ...*"

I glance down at the horseman. If I heard that correctly, then this man *murdered* people before I stumbled across him. A shiver runs through me.

The horseman meets my gaze. I wish he didn't look so damn vulnerable.

It must've been in self-defense, I tell myself. I saw his wounds with my own eyes. I'd probably kill whoever did that to me too.

"You're safe," I repeat, my heart beating madly. I'm not going to give him up now.

The room we're in is illuminated in the horseman's soft green light, and unfortunately for us, this house is not so far from the main road. Eventually, those men are going to notice the light coming from this place—if they haven't already.

Making a quick decision, I pull off my shirt and throw it over the horseman's chest. The fabric mutes the glow almost completely, making the room too dark to see.

The two of us sit in the darkness, listening.

"... *can track him ... can't be far ...*"

I feel myself go cold all over.

"... *pointless ... rain ... tracks ... morning ...*"

Maybe the rain washed away all evidence that I dragged the horseman here. Maybe we got lucky.

I think of how little luck I've had in my life. Best not to assume it will suddenly save the day now.

The voices move off, and they don't come back. Whatever they decided, it doesn't lead them back our way.

Maybe we're okay—for now.

After that, I can't sleep, too afraid of those people finding us.

My gaze creeps back to the horseman's dark form. I can't get that first image of him out of my head. He was so mutilated ... the thought still takes my breath away. It doesn't help that every so often I hear a gasp of pain in the darkness. I can no longer tell if he's sleeping or not. I go back to stroking his hair, and the action seems to calm him.

As the night wears on, the chilly air pricks at my bare skin. I don't dare take my shirt back from the horseman, even though I'm freezing. I begin to shiver, my teeth clicking together.

"You're cold." His husky voice seems as though it's pulled from the darkness itself. It makes my skin prick, though not in an unpleasant way.

"I'm okay."

I'm in such deep trouble it's not even funny. If I don't get caught in the crosshairs of those men who are looking for the horseman, men who might not mind hurting a teenage girl, then my Aunt Maria is going to disown me.

I can hear her shrill voice even now. *Thought you could spend the night with some boy, you little idiot? Well, if you think you're old enough for sex, then you're old enough to live on your own.*

And that would be that.

Or maybe she'll just beat the living shit out of me.

Not all my shivering is from the cold.

"Lay next to me."

The horseman's voice drags me from my thoughts.

I stare at where I think his eyes are as his words coil low in my belly. I can tell he doesn't mean to make the offer sexual, but between that rough voice and the fact that our torsos are both bare, my mind can't help going there.

I've never laid next to a man who I wasn't related to.

"You're hurt," I say. "I don't want to jostle—"

"If you were worried about jostling my injuries, you wouldn't have dragged me damn close to the point of death."

To be honest, I think I dragged him *past* the point of death, but apparently he can live through that too.

"I wasn't *trying* to hurt you," I say. "I was trying to help you."

He grunts, though I have no clue whether he believes me or not.

"I ... couldn't leave you," I admit, picking at a fingernail.

The room is quiet for a long moment. Then—

"Lay down next to me," he says again.

I run my teeth over my lower lip.

"I don't trust you," I confess.

"That makes two of us."

I make a disbelieving noise. "I *saved* you."

"If this is your idea of saving a man—" His voice cuts off and he takes a ragged breath, "then I don't want to know what your idea of punishment is."

"I can't believe—" My teeth chatter, "I actually felt bad for you. You're so rude."

"Fine," he says, "stay cold."

I glare at his form in the darkness. It's clear he's done talking.

I last maybe another fifteen minutes before I curse under my breath, then scooch over to his side. I bump into something wet and gooey. The horseman hisses in a breath.

Shit—

"Sorry!" I apologize.

He grunts again.

Gingerly I lay myself down next to him, bumping his arm twice more on accident. Each time he makes a low, pained sound.

Bet he's regretting his offer now.

Finally, my bare skin presses against the side of his torso. The only place to put my head is on his shoulder, and I can't help but breathe him in. This is how lovers sleep, nestled in each other's arms.

Why am I even thinking about that?

"Don't get any ideas," I say out loud, as though the horseman is the one with the dirty thoughts.

"Because your flesh is *so* tempting right now," he quips.

My face heats a little. "I don't know what you're capable of."

"I don't have *hands* at the moment. And until I reacquire them, I think you can save worrying about my capabilities."

"Wait—'reacquire them'?" I echo weakly.

The horseman doesn't respond to that. But now my mind is hyper-focused on his injuries. I can still see his horrible, mangled body lying in the mud like he'd been discarded.

"How did you survive what happened to you?" I ask.

There's a pause.

"I cannot die," he finally says.

He cannot die?

"Oh."

The silence stretches out.

"What's your name?" I ask. As far as I'm aware, there are four horsemen, and I don't have a single clue which one this is.

I swear I feel him looking at me with those frightful green eyes. In the darkness he begins to laugh.

"You don't know?" he finally says. "I'm Famine, the third horseman of the apocalypse, and I'm here to kill you all."

Chapter 9

Five years ago
Anitápolis, Brazil

Despite his words, he doesn't kill me. At least not right then.

However, he continues to laugh and laugh, raising the hairs along my arms. Now would be a really good time to move my head off of his shoulder and scoot my dumb little ass out of here.

Why do I always get myself into these messes?

Famine is still laughing and laughing and laughing. The man has officially *lost it*. Somewhere along the way, his laughter changes, deepening until he's not laughing but *sobbing*.

I lay in his arms, feeling even more awkward and uncomfortable than I did before. I don't know what I expected when I saved him, but I don't think it was this.

The third horseman of the apocalypse is having a mental breakdown right next to me.

The sound is awful, his shoulders heaving with each sob.

I don't know what to do. I thought the hard part would be saving him, but it's clear that while the horseman's body is safe—for now—his mind isn't. It's still caged in whatever prison he's been locked up in, and I don't know how to set it free.

Finally, because I can think of nothing better, I reach out and begin stroking his hair again.

"Ssshhh," I murmur, "it's okay. It's going to be okay." The empty platitudes slip from my lips. I have no clue what I'm saying. Of course nothing is okay and it won't be okay, and I should not be making *Famine* (holy shit!) feel better.

Under my touch his cries taper off until he's left taking in ragged breaths of air.

My hand stills.

"Don't stop," he says, his voice broken.

I resume my ministrations. For a long time the two of us are quiet.

"So, you're Famine?" I finally say. "What does that mean?"

"Mortal, I have no idea what you're asking." He sounds exasperated. Weary and exasperated.

"Um," I say, "do you have any special powers?" I clarify.

"Special powers," he mutters. "I can make plants perish—among other things," he says.

"I had heard stories about you. That you'd been captured. I hadn't thought they were true, but ... were they? Have you been held somewhere?"

His breath begins to speed up again. "Mhm ..."

Jesus.

I run my fingers through his hair. I really want to ask him about his captivity—where exactly he was, what they did to him, how long he was there—but it's clearly a tender subject.

"What are you going to do now that you're free?" I eventually ask.

Beneath my hand, he seems to go still.

I hear the menace in his voice when he says, "I'm going to

get my revenge."

I didn't think I was capable of falling asleep in the horseman's arms, yet I must've because I stir at the touch of soft fingertips.

I blink my eyes open, squinting at the morning light streaming in through a nearby window. A man looms over me, his green eyes piercing. After a moment, I realize I recognize those green eyes.

Famine.

I suck in a shocked breath when I truly take in the horseman.

All of him is strange and lovely.

When I found him yesterday, he wore blood and grime in place of clothing. But now he's fully dressed, and over his black shirt and pants he wears bronze armor *that definitely wasn't there last night.* The metal breastplate gleams in the morning light.

How ... ? Did he leave at some point to get his things?

But then my focus returns to his powerful build. Even kneeling, he looks intimidatingly large, and I don't have to see the skin beneath his armor to know he has a body made for battle.

That's nothing, though, compared to his face.

He's ... there aren't words for this sort of male beauty. His caramel colored hair curls around the nape of his neck, and those brilliant green eyes are made all the brighter against his tan skin.

I don't know where to look—at the sharp slice of his jawline or those high cheekbones—or those soft, sinner lips. He looks like some mythological figure taken straight out of a painting.

He is *a mythological figure.*

I push myself up, the action forcing the horseman to move away.

His fingers are what woke me, I realize. He was brushing my hair from my face much the same way I had done to his throughout the night. Now his fingertips linger on the side of my face.

His fingertips ...

"Your arms!" I gasp. Holy mother of ... "*How do you have hands?*"

Famine smiles a little, and my whole body reacts to that smile. "Are you now worried about my capabilities?"

My gaze flicks skeptically from the hand touching me to his face. "Maybe ... what are you doing?"

"I wanted to see you," he says, his gaze moving over me as though he's trying to commit my features to memory.

He stands, and for the first time I notice the other items lying next to him. One of them I can't immediately identify but the other one I recognize as a scythe, its wicked blade gleaming.

Dear God, that thing looks deadly.

He picks up the scythe, and my heart begins to patter. Last night I didn't realize just how massive he was, and now, with that weapon in hand, Famine looks especially lethal.

I edge away from him.

The horseman must see me cower because he gives me an exasperated look. "You slept on me last night. There's nothing for you to fear."

"You now have a blade—and *hands*," I say. "How *did* you get them back?"

"My body regenerates."

"Your body ..." Dear baby Jesus, he can grow back *limbs*? "And the ... the ..." I gesture vaguely at his attire.

Famine presses his lips together, either in displeasure or because he's trying not laugh. He doesn't seem like the laughing type, so displeasure it is.

"I'm not of this world, flower."

That's not really an answer, but I'm sort of stuck on the fact that he called me *flower*.

That's a compliment, right?

Looking at him, I want it to be a compliment.

Are you seriously crushing on one of the horsemen of the apocalypse, Ana?

Damnit, I think I am. But in my defense, they don't make cheekbones that pretty here on earth.

"Come on," Famine says, interrupting my thoughts, "we need to move."

"Where are we going?" I ask, hurrying after him, grabbing my basket of fruit. I have some fatalistic hope that bringing this basket back home will somehow spare me my aunt's wrath.

It's a foolish hope, but then, I *am* a fool.

Famine doesn't respond, and it's just as well. We're clearly headed back towards town, the two of us walking down the road I so recently found him on. My eyes linger on the scythe he holds; he decided to bring *that* but not the other, less threatening object, and I'm trying really, really hard not to think about the motives behind that decision. Or, for that matter, what's going to happen the moment the townspeople meet Famine.

"Last night this road was swarming with men," Famine says, more to himself than to me. "Now it's deserted."

The back of my neck pricks. "Do you think those men ... ?"

"They're setting a trap for me," he says.

The thought is downright *petrifying*.

"Maybe we shouldn't be on this road then ... we could hide ..." All I can see in my mind's eye is how much torture Famine's body endured when I first found him.

"I have waited *years* for this moment," he says. "I will not hide from them. Their deaths are mine to *savor*."

That's right about when I have my first real misgivings about Famine.

"I didn't save you so that you could kill a bunch of people," I say.

"You know what I am, flower,"—that name again—"don't pretend you don't know my nature."

Before I can debate with him more, we enter Anitápolis.

People are going about their morning when we walk down the street. They stop what they're doing, however, when they notice Famine and his big-ass scythe.

As we move towards the middle of town, a coal-black horse comes galloping down the cracked asphalt, heading right for Famine. The steed looks spitting angry, but at the sight of the creature, the horseman seems to relax.

Wait. Is that his ... ?

The steed slows, finally stopping in front of Famine.

The horseman leans his forehead against the horse's muzzle. "It's alright, boy," he says, rubbing the side of the creature's face. "You're safe now," he says, echoing the same platitudes I murmured to him last night.

I stare at the horse. Where has the creature been this whole time? And why has the steed decided to make an appearance now?

They're setting a trap for me.

Just as the thought clicks into place, I hear the whiz of an arrow.

Thwump.

The projectile makes a meaty sound as it skewers Famine's shoulder.

I expect the horseman to scream or to flinch like he did last night, but he does none of those things.

He *smiles.*

An unbidden shiver runs through me.

That is not the look of a man who's afraid. That is the look of a man bent on burning the world down.

Famine's eyes meet mine for a long second, and they're full of wicked glee. Then his gaze flicks to the men trailing behind the black horse—men I didn't notice until now. They hold bows and swords and cudgels.

"I had hoped to see you all once more," Famine says.

The horseman's nostrils flare, and the wind shifts. That's all the warning any of us get.

In the next instant the earth splits beneath the men, and strong, green shoots sprout from the ground. They grow within seconds, wrapping round and round the men's ankles, climbing higher by the second.

The men shout, their fear apparent, and several onlookers scream, many of them beginning to flee.

I, however, am still as stone, my eyes pinned to the sight ahead of me. I've never seen anything like it. All those horrible bedtime stories I used to hear about the horsemen suddenly make so much more sense.

As the vines grow larger, moving up the men's legs and torsos, they sprout thorns. Now the men start to cry out in earnest. A few of them stab at their unnatural bindings. One breaks free, but he trips, and the monstrous plant reaches out for him, moving as though it has an awareness of its own, impossible though that might be.

I glance at Famine, who is hyper focused on the men, a small, cruel smile on his lips. He told me he could kill plants; he never mentioned that he could *grow* them at will, or that he could turn them into weapons of his own making, but it's obvious that he's doing both at the moment.

The plants have now grown as tall as the men, and their many branches twine around whatever limbs they can get ahold of. Now ... now they begin to *squeeze*. First, the weapons fall from the men's hands. But it doesn't end there.

I cover my mouth. "Oh my God. Oh my God. Oh my God." It doesn't even occur to me to tell the horseman to stop.

I simply watch in horror as bones break and bodies contort. My stomach churns at the sight. I've seen my share of violence, but never like this. Never like this.

And then it's over. Too many vital things have been

broken in those bodies. Maybe Famine could recover from those injuries, but not these men. They sag in their strange cages, their bulging eyes blank, their limbs contorted.

I turn and vomit.

Dead. They're all dead.

For several seconds there's a strange stillness to Anitápolis. Even though plenty of people have fled from the gruesome confrontation, more have lingered, drawn out by their curiosity and horror.

The horseman's gaze sweeps over these people.

"Countless days I have been enslaved. Tortured and killed only to rise again. None of you helped." The silence stretches out. "Did you think you were truly safe from me?"

Wait. What?

I glance at the horseman with wide eyes as my horror begins to grow.

He shakes his head, and that smile of his is back. "You were *never* safe. Not then and *especially* not now. Your crops will die, your homes will fall. You and everything you've ever loved will perish."

I don't feel the earthquake coming. One moment I'm standing on solid ground, the next moment it seems to violently buckle, throwing me forward. I hit the asphalt hard, my basket and the jabuticabas inside scattering across the crumbling road.

Over the screams, I hear strange, groaning noises, then the ripping sounds of buildings coming down. All the while the earth continues to shake.

I cover my head and curl up on myself, waiting for it to be over.

A few years ago there was another massive earthquake that hit our town, knocking down an alarming number of buildings and burying dozens of people alive.

Now, it's happening again.

It goes on and on, and all I can do is curl in on myself and cover my head. It feels like an eternity before the earthquake finally abates.

Tentatively, I lower my arms. Dust is still settling around me, but it looks ... it looks like Anitápolis has been leveled. Just ... wiped away.

Jesus, Joseph, and Mary.

As I stare, more screams start up. I squeeze my eyes shut, trying to shut out the noise. Then that, too, goes quiet. All I can hear is my ragged breathing.

Eventually I force my eyes open and just ... take in the horror. There are more strange plants holding more limp bodies in their grips.

And now the world is truly silent.

I'm not sure there's a single soul left.

Except for me—me and the horseman.

For several long moments, I cannot speak. I keep trying to, but words fail me.

I make a sound low in my throat, something that builds into a wail.

At the noise, Famine glances my way. He saunters over and reaches a hand out to me.

I stare up at him, ignoring his hand. "You told me there was nothing to fear." My voice sounds off.

"Nothing for *you* to fear," Famine corrects. "I never promised the same for anyone else."

I take a few stuttering breaths.

How could I have just let him come here into my town?

This is my fault.

"Is anyone ... ?" *Alive?* I can't bring myself to say it.

Turns out, I don't need to.

"You are," Famine says, his expression remorseless as he stares at me.

That's ... it?

What have I done?

What. Have. I. Done?

I thought compassion was a virtue. That's what made me save the horseman. So why am I being punished for it?

This is my bad luck, showing up again.

Famine nods to the town. "Grab what you need, then hurry back. I'm eager to leave this place."

Eager to leave ... ? With *me*?

Surely he's not serious?

I give him a wild look. "What are you talking about?"

"Get your things," he says again, gesturing down what's left of the street.

I follow where he's pointing. There's nothing even left *to* gather. My entire town is nothing but rubble.

Another low moan escapes my throat. My cousins are gone. So is my aunt.

I feel a tear escape, then another. There will be no beating or disownment awaiting my return because my aunt isn't alive to deliver any of it. The thought breaks something inside of me. She always disliked me; she'd look at me like she saw something no one else did. Something bad. I suddenly feel like her disgust towards me was merited.

My carelessness killed my entire town.

"I'm not going with you," I whisper, still staring out at the destruction. Reality is beginning to sink in. I'm not sure I ever wanted to be me *less* than I do right now.

"Of course you are," Famine says.

"You just *murdered*"—my voice breaks—"the only family I have."

He gives me a curious look. "They should have saved me. They didn't."

"*They* didn't know." At least *I* didn't know—and I couldn't possibly have been the only person in this town to not know.

Nearby, Famine's horse whinnies. Guess that fucker survived the wreckage too. Bet he's a dick, just like his rider.

"Grab your things," the horseman repeats.

"I'm not going with you," I say again, this time more resolute.

He exhales, clearly impatient with me. "There's nothing *left* for you here."

My body is beginning to shake. I pinch my eyes shut, willing away the last few minutes.

I hear the horseman take a step towards me. My eyes snap open and I shrink back. "Stay away from me," I say.

He frowns. "You showed me kindness when I'd all but forgotten it existed. I won't harm you, flower," he says, his voice soft. "But now you must get up. I have lingered in these parts for far too long."

More tears are coming; they silently drip down my cheeks. "This is all my fault," I say, taking in my surroundings. Everything is so still.

"They were always going to die," Famine says, his expression turning stony. "I would've torn this town apart even if you had never cared for me."

I think that's supposed to make me feel better. It doesn't.

"Now," he says, a note of steel entering his voice. "Get. Up."

Getting up means dealing with this situation. I'm most definitely *not* ready for that. I wrap my arms around myself instead.

The horseman steps in close, placing a warm palm against my shoulder. Instinctively, I flinch away.

"*Don't touch me.*" My voice doesn't even sound like my own.

My eyes fall to the basket that's rolled meters away, and regret sits heavy in my stomach.

Near my basket a thorny bush begins to grow, rising higher by the second. Leaves unfurl, the plant fills out, and from it blooms a delicate lavender-grey rose.

Famine plucks the flower from the bush and hands it to me, thorns and all.

"I won't leave you," the horseman says fiercely. For a moment, he sounds like the Famine I got to know last night. Someone who seemed to have a heart. "Get on my horse. Come with me. Please."

I don't take the rose. "I healed you, and you killed everyone I loved. Fuck you and your rose. Just ... go." I begin to weep.

It's all finally starting to process.

Oh God, is it processing.

After a long minute, the horseman sets the rose on the broken ground in front of me.

"I won't force you to stay with me. Not after ..." He glances off in the distance, his eyes unfocused. He blinks away his thoughts, his attention returning to me. "Your choice is your own, but if you care for your life at all, then you should come with me."

And witness more death?

I'd rather take my chances in this rotten world.

My gaze meets his. *I should've never helped you.*

The horseman must see it in my expression because, for an instant, something flickers across his features. I'd say it was regret or surprise, but who knows?

It's enough to drive him towards his horse. He mounts the steed, sliding the scythe into a holster at his back. Clad in his armor and astride his horse, he doesn't look like a villain. Not at all. It's enraging.

"Goodbye, little flower," Famine says, his gaze heavy on mine. "I will not soon forget your kindness." He flashes me one last long look, then rides off.

Chapter 10

Present

Even now I taste bile as I recall the memory.

"*You*," the horseman says. His gaze searches mine. "I had wondered ..."

"What happened to me?" I say, finishing his sentence for him. "I survived."

"I'm glad." Famine takes a deep breath, the action jostling my blade. He settles himself into his chair, like he's getting himself comfortable; it's clear that whatever memory he has of me, he thinks it's going to spare him.

My anger rises like the tide. "How I hate you," I whisper.

"And yet you haven't dragged the knife across my throat," he says.

"Is that a dare?" I whisper against his ear.

My hand itches to do that very thing. To see his immortal blood spray from his neck. To see his pain. That's why I'm here. *Revenge.* There's nothing else left for me.

"Do it, flower," he taunts, echoing my thoughts.

"*Don't call me that.*"

I dig the blade in, the endearment only making me angrier.

Finish this, I urge myself. Still, I hesitate.

It's just that I've never killed anyone before.

Would it technically be killing if the horseman didn't die?

I should definitely find out. I owe it to Elvita, to my aunt and my cousins *to* find out.

I press the knife in deeper, watching as more blood slips over the blade.

"You're doing it all wrong," Famine says, his voice casual. I can feel him staring at me as though he's committing my features to memory. That angers me too.

"Shut up." I take a deep breath, gathering up my courage.

The horseman looks vaguely amused when he says, "You do realize I could stop you if I wanted?"

That causes me to pause.

The horseman openly smirks. "Girl, have you no memory of my capabilities?"

I meet his gaze.

One moment I'm in control, and in the next—

The floor bucks, the hardwood splintering beneath my feet. I'm thrown to the side, my shoulder hitting the wall. By some miracle I manage to keep my hold on my dagger. I can hear Famine's chair scrape back, and then he grabs me.

Pure instinct has me thrusting my blade forward, the point of my dagger burying itself into his chest. Famine grunts at the intrusion, grimacing as he glances down at the hilt jutting from his abdomen.

I let out a surprised yelp.

Shit, I *stabbed* him. I actually stabbed him. I stare, horrified, at the weapon protruding from his flesh. The satisfaction I was supposed to feel never comes.

The Reaper grimaces. Wrapping a hand around the hilt, he drags the dagger out and tosses the bloody blade aside.

I reach for my other weapon, but the Reaper grabs me by

the throat and hauls me over to the table, slamming my body against the polished surface, his scythe trapped beneath me.

Famine's pelvis grinds into mine as he pins me in.

"Foolish—little—flower," he clips out, leaning over me.

I reach again for the holstered dagger at my hip. The Reaper beats me to it, his hand skimming down my side as he pulls the weapon out. He tosses it aside then grabs at the longer blade strapped to my chest, giving it a cursory look before chucking it far out of reach.

Just like that, the last of my grand scheme is gone. For the third time in my life, I'm at the whim of the horseman.

"This was your plan?" he grits out, some of his blood dripping onto my chest. "To come here and kill me? You make a worse killer than you do a whore."

I spit in his face.

In response, he squeezes my throat tighter.

"Unless, of course, you *didn't* want to kill me," he says, searching my gaze. "You've seen that I cannot die, and you know what I'm capable of. Surely you're not stupid enough to think you could end me—"

Somewhere in the mansion, a door opens.

He casts a hateful glance towards the sound. I use that moment to draw my leg towards my chest, and then I kick out, ramming the fucker in the gonads as hard as I can.

Famine lets out a pained grunt, releasing me to cup himself, and I use the distraction to dash from the room.

Get out get out get out.

I leap over the dead body, round the corner—

A man stands in the way.

Shit.

His eyes widen a fraction when he sees me. I try to stop my momentum, but I slam into him anyway, the two of us going down in a tangle of limbs.

I'm desperately trying to extricate myself when I hear Famine approaching. Before I can get to my feet, the man on top of me is kicked off of my body. The Reaper's scythe goes to his throat.

"What did I tell you about staying away?" the Reaper says conversationally to what must be one of his guards.

"But—" The man's eyes dart to me.

Faster than I can follow, Famine slices the man's neck, blood spurting from his opened artery.

I scream at the sight. The man is still looking at me, his expression shocked and frightened as he reaches for his gaping throat.

Not how this evening was supposed to go.

Once more I frantically try to get up.

The horseman presses a booted foot to my chest. "You, I'm not done with."

He raises his scythe back to his side, the blade now tipped in blood.

I close my eyes against the sight, and breathe in and out, trying not to completely lose it.

"What makes you think I won't kill you right here and right now?" the Reaper says.

"I'm not afraid of death," I say softly.

"Oh really now?" Famine sounds amused. "Then open your eyes and look at it."

It's the taunt in his voice that has me blinking my eyes. I glare up at him.

He tilts his head. "There you are. Let me look at you."

If he weren't so far away, I might've tried spitting at him again.

Famine takes his time. "I wondered if we might cross paths again. You should've told me who you were. I would've spared you."

I guffaw. Like he was *ever* going to listen.

"But you didn't," I say. "Take a look at my chest and you'll see for yourself that I wasn't spared *anything*."

"Yet despite it all, you lived." He scrutinizes me, as though he can hardly believe it. "Why find me and risk my wrath yet again?"

Something warm and wet touches my shoulder then spreads down my arm and up into my hair. I realize too late that it's the dead man's blood.

I grimace up at Famine, breathing through my nose to keep my emotions under control. "I wanted to hurt you."

He raises his eyebrows. "My balls are sore, little flower, I'll give you that."

I feel my cheeks flush with anger even as the horror of my situation sets in. "Fuck you."

The horseman presses his boot down harder against me. "You tried that already, remember? I still don't want your pussy."

This is all a joke to him. My pain, everyone else's.

"You took everyone I loved from me the first time we met," I whisper. "And then you did it all over again."

He scowls. "That's what I do, mortal. It's what I will *continue* to do until I am called home."

Famine takes me in for another second. Then, removing his boot from my chest, he reaches down and hauls me up. "I thought, however, that you were different from the rest of these parasites."

Grasping me by the upper arm, he begins to haul me down the hall, pausing only to grab a length of coiled rope hanging from a mounted coatrack.

I struggle against him, letting out a frustrated noise when it gets me nowhere. For the life of me, I have no idea what's going on. Famine has had several opportunities to kill me. He's taken none of them.

Then again, maybe he's simply drawing this out.

Famine jerks me into an empty room. Tossing me inside, he kicks the door shut behind us.

I hit the ground hard, my teeth clicking together. The Reaper stalks after me.

I scramble backwards, but there's nowhere to go. I'm trapped in this room with an unearthly monster.

For a split second, the two of us stare at each other—hunter and hunted.

He's going to kill me. I can see in his eyes just how much he hates us, how much he enjoys snuffing us out one by one. He's still holding the scythe, along with the rope he grabbed.

Famine kneels down at my side, that painfully beautiful face of his illuminated by nearby oil lamps. As he does so, blood drips from his chest, where I so recently stabbed him. My gaze moves to his neck, which is also smeared in blood. Despite his earlier words, I *did* manage to hurt him.

The horseman grabs one of my wrists, and maybe it's his touch or the look in his eyes, but the hairs along my arm stand on end.

"Let me go." I jerk my arm against him, but his grip doesn't loosen.

He grabs my other wrist, pressing my two arms together before he begins winding the rope around my wrists.

"What are you doing?" I struggle against him. Once again, it's absolutely useless. He seems to have unnatural strength.

"I'm subduing you," he says. "I thought that was obvious."

Famine finishes winding the rope around my wrists, his expression placid. He leans back on his haunches and appraises me. "Will you try to kill me again?"

I pause in my struggle.

That's what this is about? He doesn't want me to get violent with him again?

I wait too long to answer.

A corner of his mouth curves up. "As I thought," he says, taking my silence as a *yes.*

In all fairness, if given the chance, I will *definitely* try to incapacitate him again.

The horseman spends the next moment taking me in.

"For a man who's scared of pussies," I say, "you're

spending an awfully long time looking at me."

He doesn't rise to the bait.

"Tell me," the Reaper says, leaning back on his haunches, "if you were in my shoes—if a girl who once saved you then tried to kill you were suddenly your prisoner—what would you do?"

This is the part where I die. Painfully. I *did* in fact squander my second chance at life.

I glare up at the horseman, defeated. "I can't say," I respond bitterly. "I'm not a monster."

Those unnerving eyes continue to assess me.

"I have never made an exception for a human before," he admits, "and I'm loathe to make one now."

I can hear the *but* coming.

"But I'm afraid there has only ever been a single instance where a human saved my life. It, unfortunately, has made an impression on me." He leans in close. "That should worry a feeble little flower like you."

Don't worry, buddy, it *does*.

He gets up, his green eyes still on me. "We'll talk again in the morning." Famine heads out of the room, but pauses when he gets to the doorway. "Oh, and if you try leaving this place, I'll make sure you regret it."

My mind flashes to the bloody body in the living room and the mass grave outside. I might be brash and defiant, but there's no way in hell I'm going to attempt an escape tonight. Famine is not exactly a man to test.

The horseman eyes me up and down. "You really should've stayed away. You may still be that same little flower who saved me, but then, I'm not known for letting flowers grow ..."

Chapter 11

"Wake up."

I start at Famine's voice, my eyes opening.

He's staring down at me, a scowl on his lips, like he's angry I'm even here.

I blink blearily, glancing around at my surroundings, before my attention returns to the horseman.

"Have you ever heard of knocking?" I say, stifling a yawn.

"You're my captive. You don't get the luxury of a warning."

"Mmmm ..." My eyes drift closed.

"Wake. Up."

"Unless you plan on cutting away these restraints—*no*," I say, not bothering to open my eyes.

Unfortunately, this isn't the first time I've slept with bound hands. However, it's *definitely* the shittiest time I've had with them. At least in the past I got paid for this sort of thing.

A moment later, Famine rips the covers off the bed. But if he thought to intimidate me, this isn't the way. I've come to expect all sorts of weird shit when it comes to me and beds. What can you do? Hazards of my trade.

I hear the metallic zing of a blade being unsheathed. "You

seem to have a shockingly bad sense of self-preservation," he says.

I force my eyes open again, shaking off the last of my sleep so that I can focus on the dagger he holds. "You're just mad I'm not more scared."

The truth is, I decided last night that Famine isn't going to kill me. I think. At least, not for the time being. That's definitely emboldened me. The rest of my attitude is simple bravado. Another knack I've picked up since I became a lady of ill repute.

Famine grabs my wrists roughly and begins sawing away at the bindings.

I stare at him as he jerks at the rope. Today, he's wearing his full regalia, his bronze armor polished to a high sheen.

"You smell like pig shit and blood," he comments.

I raise an eyebrow. "Because I care *so* much what you think."

If I'm being perfectly honest, I'm halfway enjoying not having to look and smell like a man's wet dream. It's a nice change of pace. Also, super low-maintenance.

"Keep going, little flower, you're reminding me of all the reasons I despise humans."

"First off, the name is Ana," I say, sitting up a little. "Second of all, *horseman*, let's not mince our words. You hate humans because long ago we were God-awful to you, *not* because you have a problem with my mouth."

In fact, I know I have a nice mouth—or a naughty mouth, depending on who you talk to—but it's well-liked, all the same.

He glances up at me, and I have to force myself to not be affected by his beauty.

Famine frees my hands then leaves my side. He crosses the room and opens a closet. Several dresses hang inside, the size and style of them making me think a teenager used to live in this room. I don't let myself think about what must've happened to her.

"So," I say, shaking out my wrists to get the blood flowing through them. "*Did* you decide whether I get to live or die?" Because I have to ask.

"Do you really think we'd be having a conversation if I wanted you dead?" he says, yanking one of the dresses off its hanger.

I frown at the garment, suspicious that he grabbed it for me.

Famine heads for the door. "Follow me," he says without glancing back.

I stare after him for several seconds, not sure what to make of my situation. But I really don't think he intends to kill me, and I need to wake up a bit more before I consider my next move, so reluctantly, I pad along after him.

Famine leads me into another bedroom. Resting on top of the mattress is the horseman's scythe and what I have now learned are his scales. The rest of the room is full of a stranger's things.

The Reaper crosses the room, heading to a connected bathroom, and I trail after him. There's a fancy clawfoot tub and a toilet, both which actually look as though they're connected to plumbing. The bathtub even has a lever to pump water in. Whoever these rich bitches were, I'm almost envious of them.

They're surely dead.

Maybe I'm not *too* envious of them ...

In front of the tub is a pitcher of water, which rests on a shallow basin. A washcloth lays on the lip of the bowl. There's a clawfoot tub, and yet the horseman chose a pitcher and basin to bathe with. You would've thought a presumptuous prick like Famine would at *least* try to fill up a tub.

"Living in the lap of luxury, are we now?" I say.

"That's for you," he says.

Ah. Now I understand why he skipped the tub. Heaven forbid he does anything lavish for anyone else.

"Because you stink," he adds.

"I'm blown away by your hospitality," I say, padding over to the pitcher.

What I don't say is that this situation is odd. Really, really odd. Famine still hasn't killed me, and now he expects me to bathe? In his personal bathroom, no less?

Does he plan on watching?

The horseman tosses the dress he holds onto the nearby counter, leaning against the vanity a moment later. When he doesn't leave, I realize with a jolt of surprise that *yes*, he does plan on sticking around.

How scandalous!

Ignoring the pitcher of water, I head over to the tub and try the lever. I give it a test pump. Immediately, water hisses out of the spout.

It works!

Fuck that sponge bath.

Turning my back to the horseman, I begin pumping water into the basin. He doesn't stop me either, which I half expected him too, given what a little shit he is.

It takes a long time to draw in enough water to bathe in, and the water itself is a little chilly, but eventually it fills up.

When I turn around again, Famine is still there, in the bathroom, and he makes no move to leave.

I don't know what to think of that.

I take off my shirt, then the thin bra I wear, uncaring that Famine's getting an eyeful of naked lady chest. This is just an average Tuesday for me.

The horseman's gaze drops to the wounds that decorate my torso. I actually hear his sharp inhale.

And now I think I understand his reason for lingering—he wanted to see my wounds.

He pushes away from the counter, his gaze locked on my scabbed-over wounds. "They tore you apart."

I glance down, and the memory hits me again. I can feel

those men's hands on me and I can hear the wet, meaty sound of their knives stabbing me over and over again.

"There are eleven different marks," I say. I don't know why I tell him.

"And I imagine you laid for a long time in pain, alone and frightened."

My steely gaze flicks up to him. "I wasn't *just* frightened." I was angry.

He must see the anger in my eyes when I look at him.

"*Yes*," he says, "I know that look well."

I force my emotions back down.

After a moment, he moves back, towards the bathroom counter, putting distance between us. "Those don't look like survivable wounds," he says, his voice light.

I don't bother agreeing with him. Instead, I step out of my pants, then slide off my panties, kicking them aside.

If I thought nudity would scare off the horseman, I thought wrong.

Huh.

I step into the tub and lower myself, until I'm reclining like a queen, sighing as I lean against the rim.

"How's your abdominal wound?" I ask, draping my arms over the sides. My tits are wantonly exposed. I'm honestly enjoying the hell out of this; I hope the horseman is *rattled*.

Famine narrows his gaze on me. "Gone."

"Too bad."

"My balls are better too—thanks for asking," he says.

"I wasn't worried about your balls. It seems you have no use for them." My mouth curves into a smirk as I speak. I really am enjoying myself.

The Reaper folds his arms, a wicked gleam in his eyes. "Tell me, *Ana*," he says, the sound of my name on his lips making my stomach clench, "what would you do if I let you go free?"

My gaze sharpens on him.

I could lie. But those reptilian eyes, they seem to unmask the truth anyway.

"I don't know," I admit. "I'd probably try to find you and hurt you again."

Because this life has nothing else left for me. I have no home, no job, no friends, no family. Just this vendetta.

The horseman makes a sound low in his chest. "I thought as much."

I should probably be worried at this point. But to be honest, I think I'm five cities beyond worried. I should've turned back from this long ago.

"I'll still try to hurt you," I add. "Keeping me close just makes it more convenient for me."

Now the horseman smiles, and dear God, he really does enjoy cruelty.

"I wouldn't do that if I were you," he says softly.

He doesn't say anything else, but then, he doesn't need to. The threat is implicit: if I try to hurt him, he will make me learn what true pain is.

Pushing away from the bathroom counter, the Reaper moves to the doorway. "Tomorrow we're heading out. If you try to escape, I won't feed you." He looks disturbingly delighted by that possibility.

Fucking *Famine*.

So the horseman really doesn't intend to kill me. For whatever reason, he actually wants to keep me around. So much so that he'll punish escape attempts.

I scrutinize the man. He hates humans but he won't kill me, and he hates flesh, yet he's stuck around to watch me bathe. I can't pin this guy down, and it's going to eat away at me. So to speak. But on the topic of food—

"Let me get this straight:" I say, "if I stay inside this nice-ass house, you'll feed me?" Where is the catch?

Again, the horseman's eyes narrow. "You won't starve."

Free room and board? How delightful. My toes practically

curl.

"Well then, it's settled. You have yourself a new and *very* willing captive."

Chapter 12

Despite my words, I do try to escape. Several times, in fact. Mostly because I'm fatalistically curious. I'm also bored. There's only so much to do in a stranger's room. Oh, and then there's the fact that going hungry doesn't scare me all that much.

Needless to say, I get caught—over and over again. I hadn't really planned on actually leaving this place—not when I still intend to carry out my revenge—but I *was* hoping that, while on the lam, I might find a sharp object to skewer the horseman with at some point.

We are enemies, after all.

Unfortunately, if there are weapons lying around, I don't find them.

After my fourth attempt, the horseman simply says, "Flee again and I'll use my plants to keep you in place."

Now *that* is an effective threat. I'm surprised it took him this long to truly intimidate me. My captor is the infamous Famine, after all.

So, I relegate myself to the reality of my situation: that I'll be stuck inside this room until Famine decides it's time for us to leave.

Bored and alone once again, I raid the closet, changing into an outfit more suited to my taste. The cotton dress I settle on is brightly patterned and flowy. I opt to keep my old boots, however; my feet are bigger than this room's former occupant.

I poke around at a few more of the girl's items, flipping through a few books stacked on her bookcase before I move on to a series of diaries that occupy a whole shelf. I can only assume they were written by the girl who lived here. The entries are just as entitled and inane as you might expect from a rich, sheltered teenage girl, each one signed off "*Eternally Yours, Andressa.*"

I strive for such drama in my own life. Alas, even amidst the apocalypse, I haven't managed to attain it.

What I don't expect are the salacious love letters I find hidden under the mattress, each one from *Maria*, a mysterious woman who, by the sounds of it, knew her way around a vagina. I mean, she *really* seemed to know her way around a vagina.

I need to get myself a Maria.

Those letters entertain me for a while. But there are only so many of them.

After that ... boredom. Hours and hours of boredom. So much boredom that somewhere along the way I fall asleep, sprawled across Andressa's bed, her most intimate letters and writings spread out around me.

I wake to the sound of my stomach growling. Outside the first rays of sun have lightened the sky. I can hear the low murmuring of voices, and for one second it all feels so terribly normal that I almost forget that I'm trapped in a house with a horseman of the apocalypse, and those voices belong to some of the last humans alive in this city.

My stomach growls again, and withholding food was most definitely a brilliant threat on Famine's part, damn him.

It takes another hour for me to hear the confident footfalls of what can only be the Reaper. No one else dares to walk around this place with that much confidence. They head towards my room, only stopping once they're outside my door.

Clearing my voice, I call out, "Unless you have coffee or food, I don't want to talk to you."

A moment later, the doorknob turns and Famine walks in with a glass of water and a slice of fruit in his hand.

He holds the items up to me. "Because you managed to go a whole twelve hours without trying to run," he says.

I think I'm supposed to be grateful.

But, as the poet's might put it, *fuck that shit.*

"A *papaya?*" I say, recognizing the fruit. It's not even a full papaya either; just an itsy bitsy sliver. "I'm a full-bodied woman, not a *bird.*"

"Perhaps you forgot who I am—*Famine,*" he stresses. "Feel fortunate that I'm feeding you at all."

"I want coffee. *Then* I'll feel fortunate. Maybe. Some cake would definitely make me feel grateful."

"You are a human-shaped headache," he mutters.

"What a compliment to headaches everywhere."

"Do you ever stop talking?"

"Only if you put something in my mouth," I say. "I'm partial to food, but dicks work too."

He glances heavenward.

Ah, blessed reaction.

"This is what you get, Ana," he says, setting the items on the ground. "Eat it or go hungry. I really don't care which." He backs away from the room, a scowl on his face. "Meet me in the stables. You have five minutes."

I use those five minutes to raid the house's pantry. I *do* manage to find some cake, along with a few other treats. No brewed coffee, unfortunately. I do find a knife, but there's literally nowhere to store it while traveling, except maybe my boot. But again with my luck, I'd probably end up jabbing myself with it. So I leave the knife behind.

When I finally meet Famine just outside the stables, he's frowning at me again. I think this is becoming a thing for him, where I'm concerned.

His ferocious black horse is saddled and waiting, and his men linger nearby, readying their own horses.

Not for the first time, my situation feels surreal. Forget that I've survived through the destruction of two separate cities, or that I live in biblical times. Simply the fact that I went from nursing this man to health to attacking him to being his semi-willing prisoner is strange enough as is.

I dust off the last of the cake from my fingers.

He notices the action, his frown deepening. "You're late."

A mistake I intend on repeating so long as the two of us are together.

"Just be happy I didn't run again," I say. Not that I really, truly would. Stabbing him requires close proximity.

He studies me with those unsettling eyes for a moment. Then, the corner of his mouth curves up.

Uh oh.

"If you are so determined to escape me," he says, "then perhaps I need to treat you as a proper prisoner."

I give him a perplexed look even as the Reaper moves over to his horse. "You *have* been treating me like a prisoner." What does he think he's been doing with me over the last twenty-four hours?

Famine reaches into one of his saddlebags. I hear the clang of something heavy right before he pulls out a pair of iron manacles.

Iron. Manacles.

Because of course this freak would just have a spare pair tucked away.

Crossing back over to me, he catches my wrist.

"Hey—"

I try to jerk out of his grip, but it's useless. A moment later, Famine begins clamping the heavy shackles on.

"What are you doing?" A note of panic has entered my voice.

The horseman finishes one wrist and grabs my other. "Now, if only there was something for your mouth ..."

I take a steadying breath. "Don't you think this is a bit overdone?" I say.

I mean, I *haven't* run. This is all just bluster.

My skin pricks as I feel the stares of Famine's men.

Rather than responding, the Reaper leads me towards a dark bay horse. Grabbing me under the arms, he hoists me onto the beast.

"Really?" I deadpan, looking down at him. "I'm supposed to wear cuffs while riding a horse? Now this is most *definitely* overkill."

"Not my problem," the Reaper says, walking back towards his steed.

I scowl at my horse. "You do realize that I could simply ..." I was going to say *ride away*, but before I finish the sentence I realize that the horse *isn't* wearing any reins; instead, the creature is bound by a length of rope to one of Famine's mounted men.

"So, does this mean we're going to another town?" I call out to Famine.

He ignores me completely.

"Are we?" I ask a man passing by.

He ignores me too.

"Anyone?" I say. "Anyone at all? Do any of you useless sacks of shit know where we're going?"

"Shut the fuck up," someone says.

"*Don't* talk to her," Famine warns his men.

I can't tell if he's saying it in a *how dare you talk to my lady that way* or a *don't instigate her* kind of way. Probably the latter because he's a maniacal jerk. But you never know.

It takes a little longer for the rest of the group to finish gathering up whatever supplies they need, but soon enough, the small gang of us begin to move.

The moment Famine prods his horse into action, the beast takes off like he's been unleashed. The two of them gallop ahead of us, moving farther and farther away before the Reaper doubles back, returning to us.

For a moment both man and horse look as though they're free. The horseman's bronze armor catches the light as he closes in on us. That sun seems to love him, the rays highlighting his toffee colored hair and making his mossy eyes glitter. He looks like a prince ripped out of a fairytale.

When he reaches us, he stops up short, causing his men to, in turn, halt their steeds too. Famine's ruthless gaze moves over the group of them. These are the men who helped execute innocent people—who stabbed me and killed the mayor and his family. They're the ones who have been doing this same thing to the people of every rotting city they passed through.

"Did you forget something?" one of them calls out.

Famine's eyes land on the man for a moment before taking the rest of the group in again.

"You all have been so very helpful to me," the Reaper says.

A knot of unease forms in the pit of my stomach.

"But," the horseman continues, that wicked gleam entering his eyes, "just as flowers wither away, so too does your use."

In an instant, plants break through the ground, their stalks growing impossibly fast.

I suck in a sharp breath as the first plant wraps itself around one man's ankle. Another snakes its way up a calf.

The men *panic*. One of them reaches for a weapon holstered at his side. Another tries to lift his legs out of the way. None of it is any use. The vines reach out like limbs, dragging Famine's guards off their frightened steeds.

"*Please!*" one man begs.

"*Oh God!*"

And the screams, the bloodcurdling screams.

I sit there, terrified at the sight.

A few of the horses rear up, spooked. Famine shushes the beasts, and this, oddly enough, seems to calm them down. They resettle, shuffling about only a little as their riders are attacked.

The man who first reached for his weapon now lays on his back, trying to hack away at the burgeoning *thing* wrapping itself around him. If anything, it seems to make the plant grow faster and more aggressively.

"Why?" one of the men gasps, his eyes beseeching the Reaper.

The horseman's expression is downright chilling. "Because you are human, and you were meant to die."

I hear the snap of bones and the strangled cries as the men fight for air. It seems like an eternity before they all go still. And I guess it's a small mercy that they do go still; they could've clung to life like the old man I met when I first entered Curitiba.

I make a noise as I gasp in a breath. I'm surrounded on all sides by the dead.

The rider who my horse was hitched to lays a meter away from my horse, his mouth parted in a silent scream.

I stare at the Reaper, beginning to tremble. He enjoyed killing these men. I saw it with my own eyes.

Famine hops off his horse and moves over to the other steeds, systematically removing their saddles and harnesses, humming under his breath as he does so. One by one, he releases the horses, letting them wander off down the desolate streets.

Eventually, he makes his way to me. I still haven't moved, hemmed in by the dead as I am.

"Come, flower," Famine says, his voice deceptively gentle. He steps over to my side and reaches for me.

The hair on the back of my neck stands on end. I had almost convinced myself that this man was a pushover, and pushovers can't be scary, right?

But *fuck*, I don't think he's a pushover, and no matter how disarming he is to talk to, all these bodies around me are a reminder that he's still a wretched monster.

When Famine sees my expression, he raises his eyebrows. "If you didn't have the stomach for my killing, you shouldn't have sought me out."

He's right, of course. I could've stayed far away. Besides, the men he killed might've been the few that actually *deserved* death.

Still.

I take in Famine's disarming, devilish face.

This is a creature that needs to be vanquished.

"You can either lift your arms and cooperate, or I can drag you off this horse," he says. "I can tell you which one you'll enjoy better."

Reluctantly, I lift my shackled hands, and the horseman helps pull me off the horse.

He whistles, and his own steed walks over.

I can't look at him. Not as he lifts me onto his own mount, not while he removes my former horse's trappings and sets this last steed free. Not even once he swings himself into the saddle behind me.

Famine's bronze armor digs into my back as he settles against me, and one of his massive arms drapes itself casually over my leg. His closeness only makes me tremble worse.

The Reaper clicks his tongue and his horse starts forward, picking its way past the bodies.

We've gone less than a block when he murmurs, "You're shaking like a leaf." His breath is warm against my ear. "I've told you before: you don't need to fear me—not now, anyway."

The Reaper's voice is gentle, but somehow that makes it all worse.

"Why did you do that?" My voice comes out like a croak.

There's a long pause, and I genuinely think it takes him a moment to figure out what I'm referring to.

His fingers tap against my thigh. "They would've turned on me soon enough," he finally says.

"You let them pack their things and ready their horses," I whisper. "You had them ready a horse for *me*. Why?" My voice hitches. "Why do that if you were just going to kill them all?"

"You assume my mind works like yours. It doesn't."

Thank *fuck* for that.

The two of us are quiet for several beats, the only sound the tread of his horse's footfalls and the slight jangle of my manacles. We pass by several rotting bodies, their forms caught within the grasp of more plants and trees.

"Is there any horror you are unwilling to commit?" I eventually ask.

"When it comes to you creatures?" he replies. "No."

My thoughts spin round and round. I feel untethered; my entire life is gone and now I'm here, riding alongside the horseman rather than meting out my revenge. This is ... not how I imagined events unfolding.

I wiggle my feet in my heavy boots. There aren't any stirrups for my feet, and gravity seems to be trying to pull my shoes off of me. I roll my ankles, trying to readjust my footwear to make them more comfortable. It works ... for a few minutes. But then I'm uncomfortable again.

I can't have been on the horse for more than thirty minutes or so when I draw the line. Stupid boots.

"Hold me," I say over my shoulder.

There's a beat of silence. Then, "If this is another one of your sex-starved ploys—"

Before the Reaper can finish the thought, I swing a booted foot up and into the saddle. As predicted, the effort throws my body off balance.

Reflexively, Famine catches me, his arm tightening around my waist.

"What the devil are you doing, Ana?"

My shackles clank as I unlace the leather boot. Once I'm finished, I grab the thick rubber heel and begin tugging.

"Taking off these damn boots."

I pull the shoe off, along with the sweaty sock beneath it. Setting them on my lap, I begin working on my other shoe. The Reaper doesn't say anything, but I sense his deep annoyance. Deep, deep annoyance. I'm pretty sure he finds every decision I make irritating.

Once both boots are off, I manage to open one of Famine's saddlebags—which is massively hard when you're handcuffed. But I manage it, huzzah!

At my back, I can practically feel Famine's disapproval. He doesn't stop me, however, so I press on.

Grabbing the boots, I attempt to shove the tips of both into the saddlebag, but then the manacles catch on the heel of one boot, jerking it out of the bag. I try to catch it as it falls, the action dislodging the other boot. Both tumble down the side of the horse before hitting the ground.

There's a beat of silence.

Then—

"Not my problem," Famine says.

I glance over my shoulder at him. "You *cannot* be serious," I say.

"Do I look like I'm joking?"

Damn him, he doesn't.

"I need those shoes," I say. They're my only pair.

"I'm not stopping."

"Wow." I face forward in my seat, settling myself back against him. "*Wow*."

Chapter 13

As we ride, the fields wilt.

At first, I don't notice it because Curitiba stretches on for so long, block after city block filled with buildings that cannot wither away. But eventually we do leave the city, and at some point, the structures are replaced with farmland.

But the longer I sit in the saddle with the guy, the more I realize that *the land is changing before my very eyes.*

Fields of corn and soybeans, rice and sugarcane—and everything in between—all wither away, the stalks blackening, the leaves curling. The color seems to drain away in mere seconds. By the time I glance over my shoulder at the crops we've passed, it's a sea of dead foliage.

Famine's power doesn't, however, touch the wild things. Not the grass or the weeds or the indigenous plants that greedily press up against the edges of the fields. It's our subsistence he wants to end.

"Will it ever grow back?" I ask, gazing out at the dying crops.

"Not any time soon," he replies, "and when it does, it won't be crops. This land doesn't belong to humans. It never has, and it never will."

Despite the rising heat of the day, goosebumps break out along my skin.

Life really isn't going to ever go back to the way it was. I mean, I knew that the moment Famine rode into my city, but I hadn't fully processed it until now. There will be no more farmers, no more market days. There will be no more lazy afternoons at the bordello or evenings where it's business as usual. Here in southern Brazil, farming is our main form of commerce. If Famine wipes that out ... he won't need to kill us in an instant. We'll all eventually starve.

"You've presented me with a problem," he admits, cutting through my thoughts.

"I'm going to put this in the nicest way possible:" I say, swinging my bare feet back and forth, "you can go fuck yourself and your problem away."

His grip digs into my thigh. "Is fucking your only solution to any problem?"

"Is killing yours?" I shoot back.

"My problem," he continues smoothly, as though we weren't just arguing, "is that I'm here to blight crops and starve your kind, yet I must *feed* you."

He sounds truly torn about this.

"What *will* you do?"

"You would be wise not to offend me," he says. "I have seen humans boil their belts and their Bibles' leather casing, all so that they might fill their stomachs with something representing food. I've seen them eat all manner of inedible things. I've even seen them eat their own kind. All in the name of relieving that painful ache in their guts. I don't need to make your survival easy or comfortable."

"You've actually let people live long enough to boil their belts?" I say. "I find *that* hard to believe."

I shift in the saddle, and I swear I feel the searing heat of his gaze on my legs.

"You know," I add, "you'd probably be much less bloodthirsty if you banged your aggression out."

"I don't want to be less bloodthirsty—and I definitely don't want to 'bang' you."

"I wasn't offering, though I'm sure you could find *someone* open to the idea. Probably not a *living* someone, but still, someone."

"You say that as though you didn't throw yourself at me mere weeks ago," he says, sounding exasperated.

I didn't *throw* myself at him. Ana da Silva doesn't throw herself at *anyone*; she coyly lures the unwitting into her sex den and enslaves their wills to hers ... for a time.

"I was blinded by memories of a nicer Famine," I say.

"And I have been blinded by memories of a nicer, less sexual version of you."

I raise my eyebrows, an unwilling smile spreading across my face. "I didn't realize my sexuality mattered to you."

He growls. "*Will* you be quiet?"

"Only if you put something in my mouth. Dicks are still an option," I say, just to taunt him.

"I thought you weren't offering," he says.

I open my mouth to argue, but—*oh*, he's right.

"I might make an exception just this once," I say, "for the sake of humanity, of course. A blowjob to end all bloodshed— that sounds appropriately valiant."

It really does.

A horseman was brought to his knees when a human got down on hers ...

The PR might need to be adjusted a bit, but I'm *definitely* liking the sound of that. Who knew prostitution could be such a noble cause?

"Fucking *fine*." Famine halts his horse abruptly.

Oh shit.

"Wait," I say. "Are you actually taking me up on the offer?"

I was more interested in taunting the horseman than

actually following through on my word. But now ...

Famine dismounts. A moment later, he reaches for me, cuffs and all, dragging me off his horse. My bare feet stumble against the earth, my shackles clanging as they shift.

"Alright," I say, glancing around. "Right here. Okay." I swallow, clear my throat. "I didn't realize you were so eager."

I glance at the horseman's pants. I've seen him naked before, but he was so badly hurt then that I hadn't really noticed his genitals. Now, however, I'm oddly piqued at the thought of seeing his dick, damn my curious mind.

When Famine doesn't make a move to undo his pants, I reach for them.

He glances down at me. "What are you doing?"

I can feel all that disapproving energy focused on me.

"Getting things started. If you're a little shy, we can take this slower—"

"Shy?" he echoes.

Understanding flashes in his eyes a second later, followed by—wait for it—*annoyance*.

He swats my hands away. "Stop," he says, vaguely irritated.

I give him a confused look, but he's not even paying attention to me. His focus is on a grassy patch of earth a few meters away.

I back away from him as he reaches out a hand towards the ground.

Seconds go by. Then, from the earth, a tiny sapling sprouts before my eyes, rising up gracefully, its branches and stems unfurling.

Only hours ago I saw a different batch of plants rise from the ground, and yet, this process looks wholly different from what I saw this morning. Those earlier plants grew aggressively; it was a violent, monstrous birth. This, on the other hand, looks like a slow dance.

It takes much longer for this plant to grow, partially because the tree is so damn large. As it grows and fills out, its leaves sway up and down, almost as though it's breathing. Its trunk thickens and then—wonder of wonders—beads of fruit swell along that trunk and some of the larger branches. They turn color, going from green to wine red to, finally, a violet-black.

And then, the tree settles, its rapid growth complete. I stare up at it. It's a jabuticaba tree, much like the one I picked fruit from the day I found the horseman.

Famine lowers his hand, turning to me.

"Well?" he says.

My brows draw together, confused. "Do you want me to suck your dick under there?"

He exhales, his eyes rising heavenward in exasperation.

"I'm *kidding*." Sort of. I'm still thinking about the blowjob to save all humanity.

The Reaper glowers at me. "It's food for you to eat," he explains anyway. "To get you to stop talking about sex for five seconds."

I guess his dilemma about feeding me is not much of a dilemma when sex is the other looming option.

Shame. I was half excited about his supernatural dick too.

Chapter 14

The few travelers we pass all die. The horseman makes sure of that.

The first time I see another living soul, I immediately tense. The man plods down the road, driving a small herd of goats. He doesn't notice us until we're nearly upon him, and when he does, he only has time for his eyes to widen before a twisting bush rises from the ground, ensnaring him in its grasp.

I bite back a scream as the plant kills him. Perhaps the most macabre part of it all is that even as the man thrashes in its clutches, the plant sprouts delicate, pink-petaled roses.

It's not just travelers the Reaper kills. We pass through several small towns, and in each one, the horseman's petrifying plants sprout up, trapping and killing the people in their clutches.

It's not until we enter the city of Colombo that Famine whispers in my ear. "We're staying here."

I suppress a shiver at his words. I'd like to say it's from sheer terror, but there's a sick part of me that still inappropriately reacts to the low, sultry timbre of his voice, just as I did when I was seventeen.

Our entrance is nothing like the one I witnessed back in Laguna. Crowds don't line the streets, no one waits for us. The first time anyone recognizes Famine, they scream, dropping the basket they were carrying and fleeing to their house. It happens a second time, and then a third, until it seems the whole city is in an uproar.

I guess Famine hadn't sent anyone ahead to alert the town of his arrival.

We charge forward, Famine's horse speeding up until he's galloping through the city streets. All around us—madness. People are fleeing in every direction, their goods scattering. Livestock is running loose, a few pigs squealing in panic.

Right in the middle of it all, Famine stops his horse, the steed rearing back. I have to grab onto the horse's mane to keep myself seated.

"*Stop*." The Reaper's voice rings out, echoing with supernatural force.

To my shock ... people do slow down, their frightened gazes moving to the horseman.

"I need a place to stay," he says. "The best house in the city. And I need good men who are willing to help me. Do this, and I will withhold the worst of my wrath."

At that, I glance back at Famine. His expression seems genuine enough, but then, is he even *capable* of being merciful?

A handful of people begin to come forward, ready to assist the horseman.

I guess we're all about to find out ...

By the time Famine and I eventually enter the house we'll be staying in, night has already fallen. My shackles clang as I walk next to the horseman and some of the townspeople who've been helping us over the last several hours.

The Reaper holds his scythe in one hand, and in the other

he grips my upper arm. Not so discreetly I try to shrug his hold off. Rather than releasing me, his grip tightens.

"Let me go," I hiss under my breath.

The horseman gives me the side eye, but otherwise ignores my request.

"... This is the master bedroom," says Luiz, a senior official with the Colombo police department. He's the one who's orchestrated most of our accommodations. "The owners of the house have graciously given it up for you and your, uh—" Luiz's eyes size me up, lingering on my manacles, which *still* haven't come off. Famine doesn't offer up any sort of explanation, and neither do I, "—*companion*."

The Reaper openly glares at the man, hostility rolling off him. This has been Famine's reaction ever since the two of us learned that Luiz was a part of the police force. Whoever once hurt the horseman, I have a sneaking suspicion that they were uniformed men.

Luiz leads us back to the front of the house, where an aging couple stand rigid, looking upset and uncomfortable.

The official's face relaxes. "Mr. and Mrs. Barbosa. There you are." He walks ahead of us to greet them.

Even as they take his hand, their eyes are glued to the Reaper.

Luiz turns to face us. "Famine," he says, "these are your hosts, Mr. and Mrs. Barbosa," he repeats unnecessarily, "the owners of the house."

They look both angry and alarmed.

The wife is the first to notice me. She sees Famine's grip on my arm, then my handcuffs. She eyes me from the top of my wild, curly hair, down my ill-fitting dress, and finally to my grimy bare feet. Her nostrils flare, and she grimaces, like she can sense my ill-repute wafting off of me. I wonder what she would do if she realized that I actually *was* a prostitute.

Famine squeezes my arm, then releases it, stepping forward.

"Ah, the owners," he says. "Just the people I wanted to see."

Faster than I can follow, he lifts his scythe from his back and slashes it across the couple's necks. For an instant, it looks as though the couple is wearing crimson collars. Then their heads topple off their shoulders.

I'm the first to scream, my shackled hands coming up to my mouth. A moment later, the rest of the room begins to shout as men and women grab their weapons.

Luiz comes at the horseman, and Famine spins the scythe in his hand, like it's an elaborate sort of dance. The blade arcs up, the tip of it catching the police chief low in the gut and opening him up all the way to his collarbone.

At the sight, my legs fold.

Everyone else is rushing the Reaper, weapons drawn.

"*Enough.*" Famine's voice booms.

I don't know what sort of devilish magic is at work, but for whatever reason, people listen to him. The men and women around us halt their attack, some even lowering their weapons.

"Me and my little human here—" The Reaper reaches out and jangles my manacles, "are going to be staying here. You can either help me and keep your miserable lives, or I can kill you now. Who wants to die?" His gaze sweeps over the remaining men and women who surround us.

No one makes a sound.

"As I thought." Famine lowers his scythe to the ground, holding it like a staff.

"Clean up these bodies," he orders no one in particular. "I need someone to make dinner, and I want some form of entertainment. Find me the best that this city has to offer and bring it here." *Or else.* He doesn't say it, but we all hear it.

Famine grabs my shackles and begins to lead me away. We've barely taken three steps before he pauses, causing me to nearly run into him.

"Oh, I almost forgot," the horseman says, turning back to face the men. "In case any of you are considering rebelling, let me save you the trouble—*don't.*

"Any attempts on my life will be met with *painful* retribution. I cannot emphasize that enough." Famine nods to the bodies. Luiz is still alive and moaning. "This is mercy. Just ask her." He shakes my manacles, and several sets of eyes move to me.

I don't say anything, but I imagine they can see my fear. I can certainly *feel* it seeping through my body.

"Well?" Famine says, his gaze passing over them. "Why are you all still standing there? Get to it. Now."

The horseman leads me to an empty room, following me inside. The moment he closes the door, I shudder, my muscles weakening. My legs don't really want to hold me up, but somehow they manage to.

"What do you want?" I say. My voice wavers.

"What, no sexual innuendos?" Famine says, tossing his scythe onto the bed, the blood from the blade smearing onto the comforter.

I press my lips together. Several people just *died.* I can't wrap my mind around his casualness.

All this time I was trying to get under his skin, and instead, Famine got under mine. He knows it, too. Sick shit that he is, he's enjoying the moment.

"You've been telling me that I had to put something in your mouth to get you to shut up, but it appears all I needed to do is kill a few people," he says. "How fortunate for me, since I happen to be in the business of death."

I shudder and turn away from him, moving over to the window. I can't see anything outside; the darkness is absolute.

I exhale, my breath shaky. "The day I saved you—do you know why I did it?" I ask, glancing over my shoulder at him.

"I don't care why you did it," Famine says, and yet I can see that beautiful face of his turned in my direction, waiting for me to finish my thought.

"I couldn't stand the thought that someone could hurt another person the way you were hurt."

"I'm not a person, Ana. I'm a horseman."

"Do you think that made a difference in my mind?"

He has nothing to say to that.

I turn back to the window, not wanting to look at Famine or the blood that's splattered across his bronze armor.

A moment later, he comes up to my side. Out of the corner of my eye, I see him reach into his black trousers and pull out a key. The Reaper grabs my wrists and begins unlocking the manacles.

"You're taking me out of the cuffs?" I ask.

"Would you prefer I didn't?" he asks, arching an eyebrow.

I don't say anything to that.

He finishes unlocking the thick iron shackles, and I roll my wrists. In some spots, the skin has been rubbed raw.

"I thought you didn't trust me," I say suspiciously.

"I don't," Famine agrees. "But what can you really do at this point?"

"I could hurt you," I say, my gaze flinty. I think I would really enjoy sinking another blade into the Reaper right about now.

Famine looks downright tickled at the thought. "And chance suffering my wrath? I think not," he says. "Though I welcome your attempts—meager as they've so far proven to be."

"I thought you said I was safe with you," I remind him.

"You are. I don't plan on hurting you if you don't hurt me."

Begrudgingly I admit that's fair.

"And if I run?" I ask.

"Your attempts at escape have been even worse than your attempts at murder," he says, stepping in close.

I can't help it, my breath hitches at the sight of him.

"But humor me, little flower," he continues. "Run. Go back to your poor, abandoned city, and live in your empty whorehouse. Try to earn a living again selling yourself to dead men and enjoy what scraps of moldering food escaped my reach. I'm sure you will live a long and prosperous life."

As he speaks, my hate rises, closing up my throat. I stare up at him. He's standing far too close to me. Only my clients ever got this close, but then it was for entirely different reasons.

Famine's gaze searches mine. "No, you won't run," he says. "Because running takes a certain level of courage that you utterly lack."

My palm comes up before I can help it, and I slap him across the cheek. I can feel the sting of contact against my skin. The Reaper's head snaps to the side.

In the moment that follows, neither of us does anything. I'm breathing heavily, and the horseman's face is turned away from me.

Slowly, his hand comes up, and he touches his cheek. He lets out a laugh, and the hairs along my arms stand up.

This man just killed three people, and I went and hit him.

Faster than I can follow, he grabs my jaw. "You *foolish* little flower. Have you learned nothing?" As he speaks, he walks forward, backing me up until I hit the wall. Once there, I'm pinned in. "Maybe you are courageous after all to tempt my anger."

His eyes dip to my mouth, and in the midst of his hate-fueled rant, I see something flare in those unearthly green eyes.

His gaze moves up to mine, and there's a zing of connection. "Or maybe you believe you're above punishment."

As he speaks the hardwood floor beneath me rises up like an anthill before splintering open. A seemingly harmless stem rises from the ground before probing around towards my leg.

I try not to scream at the sight of it, even as it begins to slither up my leg.

"Wh-what are you doing?"

"Reminding you why you don't try to stab me or slap me or accost me in any other manner."

The single shoot splits off into two, then three, then four, growing up and around me. Tiny thorns appear along the stem, lengthening and sharpening the bigger the plant becomes. The shrub doesn't quite wrap itself around me. Instead it grows like a cage around my body. Only once it's bracketed me in does Famine release his hold.

He backs away. "You saved me once, so I'll spare you for that reason alone," he says, "but do not *ever* test me again."

With that, he exits the room, slamming the door behind him.

I stand still for a beat, waiting for something else to happen—for Famine to come back or this cage to wither up and die.

Neither thing does.

"How the *fuck* am I supposed to get out?" I finally mutter to myself.

The answer, I find out several hours and many cuts later, is *painfully*—that's how I'm supposed to get out.

Chapter 15

I wake to screams.

I sit up too fast, swaying a little. I put a hand to my head, blinking away sleep. The screams continue, punctuated by low, agonized moans. My heart is beginning to thunder before I can truly process what I'm hearing.

I stare at the window for several seconds, thick grey clouds obscuring the morning light. The screams are coming from outside, only now they're beginning to die off. My pulse pounds in my ears.

I don't know how I get the courage to throw off my covers—covers still stained by the blood from Famine's scythe—and I slide out of bed. I haven't seen the horseman since he left me here last night, but from the sounds of it, he's been busy.

I pad around the thorny bush that caged me in yesterday and creep towards the window, dread pooling in my stomach. Outside, two people are dumping a body in what must be the home's backyard. There are already other bodies lying on the ground, some of them still moving.

I stumble back, tripping on my own heel and falling hard

to the floor.

I have to breathe through my nose just to keep the bile down.

My own memories replay themselves—how Elvita was stabbed, how I was stabbed. How crassly Famine's men discarded my body.

I wrap my arms around myself. As the screams rise, I pinch my eyes shut, my body shaking.

This is where I'm supposed to go storming out like some brave heroine and stop Famine. Instead, I'm paralyzed by fear, my mind replaying my own horrific encounter with the horseman.

That's why I've allowed myself to go along with being the horseman's prisoner—so I can hurt him again. Only now, when fighting him would make a difference ... I can't do it. I don't have a weapon, but even if I did, I don't think I could make myself walk over to him. I don't want to move at all.

Famine was right. I do lack courage—courage to do anything in the face of his atrocities.

My heart is in my throat and my breath is coming much too fast when the door to my room opens. A man comes in, one I don't recognize. My breath stills.

"Famine wants to see you," he says.

I'm still shaking, and I still can't move. When the man sees this, he comes over to me and grabs my arm, pulling me to my feet.

I wobble, and then I'm tripping forward, following the man out of the room and towards the living room, where all the furniture has been pushed aside, save for the wingback chair Famine sits in.

He lounges on it like it's a throne, his legs kicked up over one of the arm rests and crossed at the ankles. Despite the fact that it's the middle of the morning, a wine glass dangles out of one of his hands.

He looks drunk. Very drunk.

"Where have you been?" he demands when he sees me, his tone surly.

"Hiding," I reply as the man who led me here finally lets my arm go.

"Hiding is for cowards," the horseman says, kicking his feet off the armrest and straightening in his seat.

I flinch, his words echoing my own earlier thoughts.

"Besides," he continues, "I want you to get a good look at how your world dies."

I stare at Famine for several seconds.

I hate you so very, very much.

"Oh, wait," he drums his fingers against the armrest, his brows knitted together. "It seems I've forgotten something ..."

He shifts, and I hear the jangle of metal. Famine's eyes alight and he snaps his fingers.

"Ah. I remember."

He unhooks something at his side. It's only when he lifts it up that I recognize the manacles.

"You can't be serious," I whisper.

I pose no threat. If the horseman hadn't forced me to come out here, I would've probably stayed holed up in that room he left me in, coming up with excuse after excuse to explain away my inaction.

"You are clever and brash," he says, "and I like you better when I can stop your tricks."

"You could've just left me in my room," I say. I wasn't going anywhere.

The horseman sets aside his drink and rises, coming over to me with those shackles.

"I could've, but then, my mind would've dwelled on you."

I don't know what to make of *that* unnerving statement.

I don't fight the horseman when he begins cuffing me. Those earlier screams have already scared all the fight out of me.

At my back I hear the front door open and the sound of

footfalls as people enter the house.

Casting me a sly smile, Famine finishes his work, leaving my side to grab his glass of wine and return to his seat.

Stupid, evil horseman.

I begin to walk back to my room, passing what looks to be an older man and a young woman, both who loiter uncertainly in the entryway. At the sight of them, my throat tightens. This is a story I already know the ending to.

"Did I say you could leave my side, Ana?" Famine calls out, his voice grating.

I pause in my tracks, my body tensing. At his asshole-ish comment, a little of my fire returns.

I glance over my shoulder at the horseman. "Don't be cruel."

"*I* can't be cruel?" he says, his voice rising. "You don't know *what* cruelty is. Not until you have endured what I have. Your kind taught me *oh so intimately* how to be this way." The horseman says this right in front of the pair who wait in the foyer, their expressions uneasy.

"Now," he says to me, his eyes hardening, "get *back* to—my—side."

I square my jaw as I stare at him, fear and anger all churning inside me. Reluctantly I return to him, glaring the entire time. He glares right back at me.

During our exchange, the older man and young woman have hung back, watching my exchange with Famine, but now as the Reaper slouches in his chair, he gives them a haughty look.

"Well?" he says. "If you have something to say to me, *say it.*"

Tentatively the pair creep forward.

"My lord," the man says, nodding to the horseman.

Famine scowls. "I see no gifts in your hands. Why then are you here?"

Of course the prick next to me would think a human

should only approach him if they have something to offer.

I take in the horseman again, studying his bright, narrowed eyes and the way he sits in this chair like a king. He's intoxicated on wine and power and vengeance.

The older man seems to shrink on himself before gathering his courage. He places a hand on the shoulder of the young woman he's with and steers her forward.

My eyes catch on that hand.

The man clears his throat. "I thought that maybe ... a horseman like you might want ..." He clears his throat again, like he can't get the words out.

The silence stretches on.

"Well?" Famine says. "What do you think I want?"

There's another long stretch of silence.

"My daughter—" the man finally says, "is yours, if you'll have her."

Daughter. The word is ringing in my ears.

It was easy for Elvita and me to approach the Reaper. I was a prostitute and Elvita was the madam who managed my clients. But offering up *your daughter* to be used by some vengeful stranger? The thought has my stomach churning.

Famine's eyes flick to mine, and he gives me a look as if to say, *See? I do this all the time, and it tires me.*

"Humans are so *terribly* predictable, are they not?" he says.

Now that I actually think about it, this *must* happen to him all the time. In city after city he opens his doors to people who give him gifts. For a poor family, a woman's flesh might be the most valuable thing they have to offer.

I shouldn't have a problem with that—it's been my currency for the last five years.

But right now it sickens me.

Famine's gaze flicks over my face, drinking in my reaction before he casts a lazy glance back at the man. "So you didn't come to me empty-handed after all."

The man shakes his head. The girl is beginning to tremble;

she looks visibly frightened by the horseman.

"She's not much to look at," Famine notes, his gaze moving over her. "Too short and her skin is blemished."

Because she's still a teenager, I want to shout. Never mind that I, too, was a teenager when I first started sleeping with strangers. I don't have to want that life for anyone else.

"And her teeth ..." the horseman makes a face.

There's nothing wrong with this girl's teeth—or the rest of her looks for that matter—but that's beside the point. Famine is aiming to hurt.

Just like the plants he kills, Famine has his seasons. Sometimes he's light and happy, like spring. And then other times, like now, he's cruel and cold like winter.

Abruptly, he turns to me. "Tell me, Ana, what would you have me do?"

What ... the hell?

I stare at him like he's gone mad.

"Should I fuck her?" he asks me. "Or would you prefer I make an example out of her as I did you?"

I curl my upper lip, repulsed by him. "You are a monster."

"Mmm ..." The corner of his mouth lifts and he turns his attention back to his guests.

Once again, Famine eyes the girl up and down. She stares back at him, still visibly shaking.

All at once, he stands, setting his drink aside. I think that maybe he means to hurt the pair, but he doesn't reach for his scythe. Instead, he closes in on the girl.

Reflexively she takes a step back. I can't see his face, but I can see hers, and she's terrified.

"I have enough enemies," he says, glancing over his shoulder at me. "I'll spare her the worst of my torments." To one of his men, he says, "Put her in one of the bedrooms."

Chapter 16

I stare after the now crying teenager, my stomach churning. The entire time I feel Famine's eyes on me.

Don't do this, I want to tell him. *Don't use that girl the way men have used me. If it's sex you're after, I'll give it to you. If it's resistance you want—trust me, I'll make sure you know how unenthusiastic I am.*

I don't say any of those things. I have a prickly, uncomfortable feeling that the horseman would happily acquiesce and kill the girl instead. The true question is why Famine did decide to keep her around to sleep with when he's been pretty aggressively against sex with me.

Not a minute after his daughter is carted away, Famine's men lead the father through the house and out the back door.

"Where are you taking me? Where are we—let me go—" A door opens, then shuts, cutting off the older man's words.

It doesn't take much longer for his cries to start up. I pinch my eyes shut, willing away the sounds.

I made a mistake hunting down Famine. A terrible, terrible mistake. I thought I could exact my vengeance—or die. But neither of those options have happened.

"Now, now, little flower," the horseman says, his voice low and lethal, "closing your eyes won't make it any less real."

"If you let me go, I'll leave you alone," I whisper.

I don't want to listen to all this suffering. I don't want to see it either.

"Will you now?" the Reaper says. I hear his footfalls as he comes up to me. "Just when you started growing on me, too," he whispers against my ear, his breath warm.

My eyes snap open. The horseman stands unnervingly close, and as I watch him, he runs a finger down my bare arm, the touch drawing out goosebumps. He stares at my puckered flesh.

What the *fuck* is he doing?

A guard clears his throat, breaking whatever weird *thing* came over the horseman.

Another person is ushered in, and Famine shifts his attention to them, returning to his chair.

I know the Reaper brought me out here to make me uncomfortable; he seems to relish his cruelty. Two can play that game.

I might be frightened by the horseman, I might even be cowardly in the face of death, but damnit, I have been and always will be a *bold* motherfucking bitch.

Just as a man approaches Famine, I casually leave my post and sit myself down on Famine's legs like this is just something I do. And it is. I often sat myself down on men's laps in the tavern next to The Painted Angel, and plenty of those men were only slightly less revolting than Famine.

Beneath my ass, the Reaper tenses.

"What are you doing?" he hisses, too low for anyone else to hear.

I ignore the way my heart pounds or the fact that this monster has rejected me several times over. I shake my hair out, the long, wavy locks brushing against his face.

"Making myself comfortable," I say.

I adjust myself on his lap, the manacles jangling, and I make sure to cause a little extra friction.

Much to my delight, he sucks in a breath.

I can't fight Famine, or appeal to his sensibilities, but I *can* drive him mad. I'm actually pretty good at that.

The horseman grabs me by the waist. He's about to push me off, I can feel it, but for whatever reason he decides at the last minute to keep me pinned in place, his fingers digging into my skin.

The man waiting in the foyer now approaches us, fear—and perhaps a little hope—visible on his face. His clothes are tattered and patched up, and the sandals he wears look worn thin. Whoever he is, he doesn't have much, yet still he came here intent on giving the Reaper something.

When he gets close to us, the man reaches into his pocket and pulls out several rings, a dainty gold bracelet, and a necklace with the image of Our Lady of Aparecida dangling from it. The man bows his head and kneels, his hand outstretched.

"What is this?" Famine asks, disdain dripping from his voice.

"This is the only true wealth my family has," the man says. "It's yours." He looks up, and I can see in his eyes he wants to beg for someone's life, but he bites back the words.

I move to stand. For an instant the horseman resists, but eventually he releases me.

God, the Reaper is an odd bastard.

I approach the man and crouch down in front of him. "That's beautiful," I say, touching the image of the Virgin, my manacles clanking. "Does it have a story behind it?"

"It was my mother's—given to her by her mother," the man says, daring to look from me to the horseman behind me.

"She must've loved it very much," I say.

"Ana, get up."

I look over my shoulder at Famine, who is signaling to the

guards to take the man. I know what happens next.

I grab the man's wrist, not getting up and refusing to let him get up either, even as Famine's new recruits close in on us.

"This man is giving away a holy relic," I say, staring at the Reaper. "Surely you see the sacrifice in that?"

Famine frowns at me. "It's a shiny trinket dedicated to a false idol. It is less than useless to me."

I raise my eyebrows. "*Is* it false?" No one in Brazil stopped believing in the Virgin and her benevolence, not even when the world was being ravaged. If anything, she's the one thing we clung to most—proof that there's some mercy to what otherwise appears to be a vengeful God.

Famine narrows his eyes and gives me a mean smile, the expression all but saying, *Wouldn't you like to know?*

"Fine," he says. His eyes move to the man. "I accept your gift."

For a moment, I relax. But then the guards still close in on the man, one taking his offered jewelry and casting it to the ground. The rest grab the man's arms and drag him away.

He's begging to them now, though he leaves willingly enough.

I stare down at the scattered jewelry as the group of them leave the house. The Virgin and all her benevolence stare back up at me.

God is here, she seems to be saying, *but even I can do nothing.*

"I wonder," I say, staring down at the small pendant, "if you were a woman who could bear children, if you'd still be so cavalier."

"Man or woman—it wouldn't matter. I am not a *person*, Ana. I am hunger, I am pain, and no thinly veiled attempts to stop me will work."

He's right.

I interceded and it did *nothing*.

I stand up, still feeling the eyes of both Famine and Our

Lady of Aparecida on me.

I walk away from the both of them, heading back to my room, and this time no one stops me.

I stay in my room for the rest of the day. I can hear the pleading, the pained screams, and the rattling death moans. And if I look out my window, I can see the suffering as people are killed, their bodies dumped in an ever growing pile.

I'm hungry and thirsty, but I don't leave the room, fearful that if I cross paths with Famine again, he'll once again force me to stay and watch.

I consider fleeing—several times—but these damn manacles are a problem, and no one but Famine can get them off.

About an hour or so after the sun sets and the screams stop, a guard opens the door to my room.

"The horseman wants to see you," he says.

"Fuckboy can live without my company," I reply.

The man comes into my room and grabs me by the arm, lifting me up to my feet.

"I hate this too," he admits quietly as he drags me out. Even as he says it, I notice the blood crusted on his hands and splattered on his shirt.

He clearly doesn't hate the situation *enough*.

I follow after him, my arms heavy from wearing the shackles all day. In the living room, many of the guards are now milling about, clearly waiting for Famine's next order.

The man himself sits at a table overflowing with all sorts of food, from steaming cassava to fruit cut into pleasing shapes and steak dripping in its own juices. There's *bacalhau* and rice and a tray of assorted cheeses and another with various breads and crackers. There's even a dessert platter, laden with cakes and custards, cookies and sugared candies.

The smells are enough to make my stomach cramp with hunger.

The guard releases me at the edge of the dining room,

moving away to stand back at his post.

Famine doesn't look at me when he gestures for me to come closer.

I narrow my eyes. Sex work has taught me a thing or two about reading people. Self-satisfied assholes like Famine—ones who expect me to be at their beck and call—are the cheapest of the lot. The value they place on you is next to nothing.

I walk over to him, stopping just to the side of his chair.

"Entertain me." He still doesn't look up.

Casually I reach out and upend his plate, scattering food everywhere. "Go fuck yourself."

Now the horseman looks up at me, those cruel green eyes sparking with fire. I've issued a direct challenge in front of nearly half a dozen men; he's going to do something.

I should probably care more.

Before the horseman can react, however, another guard of his closes in on me. He raises his arm and backhands me, hitting me so hard I fall against the table before crumpling to the floor.

The sting against my cheek feels perversely good, just like the manacles around my wrists. They remind me who exactly the Reaper is.

There's several seconds of silence.

"Well, that was foolish of you," Famine says.

I assume the horseman's talking to me, but when I glance up, I see the Reaper's blistering gaze is focused on the man who hit me.

The guard's eyes grow wide. "My Lord, I'm sorry," he stammers out.

"'My Lord'?" Famine repeats. "I am no lord."

The Reaper adjusts himself in his seat. "What's your name?" he asks.

"Ricardo."

"Ricardo," Famine echoes. After a moment's pause, the horseman spreads an arm towards the food in front of him.

"Care to try anything?"

Ricardo's throat bobs. He gives his head a shake.

"Go on," Famine encourages.

I push myself to my knees, my cheek hot and throbbing. I and everyone else in the house watch the two men raptly. It's like seeing an accident happen in slow motion. You know it's coming but you can't stop it and you can't look away.

The same hand that struck me not a minute ago now shakes as it reaches out and takes a thin slice of cheese from one of the platters. The guard brings it to his lips, and after only pausing for a moment, he takes a bite of it.

"Good?" Famine asks, raising his eyebrows.

Ricardo nods, though I'd bet a whole night's earnings that the slice of cheese tastes like dust in his mouth.

Faster than I can follow, Famine grabs the steak knife in front of him and shoves it through the man's sternum, rising to his feet as he does so.

Ricardo makes a noise, and the bit of cheese he was chewing comes tumbling out.

"Last I recall," Famine says softly, holding the man in what appears to be an intimate embrace, "I didn't ask you to hit the woman."

Ricardo chokes in response.

"When I ask you to hit her, you hit her," Famine continues. "When I ask you to guard her fucking ass, *you guard her fucking ass.*"

The horseman withdraws the blade, blood gushing out of the wound, and Ricardo staggers a few steps, nearly tripping over me.

"Someone, take care of him," Famine says.

Up until now, none of the other men have dared to move, but at the Reaper's order, men suddenly jump into action, closing in on Ricardo, clearly nervous about disobeying the monster beside me.

"Oh, and as for the rest of you," Famine adds, his gaze

sweeping over the group of them, "don't even think about touching this woman."

Now that he's very literally put the fear of God in these men, Famine resettles himself in his seat, grabbing an empty plate from the spot next to him and placing it in front of himself.

"Ana," he says as his men drag Ricardo out of the house. "Sit."

Like a good little captive, I do as I'm told, pulling out a chair next to the Reaper and sitting down in it.

I stare passively at my place settings.

"Well?" he finally says, turning to me.

I meet his gaze, and his eyes move to my still-throbbing cheek. He frowns ever so slightly.

"Entertain me—or can you do nothing useful?" he asks.

"Oh, I can be useful," I say, "but you're not too interested in getting fucked."

The horseman cracks a smile, and the hairs on the back of my neck rise at the sight of it.

"You haven't reached for the food yet."

Unwillingly, my attention moves to the dishes in front of me. My stomach cramps at the sight of it all.

"The last person who did that got stabbed," I say. "I think I'll go hungry." Especially considering I pissed the horseman off only minutes ago.

Another sly smile slips across Famine's face, and it's like I'm finally playing the game he can't get anyone else to play.

"I'm no longer so thirsty for blood," the horseman says. He gestures to the food. "Have your fill, and I promise not to stab you."

I can feel the room's eyes on me, and I hesitate just as Ricardo did.

This feels an awful lot like a trap. Regardless, I'm too hungry to turn the opportunity down.

I go for the water first. Grabbing the pitcher in front of

me, I clumsily pour myself a glass and bring it to my lips. It's crisp and cool and I can't seem to drink enough of it. Only once I'm satiated do I move on to the food, grabbing a little of everything.

Famine watches me, his green eyes glinting in the candlelight. I half expect him to lunge for me—or at the very least to upend my plate as I did his. Maybe that's why he doesn't do either. The horseman loves himself some tension.

My fork is halfway to my mouth when the Reaper says, "Tell me about yourself."

I pause, giving him a skeptical look. "Now I *know* this is a trap."

"Why would you think that?" As he speaks, he runs his thumb across his lower lip, and it's upsettingly sexy.

I raise my eyebrows, my expression blatantly saying, *prove me wrong.*

After a moment, the horseman flashes me a wicked smile. In the short time I've spent with him, I've learned he grins when he's particularly dangerous to be around.

Famine grabs his glass of wine and props his ankles on the table. "Let me start again: what makes a young girl choose to save a horseman of the apocalypse?"

"You want to have that conversation *now?*" I ask, my gaze darting back at the men standing in the living room.

Famine just continues to stare at me, and I realize this simple question has been burning him up—maybe for years.

Has he really experienced so little humanity that he can't understand what I did?

I take a few bites of my food before answering.

"At the time, I thought what they did to you was wrong," I say, not meeting his eyes.

"You don't think so anymore?" he asks.

Another loaded question.

Now I meet his gaze. "I can't believe you have the audacity to ask that when I can still hear your victims' moans."

The horseman makes a cavalier sound in the back of his throat. "And yet you still don't hate me enough to kill me," he reminds me.

I think of the blade I pressed against his skin. How badly I wanted to hurt him—and how in the end I didn't.

"Give me a knife and we can test that theory," I say.

The horseman nods to my utensils. "Go ahead," he says.

I follow his gaze to the steak knife resting next to my plate, identical to the one he stabbed Ricardo with. I make no move to grab it.

"What would be the use?" I say. "I've seen you heal from death before."

Famine doesn't call out the fact that if I really felt this way, I would've never threatened him in the first place.

Instead, he grabs his wine and swishes it around in his cup. "So, you regretfully saved me, I destroyed some things you cared about,"—he destroyed *everything* I cared about—"and we parted ways. How've you spent the rest of our time apart?" he asks.

"Mainly with my mouth open and my legs spread," I say.

Usually, this sort of language is shocking, and I enjoy scandalizing my audience. But Famine doesn't so much as lift an eyebrow.

I *will* figure out how to push his buttons, damnit.

"That seems uncomfortable," he says smoothly.

"No more so than having to wear manacles." I raise my hands and jingle my chains just to emphasize my point.

"So, you joined a whorehouse and made a living out of getting used?" he asks, his razor-sharp attention focused on me. Between his blinding good looks and his God-awful personality, that attention is particularly off-putting.

"You disapprove," I say.

He lifts a shoulder. "I disapprove of everything you humans do. Don't take it personally."

I don't.

120

Instead, I settle into my own seat. "Don't tell me you've *never* wanted to dip your wick?"

When nothing registers on his face, I elaborate. "You know, polish the brass?"

No reaction.

"Hide the salami?"

Nothing.

"Do the devil's dance?"

Famine brings his glass to his lips. "Whatever you're talking about, it all sounds *highly* insane," he responds, "but given the idiotic pastimes you mortals are fond of, I'm not altogether surprised." He drinks deeply from his wine.

"Sex," I finally say. "I'm talking about sex."

He grimaces.

"Oh, don't act like you're somehow above the act," I say. "You seem to enjoy the rest of our things well enough." I look pointedly at his glass of wine. He's been drinking all day; clearly he approves of some human things.

Famine's mouth twists into a wry grin. "Just because you like honey doesn't mean you must also like the bee."

I frown at him, annoyed that he's making any amount of sense.

"The truth is," Famine says, eyeing his drink speculatively, "a little alcohol washes away the memory of all sorts of sins."

I study him. "You're trying to forget everything you've done?"

I don't want to linger on that thought. I can too easily empathize with it, and I don't want to empathize with any part of this horseman.

"It makes no difference what I'm trying to forget," he says, setting his drink down.

The Reaper's gaze lifts to mine, and for an instant, I see a spark of pain, and I remember all over again how I found him mutilated and discarded off to the side of the road.

I lean back in my chair and fork a piece of food and chew

it, mostly to get the taste of pity out of my mouth. Famine doesn't deserve my pity.

Out of nowhere, the horseman drops his legs from the table. Reaching out, he takes one of my cuffs in his hands, and with a single, forceful jerk he rips the metal apart, freeing my wrist.

I stare at him, aghast, even as he moves to my other wrist, tearing the manacle apart *with his bare hands*. The shackles go clattering to the ground.

Holy shit. I had no idea he was that strong.

He sits back in his seat again, acting as though he didn't just literally rip apart iron. "Why did you join a—" He makes a face, "'house of pleasure'?"

"It was called 'The Painted Angel,'" I say, still shaking off my shock. I take a drink from my water, my arms feeling unusually light now that they're free. "And you make it sound like I had a choice."

I made it to the city of Laguna half-starved, without a penny to my name. I was lucky Elvita was the one who found me and not someone else, now that I better understand how this world deals with desperate girls.

"You did have a choice," Famine insists. "You could've come with me."

"But I couldn't," I say, setting down my water. "You know that. You *know* that." My voice lowers, "I'm not the same as the people who hurt you; I can't bear the sight of pain. *That's* why I saved you. But then you killed my entire town. You became just like the people who hurt you."

Famine leans towards me, his arm moving to rest along the back of my seat. "I am *nothing* like them," he growls, his eyes ablaze. "I came to your world to end your kind because of the evil that lives in you all."

"It lives in you, too," I snap back.

He scowls at me for a long moment. Abruptly, he drops his legs from the table and stands, staring down at me. I'm struck again by how ridiculously, exquisitely handsome this monster is.

"Maybe you're right. Maybe I am evil. I was made in your image, after all."

He pushes away from me then, upending my plate on his way out.

Chapter 17

The next day, I've only just gotten out of bed when my door is thrown open, the wood banging against the wall.

Famine stands at the threshold, his armor on and his scythe in hand, looking all sorts of agitated. So, essentially, *same as always*.

"Let's go," Famine says, jerking his head over his shoulder.

"Good morning to you too," I say, biting back a yawn as I stretch.

"Ana, let's. Go."

What in the world is the rush?

"I need shoes first," I say, lifting a dirty foot. I could probably also use another bath, but I doubt I'll be getting one any time soon.

"So you can run away?" he says skeptically. "I think not."

I sigh. "I thought we had made some progress on the imprisonment front last night." He had removed my shackles, after all. I thought that was a step in the right direction. "Notice I didn't run?"

I did, however, collect every knife I could find in the kitchen and I hid them in various parts of the house. In this room alone, I have two under my mattress, two more in the closet, and another one in the top drawer of the bedside table.

Just in case.

"Am I supposed to be impressed by that? We already went over the fact that there is nowhere for you to go."

True.

"That hasn't stopped you from worrying I will run," I say smoothly.

"You are prone to stupid decisions—"

"My stupid decisions once saved your life."

"I would've regenerated anyway."

I glare at him.

He glares back.

I fold my arms. "Where's the girl?" I ask, still not moving towards him. The girl from yesterday, the one whose father heartlessly gave her away to the horseman. Last I saw of her, she was being carted away to one of this home's bedrooms. It's bothered me ever since, all the horrors he might've inflicted on her.

"What girl?" the horseman asks, momentarily distracted from our argument.

"The one you *spared*," I say euphemistically.

The Reaper's brows pull together, and I spend a traitorous moment enjoying how pretty he is. Don't get me wrong, he's still an asshole, and I wouldn't fuck him unless I was especially desperate—or you know, the whole blowjob-for-humanity bit. But he *is* pretty.

Famine's brow smooths. "Ah, yes," he says. "I almost forgot."

And then he walks away.

That's ... not an answer. And that's *definitely* not the end of the conversation.

"What happened to her?" I press, rushing after him.

"You humans are such curious, conniving creatures," he says ahead of me, striding down the hall.

"Did you rape her?" I ask. "Kill her?"

"This conversation is almost as boring as she was," the Reaper says, not bothering to turn to me.

"'Was'?" I say. "So you did kill her?" My stomach bottoms out, but of course he did. That's what Famine does.

The Reaper doesn't answer, and I'm left to imagine all sorts of horrible scenarios in my head.

I follow Famine out the front door. I can still hear low moans coming from the backyard, but I see no one—dead or alive.

Famine whistles, and a minute later his horse comes galloping out of seemingly nowhere, its hooves clacking against the broken asphalt.

I halt in my tracks. "Wait. Are we ... leaving?"

Already?

"There's nothing more I need to do here," the Reaper says as his horse comes to a stop in front of him.

Famine turns to me and, grabbing me by the waist, hoists me into the saddle. A moment later, he joins me.

"Wait-wait-wait," I say, "I haven't even had breakfast, and I need my things!"

"You don't *have* things," the horseman says calmly. He clicks his tongue, and his horse begins to trot away from the house.

I glance over my shoulder forlornly. "Not anymore." *Goodbye, knives.*

I face forward again. "Did you already kill off your guards?" I ask as we begin to wind our way through the city.

"I was tempted to," he admits, "but no. I sent them off last night."

"Why?" I ask, half turning my head.

"I hate getting blood on my clothes."

I shut my eyes against the image. "No—I wasn't asking why you spared them." Ugh. "I meant, why did you send them—"

"I know what you meant," Famine says, cutting me off.

Oh. I think that was horseman humor.

"They're going to prepare the next city for my arrival."

Just like my city was prepared. The thought sends a wave of apprehension through me.

"And," he adds, "to answer your question from earlier, no I didn't rape the girl you were worried about. I would *never* do such a thing." He says this with a conviction normally reserved for people who have been victims themselves.

Could mighty Famine have been abused? It's not too far fetched, considering all the other torture he must've endured.

"Then why would you send her to your room?"

The Reaper doesn't answer.

I try again. "Is she alive?" I ask.

"Why does it matter to you?" he says.

Because she's young and scared and I recognize bits of myself in her.

"It just does," I say.

After a moment, Famine exhales. "She's alive. For now."

As we leave Colombo, people—living, breathing people—peer out from their houses. Somewhere in the distance I hear a child laugh.

I take them in, confused. Famine doesn't leave cities intact.

Behind me, the horseman begins to whistle.

What do you have planned, Famine?

Then I hear a distant, buzzing noise at our backs.

I glance over my shoulder, and on the horizon, the sky is dark, and I swear it seems to be getting darker by the second.

"What ... what is that noise?" I ask, facing forward. It sets my teeth on edge.

He whispers in my ear. "Don't you know, though?"

I strain to listen. The noise is getting louder and louder, even as the sky continues to darken. It's not until a large bug whacks into my arm that I start to understand.

I brush the creature off, but then another three hit me in quick succession. I glance behind us again and I realize the dark sky is *moving*.

That bone-chilling sound is the collective buzz of millions of wingbeats.

It's famine in its truest form.

My eyes meet the Reaper's.

"Thus far, you seem to find my methods of killing distasteful," he says, "so I thought I'd try my hand at a more ... biblical approach.

"It will take them a long time to die," he comments. "Starvation is no quick end. Maybe some of those humans will even manage to survive ... you would like that, wouldn't you?"

"Fuck. You."

"Still not interested," he says.

I face forward again.

"Then again, I'm not sure I want to be so merciful to you humans. I really wouldn't want another Ana surviving my wrath—one is plenty enough."

I twist in the saddle once more to openly glare at him. Only moments after I do so, the ground seems to shudder, and I have to grab onto the horseman to brace myself. He gives me an arch look at the action. Behind him, the sky clears, the insects dispersing in a matter of minutes.

I don't see his awful plants sprout, and I don't hear the pained cries of thousands of people who've been caught in their clutches, but I know it's happening all the same.

I don't have it in me to be horrified any longer. It's just one more atrocity to add to the long list of them he's committed since I first saw him in Laguna.

And if I'm to travel with him, then I better get used to this horseman's perversions. I'm afraid I'm going to be seeing a lot more of them soon enough.

Chapter 18

"I'll stop three times per day," the horseman says hours later, when he's pulled his steed off to the side of the road. "You'll have to do all your humanly business then."

"What if I need to go to the bathroom more often than that?" I say.

"That's not my problem," he says, leaning back against a nearby tree.

All around us are thickly forested mountains, the terrain broken up by the occasional homestead.

"I hope you know that I *will* pee on you in the saddle if I have to," I say. "I have *no problem* with that. You may even like it too ... if that's your kink."

But let's be real, bathing in the blood of innocents is Famine's real kink.

The horseman glowers at me. "I'm hauling you onto this horse in the next few minutes, whether you've relieved yourself or not; I'd suggest you stop wasting your time."

Fun as it would be to make good on my own threat, I'm not that petty. I mean, if I had a change of clothes, then I might be, but for now ... that scenario will have to remain hypothetical.

I begin to walk away from the horseman, looking for a secluded place to do my *humanly business*, but then I pause.

"Do you not have to go to the bathroom?" I ask over my shoulder.

Now that I think about it, have I *ever* seen him relieve himself?

"I'm not talking about this with you," he says, fiddling with one of the saddle bags.

"But you *eat* and *drink*." That *must* come out.

"Not talking about it."

Fine.

With a sigh, I wander away to go to the bathroom. When I return, Famine is stroking his horse, his back to me. I pause for a moment, just watching him being gentle with his steed.

Just when I was certain the man was wholly evil, he goes and pets his horse like he cares about *something*.

"Does he have a name?"

I see the horseman subtly jolt; I guess he hadn't realized I was there.

"Does what have a name?" His voice drips with disdain, his back still to me.

"Your *horse*."

Famine turns to face me. "Are you ready to go?"

I sit down on the ground. "I mean I'm not *unready*, but I'm in no rush either." It's a lovely day, now that the sky isn't filled with locusts or the screams of the dying. I could linger.

"I don't really give a rat's ass about your concerns."

"You know," I say, tipping my head back to get a better look at his annoyingly handsome features, "it's bad enough that you're a mass murderer, but I was at least hoping that you wouldn't be such a *dick* when you weren't killing people."

"Up."

"I'll get up—but first, you have to tell me one redeeming quality about myself."

"There's *nothing* redeeming about you."

I huff. "Well, *sure* there is. I have a banging body, for one thing." I mean, that's undisputed. Just ask my clients. "I'm also easy to talk to."

"Up."

"It's okay if you're a little shy about opening up—lots of men are. It's really endemic to our culture—okay, *my* culture. Anyway, I'll go first: I think you're obscenely handsome, and your smile lights up your whole face."

Of course, that smile usually precedes violence, but ... it's still a nice smile, and there's not much else left to compliment. The man's got a shitty personality.

The Reaper approaches me, and before I can say anything else, he heaves me up over his shoulder.

"Whoa. Hey, wait—we're not leaving yet, are we? What about your neat food trick?" As if on cue, my stomach growls. "I'm hungry."

"You get two more stops," Famine says, dropping me onto the horse.

I frown at him. "I *do* need to eat, you know."

"I know what limits the human body is capable of when it comes to food," Famine says, pulling himself into the saddle. "You'll survive a few more hours of fasting."

He steers us onto the dirt road, and we resume our travels.

"So," I say as we pass a tiny farm, "you can control swarms of bugs." My tone is light, but I have to swallow down my alarm.

"I don't control the bugs, I just call to them."

Because that is just *so* much clearer ...

"How do you call to bugs?" I ask as the farm's small orchard withers away.

Famine sighs.

"I'm sorry," I say, "but do you have something better to do right now?"

"If I give you one of your damned compliments," he

growls, "will you stop questioning me?"

My eyebrows hike up with surprise. He's actually going to try complimenting me? This I have to hear.

"Sure," I say.

But in the silence that follows, I brace myself for some stinging barb.

"You have a lovely voice."

I feel an unexpected flush of warmth at his words.

I tilt my head in confusion. "But I thought you wanted me to stop talking," I say.

"About me. Talk your ass off about anything else."

"I'm sitting here with a man who says he's not actually a man, riding a horse that might not actually be a horse—"

"He's a horse."

"—and I'm supposed to not talk about any of it."

"Precisely."

There's a long pause.

"Fine. I guess that leaves me to talk about sex. Moist, thick, wet sex."

Another beat of silence passes, then—

"Would you like another compliment?"

The stars are out and the night has turned chilly and I've long since lost feeling in my ass and yet we're somehow *still* on this godforsaken horse.

"Eventually, I'm going to need to sleep," I say.

"I'm not stopping," Famine says.

"And you wonder why I didn't join you years ago."

He says nothing to that.

"I'm cold."

Silence.

"And hungry."

More silence.

"And tired."

"Deal with it, Ana."

I purse my lips. "You're really not going to stop?"

"No."

"Such a dick," I whisper under my breath.

It must be the early hours of the morning when my eyelids start to close. Then my head lowers. It knocks into my chest, startling me awake.

I thought it would've been impossible to get tired while sitting on a horse, but now I can't seem to keep my eyes open. My chin bumps my chest a couple more times, jostling me awake again and again. Without thinking much about it, I twist a little in the saddle and lean my cheek against Famine's chilly armor.

And then I drift off.

I feel myself falling when suddenly, Famine catches me, jolting me awake.

"Stay on the horse," he orders me. He sounds painfully alert, the jerk.

"You stay on the horse," I mutter, my eyes already closing.

Famine mutters something about no-good humans, but I'm already slipping back into sleep.

I wake again when I fall against the Reaper's arm.

"Are you trying to hurt yourself?" he demands, and I notice now what I didn't before—he sounds angry, indignant.

"I'm trying to *sleep*. This would all be easier with a bed."

"I'm not stopping," he says obstinately.

"Trust me, I'm aware of that."

I resettle, nestling my face close to the crook of his neck. It's an awkward angle and it puts me closer to the horseman than I care to be, but it's one of the more comfortable positions.

"What are you doing?" Famine demands. Now he definitely sounds perturbed.

"*Sleeping*," I say, my eyes already closing.

I can sense his deep, disapproving frown, but I'm hours and hours beyond caring. Gradually, I feel him relax against me.

I think my body slides a couple more times, but eventually the Reaper's solid arm comes around me, holding me to him. And then I drift off, and I don't wake.

When I open my eyes, I'm lying in a bed.

Where the hell am I ... ?

I push myself up and glance around, trying to get my bearings.

All at once, the previous evening comes back to me. Riding on Famine's horse, falling asleep over and over again only to be jostled awake. But at some point I fell asleep and stayed asleep.

And by the looks of it, we must've arrived at wherever we were supposed to during that time.

Just as I'm taking in the room, which has a couple cowboy hats hanging on the wall and a bull's skull mounted above the bed, I hear the sure stride of a familiar set of feet. A moment later Famine enters.

"Did you put me here?" I say by way of greeting.

He gives me a look. "No, my horse did."

God, he's so testy. *This* is why it's important to get a good night's sleep. Or laid. Preferably both.

"So you carried me inside this house, to this bedroom, just so I could sleep?"

Famine frowns. "Better the bed than me. You drooled on my armor."

I vaguely remember how I used him as my own personal pillow.

"Trust me," I say, "I wasn't too thrilled about the situation either."

I glance down at the blankets pooled around my waist, and I raise my eyebrows as a whole new thought hits me. "You tucked me in," I say, shocked.

"Is that supposed to mean something?" Again with that

gruff, angry voice.

My eyes rise to his, and I see it in his own gaze.

Reaper-boy fucked up. He was kind to me, and he *knows* it.

I break out into a sly smile. "Aww, you don't really hate me, do you?"

His gaze drops to my mouth, and a muscle in his jaw jumps.

"You nursed me to health once," he says, "yet still you hate me. Don't think too much on my small kindnesses."

Kindnesses. Even he's aware of what they are.

"Get up," he says gruffly, "it's time to go."

"Wait," I say. "So we're not even here?" Wherever *here* actually is.

He doesn't answer me.

Famine stopped at some random house and tucked me into bed. All, presumably, so that I could sleep.

I follow Famine out of the room and through the house, the tile floor chilly against my bare feet. I should've realized sooner that this wasn't our final destination. The floorplan is far too small.

I'm so focused on the cozy layout that I don't notice the blood until I slip in it. I lose my bearings completely and go down. My elbow bangs hard against the floor, and the liquid soaks into my dress.

Just as I'm pushing myself up, my gaze connects with a set of glassy eyes. I barely have time to register that I'm staring at a dead man before I start screaming.

Famine's arms go around my waist, and he sets me back on my feet. I begin to move, then slip again, and only the Reaper's hold on me keeps me from going down once more.

Near the dead man is a second corpse—another man, I think, though I can't be sure. The sight is too gruesome for my mind to process.

Famine steers me outside, where his dark horse is waiting, and I'm trying not to focus on the fact that blood is dripping from my dress and snaking down my skin.

We stop in front of his steed, and he nods to the beast. "Get on."

Already the horseman's scythe—the same one that must've cut those people apart inside—is strapped to the creature.

Slowly my eyes move to Famine's.

I can't do this.

"Ana—" he cautions.

I bolt.

My arms and legs pump as I make a beeline for a field lined with rows and rows of wheat that are somehow, inexplicably, still alive.

I don't quite know what I'm doing, and I don't especially care.

Run-run-run-run-run.

I weave through the plants, their stalks slapping at me. Over my heavy breath, I hear Famine's pounding footfalls behind me, and Satan's balls, the fucker is coming for me.

I strain my muscles, pushing them to their limits.

The problem is, I've spent the last few years being a soft, pliant thing that men can fall into. My muscles are nonexistent, and they're tiring fast.

It takes Famine a laughably short amount of time to close in on me. He catches me around the waist and the two of us go tumbling into the dirt.

I cough, the heavy press of the Reaper at my back making it hard to breathe. After a moment, he flips me over.

"You foolish little flower, don't you know?" he scolds me. "I kill *everything*. If you leave my side, you *will* die."

I push uselessly at his shoulders. "Then let me die, damn you!"

"*No.*"

Famine looks at me, gobsmacked; his response seems to shock him more than it does me. He searches my face, like it holds some answers.

Gentler, he says, "You saved me once. I am going to return the favor, even if it means forcing you to stay with me."

My mind flashes back to the way Famine looked at me all those years ago when he realized I had saved him. Like a drowning man clinging to a lifeline.

I think maybe he believed in humanity in that moment. Even though he shouldn't have. Even though he doesn't now.

Still, I can tell he believes in *something* when he looks at me. His cruel expression is gone, and his eyes are alight with ... well, whatever it is, it's not anger.

The horseman pushes himself off me, rising to his feet.

I lay in the dirt a moment longer, just staring up at him.

Famine dusts himself off. After a moment, he reaches out a hand to me. When I don't immediately take it, his green eyes flash.

"We can either do this the easy way—and you can willingly come with me—" he says, "or we can do it the hard way."

He doesn't elaborate on what the hard way is, but I'm not interested in finding out. I feel defeated all of a sudden. Resisting him doesn't seem to get me anywhere.

"I think your definition and my definition of *hard* are two very different things," I say, taking his hand.

He doesn't get the joke—or if he does, he doesn't react.

Famine pulls me back to my feet. Even once I'm standing, however, he doesn't let my hand go. It's not until the two of us are in the saddle and his horse begins to move that he relaxes his hold on me. But then, the arm that held me fast last night is back around my waist, pinning me against his armor. I don't think the Reaper is afraid of me diving off his horse or falling asleep.

I think, despite all the horseman's hate and anger, he doesn't half mind touching me after all.

Chapter 19

"I'm tired."

"Not this again."

For the second day in a row, the two of us have been riding late into the night.

"Newsflash—" I say, "I'm going to want to sleep *every* day. Just like eating, it's not really an optional activity for me." Even though it clearly seems to be an optional one for him.

I shit you not, the man *growls* in response.

"Also, I'm hungry," I add.

"Oh, for fuck's sake."

"Listen, asshole," I say, my irritation spiking, "if you're so determined to keep me alive, you need to fight your stupid base nature and actually help me meet my needs."

He snarls again at my words. Abruptly, he seems to alter course, directing his horse through a nearby field. We trample over some nameless crop.

"What are you doing?" I ask, shaking off my sleepiness.

"Fulfilling your *needs*," he bites out. "I can only take so much of your pestering."

Convincing him was ... easy enough. I feel a spark of

apprehension. Maybe it was too easy.

The crops we pass whack our arms and legs as we pass them. I can't see anything beyond them, not until the field falls away. Ahead of us I catch sight of a small, dark structure. We ride right up to it at full speed.

At the last second, Famine pulls on the reins, and his horse comes to a sudden halt, its front hooves lifting off the ground and pawing the air.

Everything this guy does has to be so damn dramatic.

Once the horse has dropped his feet back to the ground, the Reaper reaches down, unfastening the scythe he had strapped to his horse.

Weapon in hand, Famine swings off the horse and stalks towards the house. Only then, when I see his big-ass blade glinting ominously in the moonlight, does his awful little plan come together.

Aw *fuck.*

This is how he means to meet my needs. By killing off someone else so that we can freely use their home.

Goddamnit.

I hop off the horse and rush after him. "Famine, please, let's not do anything too drastic—"

The horseman lifts a foot and unceremoniously kicks the door in, the blow so intense I hear the metal rip from its hinges.

Inside, a woman screams.

Shit. Shit, shit, *shit.*

The horseman strides inside, looking massive and lethal, a sinister frown on his face. On the opposite side of the room an old woman cowers behind an ancient couch. I see a book on the ground, and one small oil lamp giving off weak, watery light.

"Oh my God, oh my God," she says, her voice wobbly.

As soon as Famine sees the woman, he stalks towards her, and it's obvious what he intends.

The elderly woman crosses herself, despite the uselessness of the gesture. The only divine intervention she's going to get tonight is closing in on her, and he doesn't give a shit about her life.

"Famine!" I rush after him, feeling panicked and useless.

He ignores me completely, his gaze glued to his next victim. She's still crouched on the ground, babbling something now—maybe a prayer—but I can't make out the words.

I grab the wooden staff of the Reaper's scythe, but he shakes off my hold easily enough.

"Step away, Ana," Famine commands, not casting me a glance.

Yeah, uh, *fuck that.*

He looms over the woman and pulls the scythe back, getting ready to strike.

Without thinking, I throw myself in the way, knocking the old lady aside. My eyes go big when I see the tip of that terrible scythe descending down on me.

When he realizes he's about to strike me and not the other woman, Famine jerks his arm back—

He just doesn't do it quickly enough.

The tip of the scythe sinks into my shoulder, and it's sickening just how easily it cuts through sinew.

Like a knife through butter.

For a moment, I feel like a fish caught on a hook. But then just as swiftly as the blade descended, it's gone, more flesh tearing in its wake.

It takes a second for the pain to register, but once it does, I gasp, my legs buckling.

"*Ana,*" Famine says, aghast, dropping the blade.

The woman shrieks again. Then, while the horseman is distracted, she bolts through her front door, lost to the night.

The Reaper doesn't even notice.

"You foolish woman!" he bellows at me.

He drops to his knees, reaching for me. Maybe it's my

imagination, but I swear his hands tremble a little when they touch my skin.

I cry out as he probes at the wound. I can't see his face, but I swear he recoils a little.

"Take off your dress," he demands.

"Oh, now you try to get in my pants," I gasp out.

"*Ana.*"

"I'm *kidding*," I breathe. "Geez."

"Your dress," the Reaper says, his voice angry.

I can only make out the dramatic cut of Famine's high cheekbones and those cruel, full lips of his, and I'm thankful for that. I don't really want to see whatever emotion lingers in those frightening eyes of his.

"I'm not moving my arm," I say.

A moment later Famine's warm hands grab the collar of my dress.

Riiiiiiip.

He tears the fabric apart.

Famine avoids looking at my now exposed breasts as he removes the last of my dress from my shoulder.

He reaches for the wound again. I'm assuming he's trying to help, but I'm also pretty fucking sure he has zero experience helping injured humans.

"Wait," I say, taking shallow breaths through the pain.

Famine pauses.

"Alcohol."

I feel his eyes on me. "You want to drink right now?"

I definitely wouldn't *mind.*

"To disinfect the wound," I say slowly.

Famine stares at me for a long, long moment. Finally, coming to some sort of decision, he gets up and heads to the kitchen. I can hear him rummaging around for an eternity.

When he returns, he's holding a corked jug.

I make a face. It's clearly something home-brewed and probably suspect.

Famine seems to agree. "This will sooner kill you than heal you," he says.

"Just give it to me." I go to swipe it from him, but the horseman moves the bottle out of my way.

"Hold still," he says, uncorking the lid.

I give him a skeptical look. All I've seen of Famine is his ability to hurt and kill. I have little faith he knows how to tend to an injured person.

He grabs my wounded shoulder, careful not to touch the injury itself. Gently he tips the bottle of the mystery liquor, pouring a liberal amount onto the wound.

The moment the alcohol hits, the pain becomes blinding, and a gasped cry slips out.

"This was a stupid idea," he says.

"Shut up," I grit out.

Getting up from my side, Famine wanders through the house once more, returning a while later with a couple pieces of clothing. The first one he rips into strips then wraps around my shoulder. I bite back another cry as he jostles the wound.

Once he's done, he shakes out the second garment, which looks like a shift dress.

"You don't like looking at my tits, do you?" I guess.

I am, after all, still exposed to him.

"It's cold."

"Be honest," I say, "you're uncomfortable."

"Fine, don't wear the dress," he says, backing away. "I don't care."

I do end up putting the thing on—or at least I try to. The problem is, my injured shoulder is bound up, making movement difficult.

In the darkness, I hear the Reaper exhale, then the sound of his ominous footfalls as he comes over once more. He kneels in front of me.

"What are you doing?" I ask, and now I catch a glimpse of

those luminous eyes in the darkness.

Ignoring me, he grabs the material and helps thread my arms through the sleeves.

I give him a curious look as he helps me, ignoring the pain as he inevitably bumps my wound again.

"Why are you doing this?" I ask again.

He stares intently at the fabric, and I think maybe I'm imagining his troubled look.

"I wasn't trying to hurt you," he says gruffly.

You were *trying to hurt someone*, I want to say.

But I can tell that, oddly enough, he *is* troubled by the fact that he hurt me.

"I know," I say instead. As violent and cruel as the Reaper has been, he's made a point of not inflicting pain on me. Which is confusing as hell, considering that I nearly lost my life when I last met him.

With my good hand, I run my fingers over the dress I wear. Just the feel of the cloth is enough for me to know that this shirt—big and old-lady-ish as it may be—is a thing from the world *before*.

For an instant, I'm hopelessly sad, though I'm not even sure why. I never knew that world. My sense of loss is completely made up. But from the stories, it always sounded like paradise—or, at least, a step up from the shithole world we have now.

"Thank you," I say, still rubbing my fingers over the material.

Famine grunts in response.

After a moment, he says, "You shouldn't have jumped in front of her."

I sigh. "Can't you just take a compliment without ruining it?"

"I don't need or want compliments."

Fuck it all. "Then I take it back," I say. "I'm not grateful you helped me."

The silence is heavy, and the horseman's frowns are becoming legendary enough that I can sense them in the darkness.

Maybe he cares, maybe he doesn't. He's annoyed all the same.

That's good enough for me.

"Why did you do it?" he asks.

Jump in front of the woman, he means.

"She wouldn't have done the same for you," he adds.

"You don't know that," I say.

But ... in my heart of hearts, do I really believe some stranger would've sacrificed herself for me?

No. Definitely not. People are selfish assholes.

I don't, however, admit *that* to Famine.

"I helped you once too—even though you wouldn't have done the same for me," I say instead.

A long, painful silence follows that. I feel the Reaper's searing look in the darkness.

My injury throbs, dragging my attention away from the conversation.

I try to get to my feet. After a moment, the Reaper takes my good arm and stands, pulling me up along with him.

"What now?" I ask.

"You need to sleep."

Oh. Right. In between breaking into some old lady's house and diverting her death, I somehow forgot Famine's entire reason for stopping.

I let the horseman lead me to the back room. Usually I'm the one leading the opposite sex back to a bedroom. Usually I'm the one with a plan.

Famine stops at the threshold and lets me walk into this stranger's bedroom. The air here is heavy with the smell of cloying perfume, and though it's too dark to tell, I think the room is loaded with kitschy little trinkets, because twice I bump into furniture that sends several items rattling.

I have to feel around for the bed, and even once I find it, some combination of guilt and trepidation tightens my stomach because its rightful owner is somewhere out in the darkness.

You idiot, Ana. You should've known this situation would arise. It's what happened last night, after all.

The Reaper is watching me, so mechanically, I pull the covers back and slide into the bed. The sheets are damp from the humidity, and they have an old, musty smell to them. I make a face, even as I settle in.

I mean, *technically*, it isn't the worst bed I've ever slept in, and it's better than the accommodations that old woman is going to get tonight.

Once I'm laying down, Famine retreats from the room.

I lie there in the darkness a long time, staring at the ceiling. I keep waiting for sleep to come, but my shoulder still throbs, and besides, I'm wired from the last hour.

In the room beyond mine, I can hear the horseman striding back and forth, back and forth. It should be lulling, but he sounds so damn agitated.

"Will you stop that?" I finally call out.

The footsteps pause.

"I should be on the road right now," he says.

"*I* wasn't the one who decided to stop," I say.

Now those footsteps approach the bedroom. In the darkness I see his massive silhouette in the doorway, his scythe still in his hand.

"Ungrateful human." His voice sends a shiver through me. "I should force you back onto my horse and continue riding."

"You are *so* unnecessarily dramatic," I say. I pat the mattress. "Just sit down for a second. I can't sleep listening to your pacing."

This may come as a shock, but Famine doesn't, in fact, sit down. He just continues to loom in that doorway.

With a huff, I throw my blankets off and get up.

"What are you doing?" he demands.

Instead of answering him, I cross the room and grab the Reaper's hand, pulling him forward, towards the bed. Much to my shock, he actually lets me lead him into the room.

When I get to the mattress, I push him down with my good arm. Now, however, he *does* resist.

"I am not interested in sex, little flower," he says. There's a note in his voice that raises my gooseflesh.

"I wasn't offering *anything*, you big brute," I say smoothly. "Now, *sit*." I push against his armor again.

I can perfectly imagine his insolent frown. Reluctantly, he bends his knees and perches on the edge of the bed.

"Happy?" he growls.

"Stop pouting," I say, getting on the bed as well. "Can you see me in the dark?" I ask after a moment, feeling oddly exposed.

"Would it matter?" he grumbles.

I wave my hand in front of his face.

"What are you doing?"

"You *can't* see me," I say, slightly triumphant.

"What is the point of me sitting here?" He begins to get up, but I catch his arm and pull him back down.

Before he can get up again, I begin tugging at his armor with my one good arm.

Something I've learned as a sex worker is the true nature of clothes. We wear our garments like masks. Take them off, and you strip a person of their pretenses. That's what I want to do now—strip the horseman of his pretenses, whatever they might be.

Beneath my touch, his body goes rigid.

"*What are you doing?*" Famine asks again, this time more alarmed.

"Calm your tits. I'm not trying to deflower you."

At least, not tonight.

That last wayward thought steals my breath.

What the hell, Ana? Sex with the monster is *off* the table ... or on it, depending on whether there are platters of food nearby ...

No, *no*. No fucking the scary horseman.

"You shouldn't be moving your shoulder," he says gruffly, his body still rigid beneath my touch.

"It's fine." It's not really fine, but whatever. "I've lived through worse."

It's quiet for a moment, and I know Famine's thinking about the scabs and scars on my torso.

The silence stretches on, and this is where a normal, nice person might apologize for nearly killing me. They might at the very least beg for forgiveness.

"You never should've been there," Famine says as I begin peeling away his armor.

"Where?" I say, thinking he's referring to protecting the old woman.

"Visiting me with that woman—the one who tried to *sell* you." His words drip with disdain.

"And where *should* I have been?" I ask, casting aside a bronze vambrace.

"With me."

I shiver at the low pitch of his voice, and this time there's no mistaking it, they are *good* shivers. *Problematically* good shivers.

My hands move to the armor covering his chest, my body brushing against his. I can feel his eyes on me, and even though there's nothing sexual going on, this whole situation feels intimate.

"Tell me about yourself," I say to distract myself as I work on unfastening his breastplate.

"I don't have a *self* to share."

My brows knit together. "Well of *course* you do." My gaze ventures up, and even though the bedroom is steeped in shadows, I catch sight of the pools of his eyes.

He stares back at me, and after a moment, I sense that he might actually want me to elaborate on that.

The armor comes undone in my hands. "Since you've come to earth, you've been a man—"

"I'm not—"

"You *are* a man. Just because you can't die and you can make shit spontaneously grow,"—not to mention the swarms of bugs and the not sleeping and peeing—"you have a body. You have a self."

I toss his unfastened breastplate aside, the metal clattering on the ground.

"What do you want me to say?" he finally responds. "Do you want me to tell you something human about myself? Even *if* there were a part of me that was truly human—which there isn't—your kind made sure to stamp it out long ago."

I think he's alluding to the torture he met at our hands. I almost ask him about it, but I know that conversation would put the malice back in his voice. I'm not interested in his wrathful side; I get plenty of exposure to it during the day.

"Fine, then tell me something *inhuman* about yourself."

Another long silence follows. I think I might've shocked the Reaper, though I have no idea why.

"I feel ... everything," he finally says. "Every blade of grass, every drop of rain, every centimeter of sunbaked clay. I am the storm that rolls in, I am the wind that carries the bird and the butterfly." As he speaks, he begins to gain confidence.

"The sensations are a bit muted now that I wear this form," Lightly he touches his chest, "but still I feel it all."

Forgetting about the last bit of armor that encases his arm, I inch closer to him, drawn in by his words. Say what you will about me, I like a good story.

"That's the difference between me and my brothers," he continues. "We are all meant to ravage the world, but we have our distinctions: War is the most human, Pestilence perhaps next. But even Thanatos—Death—is intimately connected to life.

"I am the one least truly alive. I have more in common with wildfires and clouds and mountains than I do anything else. So to be something that lives and breathes is a stifling, unpleasant experience. I am ... *trapped* in this flesh."

I sit back a little, trying to process his admission.

He sighs. "I just want this to be over," he confesses. "All I want is to return to what I once was."

Famine has been staring at some point between the floor and the wall, but after several moments he turns to me, as if just realizing I'm next to him.

Abruptly, he stands. "We're leaving at daybreak," he says. "Rest while you can. You won't get any tomorrow."

With that, he heads out of the room. Just past the doorway, he pauses.

"One other inhuman thing about me, flower." Famine turns his head slightly towards me. "I don't simply exist, I *hunger*."

Chapter 20

As usual, Famine makes good on his word the next day—by the time the sun has risen, we're already back on the road, and the house we stayed in nothing more than a mostly-forgotten dream.

My wound throbs as I wiggle my feet. I finally have another pair of boots on—scuffed, mud-covered boots that are certainly not mine. I took them anyway, despite the knot of guilt I felt. They fit surprisingly well.

I also happened to take a leather belt, which I used to cinch the billowy white garment I wear, which, in the light of day, is nothing more than a nightgown.

I look ridiculous, but at least I'm alive. That's more than I can say for most other people around these parts.

"The day we first reunited," Famine says, interrupting my thoughts. "Why did you seek me out?"

Here I am thinking about belts and nightgowns; meanwhile, the horseman's going all existential on me.

"I didn't seek *anything* out," I say. "You came to my town."

"You could've fled," he says.

"You would've eventually caught up with me."

"Mmm." One of his hands rests on my hips, and now it idly strokes the material there. He leans in close. "You thought I'd recognize you." His voice and the nearness of his mouth give me chills.

Yes. Of course I thought that.

After a moment, the horseman speaks again.

"I remember exactly what you looked like the day you saved me," he admits. "If I was truly looking for it, I would've recognized you, but I have spent the last five years not truly seeing anyone."

I remember how angry Famine was right before he destroyed my childhood home. I don't know the specifics of what happened to him while he was imprisoned—those secrets died with the people who hurt him—but it's obvious that whatever happened to Famine, it made an already cruel man much, much crueler.

"Why did you save me at all?" the Reaper asks.

It's not the first time he's asked me this, but apparently, he wants to hear my answer again. Or maybe he wants a different answer; I don't think human altruism sits well with him.

"Because I was young and foolish." A touch of bitterness enters my voice.

I can feel those intense eyes boring into the back of my head. I shift under his scrutiny, and I feel the need to explain myself further.

"I lost my mom when I was an infant and my father when I was twelve. After my dad's death, his sister took over raising me. She ... wasn't kind. She already had five children, and she didn't want another. She made it clear I was a burden."

I take a deep breath. "When I saw you lying there, covered in mud and blood and rain, your body ..." I can't even find the words to describe the state he was in. "It was awful." It truly was. It didn't matter who he was or what he did. No one deserved to be treated like that.

"Even once I figured out you were the horseman, I

couldn't leave you." I swallow, glancing down at my nails. "I knew what it was like to be unwanted. I spent my teenage years feeling as though my family didn't care whether I lived or died. If it were me laying on the side of the road, I would want someone to care. So I helped you."

I feel the burn of Famine's gaze. For a moment, his grip on my hip tightens.

"So you saw yourself in me," he says, his voice a little hoarse. "I should've known at the very heart of it, you'd have selfish motives."

I glance heavenward. *Lord give me strength.* "It's called empathy."

"I'm aware of what you humans consider kindness."

"Oh, and like you're some shining example of compassion," I snap.

"I never said I was—though I should point out that I *did* spare you all those years ago."

"Me and no one else," I respond. "You killed the last of my family when you destroyed my hometown."

"Was I supposed to save your aunt?" He sounds remorseless. "You said it yourself—she wasn't kind."

I glance over my shoulder at him, giving him a look like he's mad. Maybe he is. "What's the point of sparing me if there's no life for me to return to?"

Famine gazes back at me curiously, and I think he might legitimately believe that people don't need each other the way we so obviously do. "They didn't save me, when they could've," he says. "You did."

"You didn't have to kill all of them."

I feel him stiffen behind me in the saddle, his already unforgiving armor all the more uncomfortable against my back.

"Did I ever tell you how I came to be a prisoner?" he asks far too calmly.

I shake my head, a shiver sweeping down my spine.

His voice is as low as a lover's when he whispers into my ear. "I spared a family who was kind to me." As he speaks, his fingers stroke my hip, his touch menacing. "They didn't save my life—not like you—but they welcomed me into their home. They fed me, let me sleep in their bed even knowing what I was.

"Foolishly I enjoyed their hospitality, lingering a little longer than I should in one place. They didn't mind my killing so much—or at least they never complained of it. And that whole time I assumed I was above harm.

"But word eventually got out that a human family was housing me.

I left their house to lay waste to the crops surrounding a nearby village. When I returned, the family—husband, wife, and three young children—were butchered.

"There I was captured and killed. The next time I awoke, I was in an abandoned building that had been turned into a makeshift prison. And that's when the true horror began.

"There aren't words to describe what happened to me—the inflicted agonies, the twisted violations. And even if there were, I doubt a human mind could understand the depth of what I suffered. You have never had your head kicked in, your teeth ripped from your gums, your eyes gouged out, or your fingernails pried off. You've never been staked, burned, disemboweled, or dismembered—sometimes at the same time. You have never been killed, only to return to life and bear it all again and again and again." His lips are soft against my ear, even as his words fill me with second-hand dread.

"I saw the true extent of the pain and suffering humans can inflict on each other, and I endured every conceivable manner of torture." As he speaks, his voice rises.

I swallow.

"I believed in my task before I was captured, but after what I went through, *it's become personal*. Each death is reparation for the atrocities committed against *me*."

No wonder Famine savors our misery, lapping it up like cream.

"I'm sorry," I say, "that they did that to you."

Again his grip on me tightens, but he doesn't respond.

We're both quiet for some time, his words lingering in the air between us.

"So," I eventually say, deciding to lighten the conversation. "Where have you been for the last five years?"

"You mean since we first parted ways?"

I make an affirmative noise.

Famine leans back in the saddle, exhaling. "A better question is where *haven't* I been."

That has my breath catching.

Five years ago Famine left a trail of dead from Montevideo to Santiago before disappearing from South America altogether. Foolishly I had assumed ... I don't know *what* I had assumed. Clearly something far too optimistic.

"Just how much of the world is gone?" I'm almost afraid to ask.

"Much of Europe and Asia is gone, as well as some of Africa, Australia, and the Americas."

For a moment, I can't breathe. While I went about living my life, whole continents were getting decimated. I don't know how to put in words the thought of so much of the world just ... gone. So I don't.

We go over an hour in silence, and during that time I make peace with this frightening reality of mine. *We're really all going to the grave.* It makes my earlier attempt to run from the Reaper all the more ridiculous. The man was right, where would I even go? Eventually he'll kill us all.

But if that's true, what happened to his brothers? I know at least one of them had ridden the earth before Famine—perhaps two, though the reports were a bit unclear on this second one. If they were successful, why did they disappear—or did they not? And why did they leave so many humans alive?

"How is it?" Famine asks, interrupting my thoughts.

"What?" I have zero idea what the horseman is talking about.

He touches my upper arm, near my injury. I glance at it, only to realize I've been cradling the arm. At some point, the constant movement in the saddle started to make the cut throb in a funny, tearing way.

And he noticed.

I frown. "It hurts, but I'll be fine."

The Reaper says nothing, and we continue on for another minute. But then I hear Famine mutter something under his breath. Abruptly, he stops his horse.

"Has my oh-so-benevolent captor decided to give me a bonus pee break?" I say as he swings himself off his steed.

The Reaper ignores me, striding away. Without meaning to, my eyes drink in his wide shoulders and tapered waist. His bronze armor gleams under the sun.

He glances over his shoulder at me, that caramel colored hair blowing about his face, and my breath catches. He looks like a hero from some bygone age, his features painfully perfect.

Those shocking green eyes glint like jewels as they take me in. "Are you coming?"

I hesitate, not just because his beauty caught me off guard.

"My arm ..." The truth is, it hurts more than I'm willing to admit.

His expression changes subtly.

Famine comes back over to his horse. Silently, he grabs me and pulls me off his horse. I hiss out a breath as my injury is jostled.

At the sound, the Reaper's lips press together in a displeased line. He sets me down on the ground.

I begin to walk off to do my business.

"Wait," Famine says.

I turn back to him. "Don't tell me you want to watch. I didn't peg you for having *that* sort of fetish."

He gives me a hard look, like he really doesn't want to deal with my shit.

"I'm *kidding*," I say. "You're just too much fun to tease."

"Come here," he says.

I return to him, unsure what this whole stop's actually about.

He steps in close, then reaches for my shift, tugging the loose collar carefully down my shoulder.

I stand impossibly still, my heart beginning to pick up speed.

"I need you to free this arm."

"I'm going to have to take the dress off," I say.

In response, he steps back, presumably to give me room to disrobe. When, however, I begin to struggle at removing my belt, Famine steps forward again, helping me first pull it off, and then the nightgown.

I stand there, off to the side of the road, my tits out, wearing nothing but the grannie panties I also happened to lift from the house this morning.

Famine doesn't so much as blink when he sees my breasts. Instead, his focus is on my shoulder. Carefully, he unwinds my bandages. Whatever he sees makes him frown.

For my part, I refuse to look at the wound. It's one thing to feel the pain, another to see the grotesque proof of it.

The horseman reaches towards the injury, then hesitates.

"What are you doing?" I say.

He drops his hand, his cold gaze flicking to mine. "Repaying an old debt," he says.

"So you're attempting to kill me?" I ask half-jokingly.

The barest hints of a smile tug at the corner of his mouth. "I believe I already tried that once." His eyes dip meaningfully to my stomach before returning to my shoulder.

After a moment, he backs away from me, heading to his

horse. He rifles through one of the saddle bags, eventually pulling out a glass of some clear alcohol.

"You've been holding out on me," I say. I am *all* for day-drinking. Especially while injured ... and in the horseman's company.

He comes back over and uncorks the liquor. Lifting the bottle up, he tips the liquid onto the wound.

I hiss through my teeth. Shit, but that hurts.

"You don't need to do that," I rasp out.

In front of me, the Reaper stiffens, his shoulders tensing, and he doesn't look at all thrilled that I'm in agony at the moment.

"I'm *repaying a debt*," he repeats.

Semantics. He's trying to help, which is completely mind-blowing, considering the hate this man harbors for all human life.

Famine sets the alcohol down, then unfastens his breastplate, shrugging it off before setting it on the ground. His fingers go to the hem of his black shirt, and I have only a moment to wonder what he's doing before—

Riiiiip.

He removes a strip of material from the bottom of his shirt, bringing it up to my shoulder.

Famine's eyes settle on mine for a moment. "Do *not* read into this."

Oh, I'm planning on reading the entire fucking series of *Famine Acting Abnormally Kind and What it Means.*

His fingers fumble and his expression is increasingly tumultuous as he wraps the cloth around my wound. By the time he knots off the bandage, he seems openly angry.

He picks his breastplate up and slips it back on. "Let's go."

The Reaper stalks towards his horse, not waiting for me to follow.

I stare after him for a moment, before I pick up my discarded dress and clumsily pull it back on, gritting my teeth when I have to move my injured shoulder. My belt is equally difficult to secure, but this time the horseman doesn't try to help.

"Ana," he calls out again, clearly irritated that it's taking so damn long for the injured woman to dress herself.

Famine may have his moments of kindness, but he is still such an ass.

My gaze drops to the bottle of spirits lying on the ground. Over the last five years, I've drank precious little liquor, and what little I did drink was done far, far away from The Painted Angel. Elvita had a strict rule against drugs and alcohol, one she forced all her girls to comply with.

But now Elvita is gone.

I pick up the liquor bottle and tip its final remnants into my mouth, enjoying the harsh burn of it.

Another thing I'm going to read into: the fact that at some point, Famine managed to find better alcohol to clean my wound with, and he *packed* it. That's a level of consideration I can't even imagine the horseman having.

"*Ana.*"

I drop the bottle and head back over to Famine, letting him help me back onto his steed. When he joins me in the saddle a moment later, I jolt a little at the press of his body against mine. And when his hand drapes itself over my leg, I feel awfully happy about it.

Please, God, tell me that's just the alcohol's doing.

It's quiet for one tense, long minute.

"So," I finally say, "are we going to talk about what just—"

"No."

"Not even—"

"No."

"But—"

"Damn you, Ana—*no.*"

Someone's uncomfortable about tending to me.

I smile a little. "Awww, I think you don't half mind my

company."

"You're making me reconsider."

"Nonsense." I lean back against the horseman, letting myself enjoy the feel of him around me. "And guess what? I don't half mind your company either."

This really had better be the alcohol's doing.

Chapter 21

In Registro, the next big city we ride into, people line the roads of the old, crumbling highway, waiting for Famine. They cheer when they see him, their faces jubilant.

My stomach curdles at the sight, and for a moment my horror is so strong I feel like I'm choking on my breath.

What have they been told? That the horseman is going to spare them? Or did they just make that assumption like our town did? That maybe if they throw enough valuable items in his direction, he'll forget his purpose and skip them over.

Either way, Famine has too much hate inside him to do anything but kill, kill, kill.

Most of our audience's eyes are fixed on Famine, who is a head taller than me in the saddle. However, I get plenty of looks too. I can tell they're trying to figure out how I factor in. One or two of them meet my gaze, and they tentatively smile at me.

Don't be so reassured, I want to shout at them. *I can't stop him either.* My shoulder throbs then, echoing my thoughts.

"Do the people in these cities ever turn on you?" I ask, taking the crowd in.

"More often than you can imagine," Famine murmurs.

And now I'm vividly picturing an arrow spearing me through the heart. It could happen so easily. But it never comes. Just like my city, this one believes that they can win this monster over.

We wind our way through the streets, and everywhere I look, I see pre-apocalyptic buildings that've been repurposed into something else. Stables, taverns, produce markets, butcher shops, homespun clothing stores, bicycle shops, tanneries, smitheries, and on and on.

By the looks of it, Registro has done well for itself. Up until today, at least.

At some point, another man on horseback separates himself from crowd, entering the street to wave at the horseman.

I lean back against Famine. Once again, I'm vividly imagining an arrow slicing through me.

"Relax, flower," the Reaper says, reading my body language, "that's one of my men." Famine steers us towards him.

"Good to see you again, Famine," the man calls out. "We have a house on the edge of the city that we've prepared for you."

"Good," Famine says. "Take us there now."

The man's gaze moves from the horseman to me, then he turns his horse forward and begins moving.

Up until now, I hadn't thought about being seen with the horseman. Famine had me shackled and locked away like a real prisoner. But now the cuffs are gone and the Reaper has that arm draped over my thigh.

I know what it looks like. Even if I had never been in the business of sex and intimacy, I would know what this looked like.

Like Famine and I were together.

I glance over my shoulder at the Reaper, but his eyes are on the rider ahead of us. A sinister smile tugs at his lips.

Shit.

Excitement from this guy means that we're all probably fucked.

We follow the rider down several side streets. People still stand by and cheer, but the crowds are a little thinner here, now that we're off the main thoroughfare.

Soon the buildings that were once clustered together now spread farther and farther apart until it seems as though we've left the city altogether.

I've traveled farther in the last month than I ever have before, and most of what I've seen are ruins—not just of people, but of old towns and buildings too. We live in a secondhand world, one that clings to the last vestiges of that time before true hardship.

But then, alongside repurposed buildings and dilapidated houses, there are the homes like the one ahead of us. Homes that are more like palaces.

Whoever lives here, they've done well for themselves.

We ride up to the circular driveway. I see a handful of the Reaper's men loitering about the property, but it's the older couple and two sullen teenage boys that stand in front of the house that snag my attention. Next to the four of them is an ancient woman. I'm presumably staring at three generations of family, all waiting for us.

Famine rides right up to them, so close I can see the wavering smile on the middle-aged woman's face, and I can see her husband's shaking hands. They're dressed in their finest, and even though most of my life I've envied families like this—families whose privilege has shielded them from most of life's discomforts—I feel a deep sense of dread for them now. Their good fortune has gotten them noticed by the worst sort of man.

The Reaper pulls his steed up short, and I can practically sense his giddiness. Just as he's about to swing off his horse, I grab his thigh, my fingers digging into the muscle.

"Please, whatever you're about to do—don't," I say quietly.

Famine leans in close to my ear. "This is the fun part, flower. Now, *let go.*"

He jerks out of my hold, hopping off his steed, and I'm left sitting there alone.

Famine takes a moment to grab his scythe and then he approaches the family, his boots crunching ominously against the gravel driveway. He's a terrifying sight. You can't look at him for more than a few seconds without realizing that this is no earthly man.

As the Reaper steps forward, his men close in on the family.

Oh God.

The previously sullen boys now appear intimidated, and the middle-aged couple look downright terrified. Only the old woman isn't caught in the grips of fear; she looks more resigned, like she's seen this all before.

Famine steps in close to the family, his scythe looming over them. His back is to me, but I'm still tense with nerves.

"W-welcome to our house," the woman stammers out.

"*Your* house?" the Reaper says, incredulous. He cocks his head. "I'm afraid my men have lied to you if they made it seem like *I* was the guest."

I close my eyes. I can't watch this.

"Perhaps we should give you an honest reception," he continues. "Men?"

It's the mother's scream that does it for me.

"Stop!" I say, my eyes snapping open.

It might've been the mother's scream that prompted me to do anything, but it's the grandmother's gaze that ensnares me now. She and I lock eyes, and she gives me a look that says, *but what can you really do, girl? You cannot fight a storm and hope to win.*

Famine's men ignore me. Even as I'm scrambling to get off

Famine's horse, they drag the family away.

Famine, turns to me then, eyes narrowing.

I'm still trying to get out of the saddle, which is especially hard with an injured shoulder. I end up sort of just falling off the horse, crying out as I hit the ground, the action jostling my wound.

The Reaper closes in on me. In the distance, I can hear the rising voices of the family. The sound of it tightens my gut. No one thinks things are going to escalate this quickly ... until they do.

Not even I anticipated this sort of escalation, and I *know better*.

When Famine gets to me, he pulls me roughly to my feet.

"Undermine me again, and I will make the situation so much worse," he promises.

I lift my chin. "Fuck you."

In response, he grabs the wrist of my good arm and pulls me towards the ranch house's front door. Off in the distance, the screams have reached a crescendo. I'm shaking, full of fear and hopelessness. That, and a touch of anger. Smoldering, righteous anger.

Famine kicks open the front door. Inside, more of the Reaper's men linger.

"Round up the people of this city and find a building big enough to fit them all," Famine announces. "Tonight, I want there to be a celebration in my honor."

Chapter 22

I'm unceremoniously dumped into a room.

"You're to stay here," Famine says.

"Or else what?" I say defiantly.

The horseman steps in close. "Stay. Inside."

"Make. Me."

His mouth curves into a sinister smile. "Fine. Just remember you asked for it."

Before I can pick apart his words, Famine grabs me again and hauls me over to the bed.

"What are you—?"

The Reaper tosses me onto the mattress. Just as I'm scrambling to sit up he gets on the bed, his knee going to my chest.

I thrash as best I can against him; it isn't much, my shoulder still throbs and I'm tired after a day of being in the saddle.

"Get off of me," I growl.

Instead of doing just that, Famine grabs the bottom of my travel-stained nightgown. There's a momentary pause, when I realize exactly what he's about to do.

"*Don't,*" I say.

He does.

Grabbing the bottom of the makeshift dress, he rips off a strip of fabric, then uses it to bind one of my wrists to a bedpost. I tug against the binding, but it's alarmingly secure.

"So this is your kink, then?" I say, fuming. "I wouldn't have pegged you for a bondage man, but then again, I wouldn't have pegged you for evil, either."

Famine rips off another strip of the dress, and it's quickly going from an old-lady nightgown to something a bit more salacious. I don't entirely disapprove.

I flail, trying to keep my remaining wrist out of Famine's grip. But, it's the injured arm here, so my efforts are paltry. Famine captures my wrist in a matter of seconds. He handles my injured arm gentler than I expect as he moves it towards the other bedpost. It still hurts like a motherfucker.

He ties my wrist to the bedpost, then sits back on his haunches.

"There," he says, assessing his work, "now you can't get in too much trouble."

"You have *got* to be kidding me," I say.

"I'll come for you later," he says, backing off the bed. "Until then, *behave.*"

Because there's so much trouble I could get up to.

... Says the prostitute on the bed.

Okay, *correction:* there's only so much trouble I'd *want* to get up to, given my circumstances.

The Reaper leaves the room, his footfalls growing fainter and fainter as he walks away.

"*If anyone so much as looks at that door for too long,*" I hear him call in the distance, "*I will gut you and feed your entrails to you as you lay dying.*"

Jesus.

I guess I'm going to have to behave.

Damnit.

I lay there for hours, trapped on that damn bed.

Outside my room, I can hear people bustling about, shouting orders to each other. Unfortunately, the same awful procession of people comes to Famine's door just as they have in the towns before this. And just like all those other unfortunate interactions, these ones don't end well either.

I can hear the screams, but worse, I hear the crackle of a bonfire somewhere nearby, and I can smell the smoke. At first it smells as smoke should, but the longer it burns, the more ... cloying and *meaty* the smell gets.

I gag a little when I realize why that is. I lean my face into my shoulder, coughing like I can somehow get the smell and taste out of my nose and throat. That's about when I realize that I'm leaning into my bad arm, and the bandage that covered it for hours has simply ... *vanished*.

The horseman has some strange, terrible magic.

Once the shadows deepen and day turns to night, the procession of people tapers off.

For some time all I hear is the snap and sputter of the bonfire. But then, that sound is interrupted by ominous footfalls that can only belong to the Reaper. They get louder and louder until they come to a halt at the threshold of the room.

In the dying light, Famine looms in the doorway.

"Well look who it is," I say, "the asshole of the hour."

He steps inside the room, quiet. It raises all the hairs along my arm, that silent prowl of his. The closer he gets to me, the faster my breath comes. I can make out his scythe. It's strapped to his back, the blade arcing ominously over his shoulder.

The horseman makes his way to the bed.

The horseman drops something onto the mattress before reaching for one of my bound wrists, effortlessly pulling apart the material that held me captive for hours.

He leans over my body to reach for my other, injured arm,

but he hesitates when he hears my hitched breathing.

"Are you ... frightened?" His voice is so low it makes me shiver.

"You sound delighted," I say.

Okay, maybe not *delighted*, but definitely curious.

"I'll be delighted when you actually stop fighting my every decision," he replies, ripping apart my second makeshift shackle.

I shake my wrists out, trying to get the blood flowing back into them. "Then you'll be delighted when I'm *dead*."

"I'll be *relieved* when you're dead," he says, gently moving my injured arm back to my side. The movement makes it throb something fierce. "You make even an immortal's head pound."

I scoff, sitting up as Famine grabs something from the bed. A moment later, some article of clothing hits me.

"What the—? Did you just throw—?"

"Put the dress on."

"The *dress?*" I pick up the wadded up garment and shake it out. "Wait, what? *Why?*"

The Reaper sighs dramatically. For an evil motherfucker, he is so over-the-top with the theatrics.

"Must you question everything?" he says. "Because I said so."

I set the article of clothing aside. "Unless you force it on me yourself, I'm not wearing a damn dress."

The truth is, I could put the dress on; it would probably look less ridiculous than the oversized, travel-stained nightgown I'm wearing, but *fuck* this horseman and his demands.

Famine gives another long-suffering sigh. "Last time I'm going to ask nicely: Put. It. On."

"No."

In the darkness I swear I see that evil little smile of his make an appearance. "Fine."

Fine?

I'm perplexed, even as he approaches me. But then he pulls his dagger from his belt.

"What are you—?"

He grabs my dress by the collar, and—*riiiip*. He drags the blade down the fabric. As he does so, the material parts, revealing my flesh beneath.

"What the *hell* are you doing?" I almost sound scandalized.

"That was your only dress, wasn't it?" Famine says, like the asshole he is. "Pity it's ruined. Now, put the fucking dress on."

"You think I care about exposing myself?" I do. "I'll walk around bare-breasted before I put—"

"Your shoes are going next." He reaches for my boots, his blade still poised.

"Okay—*okay!*" I say, mostly because it's hard to come by a decent set of shoes these days. "I hate you, but *okay*," I mutter.

I grab the dress as he watches me with steely eyes. I know he's not going to leave, so I don't bother asking him to. I've lost enough power plays today as it is.

Slipping off the bed, I shuck off the remains of my nightgown then shake out the dress, trying to determine what it looks like. It seems to be wine colored, but I can't be sure in the growing darkness. It has enough glittery pieces to it that I can tell it's something ostentatious.

A line of buttons run up the back of the dress, and I have to pause to unbutton each one. Once the opening is wide enough, I step into the dress. I pull it up, feeling the beaded bodice and the ruffled skirt that's cut high in the front and low in the back. It's a little loose, but it works well enough.

All at once I have a flashback to my nights at the bordello, wearing dresses that cinched up the back, rouging my face in front of my vanity.

I'm getting pretty again, and I'm actually not too fond of that fact.

"Happy?" I say sullenly, turning to the horseman.

"Mmm." He makes a noncommittal sound.

"You'll need to button it for me."

"Do it yourself," he throws back.

"I can't *reach* the buttons, Mr. I've-never-worn-a-fucking-dress-before-and-have-no-idea-how-one-actually-works."

He glares at me.

"Or—I could not wear it," I add.

After a moment, he approaches me. "Where are they?"

"The buttons?" I reply. "Down my back—along my spine."

Famine tosses his dagger onto the bed, freeing up his hands. Gruffly he grabs my good shoulder and turns me around so my back is facing him. I feel the brush of his fingertips as he pulls the material together. Clumsily, the Reaper tries and tries again to get the small cloth-covered buttons through the little loop openings that edge the fabric. My stomach tightens at his touch, and I can't help but feel his breath as it stirs the hair against my neck.

I should not be reacting this way to him—not when he literally just untied me from the bed.

A hundred and twenty years later, the Reaper finishes buttoning me up. I pull out the hair that's inadvertently gotten tucked into the dress and I turn around.

The horseman is already on his way out.

"Follow me," he calls over his shoulder.

I hesitate, my eyes moving to the bed where the Reaper tossed his blade only minutes ago. On a whim I lean over the bed and grasp the weapon, tucking it into one of my boots. Days ago I wasn't brave enough to hide a knife on my person. But a lot has changed in that time.

I take a couple steps, making sure I don't slice my ankle.

Am I really going to dare the horseman's wrath by doing this?

I think of the hours spent tied to the bed while dozens of people died.

Yes, I think I am.

Dagger now secured, I trudge out of the room.

Halfway down the hallway, Famine glances over his shoulder at me. I think he just means to make sure I'm behind him, but the moment he catches sight of me, he does a double take, stumbling to a halt.

Now *that's* a reaction.

Out here in the hallway, the candlelight better illuminates my outfit, and Famine uses that light to look me over, starting with the hem of my dress—which is in fact a deep red color—and moving his gaze up. He looks like he doesn't know what hit him.

I raise an eyebrow. "Are you sure you don't like sex?" I say. "You're looking at me as though you might."

The horseman rips his gaze from my body, meeting my eyes. "I am not looking at you in *any* way"

"Yep, you are. You definitely look like you could bang one out. I'm real good at quickies—"

Famine growls—*growls!*—in response, much to my delight.

"Enough of this, Ana." His gaze drops to my borrowed boots, and his irritated expression deepens.

"What?" I say defensively. "You gave me a dress, not shoes."

He looks heavenward, then resumes walking once more. "C'mon, flower."

"You still haven't told me where we're going." Earlier, he had mentioned some sort of celebration in passing, but I haven't heard anything about it since. The dress, however, does seem to fit the occasion.

Famine doesn't respond, and a wave of trepidation passes over me. Whatever his plans are, they can't possibly be good.

Outside, his horse is already waiting for him, along with several of his men. The greasy stench of smoke and charred bodies is stronger out here, and I have to swallow back my rising bile.

Several of the guards' eyes go to my exposed legs. One of them glances from my calves to my face, and I raise my eyebrows at him.

I mean, *really?* We are literally breathing in human remains and he wants to check out a pair of shapely legs?

For shame.

The Reaper steps in front of me. "You want a dress too?" he asks the offending man.

I raise my eyebrows. I assumed the horseman didn't notice these sorts of nonverbal interactions.

Apparently, I was wrong.

The man sputters some response.

"No?" the horseman interrupts. "Then stop eye-fucking the girl."

With that, the Reaper grabs me by the waist and hauls me onto his steed. A second later he follows me up, and then we're riding off into the darkness.

I'm still processing that little exchange.

I glance over my shoulder at Famine. "You know what eye-fucking is?" I have the oddest urge to laugh.

The Reaper looks down at me. "I wasn't born yesterday."

I gaze at him a little longer, and then I grin, my lips spreading wide.

"What?" he says.

"Nothing."

"*What?*"

"If I didn't know better, I'd say you were jealous."

"Flower, I don't *get* jealous."

"Uh huh."

"What is that tone?" he demands.

"What tone?" I ask innocently.

"Do you not believe me?" Famine's voice rises with his outrage, and it is music to my ears. *This* is what I'd been missing with the Reaper. I can play a man like a hand of cards, but a horseman ... I thought I was out of my element, but it seems as though they too can behave like men.

"I'm not jealous," he insists.

"Sure," I say, tucking a lock of dark hair behind my ear.

"Damn you, Ana. Stop toying with your voice. I'm *not* jealous."

"I'm not the one getting worked up," I say, swinging my feet back and forth. God but I'm enjoying this.

Famine lets out a frustrated growl, but doesn't respond.

I smile for the rest of the ride.

Chapter 23

Eventually, we come to an enormous warehouse, something made of corrugated iron sheeting and small, smudged windows. It's clearly a structure from *before*, when large quantities of goods needed to be stored and processed.

Now, however, soft candlelight glows from within, and dozens and dozens of people are streaming into the building. By the looks of their formal attire, Famine's men didn't round them up so much as they got the word out that the horseman was hosting some sort of celebration tonight.

I don't know just how many of the city's residents were actually foolish enough to come. It looks like a lot, but then again, Registro is a large city; perhaps this is just a small portion of its citizens. I hope the vast majority of the town knew better than to fall for this horseman's tricks. I hope they're fleeing now, using this time to pack up their things and *run*.

Still, a wave of nausea rolls through me at the sight of all of the people who *did* decide to come here tonight, either out of curiosity or misplaced faith.

Have none of them noticed the burning bonfire at

Famine's new estate, or the fact that the people who went to see the horsemen haven't been heard from since?

"What are you planning?" I say to the Reaper as he rides us up to the front of the building.

"Always so fearful of me," he muses, pulling his horse to a stop. "Perhaps I simply want to enjoy myself the way humans do."

He slips off his steed, his scythe at his back. I stare at the curving blade; it looks so much more threatening here amongst all these people.

Famine turns and reaches up for me.

"What are you going to do to them?" I whisper.

"That is not for you to concern yourself with."

"Famine," I say, my eyes pleading with him.

His expression is merciless. "Off."

"I can't watch any more bloodshed," I say. "I *won't*."

The horseman grabs me roughly then, dragging me off his steed. I wince a little as my bad shoulder is jostled.

He sets me down, but rather than letting me go, he steps in close. "I'll do what I want, flower," he says softly.

And now my earlier trepidation blooms into full-bodied dread.

Famine steers me towards the building, his hand on my uninjured shoulder. I move forward like a prisoner walking the plank.

We head inside, and the people around us move out of our way.

Someone has tried to make the massive warehouse look less like some old pile of corroded metal and more like a ballroom. Bright cloth has been draped around the room and hung from the rafters. Wood and iron chandeliers hang from metal crossbeams, their candles already dripping wax.

Platters of food lay along tables lining the room, and there are basins of water and huge barrels of what must be wine resting next to a pyramid of cups.

Across the room, a lavish chair has been set up—it's the only seat in the entire building, so it's clearly meant for Famine.

The horseman steers us towards it. Nearby, several guards loiter. The horseman gestures for them, and several hustle over.

"Get me another chair," the Reaper demands.

A couple of the men's eyes go to me, and I can see their confusion. *Why does she get special treatment?*

Sorry guys, I wish I knew the answer.

They hurry off to do Famine's bidding, and within minutes another chair is dragged inside and placed next to Famine's.

"Sit," the horseman tells me, releasing my shoulder.

I frown at him but take the seat.

The Reaper moves to his own chair, removing the scythe from his back before he sits. He lays his weapon across his legs, lounging back.

"Why are you doing this?" I say, staring out at the sea of people who are quickly filling the room. They keep to the edges, standing in nervous groups. A few brave souls have dared to serve themselves some food, but most people seem to be of the opinion that it's better to leave the food alone.

Fools! I want to shout at them. *Why did you stay when you could have fled? The horseman won't take pity on you. He doesn't know what pity is.*

Famine arches an eyebrow at me. "I thought you would want me to do something more human. Don't you mortals love parties?"

That answer only causes my heart to pound harder.

"Look," he says, gesturing to the tables laden with hors d'oeuvres and drinks. "I haven't even destroyed the food."

Yet.

We both know he will. He always does.

Whatever this is, it's another one of Famine's cruel tricks.

A band begins to play sambas, and it's an awful pairing—

this joyful music with the frightened faces of Registro's citizens.

I sit in my seat, beginning to squirm the longer nothing happens.

People—mothers, fathers, friends, neighbors—all of them are beginning to relax. Slowly, the noise in the room rises as people talk to each other.

Without warning, the Reaper grabs his scythe and rises from his throne, his bronze armor glinting in the candlelight.

All at once—*silence*. I've never seen a crowd go quiet that quickly.

He raises his arms. "Eat, dance, be merry," the horseman says, his gaze sweeping over them.

If Famine thought that his words would somehow jumpstart the evening, *he thought wrong*.

No one moves. People *were* eating—some were even being merry—but now no one is budging a centimeter. Even the music has stopped. If anything, I think the horseman reminded everyone that this *celebration* is a little too surreal to be trusted.

Famine sits back in his seat, clutching his weapon like a scepter, a frown on his face. The longer people stay pinned in place, the angrier his expression becomes.

"Damn you all," he finally says, slamming the base of his scythe down against the cracked concrete floor. "*Eat! Be merry! Dance!*"

Frightened into compliance, people begin to move, some shuffling towards the tables of food, a few creeping towards the open space in front of the band. I can see the whites of a few people's eyes.

It's still silent, so the Reaper points his weapon at the musicians. "You useless sacks of flesh, *do your jobs.*"

They scramble together, some discordant notes drifting off their instruments as they rush to make music. Once they begin playing a song, people move to the dance floor, woodenly beginning to dance.

My stomach squeezes at the sight and my skin feels clammy, like I've been caught doing something I shouldn't.

The horseman glares at them all, a dark look on his face. That, more than anything, puts me on edge. The way Famine stares at them ... like a panther sizing up prey.

All of a sudden, the horseman turns to me, and my heart skips a beat at the predatory look in his eyes.

"Well?" he says.

"Well what?" I ask.

"I was referring to you too. *Dance.*" He nods to the space ahead of us.

In this mockery of a party? I don't *think* so.

"With who?" I say. "You?" I laugh, though the sound rings false. "I'm not just going to go out there alone. Dancing is for couples."

I don't actually believe that, but the thought of dancing right now makes me vaguely ill.

Famine arches an eyebrow, a slow, wicked smile spreading across his face. Rather than answering me, he reaches out a hand.

I eye it, then him, then it again. "What are you doing?"

"You wanted a partner." He says it slowly, like I'm the town idiot.

"You *can't* be serious."

The horseman stands, strapping his weapon to his back once more. He moves in front of me, then extends his hand once more.

Holy shit. He *is* serious.

I stare at that hand. The petty part of me wants to say *no*, just to enjoy humiliating the Reaper for a few seconds, but the rational, frightened part of me knows that making a mockery of this man won't end well for me.

So I take his hand.

This must be another one of the horseman's tricks. But

then he leads me onto the dance floor, where dozens of people are stiffly dancing. They give us wide berth.

"Do you even know how to dance?" I ask.

In response, Famine pulls me to him, placing a hand on my waist. The other clasps my hand.

"You act as though these irrelevant human activities of yours are somehow hard." As the horseman speaks, he begins to lead me in a dance. It's nothing formal or structured, and yet his movements have an expert flow to them. He moves like a river over rocks, and again I'm reminded of his otherness.

Haltingly, I follow the Reaper's lead. I don't know where to put my free hand. Eventually I rest it on top of an armor covered shoulder.

For a few minutes I simply stare at my feet, trying to figure out the steps. But the more I look at my boots, the more I get distracted by the dark handle of Famine's dagger.

"They're not going to disappear," Famine says, his voice haughty.

I jolt, feeling like I got caught red-handed. I glance up at the horseman, wide-eyed.

"Your feet," he clarifies.

I stare into his luminous green eyes. The candlelight makes them shine like gemstones.

"This is ridiculous," I murmur, mostly to drag my mind away from the fact that the candlelight is doing more than just making his eyes glow. Every pleasing plane of his face is highlighted by the light, and his caramel hair shines nearly as brightly as his armor.

"This is your world and your customs," he says. "I'm merely indulging in them."

Right about now, I'm supposed to snap out some cunning retort, or look away and disengage. I do neither. I'm pinned under that spellbinding gaze of his.

The intense way Famine is looking at me makes me feel

like there's lightning in my veins. And I can't help but notice how, despite the cruel curve of his lips, the Reaper is unimaginably handsome.

Finally, I tear my eyes away, staring at everyone and everything else but him.

"Uncomfortable?" he asks, squeezing my hand.

"More than a little," I admit.

"Good. It means you haven't forgotten what I am."

I press my lips together. He thinks *that's* the reason I'm uncomfortable? If only he realized that despite how awful he is, I'd still be half down to fuck the smirk off his face. And not for the sake of humanity. Staring at him makes me forget what a shitty person he is.

His gaze stays on me as we move, and I fight to ignore it. It helps that every few seconds I accidentally step on Famine's feet. That's distracting enough to ignore his gaze.

"Has anyone told you that you are complete shit at dancing?" he asks, drawing my attention back to him.

"I can always count on you for a compliment," I say sarcastically.

"Why *are* you so terrible at this?" Famine asks, curious.

"I was paid to fuck people, not to teach them the samba."

The song ends, and I pull my hands back. The Reaper, meanwhile, is slower to release me, his hand lingering on my waist.

His fingers press in, and he pulls me towards him. "Stay close," he whispers into my ear.

I narrow my eyes at him. "Why?"

The corner of his mouth curves up. After a moment, his gaze lifts from me, taking in the rest of the room. And just like that, my pulse begins to gallop away.

He brushes past me, returning to his chair, and I'm left on the dancefloor, staring after him.

"What does he have over you?" a male voice asks.

I nearly jump at the sound. I glance over at the man who's

crept up to my side. It's one of Famine's guards—I think it might be the same one who was staring at my legs earlier.

"What?" I ask, confused.

"What does he have over you?" the man repeats. "Or are you with him by choice?"

I scrutinize him. "Why do you care?" I say.

The man lifts a shoulder in response, his gaze flitting over my face. He's taken a little too much interest in me.

I edge away from him.

The Reaper lounges in his chair, one leg thrown over his knee, his fingers drumming along the armrest. His agitation is back. The horseman stares at the room full of people as though they sicken him. It doesn't seem to matter that he forced them here, or that many of them appear worried.

My heart is racing and my breath is coming fast. I'm acutely aware of the dagger in my boot.

Next to me, Famine's guard lingers, like he has more to say but he needs to recapture my attention.

I turn to him. "What are you still doing next to me?"

Ugh, I sound like the Reaper. That infernal bastard is rubbing off on me.

The guard opens his mouth, his expression caught somewhere between ire and defensiveness.

"*Enough*," Famine says, interrupting us. His voice booms across the room.

The music cuts off and the people end their chatter. In the silence, the hairs along my arms rise.

Finally the guard moves away from me—though he does look reluctant to do so—taking up post near one of the doorways.

I glance over at Famine, who still sits in his chair, his scythe in his hand. That horrible feeling in the pit of my stomach is back.

"Enough of this farce," he says softer now, his voice velvety and sinister. "You all know who I am. You all seek to placate me. But I see your excess, I recognize the hunger and greed that drives you all. It *sickens* me."

Raising his scythe, he pounds its base against the floor.

Beneath our feet, the concrete floor cracks, fissures opening along its surface, each one spreading out from the Reaper like the rays of a sun.

People let out surprised screams and many begin to rush towards the doors, but Famine's guards are barring the exits.

The horseman smiles.

It's that grin that cuts through my rising fear.

Stop him.

My heart feels like it's in my throat as I reach for my dagger. I cut my leg as I withdraw it from my boot, but the pain barely registers over the ringing in my ears.

Stop him before it's too late.

I stride forward, closing in on Famine. His eyes flick up to me, but his mind is clearly elsewhere.

Stop him. Now.

I step right up to the horseman, and I slam my knife down on Famine's prone hand with as much force as I can muster. It cuts through flesh and muscle, the blade pinning the horseman to his chair.

Immediately, the earth stops shaking and the fissures halt.

Famine sucks in a sharp breath as I stagger away. He shifts his attention to the wound.

I can hear nothing aside from my own ragged breathing as I wait for him to react.

After several long seconds, the Reaper's eyes lift, meeting mine. I expect to see anger in them; instead, I see betrayal.

"That was a *mistake*," he says he says softly.

Beneath me the floor cracks open once more, and a sharp, vined thing rises from the depths. I only have time to register that at least his ire is now focused on me before the plant wraps itself around me, squeezing and squeezing.

Desperately, I try to rip free from the plant, but the

movement only seems to make it tighten its hold. Thorns bloom along the vines, poking me in a dozen different places.

At the sight, someone shrieks, and then it sounds like *everyone* is shouting. People begin to stampede once more, moving as fast as they can for the exits.

The Reaper lays his scythe across his lap, then reaches for the dagger he's been impaled with. Calmly, Famine pulls the blade out from his hand, shooting me a considering look as he tosses it aside.

"No one's going anywhere," he says casually. Again, his voice seems to carry over the rising mayhem.

Thick, brambly shadows rise beyond the windows, growing and growing like looming specters. Someone in their desperate attempt to escape shatters one of the windows in front of these shadows, and it's only then that I realize that what I'm seeing outside are bushes—bushes that have grown so dense and tall that they effectively block off the exits.

Outside, the sky flickers, backlighting these plants. An instant later, thunder booms overhead.

Famine stands, grabbing his scythe and spinning it in his hand like he's getting familiar with its weight. His bronze armor flickers and shines under the candlelight as he moves.

"Come now," he says to the panicking room. "The party is only just getting started."

The earth trembles again, and the floor all but crumbles apart. Dozens and dozens of plants rise from the depths, ensnaring person after person, until the entire ballroom seems to be a thrashing jungle of sorts. The screams are almost deafening as people struggle fruitlessly to get out.

I strain against my own plant that binds me tight, the thorns digging into my skin.

"Stop!" I beg the horseman.

Famine glances over at me, an angry glint in his eyes. "You I'll deal with later."

He faces the crowd of trapped guests, his attention eliciting another round of petrified screams. Everything about Famine in this moment is menacing—his body, his weapon, his expression.

Outside, lightening continues to flash and thunder continues to boom. Within seconds rain begins pattering on the corrugated iron roof, getting louder by the second.

Slowly the horseman stalks forward, making his way towards a large man with heavy jowls who's bound up in a squat tree. I see the man struggle to get away, but it's useless.

The horseman grasps the man's face, his fingers digging into his cheeks. "Do *you* want me to stop?" the Reaper asks. I can barely hear him over the pounding rain and the shouts and sobs echoing through the room.

The man nods vigorously.

Famine studies him. "Hmmm ... And what would you be willing to do to make me stop?" he asks.

The man squirms under his gaze. "I-I'll do *anything*."

"Will you now?" Famine says. The Reaper glances over at me and arches a brow, like this is some inside joke.

"Are you sure about that?" the Reaper presses, his attention returning to his victim.

The man is visibly sweating, but he manages a nod.

"Alright," Famine says. "I'll stop."

The man looks relieved.

"But."

I tense. Here it is, the barbed offer I've come to expect from the horseman.

"If you want me to save all these people," Famine says. "I need something from you."

Famine might be a divine creature, but right now, he sounds like the devil of old.

"Anything," his captive says again.

"Your life for theirs," the Reaper says.

My mouth goes dry. The horseman likes doing this—testing the limits of our humanity, all so that he can prove some point about how shitty humans really are.

The man pauses. There's terror in his eyes. His gaze sweeps over the other people who are likewise caught in the grip of Famine's lethal plants.

Before the man can respond, the tree that holds him fast now releases him. He stumbles forward, just barely managing to catch himself before he falls.

"Well?" the Reaper says. "On your knees then." As he speaks, Famine spins his scythe again, the blade glinting in the candlelight.

The man is visibly shaking, his eyes locked on the Reaper's blade. He doesn't move to his knees.

Famine takes a step towards him, and the man bolts, heading for the guarded doorway.

"As I thought."

In six quick strides, the horseman is upon him. The Reaper swings that mighty scythe of his, and in one sweeping stroke he beheads the man.

The room erupts in a fresh wave of screams, these ones louder and more desperate than ever.

My nausea rises as the man's head hits the ground with a wet thud, and I nearly sick myself at the sight of his mouth opening and closing in shock.

There's blood everywhere, and the room is filled with the piercing cries of all the other trapped humans.

"You were *all* given a chance at redemption," Famine announces, his gaze sweeping over them, "but your will is weak."

The Reaper moves away from the body, towards another person, this one a woman.

She opens her mouth. "No—"

Her plea is cut short. Famine swings his scythe, separating the woman's head from her shoulders. Blood sprays as the body collapses into the plant holding her.

My screams now join the others.

The horseman has gotten a taste for death.

Famine moves onto the next person and then the next and the next, that terrible weapon cutting each one down. Mercilessly he executes the trapped townspeople until the floor shines with blood. Those he doesn't get to are slowly squeezed tighter and tighter by the trees and shrubs until I hear the snap of bones.

And now the cries aren't just terrified, they're *agonized*.

At some point my voice grows hoarse from screaming, and I have to close my eyes against the carnage. It's all so excessively cruel.

The plant caging me in has grown uncomfortably tight, but unlike some of the other people in the room, it hasn't broken any bones or crushed my lungs.

It seems like an eternity passes before the warehouse grows silent. The only noise left is the harsh patter of rain and my sobs. Even then, I keep my eyes closed.

I hear the wet thud of Famine's boots as he walks through blood towards me. A whimper leaves my lips, and a tear tracks down my cheek.

"Open your eyes, Ana."

I shake my head.

The plant holding me now releases its grip. I've been caught up in it for so long that my bloodless legs fold under me, too weak to keep me standing. Before I hit the ground, the Reaper catches me.

Now I do open my eyes and look up at his stormy ones. Behind his head his scythe looms, secured to his back once more.

I can smell the blood on him, and I can feel it in the wet press of his hands on my body.

Another frightened tear slips out. I thought I was brave, stabbing his hand earlier. I foolishly thought that if I hurt him, I might actually be able to direct his anger away from these people and onto me.

Instead I only enflamed his fury.

"You're the best of humanity I've seen so far," Famine's voice is silken, "and I have to say, I'm not too impressed."

With that, he scoops me into his arms and begins heading towards the door, kicking the odd head out of his way as he does so. Bile rises up my throat once more.

"Put me down," I say, a tremor in my voice.

"So you can stab me again?" He huffs out a laugh. I can hear the soft splash of his boots as they step through puddles of blood. "I don't think so."

The only people who are left standing are Famine's men. They stare stoically at the carnage, but inside they must be freaking out. I know *I'm* freaking out, and I've already seen this many times before.

"Why are you the way you are?" I whisper staring up at his blood-speckled jawline.

Mean. Evil.

That jawline seems to harden as he glances down at me. "Why are you the way you are?" he retorts. "You fucking stabbed me in my hand."

"So you killed an entire room for it?"

"I was going to kill them anyway." As he walks, the trees and bushes part, making a walkway of sorts for us.

"How can you possibly be a heavenly thing?" I ask as we leave the building. Outside, the rain is coming down hard, soaking me within seconds. "You meet compassion with violence, and mercy with betrayal." More tears slip out. "If there's one thing in my life I regret, it's saving you. And if I could go back and undo it all, I would."

"You would choose to not help me?" Famine says, glancing down at me, rain dripping off his face. Just from his tone and the look in his eyes, I know I've hit on something sensitive.

"After what you've done?" I say. "*In an instant.*"

"After what *I've* done?" A muscle in Famine's cheek jumps, and the rain seems to come down harder. "This is not a war I started, it's just the one I'm ending."

I glare up at him, my dark hair plastered to my cheeks. "What you're doing isn't ending some war, it's just evil for the sake of evil."

Overhead, the sky flashes, and for an instant Famine's face looks inhumanly harsh.

"How *dare* you judge me—you, who are nothing," the Reaper says, coming to a stop. "Nothing but self-aware stardust. In a hundred years you and your petty, self-important beliefs will be gone, your memory cast from the earth, and everything that makes you *you* will be scattered to the winds. And still I will exist as I always have."

"Am I supposed to be upset by that?" I say. "That in one hundred years you'll still exist as this, soulless, festering thing, while for once in my life I'll get some goddamn rest?"

Famine flashes me an angry look. A second later he lifts me up, and for an instant I think he's going to hurt me just as he has everyone else. But then I realize that his horse is right behind me, blending into the dark night.

He sets me down hard on the seat, and I've only just managed to adjust myself when Famine follows me up, his body pressing in close.

Grabbing the reins, he clicks his tongue, and his horse takes off.

The rain and wind whips against my face, but I hardly feel it. I've gone numb. Maybe that's why I don't immediately notice that Famine's cutting through fields rather than taking the main road. The crops rise around us like phantoms in the darkness.

The sky flashes, lighting up the world. For an instant I can clearly see stalks of sugarcane around us, but as I stare at them, they begin to wither, their leaves looking like long, curling claws reaching for me.

The sky flashes again and again, and the thunder seems to fill the whole sky. Rain leaks from the heavens like blood from an artery.

It's a nightmarish ride, made all the worse by the Reaper's dark, forbidding presence at my back.

I quake when I see our house in the distance, lit up by candlelight. We're going back, and it's an awful sensation, to survive all this death—like I've missed the boat to the afterlife and all that's left for me is to waste away here.

The horseman nearly rides us into the house before pulling his horse up short. A few guards meander about the property, but now that we've arrived, they start to approach us. They must see something in Famine's expression, however, because they stop several meters away from us, not daring to come any closer.

The Reaper swings himself off his steed, and before I can so much as move, he reaches up and hauls me off his horse as well.

I glare at him. "I can get off on my own."

"Can you now? That's news to me. You're always harping on getting everyone else off."

Wait, was that a sex joke?

I don't have more than a moment to process that before Famine tows me by the wrist into the house, leading me back to the room I was tied up in all day.

Naturally, I fight against his hold, trying to yank my wrist free. It doesn't deter the horseman. If anything, I get the impression that he wants a knock-down drag-out fight.

When we get to the room, he practically tosses me inside, and I stumble forward before whipping around.

If he wants a fucking fight, I will give him one. Already I'm fantasizing about slamming these big-ass boots into his nutsack.

He follows me into my room, his body dripping with rainwater. I, too am soaking wet, the water sliding down my legs.

"Well?" I say angrily. "Why aren't you leaving?"

The Reaper scowls at me, looking like he's about to say something. Instead, he walks back to the door and kicks it shut with his booted heel. Then he wheels about, unholstering his scythe and tossing it on the bed.

"I'll leave when I want to leave," he says.

Anger makes my face flush. "Get *out*."

He stalks forward, ignoring my words altogether. "You look at me like I'm a monster, but I'm not the one who spent years inflicting torture on a helpless prisoner. The horrors I endured—"

"You think I don't know pain?" I say over him. My voice comes out louder and angrier than I intend. "I lost both my parents by the time I was a teenager, my aunt abused me, and my cousins did nothing to stop her, but that didn't prevent me from mourning them all when you killed my entire town.

"And then, left with nothing, I had to fend for myself, and I consider myself *lucky* that my madam was the one who found me.

"I was seventeen when I started to sell my body. *Seventeen.* Still just a teenager."

I step forward as I talk, closing the distance between us. "You think I don't know pain? Degradation? I could sit here all night telling you about the horrors *I've* endured—the clients who beat me, who raped me, who told me I was worthless all while using me. Just because it hasn't completely broken me doesn't mean I don't understand all the ways we can hurt one another.

"So don't act like you invented pain. It's an insult to the rest of us."

The more I talk, the more Famine's anger seems to drain from his face. By the time I finish—my chest heaving with my emotions, angry tears pricking at my eyes—his expression is almost soft.

You've felt it too, his face seems to say. *The horror of suffering.* He looks both comforted and oddly devastated by that.

"See?" he says quietly. "Look how awful your kind is, that they would hurt their young. Tell me I am not justified in killing them all."

I level him a long look. "You're not justified in killing us all."

He takes a step forward, his armor brushing against my chest.

"And what *do* you think I am justified to do, little flower?"

"Leave us be. If we're awful and doomed to die, we'll kill ourselves off. If we're not, then we won't." As I speak, one of those angry tears of mine slips out. Hopefully the last one. I'm tired of crying in front of this man.

The Reaper reaches up a hand. He pauses for a moment, staring at that tear, then he wipes it away.

I don't know what to make of this situation—or of him for that matter. Not two hours ago he gruesomely killed an entire warehouse full of people. Tomorrow he'll probably finish off the rest of the city. Why is he bothering to be gentle with me? What's the point?

Famine is still standing way too close, and for a moment, his gaze drops to my lips.

It's a shock to see the obvious hunger in his eyes.

I know that look.

But just when I think he might act on whatever heated thoughts are running through his head, he takes my hand and leads me out of the room and into the living room, where a large fire roars in the fireplace. He moves us over to it.

"Sit," he says.

I scowl, but I do as he says.

The Reaper releases my hand, heading into the dimly lit kitchen. He's gone long enough for me to turn my attention to the fire.

I twist my hair, squeezing the water from the curly locks.

I'm still soaking wet, but the fire more than makes up for the slight chill.

Famine returns with a pitcher, a basin, and a cloth. He comes to my side and sets the items down.

"What are you doing?" I ask.

"You're hurt."

I do in fact have dozens of little cuts from the nasty plant I was restrained in. And then there's my injured shoulder.

"Why do you care?" I say.

"I don't know." He frowns as he speaks.

The Reaper pours the water from the pitcher into the basin, and dips the cloth in. Then, taking my arm, he begins to clean my wounds, brushing the washcloth over the small, bleeding puncture marks that dot my skin.

This is ridiculous.

I try to withdraw my hand, but the horseman holds it fast, refusing to stop, and I'm left watching him work.

Methodically, he cleans one of my arms, then the other, being extra diligent with my shoulder wound. He then moves on to my neck and chest. As he does so, I catch sight of his injured hand. It's still open, still bloody, but he's made no mention of it and gives no indication that it hurts. But it must. I know he feels pain.

And I feel a whisper of shame. Even this monster feels more remorse for what he did to me than I do for what I did to him.

You also haven't killed hundreds of thousands of people.

There is that.

Famine pauses halfway through, shucking off his armor. Beneath the metal, his wet shirt is plastered to his chest. After a moment, he removes this too.

I jolt a little at the sight of him. For the first time in five years, I see his bare flesh and the strange, glowing green tattoos that are etched onto it.

Lines and lines of them snake around his wrists like shackles, and more rows of them drape over his shoulders and around his pecs, giving the markings the appearance of a heavy plated necklace.

The symbols look like writing, but it's written in no language I've ever seen.

Famine resumes cleaning my wounds, and I continue to stare at his chest. Before, I thought that Famine looked like some mythical prince. Now he looks far more like the archaic, otherworldly creature he is.

"*Inniv jataxiva evawa paruv Eziel,*" he says.

My breath catches for a moment as the words wash over me, drawing out goosebumps.

"*The hand of god falls heavy,*" he translates. His eyes flick to mine. "You were wondering what they said, weren't you?"

I nod, my brows drawing together.

"What langua—"

"The one God speaks."

I pause, staring at the words a little longer.

"*I shall take their crops and cast them out, so that nothing may grow,*" Famine continues without my prompting. "*And many shall hunger, and many shall perish. For such is the will of God.*"

There it is, the proof that this is supposed to happen.

It's quiet for a long time. Then, softer, Famine says, "I was always meant to be the cruel one." His eyes flick to me, and for once there's something more than seething anger in those eerie green irises. "Pestilence, for all his disease, has always been perversely drawn to humans. And War was made from human desires. Terrible as my brothers are, I am worse."

After all I've seen the Reaper do, I believe him. Yet if you had asked me which of the four brothers was most awful, I wouldn't have placed Famine at the top of that list.

"How could you possibly be worse than Pestilence and War?" I ask.

He finishes cleaning my wounds, then sets the cloth aside. Sitting back on his haunches, he slings his arms over his knees. "Before your kind built fancy buildings and created technology that rivaled God—before that, I existed."

I've heard plenty of stories of the days that preceded the horsemen. But I haven't heard much about the world before *that*. The deep past that he's alluding to.

"Humans would pray to me, they would sacrifice to me, they would kill and die for me." Famine's eyes are too bright as he tells me this; he doesn't look sane. "They gave their lives to me so that I might spare the rest of their kind."

His words make me think of the man tonight—the one who was asked to die for the rest of us. He wasn't able to do it, but Famine makes it sound like others once regularly did so.

"And did you?" I ask. "Did you spare them?"

He lifts a shoulder. "Sometimes."

Sometimes is better than *never*, which is his current track record. But I get it. This horseman has always been unforgiving and conscienceless. Or maybe thinking of him like that is itself forcing him to fit some human model when he's telling me that sometimes famine just occurs in nature. Good and evil have nothing to do with it.

"I'm older than many of the mountains we've passed," he says. "I have seen the world before humans ever touched it."

And he will see the world after humans leave it.

"And what about Death?" I ask, switching topics a little.

"What about him?" the Reaper asks.

"You mentioned how you were worse than Pestilence and War," I say, "but what about Death?"

Famine holds my gaze for a long minute, then gives me a slight nod, like he's conceding a point to me. "Nothing is worse than him."

Chapter 24

We leave the next day, long after Famine's men have already headed out.

I use the extra time to find a more reasonable outfit for myself—a pair of jeans that actually fit (I'm keeping them forever) and a black shirt. I even have enough time to make myself a pot of coffee. I hum away as I heat up water over the stove.

"You seem inappropriately happy."

I scream, whirling around and clutching my chest just as Famine strides into the room, his scales in hand.

"Oh my God, give a girl some warning," I say leaning back against the stove for a split second before the hot metal has me jerking away from it.

"Is that what you say to all your clients?" Famine says, setting his scales on the table.

I narrow my eyes at him. "Is that another sex joke?"

The corner of his mouth curls up.

I look at him curiously. "But I thought ... "

I thought that Famine didn't do sex. Of course, you don't have to bang a human to poke fun at the act.

Rather than finishing my question, my gaze moves over the Reaper's face. Right now he's particularly destabilizing, mostly because he seems so ... not horrible. I don't really know what to make of it, just as I don't really know what to make of his gentleness last night.

My gaze goes to the scales on the table. Unlike his armor and his scythe, the two metal pans look old and worn.

"Why do you never keep those out?" I ask. In the time I've traveled with the horseman, I've only seen his scales a few times.

"I have them out now."

I give him a look. "You know what I mean."

He glances down at the scales, considering them. "Perhaps I care more about death than I do justice."

"Is that what they're for?" I ask. "Justice?" I assumed they were for weighing shit.

He jerks his chin to the stove behind me. "Your water is boiling."

I turn back to the pot, cursing under my breath. I feel flustered and off-kilter, and Famine is to blame.

"Drink your coffee," the Reaper says at my back. "We'll be leaving soon."

He begins to walk away, then pauses. "Oh," he says over his shoulder, "and while you're at it, pour me a cup."

Throughout our ride, I keep looking over my shoulder at Famine.

"What?" he finally demands, his gaze moving down to me.

I shake my head.

He sighs. "Whatever's on your mind, just say it."

"You're different today."

He arches one eyebrow, his green eyes glittering. "Different how?"

"I don't know," I mutter, studying his face as though it holds the answers. "That's what I'm trying to figure out."

196

Could it have simply been what I said last night? Famine has made an exception of me since we reunited, but when I explained a bit about my own troubled past, his demeanor shifted, and it hasn't shifted back.

And now he's been acting ... not *nicer*, necessarily, but—I don't know—more relatable maybe?

We spend the whole day traveling. Long after the sun has set, we're still in the saddle. Just when I'm sure Famine is going to make me sleep on his horse again, he turns off the highway.

"What are you doing?" I yawn.

"Finding a place for you to rest." He doesn't sound particularly pleased by this.

My stomach drops at that. "I don't want to stop." Not if it means Famine might kill someone else.

"Don't be ridiculous," he says. "I know you're tired."

"I'm fine, I swear."

There's a long pause, then—

"Whatever stranger you seek to protect, they will die anyway. The moment we pass them, their lands will blacken, the soil will turn unforgiving. A quick death is kinder."

I shake my head. "Please. Just ride on."

But he doesn't. A mere fifteen minutes later the horseman directs his steed to a dark structure. Famine rides up to what appears to be a home and hops off his mount.

I'm not getting off the horse, I'm *not*.

But then Famine grabs me by the waist and pulls me easily off his steed.

Setting me down, he holds me close, and I stare into his eyes.

"Please don't, Famine."

He sighs. "While I appreciate that you always assume the worst of me, you're wrong this time."

I frown, confused. "I don't understand ..."

"Go inside and see for yourself."

I glance at the ominous structure, and I almost say, *you first*. But then, I know how that story ends.

With lots and lots of dead bodies.

Swallowing down my fear, I head towards the door. It's only once I'm standing on the stoop that I understand what the Reaper meant.

Overgrown shrubs press against the doorway, almost completely blocking it from view.

Famine steps up next to me and brushes the plants aside with his hand. It's too dark to see anything clearly, but the plants seem to be curling back in on themselves to reveal the rotted front door.

Wow, uh, super uneager to touch that doorknob ...

I end up not having to. The Reaper steps past me and turns the knob. The door swings open, and then falls off completely

"Charming," Famine says.

I give the abandoned house a skeptical look. I really don't want to go in. The sexual favors I'd commit right about now for a nice damn bed.

With a sigh, I step inside.

Dead leaves crunch under my boots, and in the distance I hear something scuttle.

It smells like mildew and rot, and the few things my hands brush feel sticky, like the process of this house unmaking itself is messy.

Can one sleep standing up? Because right now I'm sort of tempted to try.

Famine enters behind me, and I hear him kick something aside with his boot. I hear a squeak and a scampering sound as some unseen creature slips away.

I wander into what must've been the kitchen. There's an old icebox in the corner, its surface banged up and tarnished. The cupboards are peeling paint and a couple of them lie on the floor.

I leave the room and wander into another, where an old washing machine rests on its side, the door of it hanging open. Pretty sure there's a nest of some sort inside the thing ...

Seriously, fuck this place.

Famine toes a broken pot. "Still want to sleep here?"

I glare at him. "You did this on purpose."

The horseman kicks the pot out of the way. "Did what? Pick an abandoned house for you to sleep in? Little flower, don't insult me—this was all your idea. But if you don't like it, I'll get my horse—" He begins to walk back towards the door.

"*Wait*," I call out after him. If it's between this and another death, I can do this.

Famine turns back to face me. "*Really*," he says, raising his eyebrows. "You really want to do this?"

"It's ... it's not so bad," I say, sweeping debris aside with my foot to make a spot for myself on the ground.

He scoffs in response.

"I thought you of all people might like a place devoid of humans," I snap, sitting down. It smells like vermin in here. *Wet* vermin. Ugh.

"How is this place devoid of humans? Everything about it was made for and by them." He makes a face, and to himself he grumbles, "The only thing worse than human creations are *festering* human creations." He punctuates his words by crushing something under his boot.

But even as he speaks, the horseman sits down near me, leaning his back against a nearby wall and crossing his arms over his chest. It can't be very comfortable wearing all that armor right now, but he doesn't complain and he doesn't make a move to take any of it off.

I guess we're really doing this.

Might as well get comfortable.

I lie down, putting my head in his lap. Immediately, his body goes rigid.

"What are you doing?" he demands.

"Calm your tits," I say, settling in. "I'm not trying to steal your virginity. You just happen to be the cleanest thing in this house."

He doesn't say anything to that, but he also doesn't push my head off his legs.

"I don't have an appetite for mortal flesh," he warns.

Imagine that—Famine not having an appetite.

"Why would you even say something like that?" I ask, curious. As I speak, I remember how he stared at my lips last night. He looked hungry then ...

"You always bring the subject of sex up," he says, "like you expect me to succumb to some base nature of mine."

"You've succumbed to your anger," I say. "Is lust really so different?"

"It's not the same thing." He sounds defensive.

"Hmmm ..." I say.

"We were talking about *your* weaknesses," he says. "Not mine."

"Ah, yes," I shift, my cheek brushing against his inner thigh. "My weakness for sex."

There's a beat of silence. Then—

"Posturing doesn't suit you, flower."

"Oh, I'm *posturing* now?" I raise my eyebrows as I speak. To give him some credit, I've fashioned my weakness into a weapon. In a world where people believe an appetite for sex is a sin, I've wielded my sexuality like a sword.

"Beneath this ... *image* you've built for yourself, you're someone else entirely," the horseman says, "aren't you?"

I glance up at him. "We are *all* someone else," I say.

I've seen men's souls laid bare in the bedroom, and the biggest thing I've learned is that people are not what they seem. I've nearly been killed by a man who had a reputation for being kind, and a local criminal paid me to hold him all night, just so that he could cry in my arms.

Famine meets my eyes, and right here in the darkness, all of *his* posturing is gone. His hate and anger are a distant memory.

We hold each other's gazes for longer than we should. Long enough to notice that even with his armor on, the glow of his glyphs still subtly illuminates his chin and cheeks.

"Is there anything about us humans that you do like?" I finally ask.

"I like your stories," he admits, his voice like velvet in the darkness.

"*Our stories?*" I say, incredulous.

"Don't sound so shocked."

"Stories are the most human thing about humans. Of course I'm shocked."

He doesn't have anything to say to that.

"What sort of stories do you like?" I ask.

"Ones where a lot of people die," he deadpans.

I reach out and give his chest a playful shove. "Get out of here. No you don't. I bet you like romance."

"No."

"I bet you do. I don't think anyone can resist a good romance."

"Stop it, Ana," he says. But I swear it sounds like there might be a slight smile to his voice.

Maybe I'm just imagining it.

"Well," I say, shifting myself to get more comfortable in his lap, "now you have to tell me one."

"No."

"C'mon, just one little bedtime story—and a head scratch. You know, as a peace offering for me not stealing your virginity."

"What makes you think I'm a virgin?" he says.

I gasp and sit up. "*You're not a virgin?*" How scandalous!

Famine pushes me back down on his lap. "Fine, I will tell you a story—"

"Tell me about your first time," I command.

"No."

"Fine. First times are always messy anyway. Tell me about your second time."

"*Ana.*"

I grin in the darkness. It was worth a shot.

"I'm *kidding*," I say. "Tell me a story you enjoy—with a head scratch," I add.

The Reaper stares down at me. "I don't even know what a head scratch is."

I take his hand and move it to my hair. "Here's my head, now, you scratch. Really, Famine, it's quite obvious."

His fingers freeze in my hair. Then, ever so slowly, they comb through my dark locks, quickly catching on kinks.

"Ow," I say.

That's the trouble with curly hair.

Ignoring me, the Reaper begins to play with my hair a little. It's definitely not a head scratch, but I'm distracted by it all the same.

"That story?" I prompt him.

"Impertinent girl," he says softly, not looking away from my hair. "Would you like me to tell you the tale of Ma'at?"

"What's Ma'at?" I ask.

"She's the ancient Egyptian goddess of harmony and justice."

"Ancient Egyptian?" I echo. I've heard of Egypt before, but *ancient* Egypt ... it sounds too far away in time and space to hold any value or meaning for me.

"Is she real?" I ask. If the four horsemen really exist, maybe other deities do too.

"The concept of her is real."

"Hmph." What a cop-out answer.

"Don't give me that noise," Famine says. "I was a concept just like Ma'at until I was given form."

"So she *is* real," I say.

"She, like me, is one of many human constructs. If God wanted her to represent divinity, He would've made her exist. It just so happens that me and my three brothers better fit His plan."

His plan to kill us all.

"Your explanation hurts my head," I say.

"You're not really supposed to understand these things."

Because you're a pathetic human.

He doesn't say that last part, but he was *definitely* thinking it.

"So do you know her—Ma'at?" I ask.

Famine sighs, like I've missed the point completely.

"Fine, fine, forget I asked. Now, tell me her story."

Famine's fingers run through my hair, snagging a bit. I wonder just how frizzy my hair is going to be once he's done.

"When the world was first spoken into creation, Ma'at was created with it. She was justice, harmony, peace and order given form—"

"So she *was* a person," I say.

"A goddess," Famine corrects, sounding a little miffed. "And only in Egyptian religion. She was a winged woman who wore an ostrich feather in her hair, which represented the straight and true path.

"To live a life in alignment with Ma'at meant to follow the spirit and flow of the universe."

Famine has a rich voice, one that pulls you in, and I listen, rapt, to the strange story he's telling.

"On the day you died, ancient Egyptians believed that your heart would be weighed against the feather of Ma'at. If you had lived a good, righteous life, your heart would be found to be lighter than her feather, and you would go on to an afterlife of eternal peace.

"But if you committed great evil, your heart would reveal its wicked deeds on the scale, and it would weigh more than the feather. Rather than moving on to a blissful afterlife, your heart would be fed to Ammut, the devourer, a hideous beast, and your soul would be forced to wander the earth, restless and lost, forever." The horseman falls silent, and I realize that's the end of his tale.

Of course Famine would enjoy that sort of story.

"Does it really work like that?" I ask. "The afterlife?"

The Reaper pauses.

"No," he finally says. "Not at all. Being human is all the pain and punishment a soul will ever endure. The rest ... the rest is much better. But only you fool humans would somehow think otherwise."

I let that soak in.

"That was a weird story. Why do you like it?"

Another pause, this one a bit longer. "I believe, if you think about it long enough, you'll figure it out."

Well, that sounds way too hard. *Pass.*

Chapter 25

The horseman must not move the entire night because when I wake up in the morning, I'm still asleep on his legs.

I blink, trying to focus my eyes.

"Fucking *finally*." Famine's voice drifts in, and blearily, I focus on him.

He stares down at me, looking very awake and very grumpy.

I sit up, shaking off the last of my sleep, then promptly groan, reaching a hand to my aching neck.

"Why didn't you push me off of you?" I complain. I'm going to have a kink in my neck *all* day.

"Oh, trust me, I fantasized about it, flower."

Now that I'm off of him, the horseman rises quickly, crossing the room like he's trying to put as much distance between us as possible.

My eyes sweep over our surroundings, and it might not be *me* he's fleeing. In the sobering light of day, this place is far worse than it was at night. The walls are covered in rings of mold and the corners of them are home to what I hope are abandoned wasp nests. The ceiling caves in precariously, and the ground is covered in droppings.

Famine saw all this and still he didn't shove me off his lap? *I* would've. I stare after where I last saw the horseman. If I didn't know any better, I'd say Famine was a gentleman.

What a disturbing thought.

I meet the Reaper outside, where he's checking his horse's straps.

"Where does your horse go?" I ask as I walk over.

Famine turns to me, his expression turbulent.

"You mean when I leave him alone?" he says. "Wherever he pleases, I imagine."

"And he just comes back to you when you need him?" I ask, rolling my injured shoulder absently; my injury feels much, much better. I guess a good night's sleep on the Reaper was all I needed. "You don't have to worry about him running off?"

"He may be a horse," Famine says, "but he wasn't born *of* horses. He was formed from the ether with one purpose and one purpose alone: to assist me in all ways."

That's all he says on the subject—it's all he says at all. He still wears that same, stormy expression when he lifts me onto his horse. Wordlessly, he gets on behind me and steers his horse back to the road.

Overhead, dark clouds gather on themselves, but it's not just the weather that feels ominous.

I can practically feel Famine's oppressive mood bearing down on me.

"So ..." I start.

Last night plays out in my mind. I still want to know about Famine's dirty little sex life—because I'm a snoop.

"I don't want to talk." As he speaks, the sky seems to visibly darken.

"But—"

"Don't push me," he cuts me off. As if to punctuate his thought, I hear a distant rumble, and one fat raindrop lands on my nose.

I glance up at the sky.

Wait. Is it possible that he has power over ... ?

"You're not a virgin," I say, staring up at the grey clouds.

"Do you suddenly not understand your own language? *I don't want to talk.*"

"Well, I *do*," I insist. "And I *really* want to discuss the fact that you've boned a woman before—or was it a man?" I gasp at the titillating thought. "Please tell me it was a man!"

Famine doesn't respond, and if anything, the sky seems to clear a bit.

Hmmm ...

"Or maybe we should talk about the fact that you let me sleep on your lap for an *entire night.*"

A fat drop of water lands on my cheek.

There we go.

At my back, the horseman goes rigid.

"One would almost think you cared about me ..." I say, baiting him.

Another raindrop hits my face—then another and another.

"*Enough.*"

The raindrops come faster and faster.

Wonder of wonders, *this is working.* And now I have not one, but two revelations to ponder over—the most obvious one being the fact that the horseman clearly has some power over the weather, which, holy shit is that spooky.

But then there's another revelation, which is somehow even more mind-blowing than Famine's ability to affect the weather.

"You *do* care about me, don't you?" I say, shocked.

Abruptly, the Reaper pulls on the reins, jerking his horse to a stop.

Without a word, he swings himself off his horse and walks away.

"Where are you going?" I call, fumbling to get myself out of the saddle. Awkwardly I do so, grimacing when the action tugs at my shoulder.

Overhead, the sky is turning worrisomely dark and the rain is coming down harder and harder, the raindrops stinging as they hit my skin.

"Wait!" I call after Famine, hurrying after him.

All at once he swivels around, facing me. "One of these days, your inability to listen is going to get you killed."

I step in so close to the horseman that our chests nearly brush. He's giving me an angry look.

I reach out and touch his cheek, for once not restraining my baser impulses. Just as he's beginning to rear back, surprised and a little horrified, my hand goes around his neck and I pull his head towards me.

Lifting to my tiptoes, I press my lips to his and kiss him.

Chapter 26

I don't know what I'm doing. I mean, I *do*—I've done this so many times I can kiss better than I can write my own name—but I don't know why I'm doing this now, with the horseman of all people.

For a long moment, Famine is stiff against my lips. Then, almost like he can't help it, I feel his mouth move against mine.

Sweet Mother of God, the horseman *knows how to kiss*—and he's responding to mine!

A bolt of lightning arcs down from the heavens. With a loud crack it hits a tree, fire and wood exploding on impact.

A surprised cry rips from my throat, and I rear back.

A split-second later, Famine stumbles away from me.

"What the *fuck*, Ana?" he says, his fingers going to his mouth.

Around us, hail begins to pelt down, the clusters growing larger by the second.

Cursing under his breath, the Reaper closes the distance between us once more, shielding my body with his own.

My eyes eventually move up to him. "You really can control

the weather," I say. I can't keep the wonder from my voice.

"What does that have to do with *anything?*" Famine says, glancing at me. After a moment, his eyebrows rise. "Is *that* why you kissed me? To test a damn theory of yours?" Even as he asks, his gaze strays back to my lips.

I can practically feel the heat of his anger. I think the only thing that might piss the horseman off more than getting kissed right now is getting kissed for the wrong reasons.

The corner of my mouth lifts. I definitely shouldn't enjoy toying with him—people tend to die when this happens—but I can't help it; he's *fun* to tease. He takes it so poorly.

My eyes drop to his lips. "That ... and I was curious."

I'm *still* curious. He felt like sin against my lips. And damn me, but now all I want is to do it again—if only to see another tree blow up.

Famine stalks back to his horse.

"What?" I call after him. "Did I say something wrong? Don't be mad—you're much less pretty when you're mad."

In response, he growls.

I grin. So much fun to tease.

The rest of the ride is full of silence—heavy, tense silence. Behind me, Famine broods away.

Even though the worst of the storm is behind us—both literally and figuratively—rain still pelts down on us. There's no escaping it, but it's not altogether unpleasant. It cools my skin against the stifling heat of the day.

We continue down the road, following one of Brazil's old highways. By the looks of it, the thing has been patched over and over again since its creation. Here the farms have thinned out, replaced by rolling fields and thick, verdant forests.

Every so often we pass by a trading post or an inn, but that's it. We don't pass by any travelers today, and for that, I'm immensely relieved. Famine's men must've done an adequate job warning people about Famine's arrival.

My own mood is light and airy until I read a sign on the road.

"We're going to São Paulo?" I say.

"If you're referring to the city ahead of us, then yes, we are."

São Paulo is one of those *big places* in my world. It's one of those cities you want to be a part of because things happened there. I always imagined that its citizens were more cultured, more sophisticated, more well-traveled—just *more*.

And now the Reaper is going to destroy it all.

As we enter the city, I can't help but suck in a breath. The place is *enormous*, and it just seems to go on and on and on. There are blocks upon blocks of skyscrapers as far as the eye can see.

However, despite its sprawl, there's a desolation to São Paulo, and slowly, I understand why. So much of what I see is rubble. There are blocks and blocks of collapsed buildings; some areas are so utterly destroyed that the debris has effectively blockaded the streets. More than once, Famine has had to turn back and find an alternate route when the original one was obstructed. It seems as though São Paulo abandoned this section of the city.

Out of nowhere, Famine says, "You're not to kiss me again."

"What?" I say, blinking away my thoughts.

"Agree to it."

"Agree to what?" I'm so lost.

A moment later my mind catches up to what he said.

"Oh, kissing you?" I state. "Naw, I'm not going to agree to that." I say it mostly to ruffle his feathers, but also because—*curiosity*.

"*Ana*." He says my name like a warning.

Just to be an asshole, I grab his hand and, threading my fingers in between his, I lift his arm to my mouth. Softly, I press a kiss to the back of his hand, then another against the side of his wrist, then—

"Damnit, Ana, *stop.*"

He pulls his arm away, and I have to press my lips together to stop from laughing at the fact that scary, horrible Famine is physically holding his arm away from me to stop me from kissing it again.

"God, calm *down*, Famine," I say. "I'm just teasing you."

"It's not funny."

"Well of course it's not funny to you," I say. "The joke's at your expense."

The longer we move through São Paulo, the more uneasy I get. I haven't seen anyone on the streets.

All the stories I heard about this place made it seem lively. Could they have been wrong?

As I look up at one of the windows, I see a figure peering out. When the woman notices me, she darts away from the window. Inside another building I see a curtain rustle.

Trepidation drips down my spine.

Perhaps, there *are* people here, after all.

"Famine, do you think this is going to be one of those cities where people try to kill you?"

His fingers drum against my thigh. "It's likely."

Well, *fuck.* That doesn't sound fun.

Famine's men clearly warned the people of São Paulo of our upcoming arrival. But now I wonder what exactly these people were told about the horseman.

By the looks of it, nothing good.

Unfortunately for Famine (and me), this city might actually have enough people to fight back.

I don't know how long we ride through that metropolis, the only sound the steady hoof beats of Famine's horse, when the rider appears. His horse moves slow, making his appearance somewhat chilling, like the calm before the storm.

He wears a large cowboy hat, and it's only once he's close that he calls out, "Hey friend, I'm here to take you to the estate where you'll be staying."

I glance up at Famine, but the horseman wears a stoic expression.

Eventually, he nods to the man, and the rider turns around, heading out ahead of us.

"Is that one of your men?" I ask.

"Maybe ... maybe not," Famine says. "You all look so alike."

"Well, that's super reassuring." I take a steadying breath. "So, is this a trap?"

"There's only one way to find out."

By walking straight into it, he means.

"That is *not* the correct way to deal with these situations," I say. Has Famine learned nothing from his time in captivity?

"It'll be alright, little flower."

I exhale. I guess it will have to be, because for better or worse, I'm along for the ride.

Following the rider ahead of us, we enter a section of the city that doesn't look so desolate. In fact, it seems as though the people here have taken pains to revitalize this section of São Paulo. You can see it in the fresh paint and the manicured gardens we pass. There are pristine parks and tiled fountains with bubbling water.

My gaze lingers on one of these fountains. Running water means pipes and infrastructure that most cities don't have the money to bother with.

The buildings around us look sturdy, and well-tended to. There are stores that sell tinctures and herbal remedies, flower shops, jewelry shops, stores that sell woven blankets and rugs.

The people who live here are still nowhere to be seen, but every now and then I hear a murmur of muffled conversation or the cry of an unhappy baby.

We move out of the city, the buildings thinning out on either side of us. Honestly, part of me thought there was no end to this place, it was so big.

The respectable shops we passed earlier have given way to gambling halls, taverns, and massage parlors. I even spot a bordello with the logo of a bare-chested woman painted onto the sign.

The moment I notice it, I feel a dip in my stomach, like I should be in *there* rather than out *here*, riding around in breeches and a shirt rather than a dress, my face dirty, and my hair wild. This is the longest I've gone without working, and I feel *guilty* about that.

Maybe because I'm so damn happy to be free of The Painted Angel. Free to not have to pleasure men with sweaty bodies and smelly dicks and bad breath. Or to listen to their mean words and put up with their rough—sometimes sadistic—ministrations. And oh God am I happy to no longer have to *fake it* from dusk to dawn. The false moans, the forced laughter and the contrived looks of lust. I'm so happy to be rid of all of that.

We come to the edge of the city, and the buildings are replaced on one side by farmland, and on the other by a huge, fortified wall. Armed men watch us from guard towers stationed along it. The moment I see them, I understand why this city is so wealthy.

Drugs.

Of course, a major city like São Paulo would be a foothold for cartels. And by the smell of it, they're growing those drugs here, too.

My eyes linger on the guards we pass, bows and arrows loosely held in their grips. They stare at us, unsmiling. No cheers, no cowering, no surprise or any other emotion. I see one of them spit out some chew, but that's the extent of their reaction.

At least they haven't shot at us yet. That would suck.

As Famine sweeps by, the farmland that I can see begins to wither, just as it always does when the horseman passes through a place.

One of the armed guards shouts, pointing to something on their side of the wall. Then several of them are yelling at each other—then at us. A few point their weapons in our direction.

"Flower, I don't think our company was adequately warned about me," Famine says.

No sooner has he spoken than the Reaper turns his punishing gaze on them.

The earth revolts, shaking the ground violently. The wall seems to weave back and forth before collapsing altogether, and the men come toppling down with it.

Now that the guards are on the ground, several plants break through the surface of the earth, growing in a matter of seconds, their vines coiling around the men.

I turn my head away before I can watch the rest. I still hear their agonized screams.

"Can I admit something to you?" Famine says conversationally. "I like it when they fight."

In front of us, our escort's horse rears back. The man manages to stay in the saddle, but before either horse or rider can get their bearings, another plant bursts from the ground nearby. It lashes out like a whip, wrapping itself around the rider and dragging him off the beast. He screams, even as more spindly shoots follow, overtaking him until he's entangled completely.

Famine passes him by without a second glance. Ahead of us there are more fields and more guards and, once we pass them, more death. So much more death. The men fall in droves, along with the wall they were defending.

Just when I think the Reaper has wiped everyone out, more appear. And with each death, I swear the horseman at my back grows giddier and giddier.

Eventually, I catch sight of a thick gate to our left, barring us entrance. As we get close, I notice strange shapes dangling from the wrought iron archway. It's not until we're about ten meters away, however, that I realize those shapes are dismembered *men*, their heads on pikes, their cleaved torsos hanging from the blockaded gate.

At the sight, my stomach heaves.

"I think I'm going to be ..."

Famine barely has time to slow his horse before I'm leaning over the side of the saddle and puking my guts out.

I've seen countless deaths at the horseman's hands; why these corpses would be the ones to make me retch is beyond me.

"Please don't tell me this means you'll need another meal," the Reaper says.

"Jesus," I say, catching my breath, "you are an asshole."

I right myself just as the horseman hands me the canteen I've taken to carrying around with me. Wordlessly, I take it from him, and swallow down enough water to wash the taste of sickness from my mouth. Even as I do so, my eyes return to the wall of their own accord. My stomach pitches again at the sight, but I manage to hold myself together.

As I stare up at the corpses, I realize that I recognize one of the faces. It's the man from the last city, the one who chatted with me at the dance right before all hell broke loose.

Unease drips down my spine. These are Famine's men. They must've warned the people of São Paulo of the horseman's arrival and made demands on Famine's behalf. And ... someone didn't take that news too well.

I lower the canteen, absently capping it.

"Better?" the Reaper asks.

I nod, shoving away my thoughts.

"Good."

Famine raises his hand towards the thick gate. Already most of the wall around it has been toppled over, the men dragged from their posts.

Overhead, the clouds darken to the color of a bruise, and the already humid air seems to grow even heavier.

That's all the warning I get.

A bolt of lightning streaks down from the heavens right in front of us and—

BOOM!

I scream at the deafening sound as the lightning strikes the wrought iron archway. The barred doors beneath blast open with a metallic shriek, shards of wood splintering off in all directions. The displayed bodies are blasted from the wall as well, disembodied limbs flying in all directions.

In the distance, I hear panicked shouting.

"Ah, much better," Famine says, a smile in his voice.

He clicks his tongue and his horse starts up again, walking over the smoking remains of the gate.

A long, palm-lined driveway cuts between fields of marijuana plants, leading up to an expansive mansion. Between here and there, people are yelling out orders. Several men are running towards the gate before stumbling to a stop when they see us.

I can see them processing the scene before them—the felled gates, the rider, the scythe, the horse ...

All at once they reach for their weapons.

The Reaper wastes no time dispatching them, his plants rising from the ground and twisting themselves around the men until bones break and blood flows. And then we're riding over these men too, and I have to physically stop myself from retching again at the wet sounds of flesh being crushed beneath hooves.

We travel the rest of the way like that, with a carpet of flesh lining our way. There are a seemingly endless amount of men, and for all of the horseman's power, I'm nervous about the cartel boss we're squaring off with.

We head up the circular driveway, my gaze taking in the palatial home in front of me. Men are moving to defend the house, bows nocked and at the ready.

An arrow hisses by, then another. I lock eyes on an arrow headed straight for me—

Quick as lightning, Famine reaches out and catches the projectile, the point centimeters from my breast.

The Reaper makes a sound deep in his chest. "That was the wrong thing to do."

Beneath us, the ground rumbles, splitting wide open. Thick, fast growing plants burst from a dozen different places, ensnaring whoever they manage to get ahold of.

Amongst the panicked cries, someone begins to clap. I glance towards the sound. An older man, his hair heavily streaked with white, is among the men caught in Famine's snares. He doesn't, however, look concerned about his predicament.

"I am not easily impressed," the man says, looking first at me, then at the Reaper, "but you, my friend, have impressed me."

This must be the home's owner. I can't imagine what sort of man he is if he can take in all this carnage and not be afraid.

"How is he still talking?" I whisper to Famine. The horseman is more of a *kill first, ask questions later* type of guy.

"I'm letting him," the Reaper replies smoothly.

"I'll admit," the man continues, sizing me up, "I assumed you'd have smaller tits."

Behind me, the Reaper snorts. Smoothly he dismounts, crossing the cobblestone driveway towards the ensnared man. Famine's scythe is strapped to his back, an open warning about who he is and the sort of violence he can wreak.

If, you know, the dead crops, the toppled wall, and the bloody bodies weren't warning enough.

"Insulting me is not going to do you any good," Famine says, casually removing his scythe from its holster as he strides towards the man.

"So you're going to kill me?" the man says.

"No," the Reaper says, "I'm going to torment you, *then* I'm going to kill you."

The older man sizes him up. All at once, he laughs. "You're bad for business, Reaper, but you would make a damn fine lieutenant. If the situation were different, I might've even tried to hire you myself."

"You killed my men," Famine jerks his head behind him, towards the remains of the gate. "Not to mention that your men tried to kill *her*." I hear the icy chill of the Reaper's anger as he jerks his head towards me. "So fuck your compliments and fuck your opinions."

"Am I supposed to apologize for defending my life and property, Reaper?" the man says. "Because if I am, then *fuck you*." He flings the oath right back at Famine.

In the wake of his words, there's a hollow, haunted silence. I swallow, preparing myself for the horseman's wrath.

Famine steps in close to him. "Men like you are the reason everyone is dying. *You* are the reason I kill."

At the Reaper's words, I feel an echo of his old pain, and my mind flashes back to the day I found his mutilated remains.

Famine brandishes his scythe, and I am bracing myself for more decapitations.

"I can help you," the man rushes to say. Now he doesn't sound quite so calm.

The Reaper pauses.

What is Famine doing?

I can't see much of the horseman's face, but I assume he's assessing the man.

"Tell me, scum," Famine says, "what use could a monster like you possibly have right now?"

"Your men are dead. Mine are not."

Yeah, the three men who are left. The rest of them lay scattered in heaps behind us.

"I can find my own men," the Reaper says. Still, he doesn't bring his blade down on the man's throat.

What is he waiting for?

"I bet they can't get things done the way my men can," the man says. "People may know who you are, but you haven't earned their trust. Not like I have."

"Is that so?" Famine says, amused.

"You need something? I can get it for you. You want something done? I can snap my fingers and make it so. All my men have to do is mention my name, and people make themselves useful."

"And what is this name of yours?" the horseman asks, derision dripping from his voice.

"Heitor Rocha."

I start at the name. Even *I* have heard of Heitor Rocha. He's not just part of Brazil's southeastern cartel; he *is* the southeastern cartel.

My heart begins to drum in my chest.

How the *fuck* did we end up here of all places?

Famine doesn't react to Heitor's words, but he also doesn't bring down his scythe on Heitor's head.

Good God, surely he's not taking this offer seriously?

The Reaper's eyes sweep over the circular driveway, past an elaborate gurgling fountain where fish swim beneath lily pads, over the last of Rocha's men, who are still caught in the grips of Famine's plants.

"Where's your wife, mortal?" the horseman asks. "Where are your children?" *Where is my leverage?* Famine seems to be saying. And if he thinks Rocha won't pick up on this, he's wildly underestimating how clever we humans are.

"Both of my wives and my only child have all passed on— but you, being all-powerful, would already know that, wouldn't you?" Heitor challenges, staring at the horseman.

The Reaper is unruffled by the accusation. He stares at Heitor a little longer, then, coming to some sort of decision, says, "I can't be killed, and any attempts on my life will be met with my vengeance."

Wait—what?

The Reaper's unearthly plants loosen their hold, releasing Rocha's men across the yard.

Oh my God, he's sparing Heitor Rocha? *Heitor Rocha?*

The cartel boss steps out of the plant that caged him in, straightening his pressed shirt.

"Do you want to keep your life?" Famine asks him.

"I believe I have made that abundantly clear," Heitor says, running a hand through his greying hair.

"Get on your knees," the horseman says.

Heitor gives him a blank look. "I don't understand."

"*On your knees,*" Famine repeats.

Reluctantly, Rocha lowers himself.

The Reaper extends his scythe towards Heitor, causing the cartel boss to rear back a little.

"Kiss the blade and swear your allegiance," Famine says.

Heitor hesitates, and now I see his pride. He hadn't anticipated this sort of debasement.

After a moment, he leans forward and kisses the blade as best he can.

Once he's done, he glances up at Famine, eyebrows raised as though to say, *are you satisfied?* His lip bleeds a little from where he must've nicked it.

"Now, your men," the Reaper says.

Heitor glances over at his men, who have hung back since disentangling themselves from Famine's plants. Rocha stands, gesturing for the others to come over.

I can see their anger burning in their eyes as they head towards the horseman. I don't know these men, but considering they personally know Heitor, they must be powerful men in their own right. And Famine is making a mockery of that power.

One by one, Heitor's men get down on their knees and

kiss Famine's scythe. The Reaper makes no move to steady his weapon as they pledge their allegiance, and by the end of the ordeal, many of the men have bloody faces.

Once the last man stands, the Reaper's brutal eyes cut to me. Right now I can see how close to the surface his violence is. He beckons me forward with his hand.

Damnit, I have to actually do something.

I move slowly off the horse, barely making a fool of myself this time when I dismount—thank God. Behind me, Famine's steed walks off; clomping across the driveway before heading off into the dead fields around us.

Even the horse has the good sense to make himself scarce.

I cross the expansive courtyard, to where the horseman waits. I have the attention of the entire gathering, and my skin crawls from it. Don't get me wrong, under the right circumstances, I preen under excessive attention. But these are not the right circumstances, and the looks I'm receiving now range from *I-want-to-hate-bang-you* to *fuck-you-demon-whore*.

What a group of fine gentlemen.

I sidle up to the Reaper's side, and his hand goes to my uninjured shoulder.

Famine's gaze moves to the mansion. "This is our house now."

Our house?

Also, what the hell, Famine? As if the target on my back wasn't already big enough.

"You will all serve us," the horseman continues. "And I expect you"—he points his scythe at Heitor—"to personally bring me dinner. And to draw my bath. And," he squeeze's my shoulder, "my companion's."

Jesus. If there was ever a time *not* to rile a human up, now would be it. But it's like the horseman is deliberately baiting the kingpin, hoping he'll snap under the strain.

"Of course," Heitor says smoothly. His eyes are frigid, but he smiles as though none of this bothers him. The sight of that empty smile is nearly as chilling as Famine's own nefarious grin.

I'm going to get my throat slit tonight. I'm sure of it.

Heitor's eyes settle on me again, moving over my body proprietarily.

"Who is this?" he asks, giving me the same kind of look a client might after they bought me for an evening. Like I'm his to do with as he pleases.

I have to fight back a scowl.

Famine's gaze moves from Rocha to me. The horseman's expression doesn't change, and yet I can see him weighing his words.

Finally, he says, "Someone important. Give her the same treatment you'd give me."

My heart picks up speed at his words, and for a moment, I remember what it was like to press my lips against him and discover that he kisses just as cruelly as he kills.

Famine stares at me for several more seconds, his gaze moving to my lips. I can almost believe that he's thinking about that kiss, too. The one he was angry about.

"Come inside and we can discuss what it is you'd like me to do for you," Heitor says, interrupting us.

I blink, turning away from Famine.

The cartel boss retreats towards the mansion, not glancing back to see whether we're following or not. His men fall into line around him, and it's clear that despite their bloody lips and pledged allegiance, Rocha is still the man in charge.

Famine starts forward, seemingly oblivious to the situation. I hurry after him.

"What are you doing?" I accuse him, keeping my voice low.

Famine's face is devoid of emotion. "What I always do."

"No, this is *not* what you always do," I say heatedly, my voice hushed. "I've seen what you always do." He chops people up, and the mouthier they are, the shittier he makes their deaths.

The Reaper's eyes cut to me. "It's almost as though you don't trust me."

Gah!

"I *don't* trust you! But more importantly, I don't trust our host—and you shouldn't either."

"I don't." The Reaper's voice is icy. He glances at me, and something in my expression catches his attention. He turns to me more fully, his eyes bright with curiosity. "But tell me, little flower: what would *you* have me do?"

Like the hunter that he is, he's sighted my own dark thoughts.

I part my lips to speak.

Kill them. Kill them just as you do everyone else.

I can't force the words out. It's one thing to see the Reaper kill, it's another thing to encourage it.

But I want these men to die. There's no sense denying it.

For the first time since we dismounted, Famine flashes me a wicked smile, looking delighted. "You've gotten a taste for blood, haven't you, little flower?"

"I'm not saying that—"

"*Enough.*" His voice brokers no argument. "I'm aware of Heitor's moral depravity. And unlike you, *I* am the hand of God, which means *I* choose when and how humans fall."

This is not going to end well. I just know it.

Not even five minutes after we enter, Famine is already deep in conversation with Heitor's men, clearly making his will known and going over logistics.

The horseman has made a habit of recruiting terrible men to do his bidding, but so far, those men have been nothing but sellouts and goons. These people, however, these are professional killers; they seem to wear their wickedness like a coat.

A figure steps in front of me, blocking my view of Famine.

"A woman like you shouldn't concern yourself with this tedious business," Heitor says.

I glance up and meet the drug lord's eyes. They're kind eyes. I wasn't expecting that—for him to have kind eyes. Not that it means anything. Plenty of men with kind eyes have been rough with me. I think I prefer Famine's eyes; he has the most truthful gaze of anyone I've ever met.

Heitor takes me by the elbow. "Why don't I show you your rooms?"

Everything about this man agitates me, from his deceptive eyes to his misogynistic attitude to his misleadingly innocent offer.

I glance over at Famine, for once wishing he'd be his usual bossy self and insert himself into my business.

Heitor follows my gaze.

"Surely you don't need his permission for everything," he says, reading my look.

"You'd be surprised," I respond.

"Come, come," the older man says, tugging my arm and ushering me along. "Famine will be right where you left him."

I'm used to catering to men's needs. Perhaps that's why I let Heitor lead me off without stronger protests.

I rub my arm as we move away from the main room, the voices behind us getting fainter and fainter. Heitor opens a door that leads out to a courtyard.

I step outside, and a moment later, he follows me. The door clicks behind us, sounding so loud. Or maybe it's just my senses that are heightened now that I'm alone with the drug lord.

His arm moves to my back, and he places his palm disturbingly low—just above the curve of my ass.

My eyes flash to his, but he's busy looking ahead, as though nothing is amiss.

"This way," he says, pressing me on.

We cross the courtyard with its manicured gardens,

skirting around a decorative pond before entering another wing of the estate.

"How does a woman like you get tangled up with a man like the Reaper?" Heitor asks casually.

I feel my throat bob as I look at him. He's still staring straight ahead.

I bet you would hurt me in bed. Much of what I've learned at the bordello is how to read people.

I lift a shoulder. "Bad circumstances."

"I'd argue your circumstances are quite good. He hasn't killed you, after all."

Now Heitor looks at me, and a chill slips down my spine. His eyes are kind—*cold* and kind. It sets my nerves on edge.

"He hasn't." *But others might.*

I let the last unspoken part of the sentence linger in the air between us.

Rocha stares at me a little longer, then abruptly, he stops, turning to a door I didn't notice.

"Ah," he says. "Here we are. Your room."

He opens the door, and I peer inside, half thinking that this whole thing is a trap and I'm about to die. But Heitor did lead me to a bedroom, a very feminine one. It has paintings of beautiful women set in gilded frames, vases full of fresh flowers, a dresser inlaid with mother of pearl, and an enormous mirror that leans against the far wall. But the most impressive feature of the room is the massive canopy bed, gauzy fabric draped along the carved posts.

This is clearly a room meant for a woman—perhaps a mistress? Whoever this woman is—or maybe there are several women—it's empty now.

I step inside, my gaze going to the ceiling, where a delicate chandelier hangs.

Heitor's hand slips down my backside and squeezes my ass. Just like that, my attention shifts from the opulent room to the man who led me here.

"Enjoy your room," he says, his eyes lingering on me, his expression saying, *I own you.*

For a moment, I don't react. Over the last five years, I've been conditioned to go along with unsolicited attention—that was how I landed new clients—but old conditioning is meeting new. I don't want the attention, not from Heitor; and besides, I think he did it to demean me.

My old programming finally snaps into place. I step into Heitor's space.

"It takes a lot more than an ass-grab to get me off," I say, my voice low, intimate, "but I appreciate the attempt, all the same."

There's a spark of ... *something* in the man's eyes. Maybe it's curiosity, maybe it's interest. Or maybe Heitor thought I was a conquerable challenge, and now he's realizing that even I come with sharp teeth.

He holds my gaze for a second longer. "You'll know when I'm trying to get you off. Perhaps sooner than you realize."

Rocha turns his back on me and walks away, his shoes clicking along the floor.

Long after he's gone, my skin still crawls.

Definitely going to die soon.

Chapter 27

That evening I sit with Famine in Heitor Rocha's grand dining room, fidgeting as the two of us wait for dinner.

"This is a bad idea," I whisper to the horseman.

He leans back in his seat, slinging a leg over his knee. "Loosen up a little, flower."

I open my mouth to fire back a retort when several of Heitor's men enter the room, each carrying a platter of food. Heitor himself is nowhere to be seen.

So much for serving us.

"And where is your insufferable boss?" the Reaper asks, noticing Rocha's absence. "I believe I asked him and not you all to serve me."

One of the men mutters something vague about Rocha being in the next town over, making arrangements on the horseman's behalf.

It's more likely that Heitor is wherever the hell Heitor wants to be; not even Famine himself can make him do otherwise.

The Reaper glares at the men, but just when I think he's going to grab his scythe and start gutting them, he leans back in his seat and lets them set the platters of food on the table.

"You there," Famine calls, pointing to one of the men.

The man's eyes move to the horseman. It's not fear I see in those dark irises—more like caution. I guess that's what you get when you're used to working around sociopaths.

The Reaper gestures for him to come over, even as the other men set down their dishes and retreat back into the kitchen.

"What is it?" the man asks, moving towards Famine.

"Grab a plate. Sit."

Maybe I was wrong earlier. Maybe Famine is planning on killing someone right now.

The man hesitates for only a moment, then he leaves the room, returning with a plate.

Tentatively, he sits across from us.

"Serve yourself," the Reaper orders. "There's plenty here, and I want you to try everything." He sounds almost benevolent, like he himself made the dishes.

The guard eyes Famine for only a second or two before he reaches for each dish, putting a little of this and a little of that on his plate until it's a heaping tray of everything.

"Now," Famine says, "*eat.*"

It takes me longer than it should to realize that the horseman isn't going to kill the man, like I assumed. He's using him as a food tester, making sure that the dishes prepared weren't laced with poison.

"And the wine—don't forget to try that," the horseman encourages.

The two of us watch the man in silence as he eats and drinks his way through the meal. The guard's eyes are flinty as he does Famine's bidding, but he polishes everything off.

When it becomes clear that he's not going to keel over, the guard stands.

"I was hoping to eat with Heitor," Famine says casually, and I'm impressed the horseman actually remembered the man's name.

"I will let him know he was missed," the guard responds. "I'm sure he regrets his absence."

"Does he now?" Famine says.

The two men stare each other down. Eventually, the corner of the Reaper's mouth curls into a lopsided smile. "You will find me Heitor, and you *will* bring him back here. He and I are to have a little chat."

My stomach dips again at the thought of one of Rocha's own men forcing their boss to do something. From everything I've heard, loyalty is a big deal in cartels. But Famine's wrath is barely leashed as it is. And I'm in the crosshairs of it all.

The Reaper sits forward as the man leaves the room, and he begins serving himself. When I don't follow suit, Famine serves me as well.

"I can't tell you how refreshing it is to sit next to you and not get bombarded with all your petty thoughts," Famine says, pouring us both a glass of wine. Setting the bottle down, he picks up his glass.

I glance at the horseman. I've been distracted today, it's true. Distracted by our violent entrance into São Paulo, by Famine's barely muzzled brutality, and by Heitor's unsolicited touch.

Before I know exactly what I'm doing, I stand.

The Reaper reaches out and places a hand over mine. "*Stay.*"

"Is that an order or a request?" I say. I don't know if it's something in the water, but like Rocha, I don't really want to follow orders at the moment.

The horseman thins his eyes at me. "Would it make a difference?" he asks, his words sharp.

I stare at him for an extra beat.

It would. It does.

And today I don't want to play games.

Slipping my hand out from under his, I begin to leave.

I think the horseman's going to call on Heitor's men to stop me.

Instead, he says, "If that's the way you feel about it, then it's a request."

I stop and take a deep breath. I know Famine conceding anything is a big deal, and maybe on another day I'd be satisfied with his response, but after Heitor's ass-grab, I'm fucking *over* being forced to fit into roles men have cut out for me.

"For this to work—truly work—you're going to have to respect me," I say, my back still to the horseman.

"A tall order from a human," he responds.

I'm not angry, but I've had enough. I begin moving towards the exit again.

"But I suppose I can make an exception for you," he adds.

I glance back at Famine, annoyance simmering just beneath my skin. But the Reaper's eyes are full of mirth. He's being playful, and for once playful doesn't involve someone dying.

It's that look, more than anything, that convinces me to stay. Not that I'm great company at the moment.

I all but stomp back to my seat.

"You're in a fine mood tonight," he remarks.

"You're one to talk," I snap back at him.

"My mood is great—or it will be, once I eviscerate our host."

There's a stretch of silence, then Famine adds, "You're still upset that I let Heitor live, aren't you?"

What's the use lying? I *am* upset, and I am beyond caring if that makes me a shitty person.

"Among other things," I say.

Famine raises his eyebrows, looking absurdly delighted. "Oh, there are other things you're also upset about? How *very* fascinating. What a magic trick it is to earn a woman's ire without trying at all."

I glare at my plate. "God, you would make a fantastic human. You'd fit right in with the rest of my clients."

"Watch your words."

"Why?" I challenge, now turning my blazing gaze back on the horseman. "What could you *possibly* do to me that hasn't already been done before? I'm tired of watching my words and watching my actions. I'm fucking *done* being careful so that other people don't have to be."

Abruptly I stand and pick up my delicate wine glass. I don't know what I'm doing until I cock back my arm and throw it at the far wall. Glass shatters on impact and wine splatters across the embellished wallpaper, dripping down its length.

It feels good to destroy Rocha's things, things that probably cost a fortune and that Famine is enjoying at the moment. It feels so good in fact that, caught up in the moment, I grab the tablecloth and yank it *hard*, sending food and dinnerware careening everywhere. Porcelain plates fall to the floor, shattering as they dump their contents. The sound of all that finery breaking is music to my ears. I can't find it in myself to feel bad for my actions. Not today and not among the wolves I'm surrounded by.

Only once it's all over do I face the horseman again, my breathing a little heavy.

"Finally," Famine says, a smile curving the corners of his lips, "a hint of your fire."

Chapter 28

The horseman stands, his chair scraping out behind him. A few pieces of food fall out of his lap as he does so, but he doesn't seem to notice them.

He closes the distance between us, looking just as scary and intimidating as ever. The Reaper steps in so close our chests nearly touch, keeping eye contact the entire time.

I'm still angry, but now there's this confusion to add to it. I assumed acting out would piss Famine off. Instead, he's looking at me like I'm wine he wants to taste.

The horseman takes my hand, his own dwarfing mine, and then he leads me from the room. And damn him and damn me, but I go along with it as though I didn't learn my lesson the first time with Heitor.

"What are you doing?" I say as he pulls me along, moving through the expansive house. "Aren't you mad?" I ask.

"That you lost control? Little flower, I'm *enchanted*. Your antics have been the best entertainment I've seen in a while."

Really now? Killing people suddenly got boring?

The Reaper and I leave the main building and cut through the courtyard.

"Where are we going?" I ask.

"To my room, of course," he responds.

I stumble over my feet.

Famine glances at me and smiles secretively, like he knows exactly where my mind is.

My gaze goes to his lips, and a sudden, shocking realization hits me: *I want to kiss him again.* Not to tease him or to distract him, but to taste those lips again in earnest and to feel the press of his body against mine.

I've absolutely lost it.

"W-why?" I ask.

He gives me another loaded glance, and I feel that look right to my core.

"Would you rather I leave you at the door to your room?" he asks.

"No," I say too quickly, and ugh, I want to cringe. I sound like a horny teenager.

The Reaper's mouth curves up on one side and the world feels like it's turned on its axis.

Famine stops at a door just down the hall from mine. He opens it, then holds the door open for me.

I step inside the room. The place is already lit by candlelight, the flames dancing in wrought iron sconces.

I move towards a side table that has a globe made entirely from inlaid stone. I spin it a little before my attention moves to the stack of books sitting next to it, their names painted along their spines.

"Why yes, please explore my room," Famine says, his voice laced with sarcasm.

"Was I not supposed to?" I say, raising an eyebrow as I turn to him. "You invited me here, after all."

Famine doesn't say anything to that, which I take for capitulation, so I continue to peruse his quarters. I toe the rugs, eye the bar in the corner of the room, stare at the mounted paintings, touch a sculpture of a nude male with a huge phallus—clearly wistful thinking on the artist's part—and eye the bed. The entire time I feel Famine's gaze on me.

I keep waiting for him to make some sort of move; he's the one who led me here after all. He was the one with desire in his eyes and suggestion on his lips. But he doesn't even try to approach me.

So weird.

As he watches me, Famine begins to unfasten his bronze armor. And now my blood heats. This is what I've been waiting for.

It doesn't take him long to remove it all. The sight of the horseman in his black shirt and breeches has me swallowing. The candlelight does nothing but heighten his beauty, dancing over his sharp jaw, high cheekbones and bemused lips. He watches me like a panther, arms folded over his chest.

The sight causes my heart to leap and my abdomen to tighten in the strangest way ...

Still, I am reluctant to move to the horseman, now that I'm acknowledging my own desire. I don't want whatever this is between us to echo every other experience I've had, but I don't know how to make it different. That's why, when my gaze snags on the Reaper's bronze scales, I move over to them instead of the horseman.

I've only caught glimpses of this device since I started traveling with the horseman.

I step up to the scales, drawn in by their odd existence. The delicate circular pans are polished to a shine. There are a series of symbols etched onto each, and I think it might be the same markings that cover Famine's body.

"Are you ever going to tell me what these scales are for?" I ask.

"They're for weighing items."

I give the horseman a look. "I figured as much." I touch one side of the scales with my finger, the shallow metal pan bobbing a little at the contact before it resettles. "Why would a horseman need to weigh anything?" I ask.

Famine runs a thumb over his lower lip, watching me for a moment, like he's deciding on something.

"It's a metric to weigh men's hearts," he finally says.

He walks to my side, unaware that I was trying to put some space between us. "The scales represent truth, order, peace—essentially, the world as it ought to be," he continues. "Whether humans are worthy of that world is for these scales to judge."

I glance over at him, my heart beating a little faster at his nearness. It takes me a few extra seconds to process what he said.

"That sounds like the story you told me," I say. The one about the Egyptian goddess who weighed men's hearts. She had scales too.

"Ma'at and I have much in common," the horseman says softly.

I touch one of the shallow pans again. Of all the beings who should wield such a device, vicious, violent Famine seems like the worst candidate for the job.

"Would you like to see how it works?" he asks.

Yes. It's an unearthly contraption that can seemingly measure something as intangible as peace and truth.

I nod.

The Reaper smiles a little and reaches around to his belt, where he's strapped a dagger.

I take a step away from him. "What are you doing?" I demand as he unholsters the blade.

"You didn't think it would be painless, did you?" he raises an eyebrow. "I need a bit of your blood for this to work." He reaches out a hand and beckons for me. "Now, let me see your finger."

I don't give it to him.

The horseman gives me a look. "I'm just going to give it a prick. Nothing more."

"I've seen your definition of a *prick*; it's a little more intense than my own definition of it."

"Fine." He begins to put the dagger back.

I watch him.

If he was interested in hurting you, he would've already done so.

"Wait," I say.

He glances at me.

I hold out my index finger.

His gaze flicks from it to my eyes. Here his gaze lingers. Without looking away, he grasps my hand and lifts his blade once more. He angles my hand over the shallow pan.

"This might sting," he says.

Before I can react, he slices his dagger across the pad of my finger.

There's a brief flash of pain, then several beads of blood drip onto the circular tray. The metal pan dips as it takes on the weight of my blood, then lifts, then dips again, until it's only a little lower than the other, empty pan.

My eyes flick to Famine. "What does that mean?"

"It means that you're a decently good person."

I give him an incredulous look. "*Decently* good?" I say. "I saved your ass once upon a time. That didn't earn me *any* heaven points?"

"You've also tried to kill *my ass*, in case you've forgotten, so no."

"Fine. Let's see how you size up then on your little holy scale," I challenge.

Famine smirks at me. Using his shirtsleeve, he wipes my blood first from the scale, then from the edge of his blade. A moment later he brings his wrist up to the tray.

In one swift motion he slices open his skin and lets his blood spill onto the pan.

I wait for his blood to weigh down his side of the scales, but it never comes. Instead, his pan begins to lift, rising higher even as more and more blood drips onto it.

The most unnerving part of the whole thing is that other, empty scale. In the horseman's story of Ma'at there was at least a feather being weighed against men's hearts. Here, there's nothing, nothing at all.

Famine stands there, bloody arm extended, those sinister green eyes watching me as the scales continue to tip in his favor.

"I may be crueler than you," he admits, "but my heart is still purer."

"Your scales are obviously broken," I say. "There's *no way* your soul is purer than mine."

If I'm really to believe that this set of scales measures truth and justice and *peace*, then Famine should be weighing his end of the scales *way* down. Out of all the devils that inhabit this earth, he's the worst of them.

Which means the scales are rigged.

God hates us and loves his evil reaper.

There's a long stretch of silence, and in that silence, I feel the horseman's nearness. All over again it reminds me that he took my hand and brought me here. That all of this is just a prelude to ... to whatever comes next.

I turn to the horseman, and I suck in a breath at the sight of him. Seeing him without all that heavy armor feels intimate. Particularly when the two of us are in his bedroom.

"Why did you bring me here?" I ask.

You know why, his eyes seem to say.

I exhale, my pulse speeding up. I've been worried since entering this room that this night might play itself out like every other experience I had at the bordello, but I realize now how wrong I was. No one—*no one*—has ever made me feel as self-aware as Famine. No one has ever made me want them so badly in spite of every awful thing they've done. Not even Martim, the first boy I loved.

Only the horseman.

My hands move to my shirt, ready to remove the garment.

Famine catches my hands. His fingers tighten over mine. I stare down at our entwined hands.

"Not everything is about sex, flower," he breathes. That low, velvety voice seems to rub me in all the right places.

Contrary to his words, my reaction to him has *everything* to do with sex.

"What else is there?" I ask.

Why did he bring me here then, if not for intimacy?

I glance up at Famine then, and in the low light, I see him as he truly is. Something ancient and full of secrets; a being that has thoughts and dreams that a mortal like me can't hope to grasp.

"Do you think I have lived for eons to be consumed by something as trifling as sex?" he says softly. "Everything comes and goes. Animals, plants—even people. You are all so very ... transitory.

"So what consumes me?" He smiles a little hollowly at that. "Things that *endure*." His gaze doesn't waver from mine, and Lord help me, I feel something in that gaze. Not lust, not attraction—though there's plenty of both—but raw connection.

He releases my hands, and I don't know what to do. I don't know what the Reaper wants, or what I want, but he basically just said *no* to sex, so I'm not sure what else ...

Famine steps in and cups my face, his gaze searching mine. At his touch, I still.

"The truth of the matter is, you're the one human I actually like."

As far as compliments go, this one is mediocre at best. But coming from Famine, I feel myself soften.

The Reaper's attention dips to my mouth, and there it lingers. Suddenly, I think Famine might be full of shit when it comes to his opinions on sex because he is giving me that hungry look again.

There's a knock on the door, and in an instant the moment and all of its unexpected sweetness is gone.

The horseman curses under his breath. "I almost forgot about that human pox, Heitor."

At his name, I stiffen.

The action is subtle, but Famine's gaze immediately shifts from the door to me.

His gaze narrows. "Why is it that every time Heitor is brought up, you get jumpy?"

"I already told you why—because he's as evil as we humans get."

The Reaper tilts his head a little, still scrutinizing me. "As I see it, *I'm* the thing you should be most scared of, not some aging human with an overdeveloped ego and an underdeveloped conscience."

"You won't hurt me," I say. "He will."

Famine studies me for a moment longer before reaching out, his hand slipping under my shirt. I suck in a breath at the contact. His warm palm runs over my flesh, then settles on the jagged scar left over from where his men stabbed me. Men who are themselves long dead.

"In case you've forgotten, I *have* hurt you," he says. "And as for Heitor, why would you think he's going to hurt you?"

"Because that's what he does," I say.

If the Reaper needs proof, all he has to do is remember how the cartel boss had Famine's men killed, dismembered, and hung for display outside his walls. We were Rocha's enemies before we arrived, and we're his enemies now. And, when given the chance, men like him eliminate their enemies.

Famine is still watching my expression carefully. "What aren't you telling me?"

Jesus, this man is relentless.

"You mean besides the fact that we know he's not afraid to kill?" I say.

Another knock comes from the other side of the door.

"Besides that," the Reaper says.

I almost don't mention my little *encounter* with Rocha. It's such a small thing, and I pride myself on handling my own business. But the horseman is not letting it go, and I don't care enough to keep it from him.

"Earlier," I say, "when Heitor was showing me my room, he grabbed my ass."

"He did what?" Famine's inflection doesn't change, but suddenly he is *way more menacing.*

"He squeezed my ass." *It was nothing,* I almost tack on, but fuck that asshole.

Again the horseman's eyes rove over my face. Whatever he sees causes a muscle in his jaw to jump.

The knock on the door comes again, and the Reaper drags his attention from mine. The cruel smile I've gotten familiar with now blooms across his face.

"It's long past time I dealt with that nuisance." He grabs his scythe and strides to the door. To himself I hear him say, "Perhaps I'll take his hands. Heitor doesn't need hands to help me. He doesn't need legs either."

Holy shit.

Famine grabs the door, then pauses. "I'll be right back," he says to me. "Stay in my room as long as you like."

And then he's gone.

Chapter 29

I don't stay in Famine's room.

There's nothing inherently *wrong* with the room, but lingering in there feels too much like waiting, and I don't really want to feel like I'm waiting on someone else at the moment.

Unfortunately, waiting is exactly what I end up doing in my bed. I'm not sure how long I thought it would take Famine to deal with Heitor, but the minutes tick by, and the hallway outside my room is painfully quiet.

I wait for the sound of footsteps—*any* footsteps—heading towards this wing of the estate, but none come. I wait so long the tapered candles have dripped down to size, getting wax all over the sconces that hold them.

I wait until my eyelids grow heavy and I drift off …

Click.

My eyes snap open, my heart racing for some odd reason. The room is pitch black, the candles having burned themselves out at some point.

I lay in bed, trying to figure out what woke me. The room is so dark it's hard to make out anything. I hear another soft noise, and I realize it's coming from the door. I locked it earlier, but now I swear it sounds like the knob is turning.

A moment later the door does, in fact, open. Low light from the hallway filters in, outlining a male figure. There's something in the hand at his side.

My muscles tense.

Famine's the only person I'd actually trust to slip into my room at night, and that's because he doesn't hide his own brand of evil like the rest of us. But if the figure were Famine, he'd be bigger, his shoulders wider and his torso more tapered.

He probably also wouldn't give a fuck about being quiet.

The intruder steps into the room, and a distant light glints off the object in their hand.

A blade.

Jesus.

The intruder doesn't even hesitate, heading straight for the bed.

Move, Ana!

There's a brass candelabra on the bedside table next to me. Silently, I reach for it, grabbing the cool metal base. And then I wait, though it just about kills me to do so.

The figure comes so close I see that it's a man. He doesn't stop until he's at the bedside. He leans in, reaching a hand for my throat, his blade coming up as well.

I can see it all play out for a moment—how he'd subdue me first, then move onto the bed. And from there ... well, I wish I didn't know what happened once a wicked man was fully in control of this sort of situation, but prostitution is no fairytale.

I lift the candelabra and swing it as hard as I can at my assailant. I miss his head, instead hitting the man's knife-wielding hand with a heavy *clink*. A familiar male voice cries out as his blade is knocked away.

The hairs on the back of my neck rise.

Heitor.

Of course it's him. He's the only one brazen enough to do this.

"*Bitch*," he curses, lunging for my weapon.

In a panic, I swing the candelabra again. This time it hits his head with a dull thud.

Heitor grunts, toppling onto me, and for one horrifying moment I think that he's attacking me. I swing again, but this time when the candelabra hits him, all I hear is a soft, guttural sound. The hand at my neck slides away, and the man above me is still.

For several seconds I lay there, breathing heavily as his deadweight crushes me.

Did I ... kill him?

I feel shockingly little remorse at the idea.

I'm more worried about the possibility that if he isn't dead, he's going to wake up and *really* want to finish what he started.

My mind is scrambled, my pulse hammering through my veins.

With a great heave, I push Heitor off of me.

He slips off the bed, landing in a heap on the hardwood floor.

Move-move-move.

I head for the door on shaky legs. It's only once I get to the threshold that I remember the knife.

Fuck.

If Heitor wakes up, *I* want to be the one with a weapon.

I hold my breath as I hurry back for the knife, keeping my eyes trained on the lump of a man collapsed next to the bed, sure he's going to pounce on me once I'm within reaching distance. But the body doesn't move as my gaze scours the bed for the weapon, nor does it move when I catch sight of it in my sheets and grab it by the hilt.

I back up, my eyes trained on the cartel boss, then I turn

and bolt for the door. Once I'm in the hallway, I run like my life depends on it, grateful I'm still fully dressed.

Where's Famine? The terrifying thought echoes over and over again through my head. Last I saw of him, he'd been planning on chopping up Heitor. But Heitor was in my room, his hands and legs very much intact.

I slow to a stop, then glance back down the hallway, forcing myself to think through the cloud of adrenaline and fear driving me onward.

I should check the horseman's room to see if he's there. That would be the logical first step.

Without another thought, I sprint back down the hall. Famine's room is right next to mine, and as I stop in front of it, I hope to hell that Heitor isn't rousing.

Tentatively I open the door. Inside, it's completely dark, and I can only assume the candles here burned down to their base.

"Famine?" I whisper, tip-toeing in.

Nothing.

"Famine?" I say again, this time a bit louder.

I fumble my way around the room, trying to feel out whether he or any of his things are still here. I'm pretty sure I touch that phallic sculpture, but my fingers don't brush Famine's scales, or his armor, or Famine himself—which I guess is a good thing. A part of me was terrified I'd stumble across his body.

I slip back out of the room and head down the hall once more.

If the Reaper isn't in his room, and he's clearly not with Heitor, then where would he be? And, more importantly, what state is he in?

I get to the end of the hall and exit this wing of the house, adrenaline still singing in my veins. Outside, the cool night air ruffles my curly hair. Candles and oil lamps glow from inside the main building of the estate. Even from here I can see figures moving inside. None of them, however, are the horseman.

I stand out in that courtyard for an obscene amount of time, debating where I should look next and just how much I should make my presence known.

Before I can make up my mind, a door from the main building opens up and a man steps out into the courtyard.

I freeze. I don't think he's seen me yet.

"*I'm just going to check on him,*" the man says to someone inside the main building.

"*Don't do it,*" someone shouts from farther inside. "*Last man who did lost a finger.*"

The guard I can see now hesitates.

"*Seriously man, let the boss have his fun, and let's have ours,*" says the guard inside.

My stomach churns. I'm pretty sure *I'm* supposed to be the boss's fun. As for the guards' fun ...

The man reluctantly reenters the building, and I hear a door click shut.

Then the only sound is my own, ragged breathing.

Dear God, what happened to Famine? Did they ambush him? How badly is he hurt?

Slowly the panic in my mind settles, and I begin to think clearly again.

One thing is absolutely obvious: I can't stay out here. If Heitor isn't dead—and it would be too good to hope that he is—then he'll return to his men. When he does, they'll all know I'm alive.

I have minutes to do something while I still have the upper hand.

It's the hardest thing in the world to approach the main building, but I force myself to do so. Slowly, I move about the outskirts of the mansion, peering through the windows. Inside, guards seem to be assembling, several of them heading out of the foyer and into the front yard.

I make my way around the massive building, holding my breath that I don't come across any more guards or—heaven forbid—Rocha himself.

My good luck holds out. I make it to the front of the building, keeping to the hedges.

On the circular driveway, among the shadowy remains of Famine's unnatural plants, half a dozen men cluster around something, a few of them jeering. I see one of them swing something, and then I hear a wet, meaty sound.

Let the boss have his fun, and let's have ours.

My stomach bottoms out, and I have to close my eyes.

Famine—awful, unmerciful Famine—is getting tortured. The same man who only hours ago touched me softly and admitted that he liked me.

If I'd given him reason to reconsider his hatred, these men have utterly obliterated it.

I watch and I try not to sick myself as they jeer and curse and hack away at the horseman. The best I can hope for is that he's already unconscious and beyond the pain.

I need to do something—*anything.*

That's when I remember the heavy weight in my hand. Through all my panic I'd nearly forgotten about the knife I'm still clutching.

Shit, am I actually going to use it?

The men's voices drift in, interrupting my thoughts.

"I'm the one who shot him, so I'm keeping the blade. You can have his armor."

"Well I fucking want something, considering I'm going to set up the body."

"You can have the horse."

"Fuck you, that thing hates humans. It nearly bit off my hand earlier."

"Where the fuck is Heitor?" someone interrupts.

"Don't wait up for him. He's dealing with the hussy this guy came here with."

Some quiet laughter.

"*Randy old bastard.*"

My grip tightens on the weapon.

I think I could use the blade after all.

While all this is going on, someone pulls up a horse-drawn cart, two steeds already hitched to it. The men have their fun for a little while longer, and even in the darkness I see them playing with Famine's scythe and grasping pieces of his armor. Almost as an afterthought they load the—*gag*—pieces of the horseman onto the cart.

Just as they're about to close up the back of the wagon, the front door crashes open and one of Heitor's men dashes out.

"The boss has been attacked, and the horseman's woman is gone."

Chapter 30

Well, fuck me up the ass.

They found Heitor—or Heitor found them—and I've frittered all my time away watching these men's sick idea of entertainment.

Almost as one, the guards race back inside the mansion, casting aside the horseman's things.

To my complete shock, they *all* leave. Every single one. Clearly they're more concerned about their boss's well-being—and his wrath—than they are about Famine.

I stand still for several seconds, waiting for one of them to return. When all is quiet, I suck in a deep breath.

Now's the only chance I'm going to get.

Heart pounding, I dash to the cart, pushing away the certainty that someone is going to see me.

When I get to the wagon and peer into it, I have to choke back a cry. There's an arrow through the horseman's head, and he's covered in blood. And like the first time I met him, he's missing appendages—though they're not far. I see his lower arm and two hands resting in the cart alongside him. I can't tell what other wounds he has, but what I can see of him is bloody and misshapen.

"Hey! What are you doing?" The voice comes from the direction of the stables.

I glance over my shoulder. A man I hadn't seen before is now striding towards me, purpose written into the lines of his body.

Shit. I turn back to Famine, starting to panic.

I was hoping to flee with the Reaper before anyone noticed, but the time for that has passed.

I can hear the guard's footfalls, quickly closing the last few meters between us.

My fear and panic dissolve away; all that's left is grim resolve.

I spin to face the man—

"*You*," the guard says, recognizing me. He reaches out to grab me.

Before, I was all hesitation. Now, I'm all action.

I lunge at him, knife gripped in my hand. It's all too easy to sink my blade into his throat.

I can see the whites of the guard's eyes as he reaches for his neck.

Holy ... holy shit.

I withdraw the blade. When I do so, a river of blood gushes from the wound.

Oh God. I take a step back as the man staggers forward, then falls to a knee.

I stare at the knife for a moment, then at the man's neck. The wound is messy, blood dripping everywhere.

I suck in a breath, and the momentary shock passes, replaced by sheer survival. Knife still gripped in my hand, I rush to the front of the cart, lifting myself into the driver's seat. Grabbing the reins, I give them an agitated flick.

The horses jerk into action. The sound of the wagon rolling over the gravel drive is noisy and our progress is painfully slow. I slap the reins again and again until the horses' pace picks up.

We leave the driveway and head towards the estate's ruined front entrance.

I glance over my shoulder. In the huge house I think I see men moving about, but no one tries to stop me. They're distracted at the moment, but even so, I doubt I have more than a few minutes of lead time. Then the men will soon notice that the cart is gone, and they'll head after us.

My mouth dries at the thought.

Facing forward again, I drive the horse onwards. We head down the long drive, dead crops to either side of us. The corpses and man-crushing plants that littered this road earlier have now been cleared away, making the ride relatively smoother.

My heartbeat is so loud it's almost all I can hear. It feels like it takes an eternity, but eventually we pass under the ruined archway, and I steer the horses back onto the main road.

My panic is building again. There's no way we can outrun Heitor's men, not while Famine is this badly injured.

What we need is time. Time for the Reaper to heal. All at once I jerk on the reins, pulling the horses up short.

Hopping out of my seat, I slip my knife into my boot, and once I'm sure it's not going to slice my ankle up, I head to the rear of the cart. Opening the back of the wagon, I grab Famine under his arms and begin to heave, gritting my teeth against the way his weight tugs at my bad shoulder. I force myself not to focus on the wet feel of his blood or his many grotesque injuries as I drag his body out of the cart and set him gently down on the ground.

Walking over to the front of the cart, where the driver's seat is, I grab the reins and flick them. Immediately the horses begin to move, and I release the leather strap from my grip as the cart jolts forward, the horses pulling it onwards.

Hurrying back over to the horseman, I grab him under the

arms and heft him up the best I can.

"I'm so sorry," I whisper. Sorry for what was done to him and sorry for the pain I'm about to inflict, hauling him away.

I drag him off the road and into the dark fields that sit across from Heitor's estate, déjà vu washing over me. I hate that Famine and I have done this before, and I hate that he and I are now forced to re-enact our first horrific meeting all over again. Most of all, I hate the panicky feeling I get every time I catch sight of the arrow protruding from his face, and the way I wince every time his body bumps over rocks and other debris.

I don't know when it happened—when I began caring for Famine. Or maybe I always *have* cared for him, even when he acted monstrous, and I just lied to myself for a time. I don't know what sort of awful human that makes me.

In the distance, I hear shouts.

They know we're gone.

I push my body to its limits, forcing myself to move faster so that I can get us as far from the road as possible.

I'm not sure how far I manage to travel, only that I drag the horseman along until I can't any longer.

My legs fold, and I collapse in a heap, the horseman's body falling on mine. After I catch my breath, I readjust the two of us so Famine isn't laying on me so much as he's cradled in my arms. Then I bow my head over him.

My body shakes from overexertion, and there's a sick feeling in my stomach, one that I try to tell myself is just fear for my own life. But every time I look at Famine, that feeling deepens.

My mind can't stop replaying all the terrible things I heard and saw those men do to the horseman in the dark. No wonder the Reaper hates us with such unholy viciousness.

I would too.

My thoughts are interrupted by the sound of horses' hooves pounding down the road. They get louder for a long time, and I wait for them to close in on us. They don't. The riders tear down the road, not stopping to peer into the dead field we're hiding in.

I let out a shuddering breath once they pass.

Safe—for now.

I glance down at the Reaper. His head is slumped over my arm, and the sight makes my chest ache in the worst sort of way.

I reach out a shaky hand and move aside a matted lock of hair, my fingers coming away bloody. That arrow is still protruding from Famine's face, and he won't be able to heal until it's out. And he needs it out. Now.

I swallow down bile, knowing what I have to do.

Moving my hands to the wound, I probe around it, gagging a little at the feel of blood and *bits*. The arrow went into his face near his eye, but it didn't go all the way through, which means I'm going to have to pull it out the way it came in.

I exhale a shaky breath. Satan's balls, but I don't want to do this. I really, really don't. But those men are still out there searching for us, and neither Famine nor I are going to be truly safe until he's awake again.

Extricating my legs out from under the horseman, I gently lay him on the ground.

Now the icky part.

Kneeling over him, I grab the arrow shaft. Biting my lower lip, I pull.

Nothing happens.

I wrap my hand tighter around the projectile, wincing at the blood oozing between my fingers, and I try again.

Still nothing.

Why me?

Finally, shifting myself to get a better angle, I pull hard, wiggling it back and forth a little. It makes awful, wet noises, but it loosens. Then, excruciatingly slowly, it begins to dislodge itself.

Thank fuck—

The arrowhead snags on a bit of flesh.

I gag again.

I tug some more, and once more it loosens before hitting more tissue

I pause to press my mouth against my shoulder.

You can do this, Ana. It's almost out.

Forcing down my nausea, I pull, wiggling the arrow shaft back and forth. With a final slick, sucking sound, the projectile slides out.

I have to swallow my cry—which is half relief, half horror—as I cast the arrow aside.

Need to check the rest of him.

God, I hate this. I hate it even more than the discovery that I actually care for this insufferable creature.

I force my hands back on Famine and, starting with his head, I run my fingers over him, looking for other injuries. One of his arms ends at his wrist, the other at his elbow. I also find gaping wounds at his neck and one of his legs, as though Heitor's men tried and failed to remove the appendages.

The entire process is awful. Famine is so still that there's no mistaking that he's dead.

Once I'm done, I reach out and touch the Reaper's face again with a bloody, trembling hand. This terrible, complex monster. Most of the time he's the evilest thing in any given place, but right now ... right now Heitor and his men hold that title.

My fingers trail along Famine's cheek. I'm so close to losing it, but I force myself to stay strong, just for a while longer. So instead, I stretch myself out next to the Reaper, laying a hand on his chest, just so that when he wakes, he won't be alone.

And then I wait.

The cool evening air stirs my hair and sways the dead stalks of sugarcane around me. It's an oddly peaceful night given how horrific it's been. I draw in several deep breaths.

I killed a man—maybe two, if Heitor didn't survive my attack.

I can still remember how easy it was to bring that knife down on the man's throat—how easily it cut through skin and sinew. I can remember how remorseless I felt in that moment, and I know deep down that I would do it again if someone found me and Famine hiding out here.

I glance over at the horseman, frowning. I'd do all of it again for this man, because wicked or not, violent or not, Famine might be the only being who has ever truly seen me and cared for me. And ... I might be the only person who has ever really seen and cared for him.

It's made us both begrudgingly loyal to each other.

That thought lingers with me as the night toils on. Every so often I hear men shouting and horses galloping up and down the nearest road, but only once does anyone stop by this field. Even then it's only for a few agonizing minutes. Then I hear their horse retreat and I breathe easy again.

I don't know how long I lay motionless next to the Reaper—out here with the endless sky above us and the vast fields around us. It feels like time drifts, but at some point, I sense Famine ... *surfacing.*

He moans, the sound tightening my chest. The tears that I've kept back are now starting to mutiny.

"Hey there," I tell him, my voice wavering. I reach out and stroke his face softly. "It's me—Ana."

He makes an undiscernible noise and tries to move his head, and the whole thing is so goddamn heartbreaking that I have to take a few breaths before I continue.

"You're safe," I say, the lie coming easily to my lips. "You were ambushed by Heitor and his men," I whisper into his ear. "They're looking for us at the moment, so we have to stay quiet."

Beneath my touch, the horseman is still.

Did he pass out again?

But then he reaches for my arm, letting out a pained sound when he realizes his own is *gone*. In the dim moonlight his eyes slid to mine. There's no faking the broken hopelessness in his gaze.

"I'm so sorry," I whisper, my tears starting to leak out. "So, so sorry." I move then and, careful to not jostle him too much, I pull the horseman into my arms and stroke his hair.

Famine is shaking, and I can only imagine his pain.

I whisper my apologies over and over. And then, holding him to me, I let myself fall apart. I cry for every awful thing that's happened to him at the hands of evil men. And then I cry for all the awful things that have happened to me at the hands of evil men, things I normally don't let myself dwell on. I give in to all the pain and suffering that feels like it's been needlessly inflicted on us.

This world is a cruel place.

"I don't blame you for hating us," I whisper. "I don't. I wish I could—it would make things so much easier—but I don't." I hold him to me again in the darkness, rocking us together.

I feel the horseman's arms come around me the best they can, and in the darkness, I think I hear him begin to cry. The sound breaks me. I press a kiss to his blood-matted hair.

The two of us stay like that for a long time, holding each other and being totally and completely vulnerable. And for once I think the cold, heartless Reaper might not actually be so cold and heartless after all.

At some point, the tears dry up, and all that's left is the comfort of each other's presence.

"This ... is ... upsettingly familiar," Famine says, pain lacing his words. His head and upper body are in my lap. My legs have long since fallen asleep, but I don't dare move him.

So I guess I finally understand the Reaper's motives when

it was *me* asleep in *his* lap.

"You ... were ... right," he whispers.

About Heitor, he means.

"Screw being right," I whisper back. "How are you feeling?"

"Like shit," he says. "What ... happened? How did you ... ?"

"Escape?" I ask, finishing his sentence for him. "Heitor came looking for me." Even now, a hot blend of fear and anger rise within me.

Famine goes rigid in my lap. "Did he ... ?"

"Hurt me?" I finish for him. "He tried, but can I tell you a little secret?" I don't wait for the Reaper to answer before I lean in close and whisper, "You don't fuck with a prostitute. We can be the things of nightmares."

"I am ... almost frightened," he says.

I crack a small smile, relieved that the horseman is well enough to attempt humor.

"How did you ... stop him?" he asks.

"I whacked him with one of his stupid candelabras."

Famine huffs out a laugh, though it ends with a wince.

It's reflexive—I reach out and stroke his hair back, trying to comfort him. And it must be my imagination, but I swear the Reaper leans into the touch.

"I don't know if he's alive or not," I admit.

"I hope he is," Famine says, and his words hold so much menace. "He and I have unfinished business."

A chill slides down my spine. How I ever thought Heitor was as scary as Famine is a mystery. He doesn't hold a candle to the Reaper.

"What else ... happened while I was gone?"

I'm quiet for a long moment, remembering all of the evening's atrocities.

"I killed a man," I admit.

I think I see Famine's eyebrows lift. He tries to sit up a little. "How did *that* happen?" He sounds far too curious.

I can't meet his gaze when I say, "He caught me right after I found you—"

"After you found me?" Famine repeats. There's a strange note to his voice, and I think he might be realizing the same thing I had earlier—that I won't just save him, I'll fight and kill for him too.

"Tell me the rest of what happened," he demands softly. "Leave nothing out."

I do just that, continuing to stroke his hair as I recount the last several hours.

He's quiet through most of it, though I swear in that silence something subtle shifts between us. I don't know what.

After I finish telling him what happened, he lays there, brooding.

"Twice now you've saved me," he eventually says. "Why? Why do such a thing when I have brought you so much pain?" He sounds desperate to know the answer.

Gently, I place my hand against his face. "I don't know, Famine. Because I am foolish, I suppose. And because I'm too curious for my own good. But most of all, because I like you every bit as much as you like me."

The way the Reaper's eyes shine in the darkness, I'm half sure that if he had hands at the moment, he'd reach out and pull my lips to his. Instead the two of us drink each other in.

"What happened to you after you left me?" I ask gently.

I know it's going to ruin the moment, but I can't not ask. He's been brutalized.

His eyes slide away from me. "I was ambushed." That's all he'll say on the issue.

Did it hurt? I want to ask, but of course it hurt. It clearly *still* hurts.

"I'm sorry," I say again, because that's the only thing I can think to say.

Famine's eyes move back to mine. "*You* have nothing to be sorry for."

"I'm not apologizing for me. I'm apologizing for humanity."

At that, Famine is quiet.

"Does God really hate us?" I ask softly. Now seems like an appropriate time for that question.

"Not as much as I do."

"That's not an answer."

Famine's face sobers up. "Your kind is running out of time," he says.

Of all the frightening things I've seen and heard tonight, that might honestly be the most terrifying. Whatever celestial test humanity has been given, we're failing at it.

The Reaper lets out a groan.

"Are you okay?" I ask, my heart jumping at the sound.

"I will be. It's just some brief pain. It'll pass soon enough," he says, his voice strained. "But, distract me, flower. Tell me about your life."

My gaze moves down to him. "You want to know about my work at the bordello?"

"I want to know about *you*," he replies, and not for the first time this evening, Famine's words send a pleasant heat through me.

"How far back should I go?" I ask.

In response, the horseman sighs, like I've taken a simple thing and made it overly complicated.

"Oh my God, calm your tits, I'll start back at the very beginning."

I can't be sure in the darkness, but I think I see him smile, just for a moment.

"I never knew my mother," I begin. "I mean, I knew her—I just don't remember it. When I was two, she died giving birth to my brother, who also passed along with her—or maybe he passed before her, I still don't know the full story on this.

"My father raised me alone, but he was a good dad. He called me his little princess and I remember he'd stop by my

school to drop off treats from the grocery store he worked at."
I hadn't remembered that story until now, and the thought of
it fills me with an aching warmth.

"What happened to him?" Famine asks.

"He died of complications from diabetes when I was still a
young girl."

There, I've covered close to the first half of my life. The
better half, if I'm being honest.

"After his death, I moved in with my aunt." Now I pause.

Famine is waiting for me to continue.

I begin to stroke his hair, more to comfort myself than
him.

"Life with her was ..." I search for an appropriate word that
won't dishonor the dead, but then I can't find any. Finally, I
shake my head. "Unpleasant."

"Why?" The Reaper's tone is carefully neutral.

"She used to beat me—for everything." She had a horse
whip she kept around for this very purpose. "I couldn't do
anything right." I still feel an old, dull burn of shame when I
remember her constant disappointment.

"Most of the time, I'm relieved that she's gone," I admit,
the words making me feel guilty.

"You mean to tell me you feel something *other* than relief?"
Famine says, and I can hear the surprise in his voice.

I frown. "Of course. She was my aunt."

"So?" Famine says. "What does that have to do with
anything?"

"She cared about me ... in her own way." She gave me a
place to sleep, food to eat, and clothes to wear. It wasn't a
joyful experience, but it was something.

The horseman makes a disbelieving noise.

"What?" I demand. "You don't think she did?"

"Not enough, flower, not nearly enough," he says. "Then
again," he adds, "I shouldn't expect any better from the likes
of humans."

"People aren't all bad," I say.

The Reaper readjusts himself a little, groaning as he does so. "Clearly you've never been tortured by them."

I press my lips together. He has a point. We're in the middle of a field hiding for our lives, and the men after us don't just delight in death—they enjoy a good dose of suffering too.

The two of us fall to silence, and we stay that way for a long time. I continue to stroke his hair. In the distance, I hear the pound of more horses' hooves. The two of us go utterly still. But, like the first time I heard the noise, these riders don't stop to check the field.

Once the hoof beats fade away, Famine says, "You never finished telling me about your life."

I glance down at him. "I know you like stories, but I'm not sure mine is what you're looking for." There's no justice, no peace and harmony, and except for the cameos Famine makes, there's nothing particularly supernatural about it.

"It's exactly what I'm looking for."

I try not to read into that statement, or the way he's looking at me as he says it. I'm going to start thinking that this man is really, truly interested in me, and that's a dangerous assumption to make when it comes to the horseman.

I exhale. "I don't want to tell you about it," I admit. I give myself a little credit for being honest.

"Why?" the horseman asks curiously.

I look away. "I'm not ashamed of what I did for a living, but ..." But in some ways I am.

"Elvita found me shortly after I arrived in Laguna." I was hungry, destitute and full of so much guilt. In my mind, I had destroyed Anitápolis. "She had an eye for desperate, broken girls.

"She took me back to the bordello, gave me food and a bed ... in return for work." I pause. I enjoy talking about sex when

I'm the one wielding it over others; I don't particularly enjoy discussing it when I'm the one who's the victim. "She ... trained me for a couple weeks," I say.

Famine has grown awful quiet.

"It's a shock to see sex like that." I wasn't completely sheltered, but I'd never been in a brothel before either. "And at some point, I joined in ..." I take in a deep breath. "And that's what I did for the last five years. I serviced men and women in most ways you can imagine—and some you probably can't."

Next to me, Famine says nothing.

"I ... don't know what else to tell you." I don't think the horseman is particularly interested in a detailed account of my many sexual encounters. "I made friends with the women I worked with. Some of them died too young, and some of them left the bordello, either for another job, or to get married or—"

"How about you?" the Reaper interrupts. "Did you ever think of leaving for another job ... or to get married?"

My gaze darts back down to him. I try to read his expression, but it's too dark.

"I almost left—once," I say. "I did fall in love ... but he broke my heart."

Famine's mouth turns down at the corners, and his eyes—his eyes look sad.

"You deserve better than what this life has given you, Ana," he finally says. "Much, much better."

I stare down at the Reaper. Of its own accord, my thumb strokes his temple. "So do you Famine. So do you."

Chapter 31

"Alright," the horseman says much later, just as the sky begins to lighten. He sits up. "I'm ready."

The Reaper reaches out, and in the dim light, I see the outline of his scythe. It's a shock to see that enormous weapon. At some point, it reappeared.

My gaze moves to the horseman's chest, and sure enough, I can just make out the shine of his armor. I imagine that somewhere near us are his scales as well.

Famine grabs his weapon, and I suck in a breath. I hadn't realized that his hand had grown back.

My gaze goes to his other arm. That one hasn't finished healing, though his forearm and hand technically are there. Still, they look a little leaner and meatier than they should.

"Ready?" I echo confused. "Ready for what?"

It takes the Reaper two tries, but he eventually pulls himself to his feet.

He glances down at me, a smile tugging the corner of his lips. "Why, for revenge. What else?"

Famine limps a little, but when I try to help him, he waves me off. With his bad arm. It's still—cringe—growing back. I can't tell what state his legs are in, but his neck wound seems mostly healed.

"Do you even know where you're going?" I say, bending down to grab the horseman's scales—which are in fact sitting nearby. I don't know why I'm bothering to grab these. Famine himself seems happy enough to leave them behind.

He makes an indignant noise. "Of course I do. I can sense the entire world through my plants."

That's ... unsettling.

But as odd as the statement is, it must be true because, not ten minutes later, we end up on the road.

The strip of land appears completely abandoned, though I know several men have ridden up and down this road over the last several hours. Famine walks towards the estate's main entrance.

"This feels familiar," I say. It's a different city and a different year, but the same brutal horseman who needs to exact revenge on the people who hurt him.

Famine stops, glancing over his shoulder at me. "I know you think I am all anger," he says as though he read my mind, "and much of the time, I am—but ..."

It's still too dark to see clearly, but I swear he's giving me another one of those hungry looks.

"I'm not going to leave you. I never meant *to* leave you the first time we met. My mind was a mess, Ana. Let me punish the people who need to be punished, so that I can think about something other than this pressing need to kill."

In the distance I hear the steady clop of horses' hooves. Unlike the earlier, pounding hoof beats, these are slow and steady. Famine turns forward again, towards the noise, which is coming in the direction of the estate.

He begins walking again, the mangled archway coming into view. I follow him, fear blooming inside me at the confrontation ahead.

The hoof beats get louder, and I hear the creak of wheels over rocks and the murmur of men's voices. The sound of those voices sends another wave of fear through me. I fight the pressing instinct telling me to run.

Famine only stops walking once we pass under the archway and re-enter the estate. He stands still under the deep blue sky, watching what appears to be a horsedrawn wagon as it approaches. He glances over his shoulder at me, then beckons me to his side.

"Why are we doing this again?" I ask.

"Calm your tits, Ana," the horseman says, using my words against me. "This is the fun part."

My stomach flips at that. Famine's idea of fun inevitably involves blood and pain.

In the dark light of morning, I can just make out that there are two men driving the cart, though by the sounds of it, more are sitting in the cart's bed.

"What is that?" I hear one of the men say.

"Get ready," Famine says as the cart closes in on us.

He doesn't give any other indication that something's about to happen. But then I feel it—the barest tremble beneath my feet.

A split second later, the ground splits open with a groan. Ahead of us, the wooden cart creaks as the horseman's plants grow beneath it, forcing it to tilt, then topple on its side. The men shout as they're thrown over. Only the horse manages to somehow stay on its feet.

Overhead, the dark sky seems to churn as thick clouds gather.

The Reaper walks around, towards the back of the cart, whistling a tune as he goes.

Several of the men are already pulling themselves to their feet.

"What the devil?" someone says.

"Not the devil," Famine says, "the Reaper."

And then he begins to kill.

The horseman brings his scythe down on man after man, whistling the entire time. A few of them are able to flee the cart, dashing in every direction.

One of those directions just happens to be my way.

I assume that the man is heading for the estate's exit, but the closer he gets the more I realize that he's headed straight for *me*.

Dropping the horseman's scales, I turn on my heel and take off, sprinting for the archway.

I've only made it a few meters, however, before the man collides against my back, tackling me to the ground. Desperately I try to drag myself away.

Before I can, a rough hand flips me over. I've barely looked up at his shadowed face when his hands go around my throat, and he begins to squeeze.

"I'll kill her!" the man shouts over his shoulder. "I'll do it if you don't let us go."

The whistling stops.

I'm choking, and all I want to do is pry the man's fingers off my throat, but *I have a knife in my boot.*

My leg is half-pinned under the man and I only manage to bring it partway towards me before he leans his weight on the leg, but partway is enough.

I grope around for the hilt, even as my vision starts to cloud. My fingers find it then, and I withdraw the blade, nicking myself in the process.

Without hesitation, I slam the knife into his side.

The man cries out, his hold loosening. I'm able to draw in a large lungful of air, but then his hands are clamping around my neck once more.

Withdrawing the blade, I stab at him again.

He grunts, but holds me fast.

266

Dear God, *let me go.*

Before I can stab him again, a booted foot kicks the man off of me.

I lay there, gasping for breath as Famine steps up to the man, his boot landing on my attacker's throat. At the sight of the Reaper, my assailant makes a startled noise.

Famine wears an unforgiving expression as he stares down at the man, his scythe holstered at his back. Behind him, lightning flashes towards the earth, illuminating the horseman's armor and hair.

BOOOOM! BOOOOM-BOOOM-BOOOOOM!

"Never, *ever* fuck with what is mine," he says.

And then he crushes the man's windpipe.

For several seconds, I don't move, my breath coming in heavy pants. Almost immediately the crackle of thunder and the flashes of lightning fade away. It's only then that I realize how ominously quiet it is.

Famine comes over to me then, and lifts me into his arms. My bloody body meets his unyielding one.

"Fuck," I say, my voice shaky as my arms go around his neck. I lean my forehead against his breastplate.

The horseman's grip tightens.

"Are you alright?" he asks.

I nod against him.

After a moment, I say, "You're good too?" I ask.

"Now I am."

I close my eyes, letting his words wash over me. He cares about me, and damn, it feels so good to be cared about—and to be held. Whatever closeness the two of us forged out in the fields around us, it hasn't left.

When I open my eyes again, I look around at the dead bodies that lay scattered.

"Are they all dead?" I ask.

He stares down at me, his gaze growing distant. After a moment, he says, "Now they are."

Once I've fully caught my breath, Famine sets me down and approaches the overturned cart. He uses his plants to right the thing, and then spends a minute soothing the spooked horses still hitched to it.

After he seems to have calmed them, Famine moves back to the cart itself and hoists himself into the driver's seat.

He pats the empty space next to him. "C'mon, Ana, let's go find Heitor and have a little chat with the bastard."

The ride back to the estate seems much shorter than the one out. Above us, the sky continues to lighten, turning a blue-grey color.

At the sound of our cart rolling in, I see several men walk forward. It's still dark enough that most of our surroundings have a deep, shadow-y hue to them; that must be why it takes them so long to recognize us.

The moment they do, Famine's plants sprout from the ground, snatching the men. A chorus of screams arise as our cart makes its way up the circular drive.

Ahead of us, the front door opens and a familiar form steps out.

Heitor.

I shrink back a little at the sight of him.

The Reaper glances over at me, taking in whatever expression I wear. When he turns his attention back to Heitor, Famine's gaze lingers on the bloody wound at the man's temple.

"What in all the devils ..." His voice dies away and he blanches at the sight of the horseman. "How are you ... ?" His eyes move over the Reaper. He staggers back. "But I saw you *die.*"

Famine stands, then slowly makes his way off the cart, his footsteps echoing in the early morning air.

"You clearly forgot what I told you earlier," he says, "so let me remind you: *I cannot be killed,* and—more importantly—

attempts on my life will be met with vengeance."

Rocha turns then, presumably to flee back inside his mansion. With a violent crack, the paved walkway beneath him parts, and a thorned bush grows up and up, its spindly branches blocking the doorway, even as they reach for the cartel boss.

Heitor stumbles back, then spins to face the horseman.

"You're not going *anywhere*," Famine says.

I can't see the horseman's expression as he closes in on the man, but just by the rigid set of his shoulders I can tell he's seething.

"I'm going to ask this once and once only," the Reaper says, his voice sinister, "what did you do to Ana?"

My eyebrows lift at the mention of my name.

Heitor stands in place, hemmed in by Famine's plants on one side and the horseman on the other.

"Who?" Rocha says. Then his eyes dart to me, and I swear something angry passes over his features for an instant. "Do you mean that bitch you're with?" he says, jerking his chin in my direction. He gestures to his temple. "*She* attacked *me.*"

It's the wrong answer.

The Reaper steps up to Heitor, his scythe holstered at his back.

"Most of the time, I don't give a shit about the humans I kill," the horseman says. "But you—you I'll make an exception for."

My breath catches.

"*Please*," Heitor says, raising his hands placatingly. "I swear this is all a misunderstanding. Tell me what you need, and I'll do it—it's as good as done."

I see Famine tilt his head. "You and I are evil men. Let's not lie to one another—we are beyond words now."

Famine reaches his hand towards Rocha. Something in the air shifts, and I wait for one of the horseman's terrible plants to grow from the ground.

269

But the earth doesn't crack open, and no supernatural flora rise from its depths. And yet, as I watch, the rancher seems to choke on his own breath.

"What are you doing to me?" Heitor gasps out.

"Did you never stop to wonder just *how* I killed crops?" the Reaper says. "If you had, you might've considered the fact that what I do to them I can do to you as well. Humans are just another sort of crop, in the end."

A chill races over me.

"What you're experiencing," Famine continues, "is the sensation of your body dying, little bits at a time. But it won't happen right away. *That* I'll make sure of."

I've seen firsthand how Famine makes crops wither. I can't imagine him doing the same thing to a human—or that he might prolong the experience to make it as agonizing as possible.

And it does seem to be agonizing. Heitor curls in on himself, crying out at some pain I can't see.

"Please," he rasps. "I can ... still help ... I'm ... sorry ... misunderstanding."

There's a pause, then I hear the Reaper's low laughter. "A *misunderstanding*? No, no, my friend. It was one thing to try to hurt me. But then you went and tried to hurt her." Famine glances over his shoulder, casting me a look. In the lavender glow of the morning, the horseman stares at me with a fervent sort of intensity.

At that look, unbidden warmth spreads through me. The horseman has now defended me multiple times, and I can't help but feel ... cherished.

Does Famine realize that's my weakness? For a girl who's never been truly beloved, this is how you ensnare me.

"The moment you touched her," the Reaper continues, "you were a marked man." As Famine speaks, the earth shakes. More of the pavement around the two men fissures open, and several insidious vines grow out of them. The plants glide with sinister ease over the dying man, wrapping themselves around his ankles and his hands. "But then you came for her—"

Famine's words are punctuated by a sickening crack, and Heitor cries out.

"Tell me, evil man," the Reaper says, "what did you intend to do to her?"

Heitor's only response is to whimper as the vines coil tighter around him.

"Did you intend to recite her poetry?" Another snap, another agonized cry. "Or to pledge your loyalty to her?" Another crack, followed by a moan. "Did you come to bring her food or clothing or shower her with praise?" *Snap, snap, snap.*

Heitor is openly weeping.

"Or to tell her how unworthy of her time you were?" *Crack.*

The man sobs, and Famine stares down at him.

I'm pinned in place, my breath caught in my throat. I have no idea what the horseman's doing, or how I feel about it, but I can't look away.

There's a pause. Then—

"No. You came to *violate* her. And my friend, we're both discovering that *nothing* stokes my rage like trying to harm my flower."

Crack, crack, crack.

More screams follow, then breathless, agonized cries.

Famine crouches next to Rocha and laughs. "You're not going to die, Heitor. You haven't begged enough yet. But you will. And even then I'll make you linger. Because, believe it or not, you are not the worst thing to walk this earth." The Reaper leans in close. "*I am.*"

Chapter 32

I have to force myself to breathe as Famine straightens.

He defended me. I mean, he tortured a man—and killed several others—so I should probably focus on how bad that is.

But I've long ago accepted that I'm no saint.

So I'm focusing on the fact that in the last couple hours, Famine has made it very clear that he feels something for me. Something deeper than loyalty. My skin tingles, my entire body electrified by the strange emotions I'm feeling.

Famine rises, walking back towards the cart. His eyes are bright with all sorts of emotions, the most prominent of them menace. But when they lock with mine, they soften, and for a moment I swear I see something both hopeful and vulnerable within them. As quickly as the expression comes, it goes again.

The Reaper moves to the side of the cart and reaches out his good hand to me. Blood is splattered across his armor, and the sight of his bloody attire is so at odds with his current chivalry.

I take his hand and let him help me off the cart. Once I'm down, he releases my hand.

"I have one last thing I need to attend to," he says softly.

I part my lips to respond, but the horseman is already turning around and stalking back towards the estate, noticing Heitor long enough for the plant that holds the broken man to slide out of the horseman's way. At the movement, Heitor cries out, the sound dying away to a whimper.

When Famine gets to the front door, the plant blocking the entrance now curls in on itself, withering away so that the horseman can get through. Famine lifts a booted foot and gives the door a solid kick. Wood splinters and the door crashes open, banging against the inside wall.

Distantly, I can hear several frightened shouts coming from the house. Famine pauses at the threshold, taking in whatever sight is waiting for him.

I start moving again, heading for the mansion just as the horseman steps inside. I pass Heitor, my eyes meeting his for a moment.

The once proud drug lord is nothing more than a broken man, his skin grey and withered, his face wan, and his limbs contorted in unnatural angles.

"Please ..." he whispers.

This is where I should feel pity. Too bad I've used it all up on the people actually deserving of it.

My gaze slides away and I walk past him, stepping inside the mansion.

Ahead of me, Heitor's remaining men are huddled in the living room, their weapons on the ground. They kneel before the Reaper, their heads bowed, like they intend to serve him faithfully.

As though last night didn't prove with painful clarity just how much loyalty they're truly capable of.

These last few men must've realized they bet on the losing horse.

"Oh, this is precious," Famine says ahead of me. "I guess shooting me was just an accident?" He's clearly remembering the same thing I am.

One of the men looks up, and my eyes widen when I notice just how sickly he looks. As though his very life were withering away before my eyes ...

This must be that same, awful talent Famine demonstrated on Heitor.

"We didn't want to hurt you," the guard rasps out, staring at Famine. "Heitor made us."

"Do you think I actually give a fuck about your reasons?" Famine asks. The ground beneath us trembles, then begins to lift, the marble floor cracking as the tiles are displaced. I stagger, bracing myself against a nearby wall as a forest of plants rise up from the ground, wrapping themselves around the men.

Even in their weakened states, a few try to run. It's useless— it's *always* useless. The branches and vines snap out like snakes striking, wrapping themselves around them.

My stomach still quakes at the crunch of bones breaking and the men's agonized shouts.

The Reaper turns from the room of guards and comes over to me. He closes his eyes, breathing in and out.

When he opens them again, he says, "It is done."

"What's done?"

The horseman gives me a meaningful look.

I don't know if I sense it, or if I just put the pieces together, but eventually I realize Famine means the people here. The people of São Paulo.

This is another thing I'll never get used to—that the horseman can mercilessly kill entire towns in a matter of moments.

There must be something in my expression because Famine frowns at me. "Come now," he says. "You mean to tell me you're actually upset about this?"

Yes. Of course I'm upset over absolutely everything except for maybe the last dozen deaths I witnessed.

Gentler than his mood seems to indicate, Famine takes my arm and leads me forward through the jungle of tangled vines and human limbs. We cross the room, then head out to the courtyard.

"Where are we going?" I say, feeling like I'm walking in a daze.

"Your room," the horseman says, and there's a note to his voice ...

I glance at him, but his face tells me nothing about his mood.

We wind our way through the courtyard and enter the wing of the estate that houses his room and mine. I stiffen a little when I see the door to my room open.

Famine releases my arm and saunters ahead of me, heading down the hall before slipping into my room. I'm slower to approach, my heart beginning to pick up speed the closer I get. It's a ridiculous reaction; I know that Heitor is imprisoned in one of the Reaper's horrific plants, but I still have to take several steadying breaths and force my legs to move towards that room.

Inside, the horseman's gaze scans the surroundings, taking in the rumpled bed, the candelabra, and the few droplets of blood on the ground. After a moment, he moves to a nearby closet and opens the door. I can see feminine garments hanging inside. Apparently Heitor kept this room stocked for whatever poor soul stayed here before me.

Famine begins yanking them off, one by one, letting them fall to the ground.

"What are you doing?" I ask Famine.

"You're staying in my room," he says, not looking back at me.

"Why?" I ask, curious. I mean, I'm not against this arrangement, just piqued that Famine's all for it.

He scoops the pile of garments up. "I would think the answer is self-explanatory," he says. "You were ambushed when you were alone. I don't want that happening again."

There's a tightness in my chest, one I'm trying to ignore.

The horseman strides past me, the light, lacy garments fluttering under his arm.

"Those aren't even mine," I say, watching him leave the room.

"Now they are," he responds smoothly.

I trail after him, into his room. I stop just inside the threshold, feeling out of place. Maybe it's all the carnage we've seen, or perhaps it's just that things between me and the horseman have shifted into uncharted territory, but suddenly I feel pulled taut like a bowstring.

Famine, on the other hand, doesn't seem to share my mood.

He tosses my new clothes into the top two drawers of a nearby dresser, then shoves them closed. Turning, he faces me once more.

My attention catches on the wound above his eye, the one that was created by that arrow. Now it's mostly healed, but it still looks a little red and raw. My gaze drops to the arm that had been amputated at the elbow. In the hours between when I found him and now, it's reformed, but it still looks meaty in a way that's not at all natural.

"Does it hurt?" I ask, nodding to the arm.

"I'll be fine," he says.

I take that for a *yes*.

He gestures to the bed. "Go ahead."

My brows draw together. "What are you talking about?"

He gives me a speculative look. "Sleep. I'm sure you need it after the night we've had."

Oh. Of course. I'm seriously questioning the state of my mind that I didn't understand his meaning. And now that he mentioned sleep, I can feel it tugging at me.

But still I hesitate.

Famine sighs. "What is it?"

"I don't really want to get in," I say, indicating to my blood-splattered, dirt-stained body.

He raises an eyebrow. "This place will be left to the vultures in another day or two. No one cares."

"I don't want to sleep bathed in your blood." And the blood of those other guys. The ones I stabbed. I suppress a shudder.

The horseman nods to the bathroom connected to his room. "That's all yours."

I hesitate for only a moment. Then I make my way to it. I turn on the faucet, a spark of wonder filling me at the sight of running water.

Stripping off my clothes, I step in as the bath fills, the water cool and refreshing. It doesn't warm, not even by the time the basin is full. Perhaps that's why I don't linger in there for long. Or maybe it's the fact that I can hear the horseman prowling around his room like a caged creature.

I scrub my skin until it's raw and wash my hair until I'm sure I'm clean. And then I'm out of the tub, unplugging the drain and wrapping myself up in a towel, my head far clearer than it was when I entered the bathroom.

When I pad into Famine's room, I find that the horseman has finally managed to settle himself. He sits in a chair next to the bed, staring at his raw hand. He has a sad, troubled look on his face, one that makes my stomach dip.

As though he senses my gaze on him, he looks up, our eyes locking. For a moment, the expression he gives me is naked vulnerability, and again, I physically react at the sight of it.

Crossing the room, I walk up to Famine and silently grab his good hand, giving it a tug.

"What are you doing, Ana?" he asks.

"For starters, I'm trying to get your ass off the chair," I say, giving his arm another tug. It feels good to curse at him, like I'm re-establishing our previous relationship.

Reluctantly the horseman gets up, though he looks wary of

me. I don't know why; we've been through hell and back over the last twelve hours. Threading my fingers through his, I lead him over to the bathroom.

Once we're inside, I push him towards the porcelain basin.

"Get in," I say.

Famine stares at the bathtub like he's never seen anything so distasteful in his life. "I don't want to bathe."

"*My God*. Just get in."

He gives me a sullen look over his shoulder, but steps in—bloody armor and all.

It's my turn to give him one a long-suffering sigh. "You need to undress first."

The Reaper's eyes flash. "This is ridiculous." But even as he speaks, he begins to undress.

First he removes his boots; then, piece by piece, he unfastens his armor, his expression saying plainly that he hates all of this. And yet there's no shyness or embarrassment when it comes to stripping. Not that he has anything to be embarrassed about ...

He levels the same displeased look at me even as he pulls off his shirt and then drops his pants and whatever he wears beneath them, tossing the last of his clothes over the side of the tub.

I'm the one who has to school my features to keep my expression disinterested, because *Holy Mother of God*, even scowling at me, Famine is the most beautiful man I've seen in all my life. Every centimeter of him is sculpted muscle, his wide shoulders tapering down to a narrow waist and a cock that is somehow pretty, despite the fact that it is every bit as displeased as the rest of Famine.

My gaze travels back up his body, lingering on his glowing tattoos, which only seem to heighten his appearance.

"Well?" he says. "Are you done staring?"

I have to stifle a smile. Moody Famine is surprisingly fun to be around—at least when there's no one present for him to kill.

I turn on the faucet and plug the drain, and then I wander out of the bathroom, grabbing a filmy white garment from Famine's dresser that turns out to be a dress that looks only to be roughly my size.

Pulling it over me, I re-enter the bathroom. The horseman is still naked and still standing; the only difference is that now he's crossed his arms over his chest.

I nod to the tub. "*Sit.*"

"I'm the one who gives the orders," he says.

As if I could ever forget.

Sauntering over to him, I swat his butt. "*Sit.*"

He flashes me a withering look, and God but I'm used to men actually liking this shit. It's weird to realize all over again that the horseman isn't most men.

But ... Famine *does* sit, slowly leaning his back against the tub even as he glares at me. I turn off the water and make my way around the basin.

There's a bench behind him, presumably where a servant might sit and help the occupant bathe. I grab a washcloth and a bar of soap and seat myself on that bench.

"Am I supposed to be enjoying this?" the Reaper says, grumpy as fuck, his back to me.

Hiking up my filmy dress, I scoot in close behind the horseman, adjusting myself so that my feet are dipped in the tub and Famine's torso is cradled between my thighs.

At the press of my legs, I feel the horseman tense.

Leaning down, I dip the washcloth into the water. On my way back up, I say softly into his ear. "You might, if you'd actually let yourself."

And then I drag the cloth down his chest.

He grabs one of my legs, presumably to remove it and the rest of me from his vicinity.

"Believe it or not," I say conversationally, "I'm not trying to seduce you."

Not that I would mind ...

The thought slips in, unbidden.

"I didn't think you were," Famine says. His hand is still on my leg, and he still seems like he's going to push me away, but he doesn't do anything for a moment.

I dip the washcloth back in the water, some of my hair brushing against the horseman's neck and shoulder as I do so.

"Then why won't you relax?" I say, continuing to run the cloth up and down his chest, trying not to let my mind linger on just how appealing he is.

"I don't like—" He seems to stop himself, then exhales. "I don't want you to take care of me."

I move to his arms, cleaning the good one, my eyes catching on the green glyphs that wrap around his wrists like shackles.

"Has anyone *ever* taken care of you?" I ask, my tone light.

"I don't need anyone to," he says, and I can hear the frown in his voice.

I don't say anything right way, instead picking up his injured arm and gently running the washcloth over the fully healed area.

"Everyone needs to be taken care of," I finally say, dipping the cloth into the water.

"Not my kind."

"*Especially* your kind."

Famine turns to look at me, the injury above his eye still red, and I use the movement to catch his jaw. I let him study my features as I bring the cloth to his face. This close to him, I appreciate just how savagely pretty he is. Pretty and feral.

Using great care, I wipe around the edges of the wound. As I do so, I feel Famine's hand slide up my leg, then down it, the action drawing out goosebumps.

That all ends the moment my washcloth touches his open wound.

He hisses at the touch, trying to jerk his head away. But

280

between my hold on his jaw and my legs pinning him in place, there's nowhere for him to go.

Apparently, this injury isn't as healed as I assumed it was.

"Stop it," he grates out, his fingers squeezing my leg.

"Just—hold still," I say, my attention on the wound.

He doesn't, instead trying to shake off my hold like a wild cat.

"Oh, for fuck's sake, stop it," I say, gripping his jaw tighter. It's not like Famine can't handle the pain. That's exactly what he's been doing for the last twelve hours. And this is nothing compared to what he endured.

The horseman's eyes flash and his gaze thins, but he listens to me.

Methodically, I finish cleaning his wound, then the rest of his face.

He watches me as I work, frowning deeply. But after a minute or so, he resettles.

I move from his face to his hair, setting the cloth aside to run my fingers through his caramel locks. At my touch he closes his eyes, and I feel a spark of satisfaction that even horsemen enjoy a good head rub.

"You haven't reacted to my nudity," he says, out of nowhere.

Oh, I've reacted. I'd have to be dead not to.

But I keep that to myself.

"Am I supposed to?" I say instead.

He opens his eyes. "In the past, people have."

That makes me pause, and I wonder again what sort of man Famine was before he was caught and tortured.

"I'm used to seeing naked men," I answer smoothly.

Though I'm not used to seeing men like Famine. He stands apart in that regard.

"Hmm ..." he muses. His hand begins to move up and down my leg again, and his touch is making me oddly breathless.

How long has it been since I've ached for someone?

I can't honestly remember. True lust is a rare thing when you've oversaturated yourself with sex. The whole process turns a bit mechanical, unfortunately.

"Would you like me to wash … the rest of you?" My voice doesn't sound like my own. It's too low.

Famine hesitates. Then—

"No. I've been done with this damnable bath since before I got in." But just like me, his voice doesn't sound as it should; it's hoarser than usual. And then, of course, there was his hesitation, as though he toyed with the idea of me touching him *lower*.

Famine stands, exiting the basin to grab a towel, and I have to force myself not to stare at his backside.

Lord help me, but you could bounce a coin off that ass and I shouldn't be thinking thoughts like this about the horseman. Especially after I made that grand statement about being unmoved by his nudity.

Because my pussy? Oh, she's *moved*.

I leave the bathroom while Famine changes, trying to be a halfway decent person.

As soon as I re-enter the bedroom, the horseman's bed beckons to me. Now that the danger has passed and my adrenaline has all been used up, I can feel my own exhaustion settling into my bones.

"Get some sleep," Famine says from behind me, toweling off his hair. "No one will disturb you."

There is no one left *to* disturb me—no one except for the horseman himself.

"What will you do?" I ask over my shoulder, even as I move over to the bed, slipping into the soft sheets.

"What I do best."

My eyes meet his.

"I'll make all those men suffer."

Chapter 33

A soft tapping noise wakes me.

I blink my eyes slowly, taking in the dusky light that coats the room.

Must've slept the entire day away.

Yawning, I sit up and rub my eyes.

There's a blissful moment of ignorance, where I can't place exactly where or when I am. And then the moment passes and my memories flood my mind.

Aw, *fuck.*

I pinch the bridge of my nose, like somehow that's going to make it all go away.

Tap-tap-tap. That sound again.

My gaze moves towards it.

Famine leans against a nearby wall, his fingers tapping along the side of the crystal tumbler he holds. He's giving me a funny look.

I sit up a little straighter, waking up fast now that I realize I have the full attention of the horseman.

"What time is it?" I ask, glancing out the window, where the sky is a greyish purple.

The Reaper doesn't respond, just taps those fingers along the side of his glass. He looks wholly untouched, like he was never butchered apart to begin with.

"You're better," I say.

"Mmm ..." he responds distractedly, those sharp green eyes still taking me in.

"What?" I finally say, because his focus is getting awkward. "Is there a big-ass bug in my hair or something?"

"Do you regret it?" the horseman asks, his voice neutral.

"Regret what?" But then I see it in his eyes.

Saving him.

I assume he's referring to last night.

"Should I?" I ask him.

He takes a sip of his drink, studying me like I'm some sort of puzzle he can't figure out.

"Why did you do it?" he asks.

"Save you?" I raise my eyebrows as I look at him. "Because you needed saving."

He frowns, and I'm pretty sure he hates how simple I've made the situation sound.

I thought we were beyond this. I assumed that last night brought the two of us closer, but now he seems skeptical and distant.

My gaze moves away from the Reaper and out the window. I can't see the main house from here, but I can sense it out there. Somewhere inside it, a dozen men are trussed up.

The thought makes me feel vaguely nauseous.

"Is everyone ... ?"

"Dead?" Famine finishes for me.

I nod my head.

He takes another drink. "Unfortunately."

I sense that if the Reaper could've, he would've kept them alive and lingering for just as long as he was once kept alive and suffering.

He lifts his glass. "Want one?" he asks, scattering my

thoughts.

"Yes," I say, before I can even consider the fact that eating first might be the better option. After the night we had, alcohol sounds like a godsend.

Famine pushes off the wall, heading to the bar nestled in the corner of his room. There's a crystal decanter already sitting out, and with a shock I realize that while I slept, the Reaper moved about the room. I should be mortified at the thought—especially considering what happened the last time a man entered my room while I slept—but all it does is make my stomach clench strangely.

Famine grabs a glass from beneath the counter and sets it next to his. Uncorking the decanter, he pours the amber liquid into both glasses. The Reaper takes his own glass, lifts it to his lips and throws it back, swallowing it in a single gulp. He pours himself another drink, then grabs both glasses.

I slide out of the bed and meet him in the middle of the room, taking the glass from him. Now that I've slept and Famine's enemies are dead, the reality of last night sinks in.

I move to the bed, sitting down heavily on the mattress. I take a long drink of the liquor. It doesn't burn as much as it should, so I take another drink—and another—my hand beginning to shake uncontrollably.

"I killed a man," I finally say, my eyes rising to meet Famine's. Dread rests like a stone in my stomach.

"I take it you didn't enjoy the experience quite as much as I do?" he says.

A small, agonized sound slips from me. I cover my eyes and bring my drink back to my lips, swallowing the rest of it in one large mouthful. It's smooth liquor, made all the smoother by my guilty conscience. At least it's beginning to warm me from the inside out, easing away a little of that guilt.

"If it's any consolation," he says, "I appreciate all that you did to help me—killing included."

I give him a hollow laugh ... and then I start crying.

It begins as a hiccup, but quickly morphs into full body sobs. Once I start, I can't seem to stop. This sadness has me in its grips. My hands still shake, and I killed a man, and so many more men are going to die, and I have no fucking clue what I'm doing or why I feel so compelled to help this demon—

"Hey," Famine says, his voice going gentle, so gentle. "*Hey*."

He comes forward and kneels in front of me. The horseman takes my glass from me, setting it aside, along with his own.

He spreads my legs apart, just so that he can move in closer, his armor rigid against my inner thighs. Then Famine takes my face in his hands, cupping my cheeks and brushing away my tears.

"Don't cry."

I lift my gaze to his, feeling miserable.

His eyes lock on a tear. He gives a fierce frown, his eyes agonized. "You *saved* me," he says.

"Is that really supposed to make me feel better?" I say, my voice hitching. "You're just going to kill more people."

His brows pull together, like maybe this is the first time he even considered that to be a bad idea.

I let out a wretched laugh. "You give God a bad name."

Famine forces out his own laugh. "You give humans a good one."

My chest tightens at that, and for a moment, I'm distracted from my sadness by the memory of his lips on mine and the close press of his body.

Just as his body presses in close now.

The Reaper continues to stare at me, his gaze intense. "Too good."

I think he might kiss me.

I'm not exactly in the best headspace for a kiss, but Famine's looking at me like he's willing to change my mind. His hands are still on my cheeks, I can feel the tickle of his breath, and his face is so close, so close. And then there's his wild eyes and wicked mouth and now I've gone still, my guilt forgotten for a moment.

Just when I think the Reaper is going to lean in, he drops his hands instead.

"You must be hungry," he says.

I feel a swell of disappointment, my misery crowding back in.

"I'm *shocked* that you'd remember I need to eat," I say.

"In case you forgot, little flower, I'm Famine. Hunger is the one thing I *never* forget," he says. He takes my hand and pulls me to my feet.

"In case *you've* forgotten," I say, letting him lead me out of the room, "my hunger has slipped your mind in the past."

He ignores me, tugging me onwards, out of this wing of the estate. We cross the courtyard, Famine's bronze armor catching the last bits of the fading light.

All over again the sight of him takes my breath away. He looks like some fabled hero with his staggering height and muscled form, all of it encased in mythic-looking armor. It's almost impossible to fathom that less than a day ago he was dead.

The Reaper glances over his shoulder at me then, catching the wondrous look on my face. The corner of his mouth curves up into a sly smile and his eyes seem to dance. I think he might tease me, but he doesn't. He simply flashes me a secretive look and faces forward once more.

It's only after we enter the main building that I remember the men Famine ensnared in his plants.

I come to a halt, my eyes going to the thick green wall of shrubs that have sprouted from the ground. Since I last saw the men, the plants have flowered, and their vines have begun climbing up the walls, almost completely obscuring the foyer. Other plants have also taken root, draping themselves over the furniture, so the place looks like some strange fantasy landscape. Amongst it all, I don't see a single body.

"Where are they?" I ask, my eyes searching the growing darkness.

"The men?" the Reaper asks. "I moved them."

I turn my attention to Famine. "How?"

He arches a brow. "Even after everything you've seen from me, you still question my abilities?"

When I don't respond, he says, "I had the plants move them."

I grimace a little at the image.

"Why would you do that?" I ask.

"As much as I enjoy the sight of dead humans, I thought it might ruin your appetite."

It undoubtedly would've, but when has that ever factored into Famine's thought process?

That was ... unusually thoughtful of him.

"You're welcome," he adds, because he can't just let a kindness go without somehow spoiling it.

I stare at the foliage a little more, marveling at the odd sight now that I know there aren't any bodies lurking within those plants.

"I was never particularly sympathetic to the plights of the living," Famine says as we gaze out at the plants. "Even before your kind got ahold of me."

I glance over at him. There's something about the tilt of his face and the gleam in his eyes that reminds me of wild, untamed places. He was right when he said he had more in common with the mountains and clouds than he does with humans.

That doesn't make me like him any less. If anything, his strangeness makes him more alluring. I know men, I know them far too well. What I don't know is this being, with his unnatural powers and otherworldly mind.

The only thing human about him is his cruelty.

Taking my hand once more, Famine leads me out of the

room. We cut through the dining room, and as I pass the giant table centered in the middle of it, I realize that it was only last night that I ruined the horseman's dinner—much to his delight. That memory feels like a lifetime ago.

We pass through a nondescript door. On the other side of it is an enormous kitchen.

Unlike other houses we've been in, there's no soul to this kitchen. It's clear from the unadorned walls and the bare countertops that only servants lingered in this space.

"There's no one left to prepare you a meal," Famine says. "We're on our own, I'm afraid." He actually sounds vaguely concerned about that.

"I think I can manage," I say. Unlike some people I know, I've had to cook for myself for the last several years. A twinge of sadness hits me when I realize I won't ever get those campy meals again, where I and some of the other girls at the bordello would pile into the kitchen, all of us talking and laughing while we cooked and cleaned.

Life at The Painted Angel wasn't all bad. It really wasn't.

Connected to the kitchen is a walk-in pantry where it looks like most of the food is stored. There are huge bags of rice and flour, jars of various fruits, dried salamis and herbs that hang from the overhead crossbeams—and on and on. There are even some pre-made items, like the basket of cheese bread that sits untouched on the shelf and the small sack of cassava chips.

Famine moves towards a wheel of cheese and peers at it. "This smells like death. I'm immensely intrigued."

I glance at the horseman. I hadn't realized he was planning on eating alongside me. This ... might actually be fun.

"Give me a second," I say to him.

He looks over at me just as I leave the pantry and re-enter the kitchen. I'm only in the room long enough to grab a knife, and then I return to the horseman's side.

Stepping up to the wheel of cheese, I cut out a wedge and

hand it to him.

"You're welcome," I say, throwing his earlier words back at him.

He takes the cheese from me, a playful spark in his eyes. Peeling back the wax, he takes a bite.

"Ugh." He makes a face. "Tastes like death too." With that he drops the rest of his slice of cheese onto the ground, his gaze moving along to the next food that piques his interest.

"What is that like?" I ask, watching him move around the space.

Famine heads to the back of the pantry, where a door is set into the wall. He opens it and disappears into what looks like a wine cellar.

"What's what like?" he calls out. "Death?" I can hear him rummaging around. "He's a dour asshole, that's what–

"Aha!"

Famine returns a moment later with a bottle of amber liquid in one hand and wine in the other, holding them up like war prizes.

"Not Death," I say, shuddering at the thought of the fourth horseman, the one Famine clearly knows a little too well. "Being Famine and eating food."

He comes in close to me. "You know, for a girl who made it her profession to lie on her back, you have a *very* curious mind."

I try not to get my panties in a bunch over Famine's description of what a prostitute does. Lying on my back! I *wish*. Fulfilling fantasies is damn hard work.

Instead I say, "Curiosity is also a handy tool for sex work." Very *handy*.

"Mmm," the Reaper responds, removing the liquor's corked lid as he does so. He takes a drink straight from the bottle.

"Ah," he sighs out. "This tastes like death too—but a much better version of it. Death at his most appealing."

That's the second time Famine has mentioned the horseman within that many minutes.

"Does he actually have a personality? Death?" I ask, intrigued.

Famine gives me a look that plainly states I'm an idiot. "Do I?" he asks.

I take the bottle from him. "Anger isn't a personality," I tease.

I don't point out that not so long ago Famine was the one who was insisting he lacked a core personality.

He takes it back from me. "But attitude *is*."

And the Reaper has boundless attitude.

"Alright," I concede, "you made your point."

"Hmm," he says, scrutinizing me as he takes a drink of the liquor.

I realize as I watch his throat work, that I *really* want those lips back on me. And those hands—hands that have cut down so many—I want them to slide over my skin.

I want them to relieve this growing ache I feel when I'm around him.

Famine lowers the bottle, giving me a suspicious look.

"What are you thinking about?" he asks.

Hell *no* am I going to admit my true thoughts.

"Just thinking about Death," I reply.

Wrong response.

His sharp gaze grows sharper still. "Whatever you think of him," he says, "he does *not* deserve that look on your face."

"What look?" I ask, touching my cheek.

"Like you want to fuck him."

It's not Death I want to fuck ...

Oh God, I really *shouldn't* want that. Because Famine has *issues*.

But I've got issues too, I guess. They just don't happen to be the murderous kind.

"So where *is* Death?" I ask.

Famine's expression darkens. "No."

"No what?" I ask, taking the bottle from him.

"No I'm not going to tell you where he is while you still have that expression on your face."

I still look like I want to bone Famine? Not good.

And the fact that the horseman cares about who I'm attracted to—also not good.

I bring the bottle to my lips and take a distracted pull from it. The spiced rum slips down my throat, taking the edge off of my nerves.

I swallow, then lower the bottle.

"Trust me when I say that I want *nothing* to do with Death," I tell him.

The Reaper must believe me because, after a moment, he looks somewhat mollified.

After a moment, Famine says, "He sleeps."

I give him a confused look. "You mean Death?" I say. "Death sleeps? What is that supposed to mean?" I ask.

"I mean that he hasn't returned to earth yet. Two of my brothers came before me. Death will follow."

Rapidly my mind is trying to piece together what he's saying. I'd heard tales of the first two horsemen, Pestilence and War, killing off far away nations. But they never came here.

"So you guys come in waves?" I ask.

He cracks a nefarious smile at my words. "Something like that."

"And Pestilence and War—the two that came before you—are they gone now?" The tales I heard of those horsemen are old and weatherworn. "Is that why you're here ... awake?"

"Essentially," Famine says.

I furrow my brows. "And Death ... is asleep?"

The Reaper nods. "Deep beneath the earth."

That's not unsettling or anything.

"Why didn't all four of you come at the same time?" I ask.

"Why draw out the process of killing us?" If there's one thing humans are good at, it's saving our own skins. It seems as though it would be infinitely easier to eradicate us all at once than little by little.

"Why indeed?" Famine agrees. "I've asked myself the same question. Let me ask you this: why don't birth and death happen at the same time?"

"That makes no sense," I say, taking another swallow of the spiced rum I hold.

"One must live before one dies," the horseman continues. "There's a certain order to things—even divine things—*especially* divine things. My brothers and I come when we do because that is the nature of our purpose—and it's the nature of your fates."

Chapter 34

The horseman is sharing a lot of himself tonight. I mean, *a lot* a lot. More than he ever has. That's what strikes me most as I rifle through the items in the pantry, grabbing the cassava chips and the cheese bread and setting them on the ground as well.

I can't decide if Famine was always willing to share these parts of himself and I'm just now comfortable enough asking him these questions ... or if he's the one who now feels comfortable enough answering them.

I grab a basket filled with dried figs, and another filled with cashews and set them on the ground. There's a roll of salami and another basket of Brazil nuts. I grab these final two item and lower myself to the floor, my back against a sack of rice.

"I'm not sitting on the ground," Famine says, scornfully staring down at me.

"Then stay standing," I reply. I mean, I don't really fucking care.

He sets the bottle of wine he still holds on one of the nearby counters. Then, without warning, he scoops me up and begins carrying me away from the food, pausing only to snatch up the spiced rum from where it rested next to me.

"Hey!" I protest. "I was comfortable."

"You'll like this better," he insists.

"Ah, yes, because you understand my desires *so* much better than I do."

Famine gives me a look, one that's heated as hell, and now I'm thinking about his mouth again ... and those other parts of him I saw earlier today.

I barely register that we've crossed through the kitchen and entered the dining room.

The Reaper kicks out a chair and dumps me into it. A moment later, he sets the rum down on the table in front of me.

"For you to entertain yourself until I get back," he says into my ear.

With that, he leaves the dining room. I can hear him rustling around in the pantry. When he returns, he brings the basket of cheese bread, the cassava chips, the salami, and the cashews.

I stare at him, brows lifted. "Are you actually ... *serving* me?"

"I'm bringing *us* dinner," he corrects me before leaving once more.

A minute passes, and then Famine returns with the wine and the last of the food, dropping the wheel of cheese unceremoniously onto the table, the knife I used now jutting out from the center of it.

"You *are* serving me," I say incredulously.

He scrapes out the chair next to me and sits down, then grabs my seat and drags it over to him. He pulls me in so close that his thighs are bracketing mine in, and there's nowhere else to look but at him.

This is ... cozy.

The Reaper reaches across the table and plucks the bottle of rum from where it sits.

I'm watching him curiously, unsure of what the horseman

is doing.

He meets my gaze, a sly smile on his lips, and then he grabs the bottom of my jaw.

"What are you—?"

The horseman lifts the spiced rum to my lips. "*This*, little flower, is me serving you."

And then he feeds me the spirits.

I watch him as I drink, and maybe it's my imagination, but his eyes seem to smolder.

I try not to stare, but the sight of him—from his tan skin to those cruel, sensual lips and his volatile gaze—is making my stomach feel light and fluttery. I don't think I've ever been around someone who was so offputtingly beautiful.

Famine doesn't remove the bottle from my lips for a long time, and I don't stop drinking, the two of us watching each other.

Again, I feel that light, airy sensation in my stomach, the one that makes me feel like I can fly.

It's the alcohol, I tell myself.

Not looking away from me, the horseman finally lowers the liquor from my lips, then brings it to his own.

Heat pools low in my belly.

The Reaper drinks and drinks ... and drinks. He doesn't stop until he's drank the liquor dry.

He sets the empty bottle down onto the table with a heavy *clink*. "Would you like another demonstration?" he asks.

"Demonstration?" I echo, lost. I'm still hung up on the fact that Famine just drank all the rum.

His mouth curves up into a smile. "I'll take that as a *yes*."

Famine stands, and before I can call him back, he heads into the kitchen. He returns several minutes later with enough alcohol to kill a small army.

He sets his loot down on the table, knocking some of our food aside.

"You have a drinking problem," I state.

Not that I blame him. If Elvita didn't have a no-substance-abuse policy in place for her girls, I probably would've fallen into the same trap years ago.

"I kill humans by the thousands, and *that's* your issue?" he says. "That I drink too much?"

He makes a fair point.

"I have a problem with the killing too." Sort of.

In truth, I should have *more* of a problem with it, especially considering all the transgressions Famine has made against me and my loved ones. But I've come to a strange sort of peace with who and what the horseman is. I want him to stop, but I can't stop him.

And if I'm being brutally honest, I don't know if I should.

Humans can be awful. Maybe this is what we deserve.

Famine doesn't stop drinking. He drinks and drinks and drinks. It's enough booze to kill a man three times over. But the Reaper seems fine. Honestly, he doesn't even appear all that fucked up.

While he works on the alcohol, I make it a personal mission to polish off most of the food in front of me. I drink a little too.

Amongst it all, we've taken to asking each other questions about anything and everything.

"How many men have you been with?" Famine asks, sipping on a glass of wine.

"Sexually?" I say, grabbing a handful of nuts. "I don't know." I pop one of the cashews in my mouth. "A lot."

"How many women have you been with?" he follows up.

"Thirty-three," I say without missing a beat.

His eyebrows go up. "You kept count?"

"They were more memorable bed partners," I say. I eat another couple nuts. "How about you?" I ask. "How many people have you been with?"

Famine takes a long drink of his wine, his gaze growing

distant. "I don't know. I don't remember the number."

I give him a strange look. "Then why did you think I would remember?"

"Because you're a human, and you give a fuck about human things. I, on the other hand, do not." With that, he polishes off his drink.

Famine leans forward to refill his glass. "Speaking of human things, what quaint little talents do you have?" he asks.

"I can fuck a man nearly blind," I say helpfully.

He exhales.

Aw, did he think I'd given up on the uncomfortable sex jokes? Poor, naïve man.

I give the Reaper an innocent look. "I can demonstrate if you'd—"

"Let's leave my eyes out of this," he says, bringing his now full glass of wine to his lips. "I already lost both hands in the last day. I'd hate for my eyes to go too."

Despite his words, I swear he looks half intrigued.

Personally, I'm far more than *half intrigued*.

"So, besides blinding men," he says, "what else do you like to do? Read? Sing? Dance? Wait, forget about that last one. I know you can't dance for shit."

It's such a rude goddamn thing to say, but a laugh slips out anyway. I've sort of developed a soft spot for Famine's asshole-ish personality.

"Fuck you," I respond good-naturedly.

"Mmmm ..." Again, he gives me a speculative look, like he's taking my words literally.

The thought heats my skin.

"I can bang out a few keys on the piano," I say carefully, answering his earlier question, "and I can carry a tune if it's simple enough."

But the horseman doesn't look like he's listening, and now my mind is back on how it would feel to have this unnatural thing on me and in me.

My thoughts are interrupted as, from the ether, Famine's scythe and scales form right before my eyes, the two items solidifying right in the middle of our makeshift feast, the scales knocking over an empty bottle.

I start at the sight of them. "Does that ... ?"

"Usually happen?" Famine says. "If I'm away from them long enough, it does."

"How long is long enough?" I ask.

The Reaper reaches out and lifts the scythe from the table. "I used to try to figure that very thing out when I was held captive."

At the word *captive*, I glance sharply at him. This is the one thing that we haven't discussed tonight. Famine's captivity. And judging by the sound of his voice, it's for good reason. Just his tone alone gives me goosebumps.

The horseman lays the scythe across his lap. "I'd wake on a pike, or in—"

"A *pike?*" I say, aghast.

His green gaze cuts to mine, and I can almost see his pain and the sharp bite of old anger. "If I was lucky, I'd simply be tied to it. If I was unlucky ..." His gaze grows distant, and I steel myself for whatever he's about to say. "If I was *unlucky* I'd be nailed to it or impaled on it."

Impaled ... ?

The food in my stomach is suddenly not sitting so well.

He lays the scythe lays across his lap, his fingers moving over the markings etched onto it.

"But it was those unlucky times when my few possessions would manifest. They'd take them away of course—not that it mattered. They kept me too injured and weak to use them or any of my powers."

My mind is conjuring up images—awful images—and it physically hurts me to imagine Famine like this. I cannot fathom just how hurt he would have to be to be unable to use his powers.

"They broke my spirit too," he admits quietly, staring at the wine in his glass. As though the reminder is too painful to bear sober, he brings the drink to his lips and swallows it all down in three long gulps.

I reach over and squeeze the horseman's leg. "I'm so sorry. Truly." I'm not a violent person, but hearing his words and seeing his expression is drawing out all my protective instincts.

He was sent here to kill humans off—presumably because we were a little too wicked for God's liking—and we somehow managed to prove to Famine that we were even *worse* than the reputation that preceded us.

The horseman covers my hand with his and gives it a squeeze. At the touch, my heart begins to race in a way that has *nothing* to do with fear or anxiety.

"How did you escape them?" I ask.

I never heard this part of the story.

"One of the men let down his guard and fell asleep as I was healing. I was able to gather just enough strength to dispatch him and the others keeping guard. Then I freed myself and ... you know the rest."

He reaches out and picks up a bottle of cachaça. Uncapping it, he takes a swig of the pale liquor.

I stare at him, taking in all of his anger and all of his pain. That's mostly what he's made from. But amongst it all, I've seen glimpses of something softer, kinder, something that grew in spite of the cruelties he endured and his own innate drive to kill us off.

Leaning forward, I grasp Famine's scythe with both hands, lifting it off of his lap.

The horseman watches me intently, but he doesn't bother stopping me. I set it aside and then I reach for the bottle of cachaça in his hand.

"Taking all my things, are we?" he asks, though he lets me

remove the liquor from his grasp.

I bring the bottle to my lips and take a long drink of it. This is, perhaps, more liquor than I've ever drank in one night.

I lower the bottle, glancing down at it. "Did you mean what you said about alcohol?" I ask, remembering what he told me all that time ago.

"What did I say?"

My eyes flick to his. "That a little alcohol washes away the memory of all sorts of sins?"

Famine cracks a smile, though there's no humor in it. "Would I drink this deeply if I felt otherwise?"

I try not to examine that too much. That maybe Famine really does have moments of regret and self-hatred, same as me.

Very deliberately, I set the cachaça down on the table, and I lean in close to Famine, my knees brushing against his inner thighs. The alcohol is making me brave.

"Then maybe it will wash away the memory of *this* sin."

With that, I kiss him.

Chapter 35

His lips are soft like satin. I don't remember that from the last time I kissed him.

And like the last time I kissed him, Famine doesn't immediately react. I think he must be shocked. The only reason the kiss continues at all is because I've nearly drunk my weight in booze, and my self-confidence is at an all-time high.

But then the Reaper's lips do begin to move, and suddenly he's returning the kiss with a passion that I'm struggling to match. He reaches out, catching me by the waist. With a deft yank he pulls me onto his lap.

I rearrange myself so that I end up straddling him. The horseman holds me tight against his body, his hands moving to my hips. All the while his lips devour mine.

I'm shocked to feel that beneath me, he's hard. I'd seen his heated looks and I'd read the interest in his body language, but this is actual proof that Famine feels desire—and for me of all people.

My hands slide to his cheeks, cradling his face. It's frightening how in this moment I can just sideline every evil deed he's done. All because at the very root of him, there's something that calls to me. Maybe it's that kernel of kindness I've glimpsed. Maybe it's his awfulness or his vulnerability. Maybe it's nothing at all, and I've simply deluded myself that we're alike.

Famine's palms skim up my sides, his fingers pressing into the flesh of my back. All while his mouth works mine. He parts my lips, and I have a moment of surprise that he actually knows how to kiss—and how to kiss *well*.

How many women *has* the horseman been with?

Famine pulls away, his breathing ragged.

Why? His eyes seem to ask. *Why did you kiss me?*

My pulse speeds up.

Why indeed?

Because I like making poor choices, and you look like the worst one yet.

Despite my very real, very powerful desire to do much, *much* more with the horseman, I begin to get off of Famine. I'm trying my hand at self-restraint.

He catches my hips. "Leaving so soon?"

Now that he has me in his grip, it's impossible *to* leave.

"I was indulging in my own curiosity."

And if I give into this, then lines will be crossed tonight that I really, truly shouldn't cross.

"Kissing you again was ..." Bewitching. Intriguing. Addicting, "*a mistake*," I say, trying to convince myself of that very fact.

I can still taste Famine on my tongue, and my lips are raw from the kiss, and all of it is addling my mind.

"It was a mistake," he agrees. "Let's make another and another. We can regret them all tomorrow."

My eyebrows lift.

Is he serious?

I study his wicked, beautiful face. It's one thing for me to give in to a handsome man in a moment of weakness. It's another for this deity to test drive his human impulses on me. And while I want him, I'm not sure I want whatever fallout might come from this.

And there *will* be fallout.

But shit, I *am* curious. Fatalistically so.

"Everything will go back to the way it was tomorrow?" I say.

Famine gives me a look like he knows he's already won. "It must."

I take in his face, and after only a moment's hesitation, I lean in, and the Reaper's mouth is back on mine as though it never left.

And I give myself over to the sensation of it.

Now that I'm not holding back and he's not holding back, it's like a spark striking kindling, catching and burning and growing. And the two of us are being consumed by it all. I'm moving against him, my body wanting more—used to having more. What I'm unused to is not being in control of my desire.

As if to make a point, I break off the kiss.

Famine all but groans. "You're thinking entirely too much, little flower."

I give him a playful shove, even as I take in his bright, heavily lidded eyes and swollen lips.

I smile a little at that. "Have I told you that I'm starting to find your abrasiveness endearing?"

Famine frowns, but his eyes soften. I take his hand, deliberately threading my fingers between his. I pause as I stare at our entwined hands. Only a day ago the hand I'm holding was gone. Now I marvel at the sight of his fingers, strong and whole. They're even a little calloused, odd as that may sound.

"They're really just as they were," I say.

My fingers move up to his wrist, and Famine watches me idly, letting me continue to explore him.

A bronze vambrace covers his forearm, vines and florets

hammered into the metal. I tug at it.

"Can you take this off?" I ask.

Wordlessly Famine does as I ask, unfastening the armor and tossing it aside. I push up his sleeve, my eyes catching on the glowing green glyphs that ring Famine's wrists.

I trace the markings, my finger tingling a little, like simply the act of making the shapes holds some power.

This is a wonder. I get the oddest sensation, like the universe is coursing through him, and I just touched the very edge of it.

"What are you thinking?" he asks.

He mocked me for overthinking a minute ago, but now he seems starved for my thoughts.

"So many things," I say.

"Enumerate them."

"I think these look like shackles," I say, turning his wrist back and forth as I stare at the markings, "but they're beautiful and they remind me that you're not human in the least, and I like that about you." Quieter, I add, "To be honest, I like far too much about you."

The alcohol has loosened my lips.

Famine stares at me with an unreadable expression. After a tension-filled second, he leans forward and grabs the back of my neck, pulling my lips back to his.

If I thought before we were a spark to kindling, it's nothing compared to the raw intensity of us now. The Reaper's fingers are tangling in my hair, catching on all sorts of knots as he angles me closer. I release his arm, my hands moving to either side of his face.

If he's the universe, I feel like I'm entering it with this kiss.

He groans against me, and it's the sexiest damn sound I've ever heard, mostly because I know how much it costs him, giving in to this strange human side of his.

His tongue sweeps against mine, and I can taste the alcohol on him.

This is a bad, bad idea.

I kiss him harder, uncaring. That light, airy feeling is back, like I might float away if he lets me go.

The truth is, bad idea or not, this *feels* right. Famine has seen my ugly, angry side, and I've seen his soft, vulnerable one. I've fought him, cursed his name, I've even tried to kill him. This seems like the last option left to us.

His hands move back to my waist, lingering there only for a moment before moving lower.

He grabs my hips and stands, lifting me in the process. The chair behind him knocks over, and my thigh bumps against the table, and hardly any of it registers as my arms wrap around his neck.

Famine carries me away from the table, and I think he might be taking me back to his room. At the thought, my core clenches.

But before we leave the room, the horseman pushes me up against a wall, pinning me in place. Famine catches my jaw, forcing me to look at him.

"Tonight, I want none of your pretty human tricks," he warns.

I exhale, leaning back against the wall. The way he's looking at me, I feel flayed wide open.

"You like my little tricks," I say, breathless, a smile tugging at my lips.

He squeezes my jaw a little tighter. "I'm not one of your weak-willed clients. I don't want your posturing. I want the raw, angry woman who tried to kill me. The same woman who saved me."

My throat works. "I ... don't have a lot of experience being genuine," I admit. I lost my virginity at The Painted Angel. I've only ever done this professionally.

"And I don't have a lot of experience being human," Famine says, "but right now *both of us are going to fucking try.*"

I don't even have a moment to look shocked before the

Reaper's lips crash against mine once more, his mouth somehow both angry and hungry.

And then, like the tide, I'm dragged under.

Everywhere he touches, my skin feels alive. His leg comes between my thighs, pressing against my core as he kisses me. At the sensation, I gasp into his mouth.

I realize being genuine isn't so hard after all. Not when you throb for the person devouring you.

My hands are in his hair, his silky, fine hair, and I'm lost in him.

At some point, he moves us away from the wall and carries me out of the dining room, past the thick knot of plants that have overtaken the estate's main room. The Reaper kicks open the door to the courtyard, and then we're outside.

The warm night air brushes against my skin. All around us, I can hear nocturnal creatures calling to one another, unaware that there's an apocalypse going on in their midst.

I know I should wait to disrobe the horseman until we reach his room, but—maybe it's the alcohol or the sexual tension, or fuck, maybe it's simply the fact that this man actually knows how to work his lips—I don't know, I'm simply *impatient.*

I reach for Famine's armor, my hands meeting the hard metal of his breastplate. He lets my body slip through his hands so that he can grab the low-cut collar of my filmy dress—

Riiiip. He tears it clean down the middle, exposing me almost completely.

I guess I'm not the only one impatient.

I give the Reaper and his armor a hopeless look. "Well, that's just not fair."

A low laugh slips out of him, and it pulls a shiver from me.

With deft fingers he unfastens his armor, shucking it off piece by piece. Once he's down to his shirt and pants, my lips are back on his, my bare flesh pressed against the black fabric still covering him.

I pull at it while I kiss him, and together the two of us hurriedly remove the last of his clothing.

Famine pulls me in close, and I revel in the feel of his naked skin against mine. He's so much taller than me that he has to lift me up to better kiss me. My hands go to his shoulders, then slide to his biceps—

"Wait, wait," I say, breaking off the kiss. "Put me down."

The Reaper's eyes are hazy, but he does as I say. Rather than staying in his arms, I back away from him.

His gaze narrows, and some of the desire clouding it now vanishes.

"What is it now?" he asks.

"I want to look at you," I say.

"You want to look at me," he repeats tonelessly.

My gaze sweeps over him, from that beautiful, wicked face that I've all but memorized to the less familiar parts of his body. His shoulders are pleasingly wide, and then there's those glowing tattoos that ring his neck and upper chest like some sort of thick necklace. The pale light of them illuminates the plants around us.

My gaze moves lower, over a muscled torso that God just gave him because for whatever reason Famine has to go around looking like a babe while he kills us all. His torso tapers off to a slim waist and—

This is a *well*-endowed man.

"Well?" he says. "Is your primitive human brain satisfied?" he says.

I flash him a wolfish smile, approaching him once more. "You're really pretty," I say.

"*Pretty?*" he says derisively.

I walk into his arms. "It's a compliment."

He grimaces at that.

The horseman scoops me up and carries me forward. But rather than taking me to his rooms, a few steps later the

Reaper sets me down on the moist earth. He spreads my legs so that he can kneel between them, his gaze moving over my own body.

Without giving me any sort of indication, Famine leans forward and presses a kiss to my lower abdomen. From there, his lips skim up my belly. His mouth pauses at the scars on my stomach, the ones his men gave me.

"Forgive me," he says, so softly I almost miss it.

I swallow. I hadn't thought the horseman would regret any action of his.

My eyes find his. "It's in the past."

He sits up a little, placing a hand on my scars even as he searches my face. "I think you are remarkably brave," he says, "and your compassion is uncommon and admirable. I owe you my life twice over, and that is no little thing.

"And, for what it's worth," he adds, "you're also pretty. Excessively so."

I feel my face heat from all the praise. "Why are you telling me this?"

His eyes are steady on mine. "Because you are human and I imagine you like compliments far more than I do. And for whatever insufferable reason I want to give you many."

My heart begins to pound loudly.

"Now," he says, a sly smile curving along his lips as he drapes himself over me, "enough of this."

He punctuates the thought by recapturing my lips. His mouth is demanding and everything about the kiss feels intimate.

I wrap my legs around him. He's hard and ready, but rather than jumping right to sex, he begins to move down my body, placing kisses as he goes.

His hands move to my breasts, his thumbs running over my nipples.

I gasp out a sound as Famine moves lower and lower—past my belly button, past my pelvis ...

He stops kissing me long enough to spread my legs wide open. I think he's just looking and admiring me the same way that I was admiring him earlier, but then he leans in to my pussy—

Fuck, *wait*.

I catch him by the hair. "You shouldn't—you shouldn't do that," I say, my voice breathless.

Oh God, I need to tell him about the grittier parts of having sex with a former prostitute. This could be a deal breaker.

"Why not." It's not even a question. My words have clearly not even begun to persuade him. He begins to dip down again.

"Wait!" I rush out, stopping him once more.

"Don't tell me you're suddenly shy?" He looks vastly amused at that thought.

Amused and impatient.

For a man who has zero respect for sex, he's sure eager to have some.

I swallow.

Oh God, how am I supposed to address this? Most of my clients just *know*.

"I've been with a lot of people," I say.

He just raises his eyebrows, like he doesn't see the relevancy. "And?"

I lick my lips, my heart thundering.

"I don't know … what sort of … diseases I might have."

I've had bouts of various ailments. Nothing that has stuck around, but sometimes with these things, *vanished* doesn't necessarily mean *gone*.

Famine's fingers drum against my skin, and my heart is in my throat.

"So, you're worried that I'll catch something from you?" he says, scrutinizing me.

My pride lay in shambles on the floor, but I nod, feeling very, very young and inadequate. I can feel the heat rising in my cheeks.

Famine's fingers dig in. "That is oddly ... touching of you to worry about me, but for the love of your vengeful God, can I please kiss your pussy now?" Even as he speaks, he leans back in and I have to catch him again by the hair.

He sighs, even as he tilts his face to me. "What now?"

"Do you understand what I'm saying?" I ask—because I'm not sure that he does.

"I cannot catch diseases," the Reaper says. "Now, will you unhand me?"

He can't catch diseases.

He can't catch diseases.

I release his hair.

Famine rests his forearms on my inner thighs. "Thank you," he says.

And then he leans in and gives me a very different kind of kiss.

Chapter 36

Holy Mother of ...

I nearly levitate off the ground.

It's been so long since anyone's lips have touched my pussy, I'd nearly forgotten the sharp, almost painfully sensitive sensation that came with it.

Famine's mouth moves over my outer lips, all but devouring me.

I try to stifle a moan. It slips out anyway.

In response, I feel him smile against me.

Oh my God.

I stare dazedly above me at the dark sky, trying to remember how Famine and I got here, with his face pressed against my core.

We were supposed to be enemies, right?

I don't think enemies do this ...

His tongue slips inside me, and I let out a yelp. My heart is thundering, and thank goodness it's beginning to drizzle because this situation is starting to make me sweat.

Famine's hands glide over my thighs as his lips work against me, and I think he's taking in the feel of me—*all* of me. But then his mouth finds its way to my clit—

I jerk away from him—or at least I try to. His hands turn into manacles, pinning me in place.

"Unless you want things to get *very* interesting, I suggest you stop squirming," he says.

I pause to eye the Reaper. "Things could get more interesting than this?" I say breathlessly. I mean, a horseman of the apocalypse is *going down on me.*

Famine responds by nipping my clit, and *holy shit.* I squirm—I squirm like my life depends on it.

The Reaper breaks away. "I do so hate following through on threats," he says.

The *liar.* He loves that shit.

The ground around us begins to tremble.

"What's going on?" I say, distracted from Famine's ministrations. I begin to sit up, and the horseman pushes me back down.

He flashes me a wicked smile. "You have always been too curious for your own good, haven't you?" he clucks his tongue. "Naughty human."

I stare at him, completely confused, when out of the corner of my eye, something moves.

Before I can register what it is, I scream.

And then it *touches* me!

"What the fuck!" I nearly slip out of Famine's hold because your girl here learned her lesson last night: I'm not sticking around to wait for bad shit to happen to me.

Famine laughs, then pins me back down, even as that *thing* wraps around my wrist; a moment later another shadowy object slips around my other wrist. And that's when I realize it's the Reaper's plants.

He literally grew plants to hold me in place.

Famine continues to laugh from where he lounges between my legs. "Did you really think I was going to do this the human way?"

Seeming to punctuate his words, another two vines wrap themselves around my ankles.

Oh this is *so* messed up.

"Are you seriously using your plants to keep me from moving?" I say.

His only response is another nip to my clit. Again I try to move away from the almost excruciating burst of pleasure, but this time I'm held in place.

By freaking *shrubbery*.

This might be the weirdest situation ever, and I've been in a lot of weird situations.

"You are a kinky freak," I tell him.

"Shhh ..." Famine says, his voice vibrating against my core.

"A kinky *control* freak," I amend.

He presses another kiss to me just as he slips a finger inside me.

Sweet Jesus.

Now that I'm unable to escape, Famine mercilessly moves his mouth on and off my clit in an absolutely *maddening* way, all while he fingers me.

This is way too much all at once, but pinned in place as I am, I can't get away.

"Famine—*Famine*—" I pant, "Please—please—please ..."

He adds another finger inside me and—

I arch into him, letting out a breathless scream as a violent orgasm rips through me. It stretches on and on, and the Reaper's mouth is on me the entire time.

Even once my orgasm is over, he hasn't relinquished his hold.

"Stop—stop!" I beg. "*Please*." I'm shaking from my climax. I don't think I can take much more.

Reluctantly, he pushes himself away, moving up my body until our torsos are flush with one another.

I feel his cock pressed hard against my thigh, and I think he's going to slip it in, now that I'm as wet as the Atlantic, but instead he chooses to just stare down at me, drinking in my expression.

He brushes back my hair. "Are you going to behave?"

"What are you even talking about?" I say, my voice still breathless.

Tilting his head, he studies my expression some more. "Hmmm," he taps the side of my cheek as he thinks, "perhaps I should torment you more. I do so *love* tormenting you ..." He begins to move back down me.

"Wait—wait!" Good God.

He pauses, his gaze sliding back to me.

"I want to touch you too."

Famine wasn't moving before, but now he seems to go utterly still. I can see him hesitate, and I have no clue what would cause a fully aroused man to mull over a woman begging to touch him.

Then, wordlessly, he lets those vined monstrosities relinquish their hold on me.

I sit up, rolling my wrists as Famine seems to retreat. He doesn't lounge back the way he usually does, expecting people to serve him. If anything, he seems a bit remote, as though he can't quite bring himself to ask this of me.

The horseman's not used to this. He's used to taking what he wants, and he's used to being taken from, but allowing someone to give him something without any underlying motive? *That* appears to take some effort.

I prowl forward, moving over to where he's kneeling. Gently, I rest my hands on his shoulders.

"Lay down," I say softly.

The man who bends to no one now follows my orders without complaint, though his eyes stare at me a bit distrustfully.

I slide my hands over his thighs, smiling a little when his muscles tense beneath my touch.

"Loosen up, this is going to be fun," I say, massaging his

legs a bit.

I move between his legs, kneeling before his cock. I can feel the dirt slipping off my hair and down my neck. This feels a whole lot more primal than what I'm used to. But in this case, different is good.

Famine's dick is tantalizingly close, and for a moment I let the tension stretch out.

My gaze meets the Reaper's, and the air is practically crackling with his nerves.

I lean in, my hot breath fanning over his erection. In reaction, it jerks.

I smile.

"Little flower, based on the look you're giving me, I feel like I should be worrie—"

Before he can finish the thought, I wrap my mouth around him, my hand moving to the base of his cock.

Famine hisses out a breath.

I don't give him a moment to recover. My mouth begins to work him, up and down, up and down.

He lets out a moan that is sexy as hell.

Famine was right of course. He *should* be worried. I'm going to make him reconsider sex. Wholly and completely.

He's going to be mine once I'm finished with him.

I use every trick I have on him, from swirling my tongue around the sensitive head of his cock, to cupping his balls, to even pressing a finger into his ass—the last one of which causes him to jerk against me.

"Jesus Fucking Christ," he swears, "what sort of witchcraft is this?"

It's my turn to ignore him, doubling down on my efforts, my mouth and hand working him.

In response he groans, his muscles clenching. His hands find their way into my hair, and he grips me like he's holding on.

With my free hand, I cup his balls again.

316

His hips buck, and his cock twitches in my mouth. "Dear Lord—you need to stop."

Um, *ignore*.

"Ana—" His voice roughens, his cock continuing to twitch against me.

Ignore.

"If you want things to progress ... Jesus ... *stop* ..."

He showed me *zero* mercy. I'll return the favor. I continue to glide my mouth over him, my hand pumping the base of his shaft.

"Fuck, *flower*—" Famine's grip tightens in my hair, and then he's thrusting against me as he begins to orgasm.

I taste him then, his cum filling my mouth for a moment before slipping down my throat. Over and over he pistons against me, and I wring him dry, working him until he's gently prying me away.

"Have mercy," he says, his hazy eyes meeting mine. His cheeks are flushed and he looks thoroughly fucked.

Beneath me, his muscles now relax.

I flash him a very wicked, very proud smile. He actually begged me for mercy. I definitely want to hear those words again.

And I want to make him feel good all over again, just for the sake of seeing his pleasure.

I push aside *that* particular thought.

He hauls me up to him, then breathes in my ear, "Ho-ly shit."

"And to think you could've been having this the entire time," I say tartly.

There's a long pause, then Famine lets out a surprised laugh. "Little flower, you are, perhaps, even more devious than I am."

His eyes spark with delight. He runs his hand over my back, seeming to enjoy the feel of my skin. But then his touch stops. It moves down a little, then up.

I stiffen against him, aware of what he's now noticing for the first time.

"*Ana.*"

My gaze meets his.

"What are these?" Famine asks, running his fingers over the lines that crisscross my back.

He's seen me naked plenty of times, yet he's never gotten a good look at my back.

"Scars."

"Scars," he repeats calmly. Too calmly. "From what?"

I've had this conversation more times than I'd like. Most men, bless their hearts, give an honest attempt at pillow talk, even when they're paying for my services. So they ask questions.

"The horse whip my aunt was particularly fond of."

"*This* is what your aunt did to you?" he says, aghast.

I nod.

He moves me a little so that he can peer at the scars. Whatever he sees makes him sit up further.

I begin to move myself, but he holds me in place, inspecting my back.

"There are *dozens* of welts," he says, horrified.

I didn't think he had it in him to be disturbed by something like this. He inflicts worse on people all the time.

"I'm aware." I remember all too clearly the sharp, lacerating burn as my skin split open, and the stiff, lingering pain that lasted for days and days afterwards as the injuries healed.

"Why would she hit you?" he says. Famine doesn't usually show his anger, but I hear it in his voice now.

I lift a shoulder. "It varied. Sometimes it was because I'd forget to do my chores. Sometimes it was because I was too slow—or too lazy. Sometimes I'd say something she didn't like, and sometimes it was just a look I'd give her."

"A look," Famine repeats. He's staring at me like he can't

fathom it. "And you still lived with her?"

"I was a child," I say a little defensively. "I had nowhere else to go."

"*Anywhere* else would've been better."

I give him a disparaging look. "Spoken like a man who has never been powerless."

"I have been powerless."

My breath catches. Of course. I don't know how I forgot.

He traces my scars some more. "And you wonder why I despise your kind."

My throat works. What he's saying is terrible, but I don't feel his hatred; right now I feel his empathy. If there was one person who understood my pain, it would be him.

"I shouldn't tell you this," I admit, "but sometimes ... sometimes—God this is perversely fucked up—sometimes I'm actually grateful you and the other horsemen are killing us off."

Famine goes still, those unnerving green eyes tracking me.

Maybe I shouldn't have said anything. I don't really want to make him believe that he's doing some good deed by wiping us all out.

I rub my temples, feeling like I need to explain myself. "When I think of all that's been done to me and others like me, when I think of every mean act I've seen—acts done without remorse or a second's thought—sometimes it feels like there's something fundamentally wrong with human nature. I don't understand why we can be so hateful to one another."

I feel shame as I speak, but then—in the wake of my words—*lightness*, like I've unburdened myself.

"Why didn't you tell me?" Famine asks.

"That I sometimes hate people just as much as you do?" I say. "Was I supposed to? Would it have changed anything?"

The look he gives me says plainly that, *yes, it would've.*

There's a long pause. Finally, the Reaper says, "If you feel this way, then why do you get upset when I kill?"

A hollow laugh slips out. "I don't *always* hate humanity. And even people who do bad things aren't always bad."

Famine gives me an incredulous look. "Like your aunt and the woman who was going to give you to me."

"Elvita," I say.

"Fuck her and her name too," Famine says. "You can't give someone away like they're a sack of flour or a candlestick. You are a *person*."

Does the horseman realize he just basically said that humans have some inherent value? That's new ...

"And you can't routinely beat someone and pretend to still love them," he continues.

"You don't know that," I say, my voice coming out as a whisper because he touched on something real and deep. "It's not that black and white."

"Are you serious?" he says, disbelieving. "We're talking about the people who *hurt you*, Ana. How can you come to their defense?" Famine looks outraged on my behalf.

"They gave me a home when no one else would," I argue.

"*I* would've," he says.

"Am I supposed to regret not heading off into the sunset with the man who murdered my entire town?"

"They were scum who abused a kid—and they abused *me*."

The moment the words are out of his mouth, his jaw clenches and unclenches.

I open my mouth to argue with him some more when he stands, scooping me up in the process. "Enough of this," he says, carrying me towards the wing of the estate where his rooms are. "I want to taste that pussy of yours again, and damn you, but the concessions I would make just to get your cunning mouth back on my dick."

Concessions? Now *that's* piqued my interest. Maybe I'll still get my moment to save humanity after all.

A blowjob to end all bloodshed. I really *do* like the ring of that.

320

Chapter 37

Late the next morning, I wake up in a bed that's not my own. Which, really, isn't all that strange, now that I have some time to process where I am.

Famine's room. Heitor's house.

I sit up, only to realize that my lips are swollen and my clothes are missing, my hair is a fucking mess, and my head—

Fuck me—I haven't had a headache this bad in who knows how long.

A moment later, the nausea surfaces.

There's a fancy toilet in the bathroom, but it might as well be in a different city, it's too far away. There's a decorative vase resting near the bed.

That'll have to do.

I barely have time to scramble over to it, buck naked, before my stomach is purging itself of everything I ate and drank in the last twelve hours.

As I retch, last night comes back to me in all its lurid detail.

And oh, was it *lurid.*

I clutch the ceramic vase to me and hurl again, though this

time I'm not sure whether it's from the alcohol or the memory of my bad, bad choices.

I can still feel Famine's touch on my skin, his lips pressed against my pussy.

I let him eat me out. Good God. I let a horseman of the apocalypse *eat me out.*

At the memory I feel myself blush. Me, the professional prostitute, *blushing*—over oral, no less.

But Father have mercy, I'd enjoyed it too. And then there was our very painfully real conversation. He saw my scars, he got angry on my behalf.

I let out a shaky breath. Has anyone truly been angry on my behalf? There were my friends at the bordello—Izabel in particular knew about the beatings and she'd cursed my aunt a time or two. But even her indignation never had the same sort of depth and weight that Famine's did. He looked at me last night like I deserved better—like if he could, he'd go back in time and erase my pain—or punish those who caused it.

And I can't help but be ... moved. So moved.

Which is awfully problematic because everything between me and Famine is supposed to go back to the way it was. That was the agreement.

So I need to stop thinking about him like things between us have changed.

When I trust that I'm not going to get sick again, I pad over to the dresser and pull out a filmy dress from the top drawer, this one the color of rouge.

There's a half full pitcher of water and some stale bread sitting next to my bed, and my throat tightens at the sight.

Did Famine leave that for me?

Warmth spreads low in my belly.

Stop it, Ana. He's just a bossy asshole that you're reluctantly friends with.

... Friends with benefits.

That's all.

I eat the bread and drink most of the water, and then, stomach sloshing, I crawl back into Famine's bed.

But when I close my eyes, all I see are the memories of what we did in this bed for the rest of the night. No sex—but everything right up to it.

At least I don't *think* there was any sex ... things got a bit blurry there towards the end.

It doesn't help that the memory of Famine's deft hands and that cruel mouth against my skin is reawakening my lust.

Everything will go back to the way it was tomorrow? I had asked.

Idiot, idiot, idiot.

My mind is *never* going to wash away those memories. And until it does, things are not going to be the same between us.

Eventually, Famine comes for me.

I hear his footfalls coming up the hall. With every step he takes, my heart speeds up. The footfalls pause outside his room, and then the door opens.

Even though I'm curled up on myself, my back to the door, I can still sense the horseman's eyes on me. My skin tingles with awareness.

Then those footfalls again. My pulse is pounding in my ears and I feel sick with anxiety and the worst sort of excitement. Oh, and legitimate nausea. That too.

Getting drunk is definitely overrated.

Famine stops a meter from the bed.

"What's wrong with you?" His deep voice raises goosebumps along my skin.

God, he's awful.

He's also clearly having no problem returning to the way things were.

I bury my face in my pillow.

Does he even know about hangovers? If he doesn't, I'm not sure I have the energy to explain.

I also hate that his voice is making my cheeks heat and my

headache pound against my temple.

"*Everything*," I mumble, drawing the blankets closer to me. "I want to forget the last twenty-four hours."

"That would require more alcohol."

I groan. "Never again," I rasp. Just the memory of all those different liquors has me gagging.

Famine continues to stand there. "Are your regrets catching up to you?"

"They caught up a while ago," I say.

"And?"

And?

I flip over to face the Reaper. "And what?"

Famine is looking at me funny, but I can't say whether it's my words or the sight of me so obviously sick. He crouches next to the bed and reaches a hand out, touching my skin. The moment he does so, I have a flashback to last night.

Tangled arms, tangled legs, his kisses down my breasts and between my thighs ...

I have to take a steadying breath, just to push those memories away.

"Did we ... have sex?"

He frowns. "You don't remember?"

"I remember most of last night ..." Enough to know the two of us let things get out of hand.

He grimaces, but he doesn't leave. The Reaper's gaze travels over my face, his entire expression full of yearning. In response, I feel my stomach clench in a very primal way.

He brushes his knuckles against my cheek, the action painfully kind.

"What?" I say eventually.

Famine shakes his head, then strolls over to my empty pitcher of water. "Do you want more? I know humans need absurd amounts of this stuff ..."

My stomach flutters.

"What are you doing?" My voice comes out a bit hoarse.

Those green eyes of his move to me. Right now they don't look nearly as apathetic as they should. "Is this a trick question?"

I don't want the Reaper doting on me. That does strange things to my mind—and my heart.

"We made an agreement last night—"

Famine sets the pitcher back down. "Fine," he says, looking unbothered. He turns his head towards the vase I vomited in and wrinkles his nose. "I'll let you take care of yourself. Grab what you need and meet me in the front of the estate in an hour."

Famine keeps his distance as I get myself cleaned up, and on the one hand I'm absurdly grateful for it, but on the other ... I don't know. His absence feels like a void has been opened up in me, one I didn't know existed, and it's making me feel restless. And that, in turn, makes me angry at myself.

"Stupid girl," I mutter. Stupid for caring *and* stupid for pushing him away.

My head still pounds and my stomach is still unsettled. Riding a horse should be fun.

I gather a few items I want to take along with me—among them Rocha's dagger, because fuck that dude. I shove them into a bag I find resting in the closet.

I leave Famine's old rooms and cross the courtyard. Lying on the ground are the remnants of last night's clothing. My gaze slides to it, and I feel heat gathering low in my belly.

Stop—thinking—about—it—Ana.

I enter the main building and nearly back out. The plants inside have run rampant, all but swallowing up the room. I glance back the way I came, and for the first time I register that outside, too, the plants in the courtyard have swelled, seeming to reclaim most of the space.

Facing the room once more, I take a deep breath.

There are no dead people in here. It's fine.

With that rallying thought, I elbow my way through the vegetation, my hair snagging on a couple outstretched branches.

When I get to the front yard, Famine is waiting for me, his horse saddled and ready. Wordlessly, he takes the bag I'm holding and secures it to his steed.

I follow behind him, taking a deep breath to steady my stomach.

The Reaper turns to me. "Before we go ..."

I wait for him to finish his sentence. Instead, he reaches a hand out, angling his palm towards my feet.

My skin tingles, and I can sense Famine's magic unfolding around us.

"What are you doing?" I ask him.

"Being naughty," he says.

After seeing what I have of Famine's normal behavior, I can't imagine what *naughty* looks like. What I do know is that I should definitely be afraid.

Only, I'm not. Despite all his brutality, I know this man isn't going to hurt me. I know it with a certainty I cannot explain.

At my feet, the moist earth shifts. From it rises a small green shoot. I watch, fascinated, as it grows before my eyes, the branches climbing, several of them twisting up my leg. Leaves and thorns sprout from the plant.

"Is this where I finally die?" I say, my voice even.

"Don't be so dramatic, little flower. I already told you—I don't intend to kill you."

Even as the plant grows, not a single thorn pricks me, though it does start to coil itself around my body like a lover.

I watch, transfixed, as in a matter of moments a rosebush comes to life around me. From it sprouts a single bud. I stare at it as the bud grows, then bursts open, revealing the delicate, smoky petals of a lavender rose.

I go numb at the sight of it.

Famine grew the same flower the first time our paths crossed. And now he grew it again.

He plucks the rose from the plant, removing its thorns. He runs a hand over the rose bush. "I know she's lovely," he murmurs to the plant, "but you must let her go."

As though it understands, the rose bush uncoils itself from me.

Just as I'm stepping away from the plant, Famine hands the rose over.

"Why?" I ask, taking it from him. Why did he grow this rose for me after he wiped out my village, and why did he grow it for me again today? It's been one of those odd, random things that's picked at me.

"Because around you," he says, "I feel the oddest urge to use my power to create rather than destroy."

We don't return to São Paulo, and for that, I'm absurdly grateful. Even from here I swear I can smell the decay in the air. I can't imagine what death would look like in a city that large.

Not that we avoid it altogether. Heitor might've lived on the outskirts of the city, but the sheer sprawl of São Paulo means that we spend kilometers passing corpses wrapped up in bushes and trees.

"Were they in pain?" I ask.

I expect a cruel response from Famine. Instead he says, "It was quick."

"Why kill them this way?" I ask. I now know that Famine can make a man wither away just as easily as he can plants.

"Preference, mostly."

That's all he says. It's almost as though, today, he doesn't savor his deeds like he usually does. I try not to think about that. It's too easy to feel hopeful, like I have the power to change a bad man one blowjob at a time.

Though I will say, my blowjobs *are* transformative.

For kilometers after we ride out, the land lies in ruins. Dead stalks of corn lean against each other in brown, brittle heaps. Fields of orange trees have all but withered away. Usually, these plants don't die until we pass them, but today as I stare out at the horizon, I see that the destruction extends as far as I can see.

It doesn't end with the crops, either. We pass through another city, and there are so many corpses on the road that Famine has to weave his way through them. Next to many of these bodies are trailers full of valuables. I realize belatedly that we're seeing at least part of the wave of people who fled São Paulo ahead of the horseman.

"When did you do all this?" I ask, covering my nose against the smell.

Not recently, that's for sure.

He makes a noise in his throat. "After I confronted Heitor, I got a little carried away."

A *little* carried away? That's putting it mildly.

But at the mention of the drug lord, my mind flashes back to that ominous night when Famine and I fought for our lives. I can still see the horseman's mutilated body even now, and the thought tightens my chest.

That memory, in turn, leads me to another—the sight of Famine fighting for me, *defending* me.

This is not what I should be thinking about right now. The fact that I *am* thinking about it right now, amongst so many dead, feels wrong.

This *all* feels wrong.

It's felt wrong from the moment I woke up. The lightness in my stomach, the intimacy that I should be regretting but don't. Or that I'm acutely aware of every part of me pressing against every part of him like I'm some virgin who's never been touched before. And now this—having soft thoughts towards the Reaper while riding through a graveyard of his own making.

That's wrong on so many levels.

When these thoughts aren't spinning through my head, my mind drifts back to last night and the way he looked at me. The way he touched me. The way he *tasted* me.

At the memory, I feel that same fluttery sensation low in my stomach. It eclipses the last traces of my nausea. For the first time I actually take note of it.

It's not desire, though that's there, too.

The last time I felt like this, it had been with Martim, the rancher who had told me he loved me and who I foolishly believed was going to marry me before he broke my heart and married a proper woman.

Oh my God.

It actually hits me then.

Fuck my tits and my asshole too.

I'm falling for this psycho.

Chapter 38

I try to walk the realization back.

Famine was just a really good lover.

You're just curious, and it's been a long, long time since you've had a genuine sexual encounter.

No one in their right mind would fall in love with a man who's wiping out entire cities.

"What's wrong?" Famine asks at my back.

Of course the horseman would notice something was off the *instant* I recognized my own feelings.

"*Nothing's wrong,*" I say way too quickly. "Why would you even ask a question like that?"

There's a long pause, then suddenly, Famine is pulling his horse to a stop.

No-no-no-no-no—

The Reaper takes my jaw, turning me to face him.

"What are you doing? Why have we stopped?" My eyes are darting over our surroundings.

"*Look at me.*"

I almost argue, but that would even be more suspicious.

I force my gaze to meet his.

"What?" I say obstinately.

Don't see it. Don't see what I've only now just realized.

His gaze narrows. "Little flower, I know something is wrong. You can tell me now, or I can figure it out on my own, but I promise you this: I *will* figure it out."

My stomach tumbles. If Famine is half as good at reading people's minds as he is at dancing, or kissing, or oral, then he's going to figure out real quick that despite our vow last night, things *have* changed between us.

"I ... am just not feeling well."

"No," he says simply.

Damn him.

"So now you think I'm a liar?" I accuse.

"I *know* you're a liar." All at once, he releases my jaw. "But keep your thoughts to yourself. I'll learn them soon enough."

This new revelation sits like a stone in my stomach.

Falling for the horseman.

I don't want to fall in love. Everyone I've loved has either died or hurt me and *then* died. My parents, my aunt, even Elvita.

And then, of course, there was that one previous time I fell in love, and that whole thing went about as smoothly as the apocalypse.

Martim had just turned twenty when he met me. I had already been at the bordello for a couple years, but in many ways I was still young and naïve when I first met the rancher.

He was all gangly limbs, but he had kind eyes and a gentle smile, and he never saw me as just some floozy to stick his dick in. His buddies were the ones who paid for our first night together, but after that he came back for himself.

The other girls had warned me not to fall for clients. So many of them had been burned in the past by men who wanted free sex or who had savior complexes. But naturally, I thought I was different, and I thought Martim was different, too.

Short story: he wasn't.

When his parents learned that he loved me, they threatened to disown him. No family, no ranch, no carefully crafted future that he had prepared his entire life for. That's what he stood to lose. He had tears in his eyes when he told me. I think he assumed I would understand.

The only thing I understood was that the world loves to kick you when you're down.

Less than a year later, Martim married a *respectable* woman. And just when I thought my broken heart had mended itself, it broke all over again.

Not too long after the wedding, Martim tried to visit me at the bordello, but not for all the money in the world would I let him touch me again, and he didn't seem to want to sleep with anyone else at The Painted Angel. So that was that.

The pain that used to accompany Martim's memory is only a shadow of its former self. Unfortunately, there's a new emotion I feel—*panic*.

I don't want to be in love again. And with the Reaper of all people.

"I *will* figure it out." Famine's breath tickles my ear.

Holy hell.

"Will you stop?" I say. "There's nothing to figure out."

"Liar."

I hate that he's right, and I hate that he's so astute. In all likelihood, not only will the horseman probably learn my secret by this evening, he'll manage to pulverize my brittle little heart while he's at it.

Because such is my luck.

The sun is setting when Famine steers us to an obviously abandoned house.

I eye the dilapidated structure. "And here I thought that you never wanted to stay in another one of these again."

"Would you prefer to sleep outside?" he asks, his fingers rubbing the obviously wet fabric of my dress together. It's rained off and on all day.

"You could always fix the weather."

He makes a derisive sound. "Of course you would ask me to change the weather just to make yourself more comfortable."

"Oh my God, Famine, calm your tits."

"I don't have t—"

"I'm not trying to make you do anything. I'm just reminding you that you threw the world's biggest hissy when we stopped at the last abandoned house," I say.

"And you threw an equally big *hissy* when we stopped at an occupied house," he replies.

I sputter. "Yeah, because you were going to kill a woman."

"And so I brought you to an abandoned house," he says slowly, gesturing to the building in front of us.

Humph.

"Fine," I say begrudgingly. "You made your point."

He guides the horse almost all the way up to the front door before stopping his steed and hopping off. After a moment, I dismount and follow him inside.

Unlike the last abandoned house we stayed at, this one is in much better condition—relatively speaking. There's even a hand pump well just outside the back of the house. The place also shows signs that other travelers have stayed in it. Used up matches, cigarette butts, a beat up book, a few empty liquor bottles, and a clay oil lamp someone left behind.

Famine turns around, his gaze finding mine. A moment later, his eyes dip to my chest. Belatedly, I realize that my rose colored dress is soaked through, molding perfectly to my breasts. Breasts that the Reaper is now staring at.

Just like that, it seems as though last night never ended. I can see Famine's hunger; it matches my own.

It looks like it takes him enormous effort, but he eventually tears his gaze away, his eyes landing heavily on mine as he exhales.

This is going to be harder than I thought, his expression seems to say. Or maybe those are my own thoughts.

The horseman brushes past me then, heading back outside.

"Why don't you just bring your horse inside?" I call after him. It's not like anyone cares about what a horse might do to this place.

The Reaper comes back in carrying several sacks and his scythe. He tosses his weapon onto the floor, the metal clattering as it skids along the ground. "Make him endure this moldy, cramped space? I may be wicked, but I am not *that* wicked."

I give him a funny look. "You are so odd."

Everything he believes—all his opinions and assumptions— are unlike anything I've ever come across.

"No, my flower, it is you who are odd. Lewd and witty and very, exceptionally odd."

He sets the packs he's carrying onto a derelict table, the wood swollen and warped. In one of them, I hear the clink of what must be Famine's scales. He, however, turns his attention to the other bag. From it, he pulls out a blanket and the remnants of last night's food.

I stare at the items with rising apprehension. "You packed," I say. "For me."

He thinks of me and my needs even when I'm not around—needs that he doesn't share. My chest tightens in an almost painful way. But the sensation is soon followed by fear.

"You look like you're going to hurl," the horseman says conversationally as he tucks the blanket under his arm.

"I'm just—that was kind of you. Is all," I say like an idiot.

He lifts an eyebrow. "I didn't realize you take to kindness about as well as I do. I'm actually strangely pleased by this."

He strides down the hall, peering into one of the far rooms. "There's a mattress back here you could sleep on, but full disclosure—there are more lifeforms growing on it than there are in the rest of the house."

That snaps me out of my thoughts.

"The floor is fine."

The Reaper returns to the living room and kicks aside a beat up coffee table before unfurling the blanket, laying it in the middle of the room.

Once he's finished straightening it out, Famine stands back, looking mighty pleased with himself. Because he made me a bed. Never mind that there's no pillow or a top sheet to cover myself with. The man who gets everyone to do his bidding went out of his way yet again to do something for me.

My heart is beating loudly in my chest.

I don't know if I can do this.

I've spent a long time working on not falling in love. I don't want that to end now—and with the Reaper no less. Because heartbreak will follow—it always does—and if gentle Martim was able to break my heart into a thousand pieces, what would terrible, merciless Famine do to it?

"Well?" the horseman says, looking at me for some sort of reaction.

Mechanically I move to the sheet and sit down.

"Thank you for this." My voice sounds wooden.

Famine scrutinizes me. "I *will* figure it out, you know."

I give him a questioning look.

"What's been on your mind," he explains.

My stomach bottoms out.

Oh right.

"Please don't," I say softly.

All he does is smile.

I'm doomed.

Chapter 39

Rain patters against the roof, and I can hear the steady drip of it from several leaks in the roof.

I sit on the blanket Famine laid out for me while the Reaper rummages around the house. My stomach is full from eating the food the horseman packed for me. Now that it's dark, I should be tired.

Instead my senses buzz. Night has always been the time I worked, so I'm used to feeling awake when most people are settling in for the evening. However, I'm not used to my heart leaping and my skin pricking with awareness at the horseman's every word and gesture.

Right now I can hear him strike a match. There's a hiss and a burst of light. A minute later he strides over to where I sit, carrying the clay oil lamp I saw earlier, a lit wick peeking out of it. He lowers himself to the ground next to the blanket, setting the lamp down beside him.

I pat the blanket. "You can sit here you know."

"That's your bed," the Reaper says.

Calling this blanket a *bed* is giving it far too much credit, but that's cute of him anyway.

"I'm used to sharing," I reply.

In the lamplight, our eyes meet, and last night silently plays itself out in our minds. Famine still hasn't moved.

"Don't make this weird," I say. "Nothing's changed between us."

The horseman gives me a sharp look, one that makes my stomach dip, but he does move onto the blanket, sitting across from me.

Seconds pass and that gravity is still in his gaze, like he is swimming in deep, deep water and he wants to drag me under with him.

I turn my attention to the house around us, listening to the steady drip of rain.

"Sleepovers in derelict buildings are kind of our thing," I say, softly.

"Mmm."

I drop my gaze back to Famine, and damnit, he's still looking at me *like that.*

"Stop it," I whisper.

"Stop what?" he says, not looking away from me.

Stop making me feel lighter than air and heavier than iron. Stop sucking me under.

"Nothing's changed between us," I insist. I don't know how I manage to say that lie in a normal voice.

The Reaper smiles at me then, his expression wry, like I'm the naïve one and he's the one with the worldly experience.

I glance away, unable to hold his gaze. I'm desperate for a distraction. Anything that might make me forget I'm incurably attracted to him.

My eyes land on the oil lamp. It's nothing more than a shallow bowl with a little pinched lip for the wick. That's all the light we have to talk by tonight.

"Can I ask you something?" I say.

Rather than responding, the Reaper waits for me to continue.

"Why did everything fail?"

I can tell that's not the question he was expecting. He was expecting a question about *us*, but hell no am I going to ask him something that will force me to confront my feelings for him.

"You mean human technology?" he asks.

I nod.

There are junkyards full of rusted automobiles and appliances and televisions and computers and those cute little cellphones people used to carry. There are landfills full of other things too—things that I don't even have proper names for, things that once worked but no longer do. I'm too young to have seen cars drive and planes fly and machines wash clothes and chill food. It all sounds like witchcraft.

Maybe that's why it all failed—I don't think God is a big fan of witchcraft.

"It all failed because humans got carried away," the horseman replies. "You were all naughty children who didn't listen when God told you in His quiet way to stop," Famine says idly. "So now He's being loud about it."

"Is that why God is punishing us?" I ask. "Because we were too ... innovative?" I've heard of a lot of sins; I didn't realize curiosity was one of them.

"God isn't punishing you," Famine replies smoothly. "*I* am. God is merely balancing the scales—so to speak."

"Because we invented too many things?" I ask.

"Because the world fell out of balance," he says. "And humans are to blame for that."

There's that word again—*balance*. The Reaper has mentioned it a couple of times now. Immediately, my eyes move to the kitchen, where I last caught a glimpse of his scales. He brought them in with the rest of our things, though he didn't properly unpack them.

"There are some good things about humans," Famine adds. "If there weren't, this would've happened long ago."

I take that in, trying to process the fact that the horseman is admitting that people have some goodness to them.

I don't say anything, caught between shock and a fragile sort of hope that maybe, *maybe* were aren't totally and completely screwed.

Famine's eyes move to mine again, and that look is back. He leans forward and reaches out, his fingers skimming my cheeks.

At his touch, I still.

"You said everything was going to go back to the way it was before," I accuse, my voice a whisper.

"I lied." There's no remorse in his tone. "I cannot forget how you saved me and all you have admitted to me since. And I cannot forget how your skin felt against mine and the look in your eyes when I touched you. But most of all, Ana, I cannot ignore the way you draw me in, again and again."

My heart starts to pound loudly, so loudly I'm sure he can hear it. These are things lovers—true lovers—say to each other, and I can't bear it. It's my weakness. Ask any girl who's known too little love in her life and she'll tell you—this is how you ensnare us.

"Don't tell me you haven't been reconsidering it yourself?" Famine says.

I glance away, picking at a loose thread on the blanket.

"*Ana.*"

Reluctantly, my eyes return to his, and he sees it. I know he does.

His eyes widen, then after a moment, he flashes me a triumphant grin. "You have." He stares at me a little longer, and I hear him inhale a breath. "*That's* what you've been keeping from me all day," he says, like he's finally figured it out.

But I don't think he has. I think if Famine knew the depth of what I'm feeling right now, he wouldn't be so pleased.

He catches my chin and pulls my face closer, leaning in

until only a few short centimeters separate our lips. "Little flower, I'm happy to give you an encore of last night," he says, his voice low. I can hear his own desire, and it is not helping anything at this point.

I stare at the horseman, unwilling to speak. I don't trust my mouth; it might blurt out every tangled, confused emotion I'm feeling right now.

"I'm used to having casual sex," I admit, "but this ... this isn't casual, Famine, and I don't know how to handle it."

The horseman's eyes are bright and deep, and part of me really wants to know what he thinks of that.

"I'm not used to handling *any* of this," he says.

He releases my chin and sits up. "Get comfortable." He nods to the blanket we're sitting on. "I'll tell you a story—with a head scratch—and then I'll leave."

I frown at the *leave* part, but then—head scratch?

I'm laying down in a matter of seconds, Famine sitting at my side.

His hand slips through my hair, and I have to bite back a very sexual-sounding moan because it feels *so good.*

"How about I tell you about the time I met one of my brothers," he says thoughtfully.

"Mmm," I say noncommittally, not really paying attention to his words until—

"*Wait.*" I begin to sit back up. "You mean here, on *earth?*"

Famine pushes me back down. "Yes."

"Which brother?" I ask, head scratch forgotten. "And what was he doing? What were *you* doing? What did you do to each other?" Oh my God, the questions I have.

Famine continues to rub my head. "I was making my way south through Europe. I'd already left the mainland, and I was crossing the Aegean Sea. I was about to arrive on Crete when I crossed paths with War." His gaze grows distant.

"In this form," Famine says, "it's hard to sense my brothers, but it isn't impossible. I knew War was close; I could feel him approaching me just as he must've felt me approaching him."

I had never thought to press Famine for information on his brothers. Clearly, I should've.

"He met me on the beach," he says.

I try to picture it in my mind—Famine meeting War, one of his brothers.

The Reaper falls silent.

"And?" I prod.

"He told me to leave."

"Did you?" I ask.

Famine's eyes slip to mine, a wry smile on his face. "One does not pick fights with War, not even in his mortal form. I left him and his family alone—"

"*Family?*" I interrupt, shocked.

What in the actual hell?

"*War has a family?*"

"So does Pestilence."

I stare at Famine, trying to process that. "You mean to tell me that *two* of your brothers have settled down and had kids?" I say carefully.

Famine nods.

"... *How?*" I finally ask.

The horseman gives me a sly look. "It's really quite simple, flower. They fucked mortal women. Those women got pregnant. Now they have families."

My eyes feel like they're bulging from their sockets. Right now, everything this horseman says is wilder than the thing before it.

"You horsemen can get women pregnant?" I ask.

Jesus. I hadn't even thought about *that*.

"I can eat and sleep and do just about everything else a human can," Famine says. "Is being able to procreate really so shocking?"

"*Yes.*"

It's really, *really* freaking shocking.

The next question slips from my lips. "Do you have any children?"

"God, no," he says, "I've made sure of that."

"You made sure—" I sit up again. "*What is that supposed to mean? Did you kill your kids?*" I can feel how wide my eyes are.

The Reaper pushes me back down.

"Would that actually shock you?" he says.

"Oh my God, *you did.*" I don't know why, but that changes *everything.*

I begin to get up, and once more Famine pushes me back down. "Calm your tits," the horseman says, and how fucking *dare* he use my own line against me— "They never lived to begin with."

I stare up at him, breathing heavily, my mind racing to catch up with his words.

"They never lived ... ?" I echo.

"I have the power to make things grow and die," he says. "I can prevent conception."

That is *so* much more information than I bargained for. But also, sex with the horseman is back *on* the table.

Jesus, did that thought actually cross my mind?

Famine stares down at me. "Are you good?"

I nod, maybe a little too quickly. "I'm good," I say, just to reassure him.

The horseman is looking at me as though I can't be trusted.

"So War lives on an island?" I start again, taking a few deep breaths to calm myself. "With his family?"

I'm trying to imagine someone like Famine being a father. I can't picture it.

"Mhm," Famine says, still giving me a skeptical look. His hand moves back to my hair, and his fingers begin rubbing my scalp once more.

"So, he loves them then?" I ask. "His family?"

"The fuck if I know," the Reaper says. After a moment, he adds, "But I imagine he does."

I lay there, trying to figure out how the hell these women managed to tame two horsemen of the apocalypse.

"Does that mean War's not killing people the same way you are?" I ask.

"He had been," Famine admits, "but yes, at some point he stopped—as did Pestilence."

"Why?" I ask, my brows furrowing.

The horseman frowns. A moment later, he stands. "Get some sleep. I'll be near."

With that, he crosses the room and opens the door. Famine slips outside, into the drizzling rain. The door clicks shut behind him, and then he's gone.

It takes far longer than it should to fall asleep.

At first, all I can think about is his parting story and all of the information he revealed. But as my shock settles, other things begin to creep in.

I cannot forget how your skin felt against mine and the look in your eyes when I touched you. But most of all, I cannot ignore the way you draw me in.

I'm haunted by the horseman's words and the look on his face when he said them.

I don't even have a dick in me, and I'm fucked.

So, so fucked.

Somewhere between one troubled thought and the next, I slip off to sleep.

BANG!

I jolt awake, trying to figure out what's happening, even as I hear shouting. Panic floods my system.

I push myself up on my elbows just as someone says, "Don't move another centimeter unless you want a hole in that pretty chest of yours."

My gaze goes first to the intruder speaking, then to the bow and arrow he has trained on me.

"Told you there was someone at the old Monteiro place," a woman behind him says.

My heart begins to gallop.

Highwaymen.

I hadn't given much thought to the bandits that roamed the roads since I began traveling with Famine. After all, anyone who came close to the horseman died.

Where the hell *is* the Reaper?

Earlier he'd said that he'd leave—and he did. I just hadn't thought he meant *permanently*. But has he come back since he left my side?

And then another insidious thought creeps in.

What if something bad happened to him again?

Another man steps out from behind the one with the bow and arrow and walks over to me. He grabs me roughly by the arm and hauls me up, then drags me to the door.

I stumble along as I'm hauled out of the house and into the rain. I can no longer see the arrow aimed at me, but I sense it at my back.

The darkness is illuminated only by the dim glow of a lantern sitting on the porch. I can just make out the group's three horses, tied to a nearby tree. Famine's steed is nowhere to be seen.

Maybe I really am alone.

I take a deep breath at that.

The man at my side presses a blade to my cheek. "Where's the other one?" he asks, his voice raspy.

"The other what?" I say. My mind can hardly keep up with the unfolding events.

"Don't play dumb, bitch. We saw the second set of footprints."

Famine and I tracked mud inside. I hadn't even thought of

that.

"Where is the man you were with?" my captor continues.

I feel fleeting relief that at least these three haven't done anything to him.

I shake my head. "I don't know."

"What the fuck do you mean you don't know?" the man growls, giving me a vicious shake. I barely catch myself from falling into the mud.

I give him a nasty look; years of barroom brawls have prepared me for men like him.

"I *mean* that I just fucking woke up, you ass-licking bastard."

The knife leaves my cheek long enough for the man to cock his fist and hit me across the face.

My legs fold, and now I do fall to the ground. I hear him spit, though I don't feel it with all the rain pummeling me.

"Bitch. We're going to have to beat some manners into you."

Distantly, I can hear the other two bandits moving through the house.

"What the hell is this?" one calls from the doorway. I glance over my shoulder as the woman saunters out, tossing Famine's scales in front of me. The metal plates clink together.

At the sight, I feel a spark of hope.

Maybe the horseman hasn't left after all.

But then I remember how he sometimes rides away without his scales, knowing they'll turn up eventually. He could still be gone.

I'm pushing myself to my feet when the bandit next to me kicks me forward, forcing me back against the ground. My hands sink into the muddy earth.

"Well?" the man says. "Answer her."

These men really have no clue who they've ambushed, even when the evidence is staring them in the face.

Not that it will save me.

I look over at the woman. "They're scales, you cunt-munching idiots."

That gets me another kick to the side. I gasp at the impact, curling in on myself.

"What did you find?" my attacker calls out to his comrades.

"Nothing much worth saving," the woman says. "At least we can trade her." She nods to me.

No.

I've been used enough in my twenty-two years; I won't let it happen again.

I hear the third bandit's footfalls as he leaves the house. "I don't want to deal with traffickers," he says, coming towards us. "Grab what you can and slit her throat."

My muscles tense at that.

The bandit reaches for me.

Acting on instinct, I kick out at the man, missing his crotch.

"Stupid bitch," he growls, lunging for me, his knife aimed at my chest.

I barely manage to roll away, the blade embedding itself into the wet earth where I was a moment ago. The man catches me by the waist and flips me onto my back, pinning my body beneath a knee.

I buck, trying to throw him off of me, but he's too heavy.

Distantly, I'm aware that the other two bandits are packing up their horses, ignoring us as though midnight scuffles in the mud are normal.

My attacker grabs my hair and jerks my head to the side, forcing me to bare my neck. Then his muddy blade is pressed against my skin once more.

I go still, my eyes moving to his.

This is it.

I survived all manner of frightening men as a prostitute—I even survived a horseman of the apocalypse—just for it to end like this.

I have the oddest urge to laugh. It all feels so pointless. So, so pointless.

Behind us, there's a rustling in the foliage that borders the house. My attacker pauses.

From over his shoulder I catch a glimpse of Famine stepping out of the shadows, fully clad in his armor, his scythe at his side.

He didn't leave.

I exhale. Never have I been so grateful to see the horseman.

He looks mildly amused as his gaze moves from one highwayman to the next; the weather, however, gives him away. The rain pounds down on us, and behind the Reaper, lightning flashes across the sky, illuminating his form.

"Well, who the fuck is this?" the leader of the group says, clearly unaware who has just joined them. I hear the slide of wood against wood as he grabs an arrow and nocks it.

"Most call me Famine, though I must admit, I have a particular fondness for 'the Reaper.'"

Another bolt of lightning streaks down from the sky, and for an instant, I can see the horseman in all his malevolent glory.

No sooner has Famine revealed himself than the female bandit takes off, sprinting across the yard.

The horseman doesn't even bother trying to catch her. Instead he throws his scythe with impossible force. The unwieldy weapon spins head over handle making a rhythmic chopping noise as it propels forward.

With a meaty *thunk*, it buries itself into the back of the woman's skull. Her legs fold, and she falls, dead in an instant.

The man above me makes a startled noise as she collapses. He turns back to me, and I see the wild look in his eyes—

The blade at my throat is moving, slicing my skin open. I cry out at the sharp bite of pain, surprise making my eyes widen. I didn't think he'd try to kill me, not now that Famine was here.

I go to push the knife away, but before I can reach it, a great, thorned plant drags my attacker off of me, and his knife falls harmlessly out of his hand.

Warm blood spills down my neck. I clutch the wound, the liquid slipping between my fingers. For a second, all I can think of is that the man must've nicked an artery, but then there would be more blood—right?

It's hard to tell what a lot is, but after a moment, I think I'm okay. And now that I can feel the edges of the wound, I can tell it only sliced part of my neck, and it's not so deep—

A hand goes to my shoulder.

I glance up and there's Famine kneeling at my side, his green eyes focused on my face. He looks so angry, so vengeful. But behind all those potent emotions, I see panic. Cloying, dreadful panic.

His gaze drops to my neck, where I'm putting pressure on the wound.

"You're hurt." There's no emotion behind the words, and yet the horseman's fingers are gripping my shoulder so tightly, and the longer I stare at him, the more distressed he appears.

"I'll be okay," I say. *I think.*

His gaze searches mine, and I can tell he doesn't know what to do.

Behind him, I can hear the cries of the two remaining bandits. I don't have to look to know what's happening to them.

I continue to stare up at the Reaper.

You saved me. I don't bother saying it. He and I both know it.

Famine cups my face, and how strange, I can feel his hand trembling. And now that I'm looking, his expression is more intense than I've ever seen it, and his breathing is a little harsh.

He searches my face, and then he very deliberately says,

"*Fuck* things going back to the way they were."

With that, he kisses me.

Chapter 40

His lips are hot on mine, and all that fear and shock and pain and adrenaline finally catch up to me. I cling to him, holding on for dear life.

He saved me. I was seconds away from a swift death, and Famine *saved me*.

What had I told him a while ago?

I helped you once too—even though you wouldn't have done the same for me.

I was wrong. Famine clearly would do the same for me.

And that realization shatters the rickety walls guarding my feelings.

Screw broken hearts. What good are they if you die and never actually get to experience anything worth experiencing?

I kiss the horseman with all the urgency I've held back until now. With all the desire and hope and all the terrible, wonderful emotions that have moved through me in the last day.

God, but this man feels like home, and that's more than a little wondrous to a woman like me, who's never really had a home.

Famine is kissing me with a ferocity to match my own, and around us, the rain is coming down in torrents, each drop hitting my skin so hard it stings. It washes away the mud and blood covering me, along with the last of my resistance.

The horseman's hands slip down my cheeks, and I wince when he brushes my wound.

His lips pause, then he pulls away. "*Ana.*" The panic is back in his voice. His gaze dips to my neck.

"It's not bad ..." But even as I speak, I feel a little dizzy, a little disoriented.

Famine's jaw clenches. "You are such a goddamned liar."

A moment later he scoops me up and carries me inside. He sets me down on the blanket he laid out for me, then quickly removes his bronze armor, the metal clinking as he sets it aside.

He pulls his shirt off, revealing those mesmerizing tattoos that glow green in the darkness.

The Reaper kneels down at my side, pressing the black garment against my wound, staunching the flow of blood.

There's nowhere to look that isn't him, and I'm confronted once again by my feelings as I take in his features. The horseman is the most excruciatingly beautiful thing I've ever seen. Usually, he looks like some proud, untouchable prince from a bygone era, but right now ... he doesn't look proud and untouchable. If anything, he looks young and uncertain and desperate.

He focuses on my injury, keeping his shirt pressed against my throat. I turn towards him, and the black cloth bushes against my cheek and nose as I do so. Even after a day of traveling, the material smells fresh, clean. If Famine were fully human, the shirt would probably smell like sweat and sour pussy—figuratively speaking, of course; the only pussy Famine's been near is my own, and I pride myself on—

"Ana."

"What?" I say, pushing away the thought.

"How bad is it?"

"How bad is what?" My gaze lingers on his lips.

"Your wound," he says slowly, looking at me like I grew two heads.

"Oh." I move his shirt away a little so I can probe the edges of the cut. "I don't know, but I don't think it's too bad." When I see the look in the Reaper's eyes, I add, "I'm not lying."

The injury hurts, I can feel the throb of it pounding just beneath my jawline, but I've lived through worse—much worse.

I stare at Famine, whose face is lit by the soft glow of his markings. His jaw clenches again, like he might be angry, and right then it really, truly hits me—

"You're worried about me," I say.

What a crazy, wondrous thing.

"Of course I am," he says, his voice so low that I almost miss the words.

I feel warmth spread throughout my body.

This, even more than his compliments, is my undoing.

I reach for him, moving with confidence. My arms wrap around his neck.

He looks at me, shocked. "What are you—?"

Before he can finish his sentence, my lips find his and I kiss him with the same fervency I did outside. For a second or two, he responds ... and then his mind catches up to him.

Famine breaks away, looking angry. "Are you just going to ignor—?"

"Yes," I say, and then my lips are back on his. Yes, I am going to ignore the fact that a man just tried to slit my throat. I fucking survived it, and now I'm floating on this adrenaline high and I need to feel the horseman against me.

At first, Famine doesn't respond, and I know he's thinking about the fact that I'm hurt and it's dark and he can't see how injured I am—oh, and that I'm a liar from time to time. The thing is, my mouth *is* a very, very good liar, and right now, it's doing its best to convince the Reaper that I'm not that hurt.

He must buy it too, because eventually he returns the kiss—and damn does he return it. His arms come around me, and he cradles me like I'm breakable, but he kisses me like he wants to break me wide open and slip inside. His lips are hot on mine.

He leans forward, his chest meeting mine. Heat radiates off of him, and despite his menacing reputation, I'm struck that, to me, everything about him is comforting. His physical warmth, his touch, his desire.

We're oil and water; we're not supposed to mix, yet here we are. His hands are wild as they dig through my hair. I can still feel them trembling, even as they hold me in place.

I feel that craze inside him. My heart beats in time with it.

I reach for his pants, tugging at them.

He catches my wrist. "Ana—"

He's still worried about my wound.

My eyes find his. "It's just a little cut, Famine. It will be fine," I whisper. "I want this. If you want it too, then let me unbutton your damn pants. Please."

He stares down at me, debating, debating ...

The horseman releases my wrist. I exhale, my heart beginning to pound.

As I begin undoing the horseman's trousers, Famine's hands skim down my body. There's a gentleness to his touch that wasn't there before, and I can't decide whether he's simply worried about my injury, or if it's something else. Whatever it is, it causes me to pause. I want to savor this. I've so rarely gotten to savor intimacy.

Buttons descend the front of my ruined dress, and one by one the horseman undoes them, slowly peeling the garment away from my body.

As soon as he reveals my stomach, his hands go to my scars. He hesitates, then places soft kisses along them.

The Reaper doesn't ask for my forgiveness again, but nonetheless I feel his apology in the brush of his lips. I feel something else too—something that seems an awful lot like adoration.

This is new, so new. I feel like so much more than my flesh is being exposed and seen. For all the sex I've had, I'm a stranger to this. Feeling valued, *adored*.

I can feel a thick knot of emotion in my throat, and my eyes begin to sting. I cover my eyes with a hand, but to my horror, it doesn't stop a tear from slipping out. Another one follows it. Then another and another.

What is wrong with you?

Famine pauses. "Ana?" he asks, and I want to laugh at the uncertainty in his voice.

It takes an embarrassing amount of strength, but I drag my hands away from my eyes. I don't know if he can see my tears in the darkness, but—

Famine's brow wrinkles as he takes me in. "Are you crying?" I can tell he doesn't know what to make of me.

"Yes," I admit.

Famine frowns. "Do you want me to stop?" he says, clearly not understanding why I'm upset.

"God no."

He stares at me longer. There's very little softness to this man, and yet, right now, he's being excruciatingly compassionate.

"I'm not human," he says. "I don't understand what you're thinking. Explain your mind."

I blow out a breath. "My clients—they never treated me like this." Not even Martim.

Sex always felt like an exchange. I was a prostitute. I wasn't getting paid to be adored. I was getting paid to slack someone's lust.

Famine's expression changes, becoming empathetic—so, so empathetic. I think, when it comes to pain and vulnerability, he sees me more clearly than anyone else ever has.

That warm, uncomfortable feeling blooms low in my belly. This time, I don't fight it.

The horseman brushes back my hair, his eyes moving between mine.

"Tonight," he says softly, "you're going to forget all the ways you were mistreated. I'm going to make sure of it."

Chapter 41

He doesn't lead, but he doesn't wait for me to lead either. Rather, every touch is met with another touch.

I stare at him in wonder as he removes my boots and the last of my dress before shucking off his own shoes and pants.

How Famine is acting right now goes against everything he's led me to believe. He shouldn't be sentimental—there's no room for sentimentality in that dark heart of his—and yet he's handling me like I'm precious to him.

Naked, he kneels at my feet. He takes one of my ankles and presses a kiss to it, running his lips over my skin.

Jesus, he's going to drag this out. It's probably not the best night to drag this out; the rain didn't wash away all the mud and blood on my skin ...

I reach for him, ready to speed things up.

Famine catches my hands and, twining his fingers between mine, he pins my arms above my head, draping himself over me. I can feel his hard cock pinned between us.

He kisses me softly. "No tricks," he murmurs against my lips. He pulls away long enough for our eyes to meet.

After a moment, I nod.

At my response, he releases my hands. His mouth returns to kissing my skin, moving down from my lips to my chin to my clavicles, sternum, and breasts.

I close my eyes against his kisses, drinking them in. Each press of his lips is unspeakably tender. This is a side of him that I didn't know existed—that I hadn't imagined *could* exist—and it's doing strange things to me.

I slide my palms over Famine's shoulders, marveling at his smooth flesh. This body of his has seen and felt so much pain, and unlike me, he has nothing to show for it. No scars, no disfigurement, just an alarming amount of nightmarish memories.

I twine my legs around his, the pads of my feet skimming over the back of his calves, trying to feel every part of him at once. My heart feels too big for my chest.

He slides his hands over my skin, breaking off his kisses to just look at me. It's the oddest thing in the world, seeing him marvel at my form like he's discovering desire for the first time. His gaze moves to my eyes, and at his expression, I still.

I don't simply exist, he once said, *I hunger.*

I see his desire now so clearly, but it's not as simple as most of the lustful looks men have given me in the past. There's a deeper element to it, and I remember something else he said to me.

Not everything is about sex, flower.

What else is going on behind those green eyes of his? Could it be ... could he feel more for me?

I force away the thought before it can sink its claws in.

Famine's fingers move to my core. The moment they touch, a naughty smile teases his lips.

"And here I thought I'd have to ready you," he says, running his finger around my entrance.

Clearly he's underestimating my own desire.

He moves his hand away, and adjusts himself until I feel his cock right at my entrance.

He stares down at me, and God, he's utterly magnificent; his glyphs illuminate those wicked lips of his and set his eyes aglow. Several strands of his hair hang down, and if I weren't so caught up in this moment, I might actually tuck them behind his ears.

But it's not just his beauty that's captivated me. He's not wearing the haughty mask he usually does during the day; he hasn't been ever since he saved me. He looks just as exposed and vulnerable as I feel.

"Flower ..."

He tilts his hips as he gazes down at me, and his cock slowly begins to push in.

I suck in a breath at the sensation of being stretched and filled, and—aww, shit—I think I'm about to have another moment.

My throat tightens, and my eyes prick.

Am I seriously going to cry right when my pussy is getting its first real taste of heaven? Is this who I've become?

Famine is looking down at me like I'm some sort of miracle he's stumbled upon and I have to bite back a sob.

Yep, apparently this *is* who I've become.

My hands move to my face again.

Don't want him to see me like this.

Famine takes my hands and moves them away from my face.

"Don't hide from me," he says. "All I want is to see you right now."

His words are unbearably kind, which is the last thing my sensitive heart needs right now.

A tear slips out.

He frowns at the sight of it. "Why are you crying?" There's a note of alarm in his voice. His hips have stilled, and it's the worst sort of agony.

I close my eyes for a moment. "It's nothing."

"Open your eyes." The alarm is still in the Reaper's voice.

Reluctantly, I do. Whatever he sees on my face causes his brows to draw together. "What's wrong?"

"Everything. Nothing."

This is unlike any experience I've ever had, and already he's ruined me, completely ruined me, for sex. My career as a prostitute is finished.

"Do you want me to stop?" he asks.

"*No*."

He looks unconvinced.

Damnit, I'm going to have to tell him something.

I take a deep breath. "I just ... I've had so many letdowns in my life, and this ... this feels too good to be true. And I feel like you can see everything on my face." Which is ironic, considering how little light there is in this room.

The Famine I met weeks ago would've openly mocked me for this. A part of me is certain he's going to mock me now.

Only ... there's no judgment in his expression. But his eyes hold a heavy sort of understanding. It makes me think that his own pain runs deep enough to recognize mine.

I see his throat work as he searches my face. "Ana ..."

I think he's about to say something big.

His lips part, but then he shakes his head, and the moment is gone.

Famine leans in and kisses me, and I feel some bittersweet mixture of relief and regret. He isn't freaked out by my words, but he's also not about to reassure me that I have nothing to worry about. He's Famine, he crushes things for fun—humans and their simpering emotions most of all.

The horseman begins to move again, and I focus on that. His cock is still stretching me in the most pleasurable way.

I marvel at him, at this.

His gaze is fixed on me as he thrusts in and out, in and out. The two of us stare at each other with wonder. None of this was supposed to happen.

"I see you," Famine says. He leans in and kisses one eyelid, then the other. "Only you."

My breath shudders out of me, and then another stupid, rebellious little tear slips down the side of my face.

Gah, my eyes need to *stop* this whole crying business.

A moment later, the horseman wipes it away.

I give him a shaky smile, and Famine's eyes catch on it.

"God have mercy, Ana, I told you no pretty human tricks," he says, staring at my mouth, his voice hoarse.

Slowly, he resumes his thrusts. Each stroke is deep, yet somehow, he makes the movement seem gentle. It reminds me of the fact that he likes to prolong all sorts of things—hunger, death, and—apparently—sex.

My hands slide down his chest, over his pecs and abdomen. Beneath my touch, his muscles tighten.

Again he pauses.

"Please—if you have any care, woman, you'll stop that now," he says, his voice hoarse. "Going to make me come too soon."

I flash him another smile. In response, his cock twitches inside of me.

My grip tightens on him.

He likes my smiles.

Famine reaches between us, his fingers finding my clit. "I'm going to have to even the score."

I laugh, but it quickly turns into a moan as he strokes me in two places at once. His pace picks up as he watches me, drinking in my expression.

"I am convinced," he says.

I can barely focus enough to say, "Convinced of what?"

"The perks of sex."

I'm hardly paying attention to his words. Sensation builds and builds inside of me as he keeps teasing my clit. My fingernails scrape down his back.

"Famine ..."

My lips part, my chest heaving as, all at once, my orgasm

crashes through me. I cry out, pulling him in close as wave after wave of pleasure ripple through me.

Famine pistons into me harder and harder as his mossy eyes drink in my reaction. He's still staring at me when, his thrusts deepen and he sucks in a sharp breath, like something has taken him by surprise. Then, with a groan, he's coming hard and fast. He looks shocked as he stares down at me— shocked and enamored.

With a few final strokes, Famine extricates himself, rolling off of me. I acutely feel his absence, but only seconds later he pulls me onto him.

Then he begins to laugh. And laugh and laugh and laugh. It shakes his whole body.

I pull away to take him in. My heart squeezes at the sight of Famine smiling, *laughing*.

I've never seen him this way. Carefree. Happy.

All because he got a little pussy.

I smile, tracing his lips with my finger. My heart is doing funny things; it feels both light and heavy.

"This is insanity," he says against my finger. "I'm having a human experience, and for once, I *like* it. Shit, I more than like it." As he speaks, he pulls me in close and kisses the side of my face.

Before I can respond, he rolls us so that I'm pinned beneath him once more.

His gaze searches mine. "This is ... I want to be in you again. And I want another smile from you. Many of them. Your smiles make me feel more like my true self."

My stomach tumbles at that. *Like my true self.* I understand that statement all too well. It's been a long time since someone saw me as anything other than Ana the prostitute, but when Famine looks at me, I remember.

I run my fingers over his cheek, and that lighter-than-air feeling passes through me.

Between us, I feel him begin to harden once more. My

eyebrows shoot up. I wasn't expecting an encore any time soon.

"I truly hope you don't have any plans to sleep tonight," he says.

I lean up and give him a kiss. "I can postpone them."

Famine grabs one of my legs, opening me up a bit, and with one strong thrust, he's sheathed himself inside me once more.

Chapter 42

"*Ana.*"

I hear the voice as though from far away.

"*Christ.*" A hand is shaking my shoulder. "*Ana!*"

I force my eyes open, shaking off sleep.

The horseman is staring down at me, and he looks—

He looks frightened.

I begin to push myself up. "What is it?"

Famine's eyes are all over my body. "Why didn't you tell me?"

"Tell you what?" I glance down at my body, but as I do so, I feel a sharp pain in my neck.

A moment later, I see the blood.

It's smeared everywhere. On me, on the sheets, and it looks like it's stained most of my discarded dress. It's even on the Reaper himself, the blood dried along his torso.

I've seen the horseman covered in blood plenty of times, but I've never seen him terrified because of it.

He tilts my face to the side.

"Jesus," he curses again, taking in my wound. "Ana, you told me you were alright last night. I was—" He rubs a hand down his face. "I was *inside* you last night while you were hurt."

I feel a flash of guilt. "It's not—"

"*Stop,*" Famine says. "It *is* that bad. Ana, why didn't you say anything?"

"I feel fine," I say.

"I couldn't wake you," the horseman says. "You're *not* fine."

"I'm awake now," I say defensively.

Awake and naked and covered in blood and grime. I suddenly feel like a naughty kid, sleeping with the horseman while wounded. Unfortunately, that's how it worked at the bordello. Getting battered by a client didn't mean any woman got to take the night off.

"You need a doctor," he insists.

"A needle and thread will be just fine—well, a needle and thread and some strong liquor." Not that I'm ready for more liquor. My stomach revolts at the thought.

Famine gives me a skeptical look. "You can't be serious."

Unfortunately, I am.

By midmorning I've washed myself clean and scrubbed out my dress as best I can. I wear the damp outfit in the saddle, my tits basically visible through the wet fabric.

Famine holds me close. I can practically feel him vibrating with anxiety. On the one hand, I'm moved by his reaction. On the other, all that we did last night has been forgotten in the midst of his worry.

We aren't on the highway for more than fifteen minutes when we come across a small trading post.

The Reaper steers his horse towards it. Before he's even dismounted, I hear a scuffling noise inside the store, followed by a scream that cuts off sharply.

I suck in a breath. That's never, ever going to get easier to bear.

Famine hops off the horse.

"Wait here," he says over his shoulder.

I don't.

Gingerly, I slide off his steed, biting back a cry when the action tugs at my wound. Not so long ago I struggled to get off this very horse after the Reaper accidently pierced my shoulder with his scythe. The horseman hadn't fretted over it like he was fretting over this injury. And sure, it was a cleaner wound, and maybe it wasn't as bad, but still.

Things really are different between us.

Famine sighs when he notices me following. "Ana, you're hurt."

"I'm *fine*," I say.

"Two words I will never again believe from you."

I enter the store behind him, wincing a little at the sight of the very obviously dead man who was working behind the counter.

"It's just a scratch," I say, moving down one of the aisles.

It's not just a scratch. I got to look at it in the mirror this morning, and it's bigger and uglier than I imagined.

Famine guffaws. "Why are you pretending it's not a big deal?"

"Have you seen my stomach?" I say. "Compared to that, *it's not a big deal*."

"It's a big deal to me," the horseman murmurs, his voice so quiet I almost miss it.

I find the first aid section before Famine does. Sitting right there on the top shelf are needles and surgical thread.

"Got it," I say, grabbing the items. Now I just need to stitch myself up.

This should be fun.

I nibble my lower lip, looking at my wound using a hand mirror I found.

"Maybe we shouldn't do this," I say.

The cut looks like it's still a little dirty, and parts of it appear to have already started to scab over. I don't know a lot about mending wounds, but I think that sealing up something that could be contaminated is a bad idea.

Famine studies the wound. "So we should do nothing?" He's clearly displeased at that thought.

"I don't know. I think if we can douse the cut in alcohol that might help."

Already, I'm cringing at the thought.

No sooner have I said it, then the horseman heads for the small collection of wines, beer, and some more potent liquor behind the counter, not sparing the dead man next to him a passing glance.

While he's back there, I grab a glass container of rubbing alcohol from the shelf. I take a deep breath while I look at it.

This is going to hurt.

Famine comes back, holding a bottle of rum and a corkscrew. I let him open the bottle and hand it to me.

Rather than pouring it over my neck, I take a long drink from it, my stomach churning at the taste.

Too soon—*much* too soon—for more liquor.

I set the rum on a nearby shelf then unstop the rubbing alcohol in my hand, passing it to Famine.

"What's this?" he asks.

"Rubbing alcohol—to pour on my wound."

The horseman looks confused. I guess he's never realized there was a difference between the alcohol human's drink, and the stuff used purely to disinfect.

"Why are you giving it to me?" he asks.

"I need you to do it. I—I don't think I have the courage to do it myself."

Famine scowls at the bottle, then looks at me. Faster than I can follow, he tilts my chin and dumps the rubbing alcohol on the cut.

"Fuck!" I hiss out, my legs nearly folding. "Motherfucking

fuck!"

I gasp out a few breaths, eyes pricking at the excruciating burn. It feels like my wound is on fire.

I glare at him. "You could've warned me."

"You're overestimating how nice I am."

I make a face, but honestly, the man has a point.

I stare at the now-empty bottle in Famine's hand. Hopefully that does the trick.

I take a deep breath. "Let me just grab some gauze, and then we can get going."

"Get going?" the horseman says. "Not while you're hurt. Tonight, we're staying here."

Chapter 43

My neck wound is not fine.

Not at all.

I first realize that shortly after I wake up the next morning, my body coated in sweat.

My cut throbs, and when I prod at it, pain lashes through me. More than that, I feel a little unwell.

It ... might be infected.

I get up and find the compact mirror I used yesterday to get a good look at it. Once I remove the gauze bandages, I angle the mirror towards the cut.

I suck in a sharp breath. The skin is red and swollen, and the wound itself is a grisly sight, the flesh a mottled mess of colors.

Definitely infected.

Before I can think twice, I grab another bottle of rubbing alcohol and, uncapping it, I douse the wound with the disinfecting liquid.

The pain is instant and intense. A sharp cry slips out of my mouth, and I nearly drop the glass.

The door to the trading post bangs open, and Famine

rushes to my side. He takes in my trembling form and the liquid dripping from my angry wound. The horseman grabs the bottle from my hands and glances at the label before his attention moves to my neck.

His brows furrow. "Is it supposed to look—?"

"I don't think so."

I see a myriad of emotions pass across the horseman's features, too fast for me to make sense of them.

He scowls, looking down at the bottle. "Will this help?" he asks.

"I hope to hell it does," I say.

The Reaper's gaze flicks back up to me. "What happens if it doesn't?" he asks.

He has no experience with this, I realize. The horseman maims and kills, but he doesn't know much about healing and the complications that come along with it.

"Let's not worry about that, Famine," I say, trying to reassure myself just as much as I'm trying to reassure him. "I've survived too many horrors for a simple neck wound to take me down."

Not that there's anything simple about it.

He stares at me for too long. Finally, he says, "I'm finding you a doctor."

I swallow.

"Okay," I capitulate.

If I'm being honest with myself, I'm a little scared at what might happen if things continue to get worse.

I finish packing, ignoring my festering injury as best I can.

Riding is another story.

As soon as we begin to move, the horse's gait jostles my injury. It happens again and again and again with each step the steed takes, and there's no ignoring the pain.

And now my nausea is rising. At first I try to ignore it, mostly because I don't *want* to deal with it. But then I'm beginning to sweat, even as a shiver courses through me. It's hot out; I shouldn't be shivering.

Famine's grip around my midsection tightens, and I let out a small noise at the pressure. My nausea is suddenly *right-here-and-it-won't-be-ignored-oh-God-free-my-midsection-from-this-torment-Amen.*

"Are you alright?" he asks, a vague note of concern in his voice.

I force down my bile and pull at his hands. "I will be if you relax your damn hand."

After a moment, he does so, and I take a few bracing breaths.

"I'm getting sick," I say. "The cut on my neck," I gesture vaguely to it, "it's not doing too well."

Famine pulls his steed up short. Carefully, he removes the bandages, then leans far enough in the saddle to get a good look at it.

He hisses in a breath while staring at the wound.

"What?" I say, getting nervous.

"It looks like it's going to grow teeth and eat my face off."

I let out a freaked out laugh. "What am I supposed to do?" I don't really mean to ask the question, but shit, I am *not* a contingency planner. Nor a doctor. And we've poured alcohol on the wound twice already, and I was really hoping that was going to work.

Worry sparks in the horseman's eyes. "You mean, besides find you a doctor? I don't know. You're the human," he says accusingly. "I don't get infections."

The two of us stare at each other, and without meaning to, I audibly swallow.

"Motherfucker," Famine curses. And then he jolts his horse into action, and the two of us ride like the wind.

Famine

Hunger makes men desperate, dangerous. It's a natural state of mine, but I haven't felt it for a while.

But now, with Ana swaying unsteadily in the saddle, that familiar panic courses through me. I realize that I hate it. Hate it with every fiber of my being.

I force my steed to ride as fast as he can, only slowing when Ana leans over to vomit.

It happens just once, but then I can feel her shivering. I hold her as close as I dare—as close as she'll let me—but my armor is hard and rigid and it can't possibly be much comfort.

This isn't good.

I knew that from the moment I first saw that wound in the light of day, but I'm understanding now that the human body shouldn't be shivering in this sweltering heat. Nor should she be retching.

With that thought, I urge my horse faster.

Someone will know how to heal her.

Ana

We're on the road a surprisingly long time. Then again, maybe we aren't, maybe the pain has just become so damn distracting that the minutes drag out. It feels like a lifetime.

Famine himself is so distracted that he doesn't bother killing off the fields around us. I would be touched by that if I thought it was somehow for my benefit, but I think he's simply forgotten, so focused on getting me help.

A hard knot forms in my stomach, and I feel real fear beginning to take root.

It can't be that bad. I don't even think the cut was all that deep. But it was long ... and jagged ... and there'd been mud all over me and who knows what on the knife itself.

You think I'd learn to clean my damn wounds better after my last experience with infection.

Even when the fever starts to get bad, I'm not too worried.

I remember this. Back in Laguna the wounds I sustained were so much worse. I laid in bed for some indeterminate amount of time, closer to death than I was to life. And still I survived.

I'm that cockroach you just can't kill.

So I lean back against Famine's jostling armor and let my eyes drift closed—just for a moment. It wouldn't be so bad to escape myself for just a little while.

I wake to Famine pulling me off the horse, and only then because the movement jostles my neck.

I cry out at the pain. It hurts so goddamn bad—so, so goddamn bad.

I try to pry myself out of his hold, but I'm groggy and my mounting fever is making my limbs stiff and clumsy.

"Where are we?" I ask.

"I'm finding you that doctor, remember?" he says, an agitated edge to his words.

Famine strides forward with me cradled in his arms. I grit my teeth at the pain each step of his causes. And then my nausea is rising.

Just want to go back to sleep ...

BANG!

My eyes snap open as Famine kicks down a door, and a moan slips from my lips as pain shoots through me.

The Reaper glances down at me, frowning deeply.

Something catches his attention and he looks up.

"I need a doctor," he demands.

There's murmuring, but I've already stopped listening.

I turn my head inward, nestling as best I can against Famine's chest. In response, his arms tighten around me protectively.

He says something else, his angry voice coming out to play.

Going real well for you, I want to joke, but I feel too shitty to tease him, and besides, sleep is dragging me under again ...

My eyelids flutter open and closed, open and closed, as I'm roused from sleep again and again. I can hear Famine's disgruntled voice and a few of his threats, and then there are the alarmed voices of the humans closing in around us.

If this is his version of help, I'm as good as doomed.

But shortly after that thought crosses my mind, Famine is ushered somewhere. He carries me the entire time, and I can't be light, but he doesn't seem bothered by my weight.

I lean my forehead against his armor, weak and tired. In response, he presses a kiss to my hair.

Things are beginning to get bad for me. I can tell because my lips are cracking and my eyes feel like they're cooking themselves and yet my teeth are chattering and I can't stop shaking.

Famine's grip has become almost painful, but I don't have the energy left to say anything.

And amongst it all is the sensation of many, many curious eyes peering at me.

My eyes slip closed, and when they open again, we're inside someone's house, Famine carrying me down a narrow hallway.

Then he's laying me down on a bed.

I cling to him. I have this nonsensical fear that the moment I let him go, I'm not going to be safe anymore.

"Little flower," Famine says softly, so softly, "you need to let me go."

Reluctantly, I do, opening my eyes long enough to see him. "Please don't leave me."

He takes my hand, threading his fingers through mine. "I won't." The Reaper says this like he's swearing an oath to me.

Now that I have his word, I relax. The bed is soft and I feel so terrible that it's easy to slip off to sleep.

I'm not sure how long I drift for. It could be minutes or hours ...

"*Why is she deteriorating so quickly?*" Famine's voice sounds far away.

I fall back to sleep before I hear the answer.

I wake to the feel of a wet cloth against my forehead. I crack my eyes open and see the Reaper peering down at me, his hands on the cool material. Over his shoulder someone else holds a basin of water. I give both of them a tired smile.

"Ana—" the Reaper begins, but I'm already fading away.

I wake again to the feel of foreign hands on me. They don't feel right. They're dry and calloused and they're moving my body around like I'm a puppet.

I try to push them away.

"*What are you doing to her?*" Famine's voice has me prying my eyes open.

A shrewd older woman leans over me. "I'm *trying* to help her—unless you've suddenly changed your mind."

Before the horseman can respond, those hands take my chin and move my head to the side.

Pain explodes through my neck and temple.

"Well, this is why she's so sick," the woman says. Her voice sounds like her hands feel—scratchy but firm and full of authority. "It's *festering.*"

"Can you fix her or not?" the horseman demands.

"You can't *fix* a human," the woman says. "We're not houses with leaky roofs or broken windows."

"No, you're all a scourge across the land, but I'm not here to play semantics with you. Now, tell me what you *can* do for Ana," he says.

"Without antibiotics? Not much," the woman says. "I can clean and bind the wound and make her a poultice to draw out what I can of the infection. But I doubt it will do much good at this point. Her body is going to have to fight this on its own."

My gaze moves to the horseman. I've never seen that look on his face—I think it might be desperation. It, more than my fever, alarms me.

"Am I going to die?" I ask as he catches my hand, holding it tightly. I don't know how I feel about that—death.

"No." Famine says it like a vow. "Not in my lifetime."

Chapter 44

Famine

It's strange, having a body. I feel too big for it. I *am* too big for it. It's the greatest relief, you know, spreading my disease through the fields. Spoiling fruit and poisoning seed. I feel more like myself.

Unlike this ... this strange human experience I'm forced to endure.

I stare down at Ana's sallow face, a hot, prickly feeling overcoming me.

It might've been fine if I never met you. If you hadn't saved me those years ago.

Your arms were too slender and your cheeks too gaunt, and yet somehow you dragged my body to shelter, and you offered me water, and I couldn't stomach any of it. A human girl hiding me from my tormentors and giving me what little she had.

You stayed by my side that agonizing night, even though I know I frightened you. And when those men were hunting me down and their voices came so chillingly close to us, all you had to do was call out and your nightmare would've been over. They would've taken me back to that prison. I might've been there still.

But you didn't call out, and despite your fear, you didn't leave me.

You saved me when you had every reason not to.

You broke me.

And in the process I broke you.

And now I fear the only way we will ever be whole again is together, all your jagged edges nestled against mine.

I hate that I want that.

But I do.

I want to be whole with you.

Ana

Bathroom.

That's the one thought I wake to. My bladder is screaming at me to be relieved.

The sheets are pulled back, and then Famine's scooping me up, his hand carefully cradling my head and neck.

I must've spoken the request unknowingly because the horseman carries me outside, past several townspeople.

He glares at the onlookers. "Leave us, or die," he says.

Within moments, the curious townspeople are gone.

I think I'm feeling better. Still feverish, still exhausted, but at least I'm aware enough to not wet myself.

Famine carries me past the surrounding homes and into the wilds that border the neighborhood, not stopping until we're alone.

I've gone to the bathroom many times while traveling with Famine. During every one of them he's given me some modicum of privacy. But now he doesn't fully let me go as he lifts my dress.

A few seconds pass. "You can let me go," I say.

I made it my business to have sex with strangers, but I can't seem to find it in me to pee in front of Famine.

"You've barely moved since I set you in that bed," he says. "I'd rather not."

I feel myself getting weepy, though I'm too dehydrated to actually cry. "I don't want you to ... see me like—"

Before I can finish, he kisses my lips once, softly, to silence me. "You're being ridiculous, Ana. I don't mind."

That's all the fight I have left in me. And so I go to the bathroom right there in front of Famine as he helps hold me up.

I'm shaking—from embarrassment, fatigue, and fever—and now I begin to sob, my dehydrated body managing to squeeze out a couple precious tears. My emotions are all twisted up.

When I'm done Famine helps clean me up and I'm caught between utter mortification and exhausted gratitude.

Why are you being like this? I want to ask him. *You're brash and mean and capricious.*

But he's not. Not when you get down to the heart of him.

The horseman carries me back into the house and resettles me on the bed. Pulling a chair up next to the mattress, he grabs a nearby pitcher and pours me a glass of water.

I watch him while he works, feeling tired and achy and just generally unwell.

"Drink," he says, handing it to me.

"So demanding ..." My voice is nothing more than a whisper. I take the water from him anyway and swallow it down. It doesn't sit well in my stomach—to be honest, my stomach doesn't feel like *it's* sitting well in my stomach—and I have to swallow several times to keep it down.

The longer I'm awake and aware, the more I realize that I'm not actually feeling better at all, just more alert. And even that is tenuous because all I want to do is go back to sleep and escape all the pain I'm in. It reminds me of the last time I fought off an infection, when the town around me had all gone to their graves.

I thought I was a goner then, too. I swear I came so close to Death I could touch him.

I set the water on the bedside table next to me. That's when I notice the small sculpture of Our Lady of Aparecida resting just behind the pitcher.

I draw in a breath. I'm not sure the horseman believes in signs, but I think I might.

"*Famine*," I say, and my voice sounds all wrong.

There are things I need to tell him. Now, before I lose the chance.

His back stiffens. "*Don't*," he says, his eyes flashing. "*Don't*," he repeats. "I already told you, you're not dying."

Maybe I am, maybe I'm not. It feels like I might be.

I take a deep breath and finally admit to him what I haven't even fully admitted to myself.

"I love you." My heart is hammering away. "I don't know when I began to, and I'm really, really upset that I do—"

"*Stop*, Ana," Famine says fiercely. There are unshed tears in his eyes.

"But I love you. So much. And I always will. I want you to know that," I say, "in case—"

"*Stop*." Famine looks angry that he can't make words wither away like he can plants. "I will kill the whole goddamn world if you don't stop."

I press my chapped lips together.

Once he sees that I'm not going to continue, the Reaper exhales, leaning his head back against his chair to stare up at the ceiling, one of his legs jiggling.

"When I told you I liked stories," he says out of nowhere, "there was one in particular that I never told you."

I give him a confused look. Fever and exhaustion are tugging me towards sleep, but I force my eyes to stay open.

"The night you saved me," Famine says, looking back down at me, "when you fell asleep, you spoke.

"You said an Angelic word, one you should have been unable to pronounce."

"Angelic?" I echo. "Is that your native language?"

He nods.

"What was the word?" I say, curious. I have no memory of this at all.

"*Gipiwawewut.*"

I close my eyes as I feel that word wash over me, drawing out goosebumps. For a moment, I don't simply hear it, I *feel* it.

Forgiveness.

"Forgive me, Ana," he says. "I know I have wronged you. Your family, your friends, your life—I took that from you. I didn't understand, but I'm beginning to, and I'm sorry, so sorry.

"Please, forgive me."

I give him a small smile. "I do," I say softly. "I love you and I forgive you ..."

I swear for a moment he looks petrified. Scary, merciless Famine, petrified.

I settle back against the bed and close my eyes, taking a deep breath as sleep begins to tug me under.

Here's to hoping I'll wake up again.

Famine

There was a moment of peace in Ana's eyes when I spoke in Angelic. So as soon as she falls asleep, I clasp her clammy hand in mine and begin speaking to her in my natural tongue.

"*I never could've imagined that I would love the slope of your nose or the space between your eyes. I know you are considered lovely by human standards, but I don't have human standards, and Ana, you are the most exquisite thing I've ever laid eyes on. Even when you sleep with your mouth open. Even when you yell at me—especially then because I love seeing your fire."*

I bring her hand to my lips and press a kiss to her knuckles.

"You were made from the earth," I whisper to her skin, *"I can feel the universe moving through you, and yet you are something else unto yourself.*

"I never wanted to love a human. I fought you with everything I had. You were everything I shouldn't want. But then, your compassion pierced me deeper than any blade.

"I have felt the earth move, I have felt the grinding of rock as mountains shift and the world changes shape. None of it could prepare me for you.

"I love you. Maybe more than all of what I am. And I don't understand why, but I do. I love you."

As I speak, her features smooth and the softest smile touches her lips. Even still, I can feel her slipping away. With horror, I realize the taste of heaven that I'm giving her is drawing her in like a moth to flame.

At once I stop speaking. She has made me selfless—to a point—but I'm still the same bastard at my core, and if the choice right now is giving Ana a comfortable death or giving her an uncomfortable life, *I'm choosing the latter.*

"You vexing woman, you are *not* leaving me."

I stand, the chair scraping back.

Need to fix this.

I stare down at Ana. I don't want to leave her—I promised her as much earlier—but I won't wait to watch her die. From, of all things, a fucking wound I could've cleaned.

Instead I made love to her.

Such a fucking bastard.

Making a decision, I storm out of the room and hunt down that doctor. I find her in the kitchen, grinding up something with a mortar and pestle.

"Heal her," I demand.

She raises her eyebrows. "I have been doing my best," she says.

"It's not good enough." *She's slipping away.* I bite back those last words.

"You didn't give me much to work with." As she speaks, she continues to grind her herbs. Not moving. Not even looking up.

Slowly, I cross the room. When I get to her, I slap that damn mortar and pestle away. The stone instruments career off the table, and herbs scatter everywhere.

"Heal. Her."

Now the doctor glances up, meeting my gaze, not cowed by my presence.

"Like I told you earlier, we can clean and dress the wound," she says, "but the infection has already progressed too far," the woman says, like that's any sort of answer.

Too far?

"Heal her," I repeat.

Her back straightens. The look she gives me is withering. "I *cannot.* Maybe before you horsemen showed up we could've saved her, but that technology is gone—you destroyed it." She pauses to let that sink it.

And it does.

Her gaze is unwavering. "It is up to your God at this point." *But don't expect much from him,* her look seems to add.

I step in close to her. "*Damn you,*" I whisper.

Without even fully meaning to, my power lashes out, wiping out crops in an instant. It skips the people, but only because killing humans takes slightly more effort and focus.

The worst part is that I don't even *want* to kill. I'm perversely grateful for these filthy humans' help, and I get no joy from taking their livelihoods from them.

The doctor stares at me, like she knows I've done

something terrible.

I stalk back to Ana's room before I can hurt anything else. There's this dreadful, yawning hole inside me.

I kneel at Ana's side. She's too still, though her chest is rising and falling fast.

Pitiful, useless human bodies. Of course they would turn frail the moment I actually *want* one of them around.

I suck in a breath as I stare at Ana's sleeping face, realization coming to me.

I've seen this trick before.

This was the choice forced upon War and Pestilence. I hadn't understood it then, when I slept deep within the ground, but I understand it now.

All of us brothers were given the choice to love as humans do, with all of the complications that entails.

One of those complications being death.

Pestilence gave up nothing in return for his love's life; War had to give up his purpose, his power and immortality stripped from him.

I expect Death would outright refuse me.

Reaching out, I trail my fingers over Ana's cheek, then trace her lips, my heart aching in a way it never has before. This is what it must feel like to *truly* be alive, every emotion so sharp it's almost painful. I've spent so long lording my unending existence over finite things that I have never given them the proper respect. Not until now.

I exhale, and even that hurts. For the life of me it feels like I'm the one getting squeezed to death by my plants. I can't breathe around this tightness in my chest.

A drop of water hits Ana's face. Then another. It takes me a second to realize they're tears. I've never cried over one of these creatures before. Not even Ana.

Ana, who's dying ...

Leaning forward, I press a kiss to her forehead, my lips lingering against her clammy skin.

"You can't go, little flower." My voice shakes as I speak. "This is one more order you're going to have to listen to."

I don't need to give up my power to get her back. She's not even dead yet.

Fuck mortal doctors and fuck Thanatos, I never needed any of their help anyways.

Carefully, I place my hand over Ana's wound. I've forsaken this part of me for so long I've almost forgotten that I can do this—

Revive.

I've stirred the skies and drawn life from the ground, but turning my power towards a human—peering inside a fleshy body and trying to make sense of what's there—it's like tasting food for the first time. Shocking and strange.

My power is really quite simple—I can make things grow and I can make things die. It's not quite War's ability to heal, and it's not quite Death's ability to give life, but somewhere in the murky waters between the two.

The infection that's racking Ana's body is just one more living thing that's doing a really, really good job of surviving. It just so happens to be killing its host in the process.

I close my eyes and allow myself to expand.

I can feel the life moving all around me; it's everywhere—in the air, on the ground, *in* the ground. The earth is teeming with living things.

Turning my attention from the array of life surrounding me, I focus on Ana. Sick, weak Ana. Immediately I sense how much closer to death she is than life, but I knew that before. I set the fear aside so I can make things right.

I hone my focus not just on Ana, but *in* her. Immediately, I sense the bacteria overwhelming her system. It's entered her bloodstream and is busy invading every little corner of her body. Not that the bacteria is all to blame. My little flower's immune system is wreaking havoc in its attempt to fight the infection.

I take a moment to appreciate the sheer magnitude of this infection. All because of a single swipe of a knife.

My moment of appreciation passes, and just like every other time I've encountered a hated lifeform, I begin to destroy it.

Ana once asked me why I was so good at dancing. The truth is that while killing is easy, miracle-working is a more complicated process. The human body is a symphony of actions and reactions all tangled together, and right now, my job is to listen to her body's symphony and move in time with it.

And that's exactly what I do.

It feels like it takes a lifetime to heal her, but it must only take mere minutes. And then it's done.

And I bring Ana back to me.

Chapter 45

Ana

When I wake, I'm alone.

I glance around me at the room, which is bare save for the sculpture of Our Lady of Aparecida and the glass and pitcher of water resting on the bedside table.

I sit up, feeling weak and hungry, but otherwise ... not too bad. After a moment, I reach for my neck. It's covered in soft gauze, which I pry away.

Last I remember, this cut had been badly infected.

The bandages and poultice fall away, and I begin to probe around my wound. It doesn't feel swollen and angry. In fact, it feels ... it feels mostly healed.

How is that possible?

I take in my surroundings again. Vaguely I remember Famine carrying me into this place, and then there was that fun pee incident outside, but everything else seems like a hazy fever dream. I think I made some pretty proclamations because I'd been sure I was going to die.

My lips are chapped and gummy, and discreetly I wipe them off before grabbing the glass of water next to me. In five deep swallows, I finish the thing off.

For a good few minutes, I sort of just sit there and let my mind catch up.

I didn't die.

Can't kill this cockroach.

I take a dainty whiff of my formerly clean dress and cringe. This outfit is the thing that needs to die.

Kicking off the damp bedsheets, I slide out of bed. My legs are shaky and honestly, I feel a little woozy, but I power forward anyway, slipping out of the room. A man passes by the hallway, and he gasps when he sees me, making the sign of the cross.

"Is this your house?" I ask.

He nods. "My wife treated you."

I give him a soft smile. "Thank you both for the care and the bed."

Still giving me a strange look, he nods.

I point towards the back of the house. "Is this the way out?"

Again, he gives a shaky nod.

"Thanks." I leave the startled man there, a little unnerved by his reaction.

Outside, the sky is full of big, billowy clouds. I breathe in the wet, earthen smell of the land. Something innate pulls me past the scattered buildings and towards the fields beyond.

The sugarcane here is a bright, blinding green. And there, right in the middle of it, is the horseman.

I've seen this before, in my dreams. Famine stands among the crops, scythe in hand, and it's like a premonition.

This is where he unmakes the world, one blade of grass at a time.

As though he senses me behind him, the horseman turns.

Right now, I see clearly that Famine is a *what* rather than a *who*. He doesn't look human. Not even a little bit. He's painfully, achingly beautiful, but he's no mortal man.

"You know," he says softly, "this entire field was dead only hours ago."

I don't bother looking at the crop in question.

"I can't bring people back from the dead," he continues. "Not without Death's help—or God's." He reaches out a hand to touch the green stalks near him. "However, I *can* control the flow of life and death in all things, like this sugarcane."

I move towards him, picking my way through the shrubs that brush my ankles.

"Did you ... do something to me?" I ask.

I don't know how I know, but I feel like maybe he did. The wound is too healed, and then there was that older man's reaction back at the house; he looked at me as though I should've been dead.

I come right up to Famine, gazing at his face, trying to read his features. At first, he won't meet my eyes, but when he eventually does, I go still.

He's looking at me like I'm his one weakness.

"Did you?" I ask again. "Heal me?"

He takes a deep, audible breath as he stares down at me, like he's drawing the life back into himself. He lets go of his scythe, letting it fall to the earth.

Famine cups my face, searching my gaze. "Yes," he says simply.

In the next instant, his lips are on mine. The kiss is fierce, almost desperate in its intensity. I kiss him back, even as I let his words sink in.

Famine healed me.

Famine, the horseman who hates humans. Famine, who loves killing and suffering. *He* is responsible for me being alive right now.

He places a hand against my cheek, bringing my forehead

to his.

"I love you," he says.

I stare at him for a long moment, my point forgotten.

I love you.

Those words are ringing in my ears. I'm sure I've misheard him.

Famine looks just as wide-eyed as I know I must look.

"What?" I breathe.

"I love you, you foolish little flower."

My heart begins to hammer against my ribcage.

"It's rather an unfortunate realization," he says, his breath fanning across my cheeks, "but despite every one of my convictions, I do."

He loves me.

He *loves* me. *Me.*

Only now is it really starting to sink in.

Famine's green eyes, which I once found so unnerving, now stare intensely at me.

"I love you," he repeats. No longer does he seem shocked by those words. That driving certainty that rules him is back.

He leans in to kiss me again.

At the last moment I bring my fingers to his lips. "*Wait.*"

His eyes focus on me.

I smile, first at his mouth, then up at his eyes.

"I love you too," I say softly. My grin widens, even as his eyebrows lift. I drop my hand. "Just thought you should hear that when I'm not running a fever," I whisper.

And then I let Famine kiss me.

Chapter 46

Several hours later, the two of us are back on Famine's steed.

I'm still reeling from the Reaper's admission that he loves me. I feel lighter than air. Has anything ever made me this happy before?

Not to mention that he healed me.

Famine holds me close in the saddle, and his lips keep brushing my temple, as though he were trying to press his adoration into my very skin. Honestly, I can't get enough of it.

Not a half hour ago I thanked and said goodbye to our hosts—who, mercy of all mercies, Famine left alive. And now, by the looks of it, he's left the rest of the city alive as well.

The two of us move through the streets of what I learn is Taubaté. Like most other Brazilian cities, this one has adapted to life after the apocalypse. Many of the old skyscrapers and highrises are abandoned, or have fallen into disrepair—if they haven't been cleared away altogether—and the majority of the population seems to have shifted the city center to what must've once been the outskirts of town.

Here the streets are lined with stalls selling everything from street food to baskets, blankets, jewelry, shoes, dinnerware, and on and on. There are restaurants that spill out of the buildings and musicians playing along the street corners.

Whatever sort of city Taubaté once was, it looks like it's remade itself into something new.

Around us, people meander about, but as we pass by them, they pause, their eyes wide. There's no mistaking Famine for anything other than what he is—a horseman.

Once we reach what seems to be the densest section of Taubaté, the Reaper stops his horse, grabbing his scythe from where it's strapped to his back.

I glance over my shoulder at him. "Why are we stopping?"

Famine smirks at me. "You'll see."

"I really don't want to," I say, because I have a feeling I know what's coming. The same thing that always comes at the end of our stays. And the last thing I want is to see these people die. Not after all they've done for me.

"Don't give me that look," Famine says. "This will be fun."

Fun?

"Your idea of fun is gutting someone alive," I remind him.

He smirks again, his eyes twinkling, and that look does nothing to calm my nerves.

The Reaper swings himself off his horse and pounds his scythe against the ground, startling the already startled onlookers. Despite the fact that it's common knowledge that the horseman is bad news, a crowd has begun to gather.

The horseman's gaze sweeps over the growing crowd. "If you wish for your town to be spared—"

"Wait, we're staying?" I interrupt.

He gives me a look that states plainly, *please shut up.*

Famine continues, "—then these are my terms: my wife—"

"Whoa, what wife?" I interrupt again. "Wait, *me?*"

The horseman doesn't even bother pausing this time, "—and I need an unoccupied place to stay, and I require offerings. Lots of offerings. Do this, and I will not destroy your lives and livelihoods."

I swear there's a collective pause, then people *scatter*.

Well, that went well.

"*Wife?*" I repeat to Famine, raising my eyebrows. "What lies have you been telling people while I've been sick?"

The look he gives me is downright nefarious. "It's only a lie if you don't intend to follow through with it."

One, that's not how lies work. And two—

"Is that ... a proposal?" I say. My heart beats faster than it should. "Because if it is," I continue, "that's going to be a *no* from me."

I think about Martim, how he promised me marriage, then broke his promise and my heart in the process.

That's not happening again.

At my words, Famine rears back. "*No?*"

"I want an actual proposal," I continue, staring down at him from the saddle. "With sex. The ring is optional. Groveling is a must."

"*Groveling?*" He lets out an incredulous laugh. "I'm not a dog begging for scraps."

"Nope, right now you're a dog with *zero* scraps. I want sex, a pledge of your undying love—"

"Now it's a pledge of my undying love?"

"*That goes without saying,*" I reply as townspeople begin to approach us.

The Reaper looks irked.

"You've gone down on me," I say, "so you're already an old hand at this groveling business."

An older man who's approaching us overhears my comment, and much to my delight, he looks properly scandalized.

"That was *not* groveling." Famine's jaw clenches.

"I don't know why you're so horrified," I say, ignoring his comment. "You've literally held me as I peed," I say. That's about as horrifying as a situation can get. "I might've even gotten some on your shoe."

Judging by the tick in Famine's cheek, I *definitely* got some pee on his shoe.

Before he can respond, the older man and several other townspeople close in on us. They carry blankets and tallow candles and jugs of oil and liquor and milk and pottery and jewelry and baskets of eggs.

"Marry me," Famine says, ignoring them as he stares up at me.

My breath catches for an instant. "No."

He looks greatly annoyed. I'm beyond gleeful.

"This isn't over," he vows.

I sincerely hope not.

By sunset, Famine has not only amassed a small kingdom's worth of goods, he's also managed to secure us a house. He didn't even have to kill anyone to get it.

"The woman who lived here died, and her children weren't able to sell the place," one of the townspeople told me earlier, when she was giving me a walk-through of the previously boarded-up home.

I understand why no one wanted the place. Not only was it built before the apocalypse—and thus full of relics that are useless at best, and dangerous at worst—but as far as practicality goes, it seems like it's more work than it's worth.

It still has a garage full of rusted out cars, and kitchen appliances that are filled with cobwebs and rat droppings, and sinks with faucets that haven't moved water in more than a decade.

At least the toilets have been updated.

Around me, half a dozen people bustle by, sweeping floors, removing moldy linens and shaggy curtains.

Beyond them, Famine stands with his arms folded, listening to some woman, a bored expression on his face.

The horseman must feel me watching, because he glances

in my direction.

His eyes brighten when he sees me. "My little flower. Do you like it?" he calls, gesturing to the room around us. It's a genuine question, and God, but he actually looks hopeful, like his happiness rests upon my answer.

I cut across the room towards him. "You've really manipulated your way into getting us the best house," I say, even though this is not the best house by a long shot.

The horseman flashes me a sly grin as I approach him. "Would you rather we stay in a different house? I'm sure any of the families here would be happy to be kicked out of their homes so that we could move in. That's always an option."

People are still cleaning the room around us, but now many of them stiffen a little.

I suppress a shudder. "Thank you, no," I say.

I step into Famine's space. "You mentioned earlier that you were trying something new," I say. I gesture to the house around us. "How is this new?"

Famine often asks people for offerings and places to stay. To me, this is the same gimmick he's always pulled.

The horseman pulls me into him. "You'll see," he whispers against my ear.

There's a chair nearby. Famine snags it, dragging it over. He sits down in it, pulling me down along with him.

"Let me go, Famine," I say, as he props me on his lap.

"No," he says casually, reaching out to play with one of my curls.

"I'm serious." This situation—Famine sitting in a chair like some sort of king—has always preceded terrible things. I don't want to be here to watch.

"As am I," he says.

Anxiety builds in my veins.

He runs a finger down my arm. "Relax," he breathes against my ear.

But I can't relax.

"What are you going to do to them?" I ask, my voice low so that the people around us can't hear.

"I already told you, little flower: I'm trying something new."

I peer at him for several seconds before realization hits me.

"You're not going to kill them?" I breathe, my eyes widening. It's too good to hope for.

The Reaper lifts a finger and traces the scab running across my neck, frowning at the sight of it. "Of course I'm going to kill them." He doesn't bother lowering his voice, and the people in the room with us flash him wide-eyed looks. "I just won't do it yet."

My gaze searches his. "Why?"

"Strange creature—would you like me to kill them straight away?"

"Jesus, Famine. No." I'm not even sure he's joking. "I just ... I'm curious." After all, the Reaper has never done anything like this before, and I want to know why.

He stares at me for a long time. I can practically see the scarred layers of himself melting away as he takes me in.

"You've never asked me to change," Famine finally admits. "Or to be something I'm not. You never needed me to be human to accept me."

I mean, I wasn't super accepting when I tried to stab him. And I don't think I've *ever* accepted his cruelty. But he *is* technically right—I never actually thought to change his behavior. I never realized that changing him *was* an option. That would be like him trying to remove the human out of me—utterly impossible.

"I don't understand where you're going with this ..." I say, still staring at him skeptically.

"I accept you as you are, Ana, with your lewd comments—"

"You like those," I interrupt.

"—and your insatiable curiosity, and your human tricks—"

"You like those too."

"—and your compassion," he finishes. "*Especially* your compassion, even in the face of cruelty.

"This is my pledge to you, little flower," he continues, "I will be at your side until my dying day, and I will hold off on the killing—for now."

Chapter 47

I stare at him for a long time.

"I don't believe you," I finally say.

He laughs. "You're welcome."

Holy shit, he *is* telling the truth.

Which means … this is a legitimate vow. One that comes as close to undying love as it gets.

I will be at your side until my dying day.

I try not to swoon. Ana da Silva does *not* swoon, especially not over scary men. But I come close to it. I come damn close.

He wants to be with me. And bonus—he's really not going to kill. And who knows how long that will last, but he's going to try. He's never tried before.

Wait a second.

I glance around at the house around us with new eyes.

I'm trying something new, he'd said. Could that actually mean … ?

"Is this house for us to keep?" I say, not daring to believe it. Famine nods.

I can't seem to get enough air in my lungs.

I focus on him again. "I want to be alone with you."

The Reaper is going to get laid. Right here. Right now.

Not looking away from me he says, "Everyone out."

Within a matter of minutes, the house is empty.

As soon as the last person's gone, I stand and pull off my soiled dress, then kick off my socks and shoes.

The horseman watches me, his eyes gleaming.

Once I'm fully naked, I nod to Famine.

"Now it's your turn," I say.

"To get naked?" he says, raising an eyebrow. "Whatever for?"

Oh my God.

I give him a look. "Do I really need to—?"

"I'm *kidding*," the horseman says, and it's unnerving how much he sounds like me.

He stands and begins removing his bronze armor. Famine is slower to get naked, his gaze drinking in my breasts ... then my waist, then my hips, then legs, then back up, his eyes lingering on my pussy as his fingers undo his armor.

"Had I known this would earn me some eager sex, I might've given up my ways much, much sooner."

I guffaw at that. We both know the Reaper fought his physical urges to the bitter end.

It only takes him a little longer to pull off the rest of his clothing. In the light of day, I see every exposed centimeter of him. I'm used to his nudity, but it still takes my breath away.

Famine's wide shoulders give way to his rounded pecs and tapered waist. His abs are a thing of glory, but even they can't hold my attention for long.

My gaze moves to his erection.

Cocks are kind of my thing. I've seen hundreds of them—fat ones, skinny ones, long ones, short ones. I've seen penises so small that I could barely fit two fingers around them and penises so large they never fully fit all the way inside me, no matter the position. There were dicks that swung to one side and some that grew to twice their normal length; there were some that were bulbous and fleshy and some that were utterly outshined by their owner's enormous balls. And there was everything in between.

Famine's cock is, like the rest of him, annoyingly faultless—thick enough and long enough to make a girl feel thoroughly loved, but not overly endowed to make her regret it the next morning. His cock even slopes with just enough arch to hit a woman's G-spot.

As I stare at him, a grin spreads across my face.

This might be the most blasphemous thing I've ever thought, but God clearly made this man for fucking. Sure, killing too, but I'm just saying—this dick has enough bells and whistles to play itself a song.

"That look of yours always makes me nervous," Famine says, reaching out and pulling me against him. He traces my lips, his pretty cock trapped against my belly.

"Say it again," I say.

Famine lifts me up once more, forcing my legs to wrap around him again. "That look of yours—"

"Not that," I laugh. "That you love me."

The Reaper's eyes grow heated as he carries me forward. "I love you, Ana." When I smile he says it again. "I love you, I love you, I love you. Do you want me to keep going? I can do this all—"

"I love you," I interrupt, placing a hand against his jaw. "And I can't believe I get to have you, you sadistic little shit."

As though to emphasize my point, I lean in and kiss him. I think Famine meant to take us back to a bedroom, but only seconds after my mouth meets his, my back bangs against one of the living room walls, the Reaper's chest pinning me in place.

He stares at me as he lifts my hips, then lowers me down against, him, driving his cock into me.

I hiss out a breath at the sudden intrusion. For a moment, I can't move, my core throbbing around Famine's dick.

He shifts, sliding out of me. I make a sad sound, but then he thrusts back in and I let out a long, very unflattering moan.

A wicked grin splits his features and—

"*Wait*."

Famine pauses, arching a brow.

I take a shallow breath, trying to think past the big fucking dick that I'm skewered on.

"Just so we're clear—" I say, "I don't want a child." I now know he can work his contraceptive magic to make that happen.

The Reaper gives me an unreadable look.

"You being inside me is sort of contingent upon that." Probably should've discussed this the first time we were intimate. "Understood?"

His hand comes between us and squeezes a tit. "Understood."

He grinds into me, and that answer is going to have to do because holy shit, this man knows what he's doing.

He should not be good at this too; this is *my* profession, not his. Which I know is completely ridiculous because Famine is making me feel fucking amazing and I should not be complaining, but the man with the perfect body and the perfect penis is really good at using both.

He must read my thoughts from my face because he says, "You've had all this practice pleasing people and no practice being pleased."

I give him a look. "There's no way you've *ever* pleased anyone besides yourself before now."

He gives me a revealing smile. "Alright, you caught me. But—" He begins to piston in and out, in and out, drinking in my expression with heavily lidded eyes, "am I not a quick study, little flower?"

I don't bother answering him. Those wicked lips of his have taunted me for weeks and weeks. I wrap an arm around his neck and pull him in close, kissing him as our hips meet again and again.

He pulls us away from the wall and, never fully withdrawing from me, moves us down to the ground.

Famine stares down at me as his thrusts begin to speed up, his hips slamming against mine as his cock drives deeper and deeper. He flashes me a wolfish grin, his caramel-colored hair dangling down.

"What?" I ask.

The horseman shakes his head. "You are so fucking gorgeous, and I like this look on you."

As he speaks, sensation is building in me, rising and rising.

"What look?" My voice has gone annoyingly low and breathy.

"Tousled hair, swollen lips, and bright eyes," he says, devouring my expression as his cock continues to stroke me, faster and faster.

"You like the way I look all sexed up," I say, a smile spreading across my face.

He stares at my lips, transfixed, and almost as though he can't help it, he begins to smile back.

I reach up and cup his face in my hands, staring at him as he works me. His hair is caught in my fingers and his sweat is already beginning to mingle with mine, and amidst it all, I feel a deep connection with Famine.

"I love you," I say. I can't help myself. And I need him to hear it over and over again until he fully stops hating himself. And even then I'll say it because those words feel like basking in sunlight.

The Reaper pauses, and I make a sad, disappointed little sound.

He grins back at me. "So impatient."

Around us, I hear tile crack. The floor shifts, and I feel the brush of a plant. It brushes against my hair even as I hear more tiles around us crack, lifting up and sliding aside as more shoots push through.

And this is the part of Famine that I might just love most. He will always be inhuman, and do weird, inhuman shit—like grow *plants* while he's inside me.

Leaning in, the horseman kisses me, while around us the foliage continues to grow. His kiss deepens, and I am consumed by the sensation of Famine in me and above me and around me and—

All at once, my climax crashes through me. I cry out into the Reaper's mouth, pulling him in close as I ride out my orgasm.

He strokes me deeper and deeper, faster and faster, his balls slapping against me until I feel him thicken.

Famine groans against my lips as he comes inside me.

Eventually, his thrusts slow, turning gentle. The horseman rests his head against mine for a moment, his breathing ragged. I can tell he wants to say something about how amazing sex with me is (because let's face it, my pussy is a man-slayer), but I'm not sure he trusts himself enough yet to do so.

Instead, he says, "I love you."

And that is far, far better.

He slides out of me, pulling me against him a moment later. Only now do I get a good look around me. I'm surrounded by a thicket of flowering plants. Even as I watch, another bright bloom bursts to life.

So much for our living room.

I catch sight of a familiar flower—the same ashen rose Famine's grown for me in the past.

"This is ..." I look for the right words, "strange and lovely."

"That's your flower." He pulls me in closer.

"I get my own flower?" I say, raising my eyebrows.

Famine traces my lips. "If I can't make things grow in you, then I'll have to make them grow around you."

"Is that supposed to flatter me?" I say. "Because that sounded creepy as fuck."

"I'm glad that you haven't entirely forgotten that I am 'creepy as fuck.'"

I grab the lavender rose and give it a yank. After some resistance, it rips free.

Famine makes a disapproving noise. "You are such a human—needlessly tearing apart a perfectly good plant."

"You have *literally* done the same thing before." I turn to give the horseman a look, but once I do so, I can see the mirth in his eyes.

A laugh slips from his lips, and he gives my ass a squeeze. "I think riling you up might be a new favorite pastime of mine." Famine leans over to give me a kiss.

I kiss him back, then tuck the pale purple flower behind his ear. Pulling away, I admire the horseman's beauty.

He watches me the entire time. "You make me feel things in the most exquisite way," he admits. "I've lived eons, and yet with you I feel young all over again."

"Is ... that a good thing?" I ask. I can never tell what Famine thinks a compliment is.

"What do you think?"

I don't know. Maybe.

But then again, I'm a fucking idiot, so who knows.

What I *do* know is that the horseman has spent all this time on earth gorging himself on cruelty, but there are so many other experiences Famine hungers for.

Maybe love most of all.

Chapter 48

That night, I stare at the bed in our bedroom for a long time, the lanterns giving everything a soft glow.

Our bedroom.

This is so weird.

"It's not going to grow thorns," Famine says from behind me, making me jump. I didn't hear him walk up. "Unless, of course, that's your thing. Because I *can* make that happen."

I let out a laugh before falling silent once more.

Beds are one of those ordinary things most people take for granted. For me, however, they're sort of a moving target. I've slept in them, fucked in them, been beaten and assaulted in them, and just about everything in between. Beds are a bit of a battleground for me.

But staring at the bed in front of me, with its soft sheets, I'm facing a new reality. It's not just Famine whose world is changing.

"You're really going to sleep right there. With me," I say, nodding to the mattress.

I can feel the horseman's gaze on me. "We don't *have* to sleep."

Another laugh slips out. I can't even say *what* I'm feeling at the moment. There's hope and fear and an anxious sort of excitement.

"Is this where you decide to give groveling a go?" I ask. He's already pledged himself and sexed me up. All that's left is groveling—well, that and actually proposing to me.

"Petulant thing." Famine grabs me by the jaw and gives me a ferocious kiss. He walks forward, into my space, forcing me to back up until I bump into the wall. "Just for that, I think tonight I'm going to make *you* beg."

I wrap a hand around the back of Famine's neck. "You can try," I say.

He grabs one of my legs and hooks it around his waist. Famine's reaching for my other leg when I catch his hand. "Just—don't ruin our bedroom floors."

The Reaper gives me a wicked look. "Floors are overrated," he says, grinding into me.

"*Famine.*"

"*Ana.*" He grinds into me a little more, and I forget the point I was making. "Besides," he adds, "you like me a little wild."

This is true.

"Fine, but if you break the floors, you're going to have to fix them too," I say, releasing his hand.

"Is this what domesticity is going to be like?" Famine asks. "Long discussions about floors? Because if that's so, I suddenly see the perks of fucking you speechless."

I guffaw. "You're not that good a lover."

He pauses. "*Excuse* me?"

I fight back my smile. "You heard me, Reaper. You're not that good."

Lies. All lies.

Famine knows it too.

"Take it back," he demands.

"No."

He presses deeper against me. "Take—it—back."

"*No.*"

"Fine."

He reaches up the new dress I'm wearing and rips my also new panties clean off of me. It takes a little more effort for him to unbutton his pants, his erection springing free. The Reaper doesn't even fully step out of his trousers, just pushes them down far enough to give his dick some room to breathe.

I raise an eyebrow.

Famine still has me pinned against the wall, but now he pulls his hips away long enough to align himself with my core.

And then he drives his cock into me.

I gasp at the overwhelming feel of him inside me. Everything about his presence is demanding. His grip, which has me pinned in place, his dick, which is forcing my pussy to give way for it, and his eyes, which are all but telling me to recant.

When I don't, he gives me a challenging look. At my back, the wall shifts a little, then—

Crack-crack-crack!

The tile flooring breaks in a dozen different places. I smell the sharp scent of wet soil before I see the spindly plants rising from the ground.

"Damnit, Famine," I rasp.

The horseman doesn't respond, too busy thrusting in and out of me, each movement slowly forcing my pussy to better accommodate him.

I part my lips, a dozen different responses at the ready, but then the horseman begins laying into me, his hips slapping against mine, making my body jerk with every aggressive thrust.

My breath comes in shallow pants. The two of us stare at each other as he rails me.

All at once the Reaper pulls out. Still holding me up, he carries me over to the bed that was brought in only hours ago.

He tosses me onto the sheets.

Around us, the room has morphed into something fantastical. Several small trees now crowd the space, their branches fanning out across the ceiling. And in the midst of it all there's Famine, with his glowing tattoos. He's much like this room—fantastical.

Before I can do much more than take him in, he grabs me by the ankles and flips me onto my stomach. The bed dips as he joins me, and I feel his lips skim the up curve of my back.

He brushes the hair away from my neck.

"Take it back," he whispers into my ear.

Is he still thinking about my comments on his skills as a lover? Because if he is ...

I arch into him. "No," I breathe.

The horseman kisses my shoulder, and I feel his smile against my skin. Then he drives into me.

I let out a small sound, my body going boneless as he fits himself back into me. His cock pumps in and out relentlessly, and I can barely do more than fist the sheets.

I am all sensation, powerless to do much more than enjoy each deep stroke of his.

"I was going to make love to you slowly," he says against the shell of my ear. "I was going to be gentle—and you know I'm not gentle by nature—but now I have a point to prove."

I shudder at the sound of his husky voice. Even it has the power to pull me deep under his spell—it always has.

"Are you going to prove it?" I pant. "Or are you going to waste all your time chatting with me?"

His hips go still, and I can feel that unnatural gaze on my back.

I hear his laugh, and a very real chill runs up my spine.

Famine slips a hand between my stomach and my legs. He finds my clit, even as he's hammering into me. The horseman rolls it between his fingers, and *Jesus.*

A low moan escapes me before I can stop it.

Oh God, he's going to end this for me way before I'm ready. Everything feels so unimaginably good.

"Famine," I gasp. My climax is *right there*. Another stroke or two and I'm done. "Famine, I ..."

Suddenly, his fingers are gone.

My orgasm, which had been building up, now falters.

"Say it," he says.

"Damn you." This bastard.

"Just tell me the truth, little liar—that I am an exceptional lover—and then I'll give you your orgasm."

"No," I say. I didn't even want to come at the moment.

"Fine."

His fingers are back on my clit, and somehow his heavy, punishing strokes deepen.

Once again my orgasm begins to build, coiling up inside of me—

He removes his hand.

"*Say it.*"

I'm not proud of it, but I think a sob slips out.

"Stop toying with me," I say.

"Flower, you *invented* this game. Now, say it." He's still moving lightly in and out of me, but he's withholding his powerful thrusts—the ones that will make me come.

"You are the devil."

"Nope," Famine responds smoothly. "He's nicer than me."

The horseman's hand moves back to my clit, and it begins all over again. I've been having so much fun baiting the Reaper that I didn't realize *he* had been baiting *me*.

I exhale, then arch against him.

"You're not a great lover—" I begin.

Already, I can feel Famine reacting, ready to torment me some more.

"—you're the best lover I've ever had."

It's easy to admit because it's the truth. Everything about the sex we have is entangled—our limbs, our wills, our very personalities.

I feel his breath at my back. Finally, he kisses the juncture between my shoulder and neck.

"Thank you, flower," he says. "You're not half bad yourself."

The fuck?

But then his adept fingers find my clit and he's driving into me and touching me and touching me and it's impossible to fight—

I cry out as my orgasm goes off, lashing through me. Famine continues to stroke my clit, stretching my climax out. But as he does so, I feel his body tighten. And then, with a groan, he empties himself into me, pistoning in and out until he's spent.

Famine finally withdraws, and then all of that intensity transforms into something that is gentle. His palms glide over my arms and he kisses my shoulders and my scarred back.

"So beautiful," he murmurs against me.

I flip over and touch his cheek, my thumb rubbing against his skin. He turns his head to kiss my palm.

I can't believe I get this man. Or deity. Not even sure at this point what he is.

"Tell me what you're thinking," Famine says, staring down at me.

I swallow, looking back up at him. "This is too good to be true. *You're* too good to be true."

He laughs at that. "Too good to be true? You wound me, flower. I haven't built a reputation of violence and destruction to be so easily complimented."

After a moment, he asks, "Are you still scared of this bed?"

I furrow my brows. He remembers my hesitation?

"I was never scared," I admit.

He lays down next to me and pulls me close. "Then what were you thinking about when you were staring at it?"

"Like I said, this is all too good to be true. And good things don't happen to me."

Famine's eyes go soft, and it's an attractive look on him. "That's not true. Not anymore. Not for either of us."

He holds me tight, and that's how I begin the first night of truly living with the Reaper—in his arms, in our bed, with his wildness all around us.

Chapter 49

It doesn't take long for the house to be brought back from the dead. Eventually all of the home's old furniture is either cleaned and used, or discarded. All the leaves and nests, trash and animal remains that once lay scattered on the floors are neatly removed.

For perhaps the first time, I see a truly gentle side of Famine emerging. He's the one responsible for coaxing out the last of the living animals who've taken up residence in our dilapidated house. At the moment, he's found a colony of mice in the walls.

He leans into an exposed wall, reaching for the small animals. Famine's armor is gone, and his scythe and scales are laying haphazardly in our bedroom. This is about as normal as the horseman ever looks, and I have to say, he still doesn't look that normal.

He's too sexy—much, much too sexy—to ever just blend in. Not to mention that his sleeves are rolled up, showcasing the glowing green tattoos on his lower forearms.

I watch him as he retrieves one of the squeaking animals, cupping it in his hand.

"You're just going to draw them back in with those fruit trees of yours," I say as he pets the thing's forehead with his thumb.

Because of course the trees Famine grew on our first night produce fruit. Fruit that will drop and rot on the ground and draw in rodents and all other sorts of wild critters.

Rather than removing the *highly* problematic trees, the horseman hired people from the town to open up our roof so that they could better grow. Apparently the horseman isn't worried about the fact that it rains often here. His response had been, *I like you wet.*

Now he says, "Don't act like you disapprove. I know you have a soft spot for displaced creatures."

Creatures like the horseman himself.

I continue to watch his rescue mission. "If I wake up to bird poop on me, you and I are going to have a problem." Or a scorpion in my bed. I will *shit bricks* if I wake up to a scorpion in my bed.

"Come now, flower," he says over his shoulder as he takes the rodent outside, "you've peed on my boots. What's a little bird poop? Besides, it will keep you humble."

Humble?

I like my overinflated ego just fine, thank you.

Famine heads towards the tree line of our new property, and the trees are another thing: with every passing day, the thick forest growing kilometers away seems to be creeping closer to our house. I know that one day soon, the foliage is going to be right at our doorstep.

As I stare off at the horseman, I feel that familiar lightness in my belly all over again.

I can't believe I'm doing this—that *we're* doing this. A retired prostitute and her apocalyptic boyfriend.

Life is strange.

I head back inside, and it's as I'm passing by the living room I notice a new vine snaking up the back wall. I have to take a second look at it, just to make sure it's not a snake, but nope, it's another plant growing in yet another room of this house.

I hear the front door open and close behind me.

"Is this going to become a thing?" I ask, gesturing to the vine. Surrounding it are the other plants that sprung up when we first christened the place.

"Undoubtedly," the horseman says smoothly.

I guess this is what happens when Famine is happy. Rather than killing things, he makes them grow. I mean, technically he *did* grow plants even when he was determined to kill all us humans, but that was different; those plants were his weapons, these ones are his houseguests.

The horseman comes over to me. He should be covered in sweat, but when his arms wrap around me, his skin is only slightly sticky, and even then, I'm pretty sure that's a result of the humidity, not him.

"Does that bother you?" he asks, his voice bored. I'm not sure what to make of that tone. Sometimes his calmness is a trap set to spring, and other times it just is what it is.

"Probably no more than my ways bother you," I reply.

I practically feel Famine's pleasure at my response.

I begin to smile, but then a thought slips into my head that drains away my good mood.

There's a question I've wanted to know the answer to ever since we moved into this house. Up until now I'd avoided asking it because a part of me is terrified of Famine's response. But it's time I finally asked.

I exhale. "Are you still going to keep killing off people and their crops?"

Famine moves around to face me, his gaze intense.

"Your fellow humans get a single lifetime to prove to me that their miserable lives are worth saving," he eventually says.

"A single lifetime?" I repeat, confused by his wording.

It hits me a moment later: Famine is speaking of *my*

lifetime—that's the lifespan he's referring to.

He takes in my expression, the corner of his mouth curving up. The Reaper crowds me, his lips coming to my ear. "I want to see this pretty skin get old."

"You really want to be with me for my entire life?" The thought nearly steals my breath away. "What if you change your mind?"

"About you?" he asks, and now he looks amused. "You silly little flower—don't you realize I've spent all this time trying to do just that? I have had eons of disdain for humans and years of torture to cultivate my hate. Yet here I am, by your side, and God Himself couldn't rip me from you.

"I am not human, Ana. Old age and wilted beauty do not repulse me. They are part of the life cycle—they are a part of what makes me, *me*."

I actually hadn't even thought that far ahead, but the brutal honesty in his words eases my fear.

I take in those eerie green eyes. "And what if *I* change my mind?"

Famine rears back a little. "About me?" He raises his eyebrows, as though the thought is preposterous. "Then I suppose I'll just have to threaten to kill off more towns. I imagine that will get you to stay."

"Oh my God," I say, "living with you is an awful idea."

"Truly, it is," he agrees.

He reels me in close and kisses the tip of my nose. "I suppose I could give you no reason to leave. That's the less fun option, but I'm quite charming when I want to be."

"I think you're confusing my wonderful personality with your own," I reply.

The horseman laughs at that. "Hmmm, maybe."

Then he leans in and kisses me. It's short and sweet and all too brief.

The horseman pulls away just enough to lean his head against mine.

"I've never felt so alive before, Ana," he admits. "It's wonderfully messy. I think I might like being human after all."

Two nights later, I find myself on my back, Famine's head between my thighs, my fingers wrapped up in his hair.

Since the two of us started living together, I've discovered something about Famine: he loves going down on me. Loves, loves, loves it. Which, I'll be honest, I have mixed feelings about.

Obviously it feels good, but I'm also so self-conscious. It's more than just feeling like my vagina has seen some shit, and I don't want his mouth down there. It's also that I am unused to selfishly receiving pleasure.

I think that might be part of the reason the Reaper likes this so much. I'm pretty sure he's determined to replace my old conditioning with something new.

He pauses now, his face moving away from my core.

I'm panting, still staring up at the tree branches above our bed, when he shifts himself, draping his naked body over mine, his erection pressing against my thigh.

He stares down at me.

"Marry me," he whispers.

I freeze, taking in his features. His eyes are bright and he looks eager and hopeful, his normal arrogance wiped clean from his expression.

"Please," he adds.

My heart lurches.

I think this is him groveling.

My throat constricts, and my pulse is speeding up. "Why do you want to marry me?" I ask. I find that I'm actually afraid of his answer.

The Reaper's lips quirk. "Little flower, don't you know? I happen to enjoy it when you pee on my boots, and you sing songs off-key, and when I wake up to your atrocious morning breath—you know, you also fart in your sleep."

Jesus.

"This is the worst proposal I have literally ever heard," I say.

"I like it when you heckle me for saving small creatures, and I want to keep growing plants inside this house just so that you'll give me shit for it. I happen to love you—*all* of you— and I always will. And I want you to always love me too."

"You know I do," I say quietly.

"Marry me," he says again.

My heart is pounding way too loudly. "Marriage is for humans," I say.

"I don't give a damn. I want you to be mine under the eyes of all of these deceitful little assholes we live alongside.

"Please," he repeats.

Still I hesitate.

"I'm afraid," I admit. Afraid of loving something this much, of having it this good. I'm afraid of actually getting everything I've ever dreamed of because I've never gotten anything of substance before in my life.

"No one will ever hurt you again," Famine vows, misinterpreting my words. "It's us against the world, Ana. Marry me."

A moment later he reaches under the mattress and pulls out a ring. Sitting right in the middle of it is a fat-ass diamond. The thing isn't some modest stone, this thing is a goddamn *boulder.*

My gaze moves to his. "Who did you kill to get that thing?"

"*Ana,*" he says, his voice beseeching me to take this seriously.

This *is* too good to be true, but for once, I don't let that stop me.

I smile up at Famine, my grin so wide it hurts my cheeks. I tuck a lock of his toffee-colored hair behind his ear, and then I lean up and kiss him.

"Yes," I say against his lips. "Yes."

Chapter 50

Famine

The days become weeks, the weeks become months. My scythe doesn't rust and my muscles don't grow soft, but I have gone to seed, my purpose set aside.

Just for a moment, I told myself when we settled in. *Then I will get back to my task.*

I knew I was telling myself a lie, but it was alright at the time. I wanted to give Ana a respite; she asks for so little.

But the truth is, I actually like this derelict little house of ours, and I'm curious just how overgrown I can make it before Ana actually loses it.

I expected the townspeople to plot against me, to rebel and fight for their lives. I was *ready* for that confrontation. But while I sense their deep and abiding fear, they have left me alone. I even get the impression that they respect me.

Ana, on the other hand, is openly adored. The same people who cast me fearful glances will happily pull her aside to chat about this or that. I would die before I admit it, but a part of me is proud of how beloved my fiancée is.

And now I've come to the ridiculous decision that maybe I'll hold off killing them altogether—at least while Ana lives. Only then will I resume ravaging these lands.

My throat closes up at the thought of Ana one day dying.

What *will* happen when that day comes? Once she's given me children—assuming, of course, that she ever wants them—and she grows old and passes. She'll be gone, and ... and ... I will be forced to feel the earth take her body back into itself. I will feel it pick her apart and disperse that beloved skin and that beautiful hair and every other bit of her into the ground, food for some other, newer life. The world will go on, *I* will go on, even if she won't.

I find I can't breathe at the thought. It cuts too deep. Much, much too deep.

Why have I never considered this?

It's not even her dying that causes me grief; it's the lingering on without her. Lingering on and on.

I stand out in our yard, taking in my surroundings with a sort of helpless fear I've come to despise. I can hear Ana somewhere in the house, humming while she burns the dish she's trying to make.

I still can't get enough air in my lungs.

How will I ever possibly take back up my scythe once she's gone?

I *won't*.

I can't.

It's as simple as that.

What a fool I've been to believe I didn't have to choose between Ana and my task. Choosing her *was* the end of my task. There's no moving on once she's gone.

But—if I'm made mortal—I'll age with her, die with her, move on to whatever comes next *with her.*

I want that. I want it bad.

But mortality would mean living in this body I have long

despised, a body I've only recently been reconsidering. And it would mean giving up my powers.

That's a staggering tithe—one my brothers have already paid.

I finally understand why they traded in their weapons and their immortality. There is nothing quite like being human. This damnable, deranged experience actually has some perks.

I find I don't care nearly enough about my power to shake away this notion that I could be mortal with Ana.

I want to do it. Right now. Before I lose my nerve and retreat back into my usual, apathetic self.

However, there is one more thing that stands in my way, one other thing that's always stood in my way.

Forgiveness.

The word rings in my ears like God Herself spoke it.

Forgiveness.

I suck in a sharp breath. Ever since I first heard Ana speak that word in her sleep, a word her vocal chords shouldn't have even been able to produce—it's been there, taunting me.

I'm not sure who I'm supposed to forgive, but I imagine it's everyone. God would expect no less.

It's not even in my nature to forgive. I'm apathetic at best, vengeful at worst. And after everything humans have done to me, to Ana ...

Forgiveness is preposterous.

I don't need to do it. Not today, not ever. I still get to have Ana.

Ana, who every second is losing bits of her life, the clock counting down to her end.

My steady pulse grows frantic.

I don't need to decide today.

I don't.

But the longer I wait, the closer to death she'll get. Is it wrong that I want to age with her?

Forgiveness. I turn the word over and over in my mind.

Forgive these petty, wicked creatures.

It's so wholly oppositional to what I've been doing this entire time.

Above me, storm clouds gather, the thick plumes of them darkening the sky. The ground is beginning to shake—just a little.

I think of Ana. Ana, who asks nothing of me. Ana who saved me before she knew what I was—and then saved me again once she did know.

Ana, who I forgave long ago—I forgave her the very night we met. And I've forgiven her every day since—for harming me, for hating me, for every slight she's inflicted. It's easy enough to forgive someone like Ana, who is kind when she doesn't need to be. Ana who is radiant and thaws my cold heart.

It's much harder to forgive everyone else, especially when everyone else includes the people who once hurt me.

They made ribbons of my skin, they disemboweled me, they stabbed me—over and over—and burned me alive. Those men and women made pain an art form.

And the very night Ana saved me, my body still mutilated, God forced me to consider that damnable word.

Forgiveness.

You ask too much, I'd whispered into the darkness, my voice broken. *Far too much.*

I hadn't been able to forgive this teeming mass of humanity then. I *still* haven't been able to do it. But I know intuitively that I don't get mortality until I do this.

I swallow.

A raindrop hits me. Then another. The ground beneath me is shaking.

If I forgive humanity, then what?

I think of these wretched people, with their crudely-dug wells and their rickety corrals full of bored looking animals. I think of the crumbling cities overgrown with plants.

Human hearts are spiteful and selfish; they are what bid me and my brothers here.

As though aware of my thoughts, my armor materializes on my body, and my scythe and scales appear a mere arm's span away from me.

I feel the weight of not just my armor, but my hate and anger, my task and my immortality—all of it—on my shoulders.

I drop to a knee and place a fist against the trembling ground, even as raindrops begin to patter against my armor, coming down faster and faster. My breath is labored and my ever steady heart is quickening.

Something's happening to me. I don't know if it's as simple as my mind changing, or if the forces that brought me here, the forces that made me a man and forged my purpose into form are now transforming.

"Famine?"

I jolt at the sound of Ana's voice.

My gaze flicks up from the ground, where small plants have started to flower and twist up my wrist.

She stands outside our doorway, her cotton dress whipping in the wind. Rain is pelting her, and her eyes look spooked.

Still, she's so goddamn radiant that it makes my chest tight looking at her.

At what point did she become my purpose?

Her gaze roves over me. "What are you doing?" she calls out to me.

I don't ... I think ...

Fuck, I'm uncertain. I hate being uncertain.

Forgiveness.

That bloody word echoes through me.

"I'm ... relinquishing my purpose."

Chapter 51

Ana

Famine has barely spoken the words when—

BOOM!

It sounds like the world is cracking itself wide open.

I stagger towards the horseman, the ground trying to throw me off like a wild horse bucking its rider.

Another earthquake.

I remember the last one well enough. Famine had caused it then, too.

Around us, the earth heaves, and trees from the forest that now surrounds our house snap by the dozens, their trunks crashing to the ground. That's the only sound I can pick out, but there are others too—too many others. I think our house is making some of them.

Rain turns to hail and lightning flashes from the heavens—coming so fast and from so many places that I can't make sense of it.

I cover my head as a bloodcurdling howl rises from the

depths of the earth, the sound filling the sky, so deafening that it drowns out the roar of the storm.

Far in the distance, several of Taubaté's derelict skyscrapers begin to fall.

I swallow my scream at the sight. They crumble apart as they collapse, kicking up plumes of debris in their wake.

At some point, the unearthly howl dies away, leaving my ears ringing. Slowly, I hear the sounds of frightened animals. Thousands of birds and bugs have already taken to the skies, but they fly in a confused, agitated sort of way, like neither land nor sky is safe.

A short ways from me, Famine is still kneeling on the ground.

His face is wiped clean of all expression.

Fear—true, undiluted fear, the kind you feel as a kid—floods my system.

"What was that?" I breathe.

I'm not sure he heard me; my voice is too quiet and our surroundings are too loud.

But then the Reaper's unearthly green eyes move to mine. He holds my gaze for several seconds.

"My brother is awake." Famine's face is pale. "Death ... *lives*."

Chapter 52

Ana

Death lives.

The hairs on the back of my neck stand up.

My pulse is pounding between my ears, and at the back of my throat I can taste the acrid tang of bile.

"Death?" I echo. "As in ... your brother?"

He doesn't even need to answer. There's no misinterpreting the Reaper's words.

Just the thought of the fourth horseman has my skin turning clammy. Death doesn't seem like a lenient horseman.

"But ... I thought that you said ..." Famine said he was relinquishing his purpose.

Like Pestilence and War.

Oh God.

The Reaper lifts a hand, hovering it over the ground. From the earth a wispy stalk rises. Within seconds, a small bud forms at its tip. It bursts open, a delicate white flower unfurling.

"I didn't lose my power," the horseman murmurs.

"Were you supposed to?" What is going on?

When I first noticed the unnatural storm brewing above us, I came out here wanting to know what pissed the horseman off. But he didn't look angry then so much as agonized, and if what he's shared so far is any indication, he was trying to give up his task. Presumably for me.

"Why would you do that?" I ask before he can answer my previous question. "You don't need to be mortal for me. You hate being mortal."

His gaze meets mine. "Not anymore. Not with you," he says.

I take all of him in, rain still pelting the two of us. He's wearing his armor and his scythe and scales are at his side.

"But it doesn't matter," he says. "It didn't work."

"It didn't work?" I echo. "Should it have?"

Famine pushes himself off the ground, the plant slipping off of his forearm. He gives me a strange, intense look.

The Reaper closes the distance between us and cups my face, pinning my hair to my cheeks.

"He's coming here."

"Who?" I ask, my heart galloping away.

But I know. I know.

I search the horseman's face. *Tell me everything is okay*, I will him. *Tell me the world is not about to end.*

Famine's gaze is fierce. "There's something I need to show you."

He's still not acting right.

Famine drops his hands from my face, then moves away to grab his scales. After he scoops them up, he takes my hand, leading me back towards our house.

"Death is awake, and he's coming here."

There it is.

"Why would he come here?" I ask. Famine made it pretty clear when he told me about his encounter with War that the horsemen try to keep to their own corners of the world.

"Because I've been naughty," the Reaper says.

"You're always naughty," I say. "Why is today any different?"

Other than, you know, Famine trying to relinquish himself of his duty.

"You'll see."

That sounds ominous.

We enter our house, and he pulls me towards the kitchen. On the countertop are ingredients from my failed attempts at baking—eggs and flour, butter and milk.

With a single sweep of his arm, Famine sends the ingredients careening off the counter. The glass jar of milk explodes and the eggs splatter, and Famine notices none of it.

Instead, he sets the scales on the cleared surface.

I stare at the bronze device. It's the one possession of Famine's I usually forget about. Now, however, he's giving the thing an inordinate amount of attention.

From a nearby drawer, the Reaper withdraws a knife with a wicked sharp blade.

"What are y—?"

Quick as lightning, he slices his forearm, then holds it directly over one of the bronze pans.

The scale wavers, bobbing up and down, up and down. Like last time, the pan with the horseman's blood rises higher than its empty companion.

Famine wipes the blade on his sleeve. Then, he grasps my hand.

"*Famine.*"

His eyes hold mine, and they're lethally steady. "Just trust me." Even as he speaks, his cut continues to bleed everywhere.

He doesn't look away from me, not until I give him a reluctant nod. I don't know what's going on, but I do trust him. I trust him with my life.

He takes my index finger, and using the tip of the knife, he pricks it.

Instinctively my hand jerks back, but the horseman holds it fast. Moving it over the scales, he squeezes out one—two—three drops of blood from the tip of my finger, each droplet hitting the saucer across from his. Last time we did this, Famine had weighed my blood against an empty saucer. Now he's pitting it against his.

I expect my side of the scales to dip as it did before. I expect to see Famine's blood rise above mine like it did last time.

Instead, the tray holding my blood rises and rises. It shouldn't be a strange sight. There's more blood on Famine's saucer after all; his side is heavier. But his scales have never weighed the literal mass of things.

I suck in a breath. "How ... ?"

How could I possibly be holier than you?

"It was my mind all along that ruled the scales, not God's," Famine says.

My eyebrows draw together in confusion.

He's still holding my hand and blood is slipping down my fingers and onto his skin and the look he's giving me ... like he's trying to will the answer into my head.

"It's not you who has changed," he says, "*It's me.*"

I search his eyes. "But ... you still hate humanity," I say. Because those scales were never just about me. They were about what I represented—humankind.

"Not anymore," he says, repeating his earlier words. "Which is why my brother has risen."

I still don't understand that. I don't understand any of this. Famine supposedly tried to give up his task ... but maybe it didn't work? And now the fourth and final horseman has awoken and ... he's coming here? The more I process what's happening, the sicker I feel.

"What does he want?" I ask.

"There is only one thing Thanatos ever wants," Famine

says. "Death."

Famine

Death doesn't show himself. Not in the hours that follow. Day turns to night and still he hasn't arrived.

I can feel him out there. There's no agitated energy, just cold, emotionless determination. He's coming closer and closer, but there's no urgency.

I stare down at Ana from where I sit on the bed. She's finally managed to fall asleep, our sheets tangled around her legs. She's absolute shit at sharing blankets. Just that one small detail has my chest tightening.

How many more things have I yet to discover about her? There's an entire world contained beneath that skin of hers, and I hunger to explore it all.

But I might not get a chance to.

Not without facing my brother first.

I cannot tell what his intentions are—nor God's for that matter. That was part of the deal: once we're human, we live as humans do. The only divine intercession I've felt since I arrived was the Angelic word Ana spoke—and perhaps Ana's miraculous recovery from the injuries my men wrought on her.

Of course, if Death awoke, perhaps it was God who woke him. I cannot recall what woke me, only that it was time.

Ana murmurs in her sleep, then shifts. Without intending to, I move over to her and kneel at her side.

I brush her hair back from her face, my thumb stroking her temple.

I didn't know it would be like this. That it *could* be like this. I had seen humans' hate, and I had felt the depths of it, but I never imagined they could love this deeply. That *I* could love this deeply.

It's frightening and it's making me obsessive.

"Nothing will happen to you," I breathe. "On my very existence, I swear it."

Death can come, but he will not take my Ana.

My brother doesn't come that day or the one that follows—or even the one that follows that. It takes him two weeks to arrive in Taubaté. But the moment he does arrive, I know it.

His power detonates, the force of it so strong that I drop the dagger I was sharpening.

In an instant, the entire city of Taubaté is just *gone*, humans dropping dead where they stand. I sense their lifeforces all snuffed out like a candle. Thanatos doesn't have to touch them to kill them—he doesn't even need to make their flesh wither away as I must. He simply wills their souls to leave their bodies, and they do.

It's that easy for him.

I'm still reeling from the display of power when I realize—

"Ana."

All at once, I rise to my feet, the kitchen chair clattering to the ground behind me.

"Ana!" This time I shout her name. And then I'm racing through the house, panic rising like a swell within me. "Ana!"

What if she's dead? What if he took her and—

She comes running out of our bedroom. "*What's wrong?*" she says, breathless, her eyes wide with worry.

At the sight of her, *alive*, my legs buckle, and I fall to my knees.

"Famine?" Now she's the one who sounds afraid.

She runs over to me. I catch her by the waist and hold her close, my face pressed against her stomach.

Alive, I remind myself again.

"I thought he took you," I say against her.

"Who?" she says, her fingers slipping through my hair. She

tilts my face so that I'm looking up at her.

"Death." Even as I speak his name, my fear begins to rise all over again.

If he didn't kill Ana, it's because he has some plan for her. A plan I want no part of.

"He's here?" she says.

I nod.

Even now I feel him like a pulse off in the distance, though I can't sense precisely where he is. He must be keeping to the sky, where he knows I can't pinpoint him.

"And he's close," I say. I don't bother telling her that everyone else is gone.

The expression is wiped clean from her face.

I take a deep breath and stand. I've gone over this moment every day for the past two weeks. What to do, what Ana's to do.

"Listen to me carefully," I tell her now. "I want you to hide far away, beyond the fruit trees."

"But you said—"

I said a lot of things in the last two weeks, some of them lies and some of them truths. Amongst them all, I told her that running and hiding were pointless, which they are. Death knows all souls. He'd find us. He'd find her.

"Fuck what I said. If you stay here, he will kill you," I say. "That is what he does."

It's not the complete truth. Thanatos could just as easily kill her here as he could several kilometers away. The actual truth is that I want Ana to be far away when I face my brother because I want his focus to be on me and me alone.

"What will he do to you?" she asks. Her voice wavers.

"I'll be fine." Now I *am* telling the truth.

"Can he kill you?" she asks.

Can Death himself remove me from the face of the earth?

God help me, but—

"Yes." I wouldn't die, but it would be the end of my

existence in this form.

"I'm not leaving your side," she says fiercely.

I feel a swell of love so sharp it's almost painful.

"Damn you, Ana," I say, "don't make me force you away."

Emotions flicker across her face too rapidly for me to follow.

"I'm not leaving you," she says stubbornly.

This woman of mine.

I pull her in close and kiss her, my mouth rough on hers.

"I'm not going to die," I tell her. "He's my brother, and I know how to handle him. I cannot, however, face him while worrying about you."

"I am not a liability, Famine, and I'm not going to let him ..."

She keeps talking, but I don't hear her words.

She's not going to back down. Damn her and her stubbornness.

Before Ana can finish making her point, I scoop her up and carry her outside.

"Famine, put me down." She tries to wriggle out of my arms.

Only once we're outside do I set her back down.

Ana huffs, pushing a stray curl out of the way. "Do *not* manhandle—"

Before she can finish, I flick my wrist. In seconds, a soft, waxy-leafed bush bursts from the earth, twining itself around her as it grows.

Ana's been a victim of this trick often enough to know she's not going to like it.

"*Famine*," she hisses. "What are you doing?"

"Hiding you," I tell her, "because you won't do it yourself." As I speak, a line of plants burst from the ground, creating a road of sorts from Ana all the way to the nearby forest's tree line.

Ana's eyes flash, and the look of betrayal she gives me

nearly makes me waver. If I wasn't such a cold-hearted bastard, I might've actually lost my nerve.

Instead, I flick my wrist again, and the plants begin to move, each one systematically grabbing her before handing her off to the next bit of foliage in line. It's a strange and unnatural sight, watching the flora spirit away a grown woman into the forest beyond. It's the thing of human myths.

What's not so mythical are the curses pouring from her mouth.

"*You goddamn bastard!*" she shouts. "*Let me fucking go! Famine, I swear upon your God, I will kick you in the dick so hard you'll feel your balls in your throat.*"

Normally, the sadist in me gets quite a bit of pleasure from her protests. But right now there's no joy in it. I stare after her until even her voice fades away.

I go back inside the house long enough to grab my scythe before returning to my front yard. My gaze goes to the heavens, where thick storm clouds have amassed.

He's still out there. Still circling. And damn me, but I cannot pinpoint him with my senses and I cannot clear this sky enough to spot him with my naked eye.

If I had been level-headed, I would easily blow away the incoming storm. But my feelings are inextricably bound up in Death's arrival, and my anxiety cannot do more than intensify the already thick cloud cover.

So I stare at the heavens and focus as best I can on where he might be.

Minutes pass.

"Come on, brother," I murmur. "Let's end this."

As though he heard my words, I sense him lowering himself from the sky. I still can't spot him.

In the distance, I hear my steed snort, then the dull pound of his hooves galloping towards me.

Off in the opposite direction are another set of pounding hoof beats. I drag my gaze away from the sky.

There, charging up the road is a dappled grey steed. His empty saddle is made of black leather and limned in silver, chthonic images styled across the seat.

Death's fabled horse.

At last, Thanatos has found me.

Chapter 53

Ana

I sit in a cage made of plants, seething. There are sticks in my hair, leaves down my shirt, and stalks up my skirt.

The plants around me are no longer manhandling my ass, and they are no longer wrapped around my limbs, but the thick, barbed bush that encapsulates me is obviously meant to be a cage.

After a minute, I stand up and brush myself off, my head skimming the branches that arch overhead.

Will this plant release me if I put up a fight?

I give it a test kick, just to see. When it doesn't fight back—also, yay for living in a time when plants fight back—I begin to push my way through the foliage, elbowing back branches and ignoring the nicks and scrapes I get from the thorns.

It takes me several minutes, but I get out of that stupid cage Famine wrought.

Oh man, am I going to rip him a new asshole.

I begin stalking back the way I came when I hear a loud,

thumping noise overhead.

Whomp—whomp—whomp.

I glance up at the object descending from the sky. At first glance, it looks like an enormous black bird, but after several seconds, I realize it's a winged *man*.

The dark angel lowers himself to the earth, his massive black wings beating behind him, causing his dark hair to ripple. I catch a glimpse of glowing glyphs crawling up his neck, but it's his beautiful, solemn face that snags my gaze.

His feet touch the ground, and his dark wings fold up behind him. He doesn't carry a sword or a scythe or any other weapon, but I feel as though I can't draw in enough breath.

The hairs across my arms stand on end; I don't believe I've ever encountered a being that seems as lethal as this one does—Famine included.

He strides forward, silver armor gleaming, his gaze trained on me.

Around him, the underbrush withers away, their leaves curling up and their stalks turning brittle.

It's the same sick power that Famine has.

Only this isn't Famine.

There's only one creature in existence who this could be.

"Death," I whisper.

And he's coming for me.

Famine

I realize my mistake the moment my brother's feet touch the earth. I sense him, not near me, but near *her.*

Ana.

Scythe in hand, I'm suddenly *sprinting*, cutting across thick vegetation, the bushes and trees bending out of my way. I run like my very life depends on it.

But it's not my life I'm worried about.

It takes less than a minute for me to arrive where I so recently left Ana.

Death stands among withered vines and shrubs, facing me off, his wings folded at his back. Kneeling in front of him—

"*Famine!*" Ana chokes out. She lunges forward at the sight of me, but Thanatos catches her by the shoulder, jerking her back in place.

The sight of him manhandling her has me rolling the scythe in my hand. I storm forward.

"Don't come any closer, brother," Death says calmly, his fingers tightening their grip on Ana's shoulder.

I jerk to a halt, my eyes focused on where he holds her in place.

Thanatos moves his hand to stroke Ana's face, his fingers trailing over her cheekbone. Beneath his touch, she pinches her eyes, grimacing.

He could take her from me in an instant, and I would be powerless to stop it. I *am* powerless. The thought stirs up violent thoughts. But just beneath that is another, sickening emotion—*dread*. Deep, existential dread for Ana.

I can barely breathe around the thought of her *dying*.

Ana exhales and opens her eyes again, her gaze finding mine. She looks oddly calm, but her breath is leaving her in ragged gasps, like she's only barely controlling her fear.

"Dear brother," Thanatos says, "I was hoping our reunion would go a bit differently."

I clench my jaw, my focus moving to him.

"Why are you here?"

"You *know* why I am here," Death says. After a moment that stretches out, he adds, "We were made to end these creatures, not to *give in* to them."

His fingers continue to pet Ana's cheek. Her body is shaking, and a single, frightened tear escapes from her eyes.

I grip my scythe tighter. At the sight of her fear, that old hunger rises in me—the one that needs to suck the marrow from the earth. Overhead, clouds stir and churn.

Death tilts his head, his expression placid. "You surprised me, you know. The others, I was expecting to fail to some degree. War, after all, is made from men's wicked desires, and Pestilence—well, he has an unnatural curiosity for humans as well. It came as no great shock that that they were felled by these women of fire and clay.

"But you, dear brother, the great Famine himself, who has killed millions of humans without pause or remorse. I thought that surely you wouldn't be so easily swayed."

Thanatos glances down at Ana, and I have to physically hold myself back from intervening.

"I cannot fathom what it is about them that draws you in," he says, sounding oddly intrigued. "I suppose it *is* in your nature to hunger for things—even things you shouldn't."

He's still stroking Ana's face.

"*Brother*," I warn. I can feel myself beginning to tremble. I'm losing my patience and my control.

But Thanatos has a fire in his eyes. "You and I, Famine, we blink our eyes and civilizations have risen and collapsed. The centuries fall away like petals of a flower. You are the bearer of the divine scales; you know the price of all things. Surely it must be obvious that a single, insignificant life isn't a worthy trade for your immortality."

Finally, we arrive at the reason for this reunion. It must shake even unflinching Death that three of his brothers would choose mortality over duty.

"I am the bearer of the scales, and I do understand the worth of all things," I say. "It is for me to decide what a worthy trade is. And I have decided."

Death studies me for a long time. After a minute, he takes Ana by the chin and tilts her face up to him, studying her features. She meets my brother's dark gaze, another tear slipping from her eyes.

The gathering clouds above betray my emotions. I feel a

drop hit my cheek, then another splash against my temple.

"She has a pleasing enough form," Death admits, "and her spirit *is* resilient and forgiving, but she will die soon enough. It is the way of these creatures. Even I cannot keep her here forever."

She will die soon enough?

She won't if I am by her side.

"I don't care, brother," I say resolutely. "I have made my choice."

Thanatos sighs, moving his hand back to Ana's cheek, those maddening fingers stroking her skin once more.

"I will relieve you of your scales and your scythe," he says, his voice full of mocking disbelief.

Still, I nearly stagger.

He will help me after all.

"I will even allow you to strip yourself of your immortality and your duty," he continues, "because you so love humanity."

I hadn't asked for his permission when I first tried to cleave away my immortality, and I didn't ask for it now, but I'll—begrudgingly—take it all the same. This is what Death does, after all—he can strip men's souls from their bones, and he can strip my immortality and purpose from mine.

"*But—*" Death adds.

But.

That single word steals my breath, and I feel the weight of his tithe.

"—but your mortality comes at a price."

Not many things shake me, but this does. What other hells must I endure?

"I thought the price was steep enough as it is," I say. Thanatos himself had been the one to say this was an unworthy trade.

"You're in the land of humans. There is no fairness here," my brother replies.

Damn him, but I cannot disagree.

"You want mortality?" he continues. His hand moves to Ana's shoulder once more. He squeezes it. "Then your female comes with me."

To the afterlife, he means.

"*What?*" I take a step forward, alarmed, just as Ana bites her lip, a couple more tears silently slipping from her eyes.

"Ah, ah," Thanatos says, his black wings unfurling. They come around Ana, further isolating her from me. I stiffen at the sight of her in Death's embrace. "That's not how this works, brother."

I try not to panic. It would be effortless for him to take her from me. Worse, he'd consider it a mercy to deliver her from this world.

"Fuck you, Thanatos," I say, "That is no trade."

The only reason I want to rid myself of my immortality is so that I can live and die alongside Ana. What would be the point if she were already dead and gone?

"But I thought you wanted to save humanity?" Death says, his eyes gleaming.

To hell with humanity. I don't much care about all the other humans out there.

My brother's eyes narrow. "I see. You wouldn't save humanity if this woman couldn't be saved, too," he says, echoing my thoughts.

"Does it matter what my reasons are?" I say.

"Of course it does," Death says. "You are the bearer of the scales. You know better than I do that motives are *everything*."

I take a step closer. The last of my reasonableness is burning itself away. I've stayed my hand, I've been more goddamn civil than should be expected of me.

Now the heavens open up. Rain begins to pelt down, and the sky flashes.

BA-BOOM!

The thunder rattles above me.

"Listen closely, brother," I say. "The woman you're holding is the *only* thing that matters to me. If you hurt her at all, we will have a problem, Thanatos. Your duty won't mean shit in the face of my wrath."

Death looks sad. "You have lost sight of who and what you are, Famine, to so easily turn your back on your task," he says.

A bolt of lightning strikes a nearby tree—

BOOM!

The trunk explodes, fire and sparks bursting from the wet wood, and the small clearing we're in lights up.

The corner of my mouth lifts into a smile.

"Have I now?" I say, gripping my scythe tighter as rain comes down in torrents. "And you would know, wouldn't you?" I say, as my anger mounts. "You, who have not felt my pain or my anger or lived through—"

"Every human feels pain," Death says. "I don't need to know yours—"

"I suffered here for years, brother," I say, cutting him off. "*Years.* Where were you then? Why didn't you slay my oppressors and save me so that I could return to my task?"

Death is quiet.

I point to Ana with my scythe. "It was this woman with her *pleasing enough form*—"

Ana—God bless her vanity—frowns at that.

"—who saved me," I say. "So, you and your offensive trade can fuck—right—off."

I will find another way to be mortal—or I won't. Perhaps I'll keep my immortality right up until Ana's death, and then I'll make the trade.

Thanatos's fingers dig into Ana's shoulder. She glances up, giving my brother a look that would shrivel the balls off a lesser man, and tries to jerk her shoulder free. It doesn't get her anywhere, but I admire her all the same. The knot of worry that sits in the pit of my stomach loosens just a little.

"Do you really think I'm going to let the two of you just

walk away to continue on as you were?" Death says, raising his eyebrows. "Whatever you've been doing in this corner of the world, it ends today."

Rain is coming down in torrents and the wind howls through the forest. More lighting flashes, hitting neighboring trees and setting the lumbering plants on fire before the rain douses them out.

I can no longer tell if Ana is crying, but her eyes are agonized.

It was too good to be true, her face seems to say.

I want to prove her wrong, but Death is one entity I cannot so easily vanquish.

"You heard my first offer," he says.

I scowl at him, squeezing my scythe so tightly that my knuckles are turning white.

"Here is my second: Resume your task. Ride with your—" his upper lip twitches with distaste, "*woman*. Use your powers as they were meant to be used."

Even as he speaks, the memory of the wind in my hair and the pound of my steed's galloping body is so sharp it feels as though I could reach out and touch it. Most of me aches for that wild freedom.

Thanatos continues, "I will ensure that your female is one of the last humans to go. All you must do is take up your task once more. Let's finish what we've started, brother."

As if on cue, Death's horse trots into the tiny clearing, followed by my own steed.

I can see it now: The three of us riding to the ends of the world. Thanatos would take humans right where they stood, and I'd blight the crops of any individuals who escaped his attention. We'd cut down humanity one city at a time.

Even now I can feel the oily urge to mount my steed and do just that. Domesticity was never a natural state for me.

Ana would be with me. It would be alright, for a time—

"*Famine*," Ana says.

My gaze moves to her, still in Death's grip. Around us the thunder has quieted, and the rain has lightened up to a thoughtful drizzle. I stare into her eyes.

"Don't," she says.

I can tell it takes a lot for her to say that. Her will to live has always been a dominant force.

I take a deep breath.

If I take what Thanatos offers, she would survive. But if I drove my steed across the world and made Ana watch death after death ... well, that's not without its own consequences.

She might live, but she might also come to hate me. I would make her into something terrible. I'm not sure either of us could survive that.

And even if—by some miracle—I didn't lose Ana's love, eventually the world *would* still end—maybe in one year, maybe in ten, maybe in fifty—and Death would kill her then, before her time was up. He would kill all his brothers' wives. Death would finish the task that the rest of us turned our backs on and take our women at the end of it. They might be the last humans to go, but they would still go.

"Remember what you told me," Ana says, her voice wavering, forcing me to turn my attention back to her. "*Forgive.* That's what you're meant to do. Even if—" She chokes on her next word, and has to restart again. "Even if it kills me."

She would sacrifice herself. She broke me once, and she's breaking me all over again.

But if we break, we break together.

My attention moves to Death. "I don't want either of your offers."

My brother holds my gaze for a long moment. "So be it," he finally says.

I feel a shift in the air. Then, under Thanatos's touch, Ana's eyes roll back in her head. Her body sways, then collapses on the ground.

Dead.

Chapter 54

Famine

"Ana!" My voice sounds so far away.

I feel like the earth is disintegrating around me, that I am in free fall.

Can't breathe.

Can't think.

In an instant I close the distance between me and Ana. I fall to her side, my arms slipping under her torso. I cradle her in my arms.

There's no pulse, no sense of life left in her.

"What have you done?" I say to my brother, my gaze pinned on Ana's face.

I choke on my breath, unable to process—to accept—what I'm seeing.

"Ana," I say, shaking her like an idiot. I cup her cheek. "Ana." A tear slips out, hitting her chin.

I press my lips to hers, trying to breathe life back into her. Nothing within her stirs. I could make her body grow, but there's nothing wrong with it. It's simply that the soul residing in it is now *gone*.

I am being unmade.

Distantly, I'm aware of the gusting winds and the shaking earth. I'm aware that trees are snapping and plants are dying and it's my doing.

My brother took her, just as he promised. No discussion, no negotiations, no interest in hearing the rest of what I was going to say.

"What have you done?" I repeat.

"You've seen death often enough, Famine. I assumed you understood."

"Bring her back." I'm beginning to shake. A low, moaning noise tears itself from my throat. "You gave all of my brothers a fair trade. That's all I want."

"War and Pestilence were both willing to save humanity. You are not."

I know for a fact War and Pestilence would've happily razed the earth, no questions asked, if it meant keeping their wives. That's simply the way we work.

My grip on Ana tightens.

Slowly I look up at Thanatos, and I am filled with menace. There is a reason men don't cross me and live.

"*Bring her back*," I demand. Once again the rain is picking up and lightning is flashing overhead, and the earth is openly revolting and every blade of grass around us is dead.

BOO–BOOM! The thunder roars.

My brother stares at me piteously.

"You have my terms."

I stare down at Ana's lovely face, and her shining, sightless eyes.

Next to me, Death looms. "My other offer still stands."

His offer.

His ridiculous, shitty offer.

I let Ana go, her body slipping from my arms, the ache

inside me growing and growing.

"I wasn't lying when I said that hurting her would be the end of everything," I say as I rise to my feet. Already I can feel the land dying, and the last of Taubaté's skyscrapers falling to the ground under the quaking earth. The wind swirls around me and hail pelts at the dead foliage.

I hadn't realized I cast aside my scythe. I pick it up now, spinning it in my hand, and approach my brother.

"You would hurt me?" Death says.

In response, I swing my scythe, aiming for his neck.

Thanatos barely moves in time.

I lean into my follow-through, spinning with the arc of my weapon. I bring the scythe up overhead before arcing it back down, the tip angled to impale Death's chest.

My brother has to leap back, his expression alarmed.

"Famine—"

Rolling my wrist, I swing the scythe around, seamlessly readying another attack.

One of Thanatos's black wings snaps out, hitting my arm with enough force to knock the weapon from my grip.

No matter.

I come at him again, bringing my arms up and fisting my hands. I have a dagger strapped to my side, but I don't bother going for it. I want to feel the burst of pain as my flesh lays into Thanatos.

My arm snaps out, and I punch Death in the chest so hard his silver armor dents inward.

He grunts, but has barely any time to recover before I follow the hit up—

Another damning blow, another dent in his armor.

I am not a man, I am something else, something bigger, and all I feel is pain and anger.

Again and again the blows come, each one landing against Death's chest and caving in his armor. He barely has time to catch his breath—a sensation that is strange and foreign to him—as he stumbles back.

Fall, damn you.

Lifting a booted foot, I kick out at his knee.

He moves out of the way, his hand at the edge of his armor. I can hear the fastenings ripping clean away as he tears the breastplate off of himself.

"I wouldn't remove that if I were you," I say. "This is going to hurt a lot worse."

Vaguely I remember the first time I felt pain. There's nothing like it. It's terrible to endure and a shock to a newly wrought horseman.

Death casts it aside anyway.

"You wish to fight me, brother?" Thanatos says. "Fine."

He waits for me, and I descend on him again, fists at the ready. I throw another punch, my grief and anger consuming me.

But the blow never lands.

Death catches my closed fist. His dark eyes meet mine as his hold tightens. All at once he twists my hand until—

Snap.

I grunt at the sharp, shooting pain of my broken bone. Thanatos releases my fist then, and I clench my teeth, my breath hissing out of me as my arm falls uselessly to my side.

If he thought a mere broken bone would stop me, *he thought wrong.*

I bring up a booted foot and I kick him square in the chest, the force of my blow so powerful his feet leave the ground.

Death pitches backwards, hitting the earth hard, his wings pinned beneath him. Nearby, his horse whinnies, shuffling away from us.

I'm on my brother in an instant, my good hand going to his throat. His breath comes in ragged gasps, and I can see him wincing from the pain.

I tighten my hold on his neck, and he reaches up with his hands, clawing at my grip. He lets out a strangled noise.

I smile malevolently at him. Now he knows what it means to be powerless.

Under my will, earth splits apart violently, opening up beneath my brother. Mud begins to slip over his wings, pulling him down, down.

I'll bury him alive. Then he will understand the crushing, suffocating feel of grief.

Right when he's sure he will die, I will make my own bargain with him, one where Ana lives and I don't have to destroy the world as payment for it.

Death grabs my good arm, his hold tightening.

In the next instant, I feel ... *odd.* Weak and tingly. I choke a little on the sensation before I realize—

He's sucking the very life out of me.

It's the same ability I have, only his is much, *much* more powerful.

I choke again, my hold loosening around his neck. It's a struggle simply to breathe as I try to force my body to *revive* itself.

Death pushes me off him easily then. Now it's his turn to loom over me. He places a boot on my chest to hold me down.

"Do you still want to fight me?" he says, his black wings spreading wide behind him.

In response, I kick out at him, a blow he easily dodges.

He laughs, bending down to grab me. He drags me up by my shirt. My feet touch the ground for only a moment before I hear the great thundering thump of Death's wings.

Then he's lifting us both into the sky, our bodies rising higher and higher.

My breathing is still ragged, and though my anger burns hot, my life is still ebbing away from me.

The weaker I grow, the more my grief batters at me. I feel painfully human.

We rise high above the treetops as Thanatos drives us into

the heavens. The sky around us is ablaze with lightening and wind. Hail pummels our skin and our hair sticks to our faces.

We're covered with mud, the two of us a little worse for the wear.

"Brother," Thanatos says, his face solemn.

I meet his depthless eyes.

"You may have started this fight," he says, "but you know it is I who finish all things. *Forgive me.*"

With that, Death drops me.

For a moment, I'm weightless—so much so that I almost forget I have a form. I am the wind and the rain and the earth once more.

But then the lacerating pain of my injured arm reminds me—*I am alive, Ana is not.*

It takes the merest thought, and a plant begins to grow. It's thin and malnourished because I have so little left in me *to* grow life, but I manage to make it grow tall enough for my purposes.

It reaches out and lovingly catches me from the sky. Its spindly arms lower me until my feet touch the earth.

I'm dusting myself off when Death slams into me, knocking me back down to the ground. I grunt as the pain from my broken arm radiates through me, the agony so sharp my vision clouds.

I blink away the darkness, and once again there's my brother, looming over me. He gazes down at me, looking as patient and steady as ever, damn him, and his eyes are full of pity.

The pity undoes me.

I've burned my anger out. All that's left is a weakened, broken man whose heart is full of grief.

I tilt my head a little, and out of the corner of my eye, I see Ana. Maybe it's a trick of the light, but already she's beginning to truly look like a corpse.

A keening sound works its way up my throat

Everything hurts. It all hurts so damn bad.

"Please, brother," I say.

Death rearranges himself, pressing a knee on my chest. His dark wings are splayed wide, hiding the sky from me.

"I won't bring her back, Famine," he says, gazing down at me. "Not without your agreement. You can hate me, you can fight me, but you cannot change my mind."

A few years of torture might make Death reconsider, but I won't dare do to my brother what mortals did to me.

We are not the real problem, after all.

I turn my head and look over at Ana again. Lovely, vivacious Ana.

A tear slides down my cheek.

I won't let her slip away. Not now. Not ever.

All I want is to have her back in my arms.

That's all.

My gaze moves to Thanatos. I close my eyes and swallow.

"Alright, brother. You win—I accept. Just bring her back."

Chapter 55

Ana

I gasp in air, my eyelids fluttering open.

Famine stares down at me, my body cradled in his arms. As soon as he sees me awake, he pulls me into a tight hug, crushing me against his armor.

Of their own accord, my fingers thread themselves into the horseman's hair, holding him to me.

"What ... ?" *What happened to me?*

"I'm sorry," the Reaper whispers, his voice broken.

"Sorry?" I say, confused.

My mind is groggy. There's a metallic taste at the back of my throat, and I have this deep-seated and inexplicable feeling of being *off*.

I turn to the Reaper. "How did you get to me so quickly? Did I faint?"

The last thing I can remember is that Famine stood across from me and ... *Death* ...

I pull away from Famine, searching for his brother.

Death meets my gaze, his expression pensive.

Famine cups my jaw with his hand, and he's looking at me like I'm the most precious thing in the world.

"No," he says simply.

"Then what happened?" Even as I say it, my voice wavers.

The answer is right there, in that taste at the back of my throat. Or maybe it's my skin, which is cold and clammy in the most unnatural of ways.

But I want the Reaper to deny it.

To deny that I died.

He takes me in for a long time, and then he slowly nods his head.

I shudder, my spooked eyes moving back to Thanatos.

He killed me, and he did it so quickly that I didn't even realize it. I try to recall anything that came after that ... but there's nothing there.

I couldn't have been dead for very long. We're still in that same bit of forest I last remember seeing, and the stormy sky looks about the same.

But if Thanatos killed me, then why am I breathing—?

The second awful realization hits me.

My gaze snaps back to Famine.

"You *agreed* to it," I say. Death's second offer. That's why he's apologizing to me.

The Reaper squares his jaw. "I did." There's no remorse in his voice.

It took months for Famine to set aside his murderous ways, but apparently only a few minutes to pick it back up.

All because of me.

I would've never imagined that the fate of the world might *actually* depend on me one day. I've always assumed my life was fairly insignificant. But somehow, without my say, I've now fucked everyone over.

I grip Famine's arm. He winces, his arm jerking under my touch. I glance down. Seeing the odd bend to it, I release it immediately.

What happened to you? I want to ask. It's clear there's more to the story that happened while I was ... *gone.*

"Why did you agree to it?" I ask instead, uncaring that we have an audience.

I don't want to go back to the way things were. I barely coped with the horrors I already witnessed. I don't know how much more I'd be able to bear.

Famine's face is grim. "Because, despite how much or how little I care for humanity," he says, touching my face again, "I still care for you much, much more."

That's the most beautiful, terrible thing he could have told me. It's a compliment and a sentence all rolled into one.

The Reaper pulls me in close, pressing his lips to my ear. "All is not lost, little flower," he says, his breath harsh against me. "Let Death see what it means to be human. If I can be swayed, so can he."

Famine pulls away a little to meet my gaze. Keeping his voice low, he adds, "There is still hope for your world."

"More people will have to die," I say. My voice has grown rough.

"More people will die, regardless," Famine says.

I hear the clatter of metal, and my gaze moves from him to Thanatos. The final horseman is picking up his armor and wiping the mud off. He inspects the silver breastplate, which looks badly dented, before tossing it aside. Death moves over to the two horses that wait nearby. He grabs their reins, then heads over to where Famine and I sit, leading the horses along behind him.

He steps in far too close to me, his presence stifling. I can still remember that lethal hand on my cheek.

Death is huge and muscled like Famine—truth be told, he might be slightly bigger—and he has that same sharp beauty that is somehow too pleasing to the eye to be fully human. His skin is pale, his cheekbones are high and his jaw is sharp.

Those deep eyes of his are old—so old I can't bear to look at them for too long—but his lips have a rueful curve to them. His hair is so dark I imagine it shines blue in certain light. Now however, the rain has plastered that hair to his face.

Where Famine is capricious and conniving, Death seems solemn ... and *ancient*. ... He's beautiful in an enigmatic sort of way.

My gaze moves back to Famine, and for a moment, I simply stare at the two of them. They are leviathans, and I am nothing.

But that's not true.

Death hands the reins to Famine. "Mount your steed, brother."

The Reaper looks at the proffered rein for a moment before taking it. I can practically feel the weight of Famine's task falling back on his shoulders.

An aching sort of despair fills me. This is all because my life means more to Famine than everyone else's. If that suddenly weren't the case, maybe the Reaper wouldn't agree to Death's terms ...

My gaze cuts to a dagger sheathed at Famine's side.

For about two seconds, I consider doing something self-sacrificing for the benefit of humanity, like falling on Famine's blade, but ... I'm not that broad.

I'm a bar-fighting, pussy-hustling, scrappy-ass bitch, and I'm not going to just go along with this quietly.

So I grab the hilt of Famine's sheathed dagger and withdraw the blade. Weapon in hand, I spin on the other horseman beside me. Then, I do to Death what I could never do to Famine.

I stab that motherfucker.

Chapter 56

Thanatos stares at me for several seconds, an odd, surprised look on his face. I'm still holding Famine's blade, even though it's embedded itself into the horseman's abdomen.

"Ana!"

I ignore Famine's alarmed voice, focusing all my attention on the horseman in front of me.

Death's hands go to the wound just as I withdraw the blade.

He hisses in sharply and gazes down at the wound. There's not much to see, other than a growing wet stain on the black shirt he wears.

"*Ana*," Famine says again, only this time he grabs me by the arm and drags me away. "What have you done?"

My gaze is still locked on Death.

I should feel some remorse. It's odd that I don't. Then again, my cheeks are wet and maybe it's the rain but maybe it's my eyes. I don't know. I don't know. It's been a weird, awful day.

"If he thinks we should all die, then it's only fair he knows what it feels like," I say, staring at the final horseman as though in a trance.

Death makes a choked sound, his hands moving to the wound, and I smile.

I fucking *smile*.

It took an apocalypse, mass murder, and a few near death experiences, but I think I finally lost it.

Using Famine's dagger, I point at the wound. Blood is slipping down Thanatos's fingers. "That's for taking my parents. And everyone else, you fucker."

Famine drags me back with his good arm, and I can feel him trembling. He grabs the blade from my hand, wipes it on his trousers, then sheathes it at his side once more.

Beyond the Reaper, Thanatos sways, then drops to his knees. He's making pained noises, and even from here I can see his limbs shaking, undoubtedly from the pain.

"You've never been on this side of death, have you?" I call out to him as the Reaper hauls me onto his horse the best he can. I can still remember with perfect clarity the awful sensation of the blades that entered and exited my own body. "Feels like shit, doesn't it?"

"Ana, stop," Famine says.

Thanatos focuses his gaze on me. I expect him to look angry, but those ancient eyes are agonized. Reaching out, Death angles his palm at me.

"*Brother*," Famine says sharply, "stay your hand. We have a deal."

"Her ... stabbing me ... wasn't ... part ... of it," he rasps out.

The Reaper's hand settles on my thigh.

He stares down at his brother. "And like you said, this place is not fair. Welcome to the land of the living."

Famine clicks his tongue and, turning his horse around, the two of us take off.

Chapter 57

"You little firebrand," Famine says once we're out of earshot. And then the wicked love of my life laughs. "Remind me never to cross you."

Now that the adrenaline is wearing off, I'm beginning to shake. In response, the Reaper pulls me close.

"Are we really just going to leave him back there?" I ask, looking over my shoulder.

I'm beginning to feel the first tendrils of remorse. Or maybe it's fear.

The Reaper gives me a look like I'm the most insane human he's ever crossed paths with. "You *stabbed* him. Would *you* like to go back and see how forgiving Death is?"

A shiver works its way down my spine. "No thank you." I've already died enough times today.

The two of us cut past our house, which looks a little worse for the wear, now that it's endured several earthquakes and a supernatural storm. Famine doesn't bother to slow. I barely get a moment to glance at it before we pass it by and head for the nearest road.

Oh God, we're really doing this.

I take a deep breath, but there's no bracing myself for all the traveling and killing that lies ahead of us.

"Where are we going?" I ask, dreading Famine's answer.

There's a long pause.

Then—

"We're going to get my brothers. It's time this ended, once and for all."

Acknowledgements

I think I say this every time I put out a new book, but it always remains true: thank you all so much for reading my novels and getting lost in my world. I hope you found a soft spot in your heart for my third—and perhaps wickedest—horseman and the woman who tamed him. I kept pretty quiet about both Famine and Ana because, well, both of them are a little rough around the edges.

To my beta and ARC readers—I deeply appreciate all that you've done to help me with this release. It came down to the wire! To my author friends who cheered me on during the year that it took me to write this (and who gracefully put up with my periods of radio silence), thank you for being my people.

To my family and friends, thank you for your constant support and love and just being genuinely accepting of my weirdness. To my husband—I can't tell you how much it means to me that you're my biggest fan and always my first reader. I love you, I love you, I love you. And to my two nuggets, thanks for always keeping it real.

I can't believe there's only one horseman left! Hopefully humanity makes it out alive. I'll keep my fingers crossed. Until then—

Hugs and happy reading,
Laura

Keep a lookout for the next book in Laura Thalassa's *The Four Horseman* series:

Death

Coming soon.

Never want to miss a release?
Visit laurathalassa.com to sign up for Laura Thalassa's mailing list for the latest news on her upcoming novels.

Be sure to check out Laura Thalassa's new adult paranormal romance series
Rhapsodic
Out now!

Be sure to check out Laura Thalassa's new adult post-apocalyptic romance series
The Queen of All that Dies
Out now!

Be sure to check out Laura Thalassa's young adult paranormal romance series
The Unearthly
Out now!

Other books by Laura Thalassa

THE FOUR HORSEMEN SERIES:
Pestilence
War

THE BARGAINER SERIES:
Rhapsodic
A Strange Hymn
The Emperor of Evening Stars
Dark Harmony

THE FALLEN WORLD SERIES:
The Queen of All that Dies
The Queen of Traitors
The Queen of All that Lives

THE UNEARTHLY SERIES:
The Unearthly
The Coveted
The Cursed
The Forsaken
The Damned

THE VANISHING GIRL SERIES:
The Vanishing Girl
The Decaying Empire

THE INFERNARI SERIES:
Blood and Sin

NOVELLAS:
Reaping Angels

FOUND IN THE forest when she was young, Laura Thalassa was raised by fairies, kidnapped by werewolves, and given over to vampires as repayment for a hundred year debt. She's been brought back to life twice, and, with a single kiss, she woke her true love from eternal sleep. She now lives happily ever after with her undead prince in a castle in the woods.

... or something like that anyway.

When not writing, Laura can be found scarfing down guacamole, hoarding chocolate for the apocalypse, or curled up on the couch with a good book.